Praise for

THE THERAPIST

A *USA Today* Bestseller
A July 2021 Indie Next Pick

"As the story progresses, the reader learns new information, and Alice soon suspects everyone around her as the possible killer. The readers are right there with her wondering who to trust or if anyone is even trustworthy. The plot twist will come as a surprise and keep you flipping through the pages until the very end."
—*Mystery & Suspense*

"Psychological thrillers don't get any better than B. A. Paris's scorching *The Therapist,* one of those books that make you want to draw the blinds to make sure nobody's peeking inside."
—*The Providence Journal*

"There's plenty of guessing and twists in this story of obsession that will leave readers wondering who to trust."
—*The Parkersburg News and Sentinel*

"A delicious web of lies." —Jane Corry, bestselling author of *My Husband's Wife*

"Tense and compulsive." —Louise Candlish, bestselling author of *The Other Passenger*

"Suspicion, betrayal, and dark secrets abound in this tense story—all hidden just beneath the surface of a seemingly perfect suburban life." —T. M. Logan, author of *The Vacation*

"A daring, stay-up-all-night love story. This should be next on your reading list if you love to read thrilling love stories."

—*The Washington Book Review*

"We're in a new golden age of suspense writing now because of amazing books like *Bring Me Back,* and I, for one, am loving it."

—Lee Child

Praise for

THE BREAKDOWN

A Barnes & Noble Best Book of 2017: Mysteries and Thrillers

"A story with a ratcheting sense of unease—a tale of friendship and love, sanity and the terrible unraveling of it."   —*USA Today*

"In the same vein as the author's acclaimed debut, *Behind Closed Doors,* this riveting psychological thriller pulls readers into an engrossing narrative in which every character is suspect. With its well-formed protagonists, snappy, authentic dialogue, and clever and twisty plot, this is one not to miss."   —*Library Journal* (starred review)

"This psychological thriller is even harder to put down than Paris's 2016 bestseller debut, *Behind Closed Doors*; schedule reading time accordingly. . . . A skillfully plotted thriller. With two in a row, Paris moves directly to the thriller A-list."   —*Booklist* (starred review)

"British author Paris follows her bestselling debut, 2016's *Behind Closed Doors,* with another first-rate psychological thriller."

—*Publishers Weekly* (starred review)

"B. A. Paris has done it again! *The Breakdown* is a page-turning thriller that will leave you questioning the family you love, the friends you trust, and even your own mind."   —Wendy Walker, author of the *USA Today* bestselling novel *All Is Not Forgotten*

Praise for

BEHIND CLOSED DOORS

August Amazon Best Books of the Month: Mystery,
Thriller & Suspense
August 2016 Indie Next Pick
August 2016 LibraryReads Selection
Real Simple's Best Book of the Month for August
iBooks Best Books of August

"Newlyweds Grace and Jack Angel seem to lead a perfect life in British author Paris's gripping debut, but appearances can be deceiving.... Grace's terror is contagious, and Millie's impending peril creates a ticking clock that propels this claustrophobic cat-and-mouse tale toward its grisly, gratifying conclusion."

—*Publishers Weekly*

"Making her smash debut, Paris [keeps] the suspense level high. In the same vein as *Gone Girl* or *Girl on the Train,* this is a can't-put-down psychological thriller." —*Library Journal* (starred review)

"A clever heroine." —*Kirkus Reviews*

"Debut novelist Paris adroitly toggles between the recent past and the present in building the suspense of Grace's increasingly unbearable situation, as time becomes critical and her possible solutions narrow. This is one readers won't be able to put down."

—*Booklist* (starred review)

"A gripping domestic thriller ... The sense of believability and terror that engulfs *Behind Closed Doors* doesn't waver."

—Associated Press,
picked up by *The Washington Post*

"If you're hunting for a thriller to give you chills in August, look no further than this book, which is already a big hit in the UK."

—*Real Simple*

"*Behind Closed Doors* takes a classic tale to a whole new level. . . . This was one of the best and [most] terrifying psychological thrillers I have ever read. . . . Each chapter brings you further in, to the point where you feel how Grace must feel. The desperation, the feeling that no one will believe you and yet still wanting to fight because someone you care deeply about will get hurt."   —*San Francisco Book Review*

"Paris grabs the reader from the beginning with a powerful and electrifying tale. *Behind Closed Doors,* a novel sure to make one's skin crawl, also reveals no one truly knows what does go on behind closed doors."   —*New York Journal of Books*

"B. A. Paris takes the cliché about not knowing what goes on beyond closed doors to a nightmarish place. . . . Each chapter escalates the tensions and stakes faced by Grace in the nightmare that is her new 'perfect' marriage to Jack."   —*HuffPost*

"This debut is guaranteed to haunt you—especially if you're about to tie the knot. Paris's thriller asks the question: 'The perfect marriage or the perfect lie?' Jack and Grace, the couple at the center of this totally enthralling novel, are so clearly not what they seem you'll have no choice but to read and read and read until their darkest secrets are revealed. Warning: Brace yourself."

—*Bustle* (10 New Thrillers to Read This Summer)

"This dark and twisted thriller will keep you on your toes and have you wondering exactly what goes on behind your neighbor's door."
—*BuzzFeed* (6 Thriller/Mystery Reads That Will Have
You Sleeping with the Lights On)

"In B. A. Paris's hair-raising debut, a woman falls in love with a psychopath, only realizing his true nature when she's hidden from the world and suffering unthinkable horrors at the hands of a seemingly perfect man. *Behind Closed Doors* is both unsettling and addictive. . . . I raced through the pages to find out Grace's fate. A chilling thriller that will keep you reading long into the night."

—Mary Kubica, *New York Times* and *USA Today* bestselling author of *The Good Girl*

ALSO BY B. A. PARIS

THE
THERAPIST

B. A. PARIS

ST. MARTIN'S GRIFFIN
NEW YORK

Published in the United States by St. Martin's Griffin, an imprint of St. Martin's Publishing Group

THE THERAPIST. Copyright © 2021 by Bernadette MacDougall. All rights reserved. Printed in the United States of America. For information, address St. Martin's Publishing Group, 120 Broadway, New York, NY 10271.

www.stmartins.com

The Library of Congress has cataloged the hardcover edition as follows:

Names: Paris, B. A., author.
Title: The therapist / B.A. Paris.
Description: First U.S. Edition. | New York : St. Martin's Press, 2021.
Identifiers: LCCN 2021006611 (print) | LCCN 2021006612 (ebook) |
    ISBN 9781250274120 (hardcover) | ISBN 9781250277640 (international, sold
    outside the U.S., subject to rights availability) | ISBN 9781250274137 (ebook)
Subjects: GSAFD: Suspense fiction.
Classification: LCC PR9105.9.P34 T48 2021 (print) | LCC PR9105.9.P34 (ebook) |
    DDC 823/.92—dc23
LC record available at https://lccn.loc.gov/2021006611

ISBN 978-1-250-78405-6 (trade paperback)

Our books may be purchased in bulk for promotional, educational, or business use. Please contact your local bookseller or the Macmillan Corporate and Premium Sales Department at 1-800-221-7945, extension 5442, or by email at MacmillanSpecialMarkets@macmillan.com.

Originally published in the United Kingdom by HQ, an imprint of HarperCollins Publishers Ltd.

First St. Martin's Griffin Edition: 2022

10 9 8 7 6 5 4 3 2 1

For Margaux, for making this book so much better

PAST

My office is small, perfect and minimalist. It's decorated in calming shades of gray, with just two chairs; a cocoon-style gray one for my clients and a pale leather one for me. There's a small table placed to the right of my chair for my notepad, and on the wall, a line of hooks to hang coats, and that's it. My relaxation treatment room is through a door on the left. The walls there are the palest of pinks and there are no windows, just two ornate lamps that cast a golden glow over the massage table.

Through the slatted blind shading the window of my office, I can see anyone who comes to the door. I'm waiting for my new client to arrive, hoping she'll be punctual. If she's late—well, that will be a black mark against her.

She arrives two minutes late, which I can forgive. She runs up the steps, looking around her anxiously as she rings on the bell, her shoulders hunched up around her ears, worried that someone might recognize her. Which is unnecessary, because there is no plaque on the wall advertising my services.

I let her in, tell her to make herself comfortable. She sits down in the chair, places her handbag at her feet. She's dressed in a navy skirt and white blouse, her hair tied back in a neat ponytail, as if she's come for a job interview. She's right to treat it as such. I don't take just anyone. The fit has to be right.

I ask her if she's warm enough. I like to have the window open, but spring hasn't quite shifted into summer yet and I've had to put the heating on. I gaze out of the window, giving her time to settle, my attention caught by an airplane trailing through the sky. There's a polite cough, and I turn my attention back to my client.

I angle my body toward her and, in full therapist mode, ask the standard questions. The first meeting, in some ways, is the most boring.

"This doesn't feel right," she says, when I'm only halfway through.

I look up from my pad, where I've been taking notes.

"I want you to know, and remember, that anything you say in this room is confidential," I tell her.

She nods. "It's just I feel incredibly guilty. What could I have to feel unhappy about? I have everything I want."

I jot the words "happiness" and "guilt" on my pad, then lean forward and stare directly into her eyes.

"Do you know what Henry David Thoreau believed? 'Happiness is like a butterfly; the more you chase it, the more it will elude you. But if you turn your attention to other things, it will come and sit softly on your shoulder.'"

She smiles, relaxes. I knew she'd like that one.

ONE

The sound of excited voices draws me away from the box of books I'm unpacking. It has been so quiet all day that it's hard to believe I'm actually in London. Back in Harlestone, there would have been familiar external noises; birds, the occasional car or tractor, sometimes a horse going past. Here, in The Circle, everything is silent. Even with the windows open there's been only the occasional sound. It isn't what I was expecting, which I guess is a good thing.

From the upstairs window in Leo's study, I look down to the road outside. A woman with a white-blond pixie cut, wearing shorts and a vest top, is hugging another woman, tall, slim, with coppery red hair. I know the smaller woman is our neighbor, I saw her late last night outside number 5, pulling suitcases from the back of a car with a man. The other woman I haven't seen before. But she looks as if she belongs here, with her perfectly fitting navy jeans and crisp white T-shirt hugging the contours of her toned upper body. I should move away, because if they look up at the house, they might see me standing here. But my need for company is too strong, so I stay where I am.

"I was going to call in on the way back from my run, I promise!" the small woman is saying.

The tall woman shakes her head, but there's a smile in her voice. "Not good enough, Eve. I was expecting you yesterday."

Eve—so that's her name—laughs. "It was ten in the evening by the time we arrived, way too late to disturb you. When did you get back?"

"Saturday, in time for the children going back to school today."

A sudden wind rustles the leaves of the sycamore trees, which line the square opposite the house, and snatches away the rest of her reply. It's very pretty here, like a movie set depicting an enviable life in the capital city. I didn't really believe places like this existed until Leo showed me the photos and even then, it had felt too good to be true.

My attention is caught by a delivery van coming through the black gates at the entrance to The Circle, directly opposite our house. It turns down the left side of the horseshoe-shaped road and drives slowly around. Leo has been filling our new home with things I'm not sure we need, so it could be for us. Yesterday, a beautiful but unnecessarily large glass vase arrived, and he spent ages wandering around the sitting room with it in his arms, trying to find a place for it, before finally depositing it by the French windows that open onto the terrace. But the van continues past and comes to a stop at the house on the other side of us, and I move nearer to the window, eager to catch a glimpse of our neighbors at number 7. I'm surprised when an elderly man appears on the driveway. I don't know why— maybe because The Circle is a newish development in the middle of London—but I'd never considered older people living here.

A few moments later, the van drives off and I look back to where Eve and the other woman are standing. I wish I felt confident enough to go and introduce myself. Since we moved in ten days ago, I've only met one person, Maria, who lives at number 9. She'd been loading three little boys with the same thick dark hair as their mother, plus two beautiful golden Labradors, into a red people carrier. She'd called "hello" to me over her shoulder, and we'd had a quick chat. It was Maria who explained that most people were still away on holiday, and would only be back at the end of the month, in time for school starting again in September.

"Have you met them yet?" Eve's voice pulls my attention back, and from the way her head has turned toward the house, I realize she's talking about me and Leo.

"No."

"Shall we do it now?"

"No!" The force of the other woman's reply has me stepping back, away from the window. "Why would I ever want to meet them?"

"Don't be silly, Tamsin," Eve soothes. "You're not going to be able to ignore them, not somewhere like this."

I don't wait to hear the rest of what Tamsin says. Instead, my heart pounding, I escape into the shadows of the house. I wish Leo was here; he left for Birmingham this morning and won't be back until Thursday. I feel bad, because a part of me was relieved to see him go. The last two weeks have been a bit intense, maybe because we haven't got used to being with each other yet. Since we met, just over eighteen months ago, we've had a long-distance relationship, only seeing each other at weekends. It was only on our first morning here, when he drank straight from the orange juice carton and put it back in the fridge, that I realized I don't know all his quirks and habits. I know that he loves good champagne, that he sleeps on the left side of the bed, that he loves to rest his chin on the top of my head, that he travels around the United Kingdom so much that he hates going anywhere and doesn't even have a passport. But there's still so much to discover about him and now, as I sit at the top of the stairs in our new home, the soft gray carpet warm under my bare feet, I already miss him.

I shouldn't have been eavesdropping on Eve's conversation, I know, but it doesn't take the sting out of Tamsin's words. What if we never make friends here? It was exactly what I was worried about when Leo first asked me to move to London with him. He promised me it would be fine—except that when I suggested having a house-warming for everyone on the street so that we could meet them, he wasn't keen.

"Let's get to know everyone before we start inviting people over," he'd said.

But what if we don't get to know them? What if we're meant to make the first move?

I take my phone from my pocket and open the WhatsApp icon. During our chat, Maria had offered to add me and Leo to a group for The Circle, so I'd given her both our numbers. We haven't messaged anyone yet and Leo had wanted to delete himself when notifications kept coming in about missed parcels and the upkeep of the small play area in the square.

"Leo, you can't!" I said, mortified that people would think he was rude. So he'd agreed to mute the group instead.

I glance at the screen. Today, there are already twelve new notifications and when I read them, my heart sinks a little more. They are full of messages from the other residents welcoming each other back from holiday, saying they can't wait to catch up, see each other, start yoga, cycling, tennis again.

I think for a moment, then start typing.

Hi everyone, we're your new neighbors at number 6. We'd love to meet you for drinks on Saturday, from 7 p.m. Please let us know if you can come. Alice and Leo.

And before I can change my mind, I press send.

TWO

"There you are," Leo says, coming into the kitchen, a stack of dirty glasses in his hands. He puts them down next to the sink, pushes his hair from his forehead. "Are you coming out to the garden? You're missing all the chat." He raises an eyebrow. "I'm currently being warned about our bins being visible on the drive on collection day, not tucked away at the side of the house."

"Wow," I say, smiling. "I wouldn't even know what to say to that." I open a bag of crisps, tip the contents into a bowl, rescue a couple that spill over the edge. The scent of truffle, artificial, catches my nose. "I'll join you as soon as everyone has arrived, I promise. Someone needs to be here to answer the door."

He eyes the bowl doubtfully. "What flavor are those?"

"Try one."

He takes one, crunches it in his mouth and wrinkles his nose.

"Dead bodies," he says. "It tastes of dead bodies."

I laugh, because I get what he means. They're pungent, earthy. He takes another bite and grimaces exaggeratedly, and I'm glad he's finally relaxed. He'd been annoyed when I told him I'd gone ahead and invited people for drinks. I'd sprung it on him on Thursday evening, when he came back from his three days in Birmingham. It had been another scorching day and he'd looked hot, and cross.

"I thought we'd agreed to wait," he'd said, tugging at the neck of his shirt.

Guilt had me reaching for a bottle of wine, hoping to pacify him.

"It's only for drinks," I told him, knowing I needed to avoid the word "party."

"Who have you invited?"

I handed him the bottle while I dug in the drawer for the corkscrew. "Just the people from here."

"What—everyone?"

"Yes. But the people from number 3 can't come and only Maria or Tim from number 9 are coming, so that's twenty-one at the most."

"When is it?"

"Saturday."

"This Saturday?"

"Yes."

He'd been silent all evening and yesterday, he'd gone to see Eve's partner, Will. I watched from the window as they talked on the doorstep, worried he was telling Will there'd been a mistake and that we had to cancel. But when he came back, he said he was going out to buy beer and champagne, and I'd breathed a sigh of relief.

"How's the champagne going?" I ask now. "Will we have enough?"

"Not at the rate I'm drinking it!"

Recognizing Eve's voice, I look over Leo's shoulder and see her standing in the doorway, an empty glass in her hand, a pink flush staining her cheeks, matching the pink tips she's added to her white pixie cut. "It's delicious! I'm not sure Prosecco is going to cut it for me in the future."

I met Eve properly the day after I overheard her and Tamsin talking outside my window, and I instantly liked her. It wasn't just that—unlike Tamsin—she seemed eager to get to know me and Leo, it was also that she was warm and caring, understanding that it wasn't easy moving into a street where everyone already knew everyone else. She and Will only moved to The Circle eighteen months ago, so things are still relatively new for her too.

Leo turns. "Has everybody arrived, Eve, do you think? Alice is worried she won't hear the bell from the garden."

"Will's just arrived, his rehearsal ran over, so I think everyone is here, except Maria and Tim," she says. "But didn't I see a message on the WhatsApp group saying they have babysitting issues?"

I take three bottles of champagne from the fridge and hand one to her, two to Leo. "Yes, Maria said that one of them would come along if they could."

Eve laughs. "They have three boys, so that could explain their babysitting issues. Lovely, but noisy."

"Edward and Lorna aren't here either," I say, now knowing the name of my elderly neighbor, and his wife. "I went over to introduce myself, and to make sure they'd seen the invitation, and they said they weren't sure they'd be able to come."

"I'm not sure parties are their kind of thing," Eve says doubtfully. "I honestly don't think anyone else will come now, but why don't you leave the door ajar?" Eve hugs the bottle to her chest like she's scared someone will steal it. "Then if Tim or Maria come along, they can let themselves in."

I hesitate a moment. Back in Harlestone, I wouldn't have a problem leaving the door open, but living in a city is different. Sensing my unease, Leo kisses the top of my head.

"It's fine," he says. "We're in a gated street, no one can get in unless they're let in."

I give him a smile. He's right, and anyway, I need to shake off my preconceptions about living in London. I go through to the hall, but before I can unlatch the door, there's a ring on the bell. "I'll be out in a minute!" I call over my shoulder to Leo. "I'll just get this."

I open the door to a tall, good-looking man dressed in smart chinos and a beautiful linen jacket. He's standing a few steps back, looking down at me from slightly hooded, deep-set gray eyes.

"You must be Tim," I say, smiling. "I'm Alice—come in."

"Hi, Alice, lovely to meet you."

He steps into the hall, ducking his head below the glass pendant lightshade. For a moment, neither of us speaks.

"Did you know the house before?" I ask, breaking the silence.

"No, not really. I know you've had some work done, though."

"Only upstairs. We created a bigger bedroom by knocking down a wall."

"Sounds fascinating. I'm trying to imagine it." He looks toward the stairs. "At the front or the back?"

"The back. I can show you if you like," I add with a smile, because it isn't the first time I've traipsed up the stairs this evening. All twelve houses in The Circle were originally identical, although some have been extended since. People are interested to see how we've used the same space.

"Great, I'd love to see it," he says, following me up.

"So, Maria drew the short straw," I say, when we reach the landing.

"Sorry?"

"She got to stay home and look after the boys. She said you were having trouble finding a babysitter."

He nods. "That's right, we couldn't. Beginning of the school year, so I guess they prefer to catch up with friends."

I open the only door on the right-hand side of the landing. As he follows me in, the sound of people chatting and laughing in the garden floats in through the open windows.

"Amazing," Tim says, looking around. "I don't think I've ever seen such a big bedroom."

"It was Leo's idea," I say. "We didn't need three bedrooms, so he had two of them knocked into one."

"I hope this doesn't give Mary ideas."

"Mary?" I can hear Eve's infectious laugh and suddenly, I'm desperate to get out there and be part of it. "I'm sorry, I thought your wife was called Maria."

He smiles. "She is, but I call her Mary. It started off as a joke because she went to a convent school, and it kind of stuck." He looks at the wardrobe, which runs half the length of the wall opposite the windows. It's extra deep and has beautiful wooden-slatted doors. "I wouldn't mind a wardrobe that size."

I laugh and he moves out of the room, letting me go past him down the stairs.

"Thank you," he says gravely when we get to the hall. "For the grand tour."

I point toward the garden. "Everyone is outside, so grab a glass and help yourself to anything you like. I'm just going to close the door."

I take a moment to breathe in the quiet air at the front of the house before going to the garden. As I pass the kitchen, I see Tim at the sink, filling a glass of water from the tap. I want to tell him that there's chilled, bottled water in the ice-bin outside but I can see Leo waving at me, so I start to weave my way through the throng of people. He's standing with Will, who is gesticulating theatrically with his hands as he explains something to Leo. Will is an actor, a rising star and, with his thick dark hair, roman nose, and chiseled lips, on his way to becoming a rising heartthrob. Eve complains that they can't go out without him being recognized, but I can tell she's secretly thrilled.

As I get nearer, they're joined by Geoff from number 8, who's divorced, and—no, I can't remember the name of the other man with the tawny hair. He came with Tamsin, so I'm a bit wary. To be honest, after what I'd overheard, I was surprised when she eventually replied to my invitation on the WhatsApp group and said she and her husband—Cameron? Connor?—would see us on Saturday. Maybe Eve persuaded her to come.

I smooth my white sundress self-consciously, scanning the garden for someone standing on their own. But there are only groups of people who've known each other for years and are happy to catch up with each other after the holidays. I'm a stranger at my own party, I realize.

"Alice, over here!"

I see Eve standing on tiptoes, waving in my direction. Grabbing a bowl of crisps from the table, I make my way over.

"Nice dress." Looking up, I see the man with tawny hair standing in front of me. Judging from the four glasses he's holding in one giant hand, he's going to get refills.

"Thanks." I give him a smile. "I'm sorry, I didn't catch your name."

"Connor. I'm Tamsin's better half." His voice has the trace of a Scottish accent.

"Well, I haven't met her properly yet, but I'll keep that in mind when I do," I say.

He laughs and moves away.

Creep, I think, watching him go. Then I feel bad, because he was only having a joke.

I carry on to where Eve is standing with her friends and I could swear Tamsin's eyes narrow a little when she sees me.

"We were just saying how brave you are, moving in here," she says, and gets a nudge from Eve in return. With corkscrew curls framing her face and her pale green eyes, Tamsin really is stunning.

I give her a smile. "I'm sure I'll get used to it. Especially with lovely neighbors like you," I add, in an attempt to get her on my side.

She frowns and I sense it then, she doesn't like me. My heart sinks. Maybe Tamsin is one of those women who guard their friends jealously and my remark has made me seem presumptuous in thinking I can join their group. I need to take things more slowly.

"Why don't you get a drink?" Cara, a pretty brunette says. I know she came with Paul but I can't remember what number they live at. Two, maybe? She dips her hand into the bowl I'm holding. "These crisps are delicious. Where did you find them?"

"From the delicatessen in Dean Street," Tamsin says, beating me to it. She gives a tight smile. "I've bought them there before."

The rest of the evening passes in a whirlwind. By the time the last guests have left, I feel more at home than I thought I would.

"Everyone is so friendly," I say to Leo as we stack glasses into the dishwasher. "We should start having people around to dinner in small groups so that we can talk to them properly."

He raises an eyebrow. "Let's take the time to work out who everybody is first."

"I already know who everybody is," I tease. "Did you meet Cara and Paul from number 2? They seem really nice."

He straightens up. "I'm sure they are. But don't make snap judgments about people, Alice. And be careful what you share about yourself. I don't want this to be like Harlestone."

I stare at him, thrown. "Why not?"

He pulls me toward him, wanting to take the sting out of his words.

"Because I don't want anyone knowing our business. We're fine on our own, Alice." He kisses my mouth. "We don't need anyone else."

THREE

We've had a lazy Sunday morning, staying in bed late before going out to the garden, where we're lying side by side on wooden loungers under an orange parasol that Leo found in the garage. The air is heavy with the heady smell of jasmine and the book I was reading is lying on my chest. I turn my head lazily toward Leo. He's checking messages on his phone and, sensing my eyes on him, he looks over at me.

"Paul has invited me to play tennis with him next weekend," he says. "And Connor has messaged to remind me about a Residents' Association meeting on Thursday." He puts his phone on the grass and reaches for my hand. "Luckily, I'm not sure I'll be back from Birmingham in time."

"I can always go," I murmur, closing my eyes at the feel of his touch.

"I think it's more of a man thing."

My eyes fly open. "Wow, I didn't realize we'd regressed to the 50s by moving in here."

He grins and rolls onto his side, his blue T-shirt exposing a line of skin at the top of his shorts. "Don't blame me. From what Connor said, everyone goes back to his for whiskey after. He's a whiskey trader and has an amazing collection, apparently."

"And women don't drink whiskey," I say, dryly. I lean toward him and give him a kiss, happy to see him so relaxed. "When do you think your work in Birmingham will be finished?"

"In another few weeks, I hope." He smiles. "I can't wait to be able to come home to you every evening. Ever since you reversed into the front of my car at those traffic lights, it's all I've ever wanted."

I can't help laughing. "Good try. We both know that it was you who smacked into my car."

"I did not *smack* into your car!" he protests, but he's laughing too. "I bumped, and it was a very small bump."

He's right, it was such a slight bump that I decided not to bother getting out of the car to check it for damage, mainly because it was a horribly wet January day. But he had come to my window and knocked on the glass, gesturing at me through the rain to open my window.

"I'm so sorry," he said, drops of water rolling down his face. The lights had by this time turned to green and as the cars began to pass around us, he bent closer and I found myself looking into brown-green eyes that managed to be both admiring and apologetic at the same time.

"There's no harm done," I told him. "Really, I hardly felt it."

"There might be harm done," he replied. "I must have damaged your car at least a little bit."

"Honestly, it's fine." I liked the way his hair, damp with rain, clung to his forehead, the hint of stubble on his chin, and began to wish he had done some damage, so that I'd have a reason to carry on the conversation. Maybe I should check. I unbuckled my seatbelt. "If it will put your mind at rest, shall we have a look?"

I walked to the back of the car, the collar of my coat pulled up against the rain, and bent to inspect the bumper. There was only the smallest of marks and I couldn't swear that it hadn't already been there because a few weeks before, I'd backed into my friend Debbie's horse-trailer.

"There might be some internal damage that you can't see, so shall I give you my details in case your bumper falls off further along the road?"

I smiled. "If you insist."

"I do." He took a card from his wallet and handed it to me. "And can I insist that you give me your details, in case your bumper does fall off, and you're too polite to tell me?"

Leo Curtis, I read, looking at the card. Risk-management Consultant.

"I don't have a card but I can give you my cell phone," I told him. He called me that night.

"I just want to make sure you don't have late-onset whiplash."

"I'm fine, the car's fine," I reassured him.

"Then perhaps we can celebrate that fineness together," he suggested, making me laugh. "Can I take you out for dinner?"

"I think that might be a bit difficult," I said regretfully.

There was an embarrassed pause. "I'm sorry, I should have guessed—"

"No, that's not what I mean," I interrupted hurriedly. "It's just that I presume, from your card, that you live in London. I live in East Sussex. Meeting for dinner won't be easy."

"Don't worry—have car, will travel. Tell me, is there a wonderful restaurant not too far from where you live where I could take you to apologize for crashing into your life?"

"Believe it or not, there is."

And that had been the start of it all.

Now, Leo nods toward my cell phone. "Anyone message you, or am I the favorite?" he jokes, which niggles a bit but only because of how unfriendly Tamsin was.

"Just one from Cara thanking us for last night, which is lovely of her as she already posted a message on the WhatsApp group—as did everyone else. They're obviously very polite here. Did you see all the 'New Home' cards we got? I put them in the sitting room, along the mantelpiece."

"Yes, I saw them. I suppose they'll be there for weeks," he adds with a smile, referring to the way I keep birthday and Christmas cards on display for ages.

"I know it's weird, but people generally put a lot of thought into choosing cards so I can never bring myself to throw them straight into the bin." I give my body a stretch, then stand up.

"Where are you going?" he says, reaching a lazy hand toward me.

"To make a salad to have with the steaks."

He gives a contented sigh. "Sounds wonderful."

I'm woken by a sudden movement, Leo sitting upright in our bed.

"Who's there?" he shouts, his voice loud in the quiet of the night. It's late, the shadows sitting heavy in the dark of our bedroom.

"What's the matter?" I whisper. It feels like I've only been asleep for ten minutes. What time is it, anyway? I try and pull him back down but he shrugs me away impatiently.

"There was someone here." His voice is sharp, urgent.

"What?" My heart jumps. I sit up, wide awake now, adrenaline surging. "Where?"

"Here, in the bedroom." He fumbles for the switch on his bed-side lamp, and the artificial white light momentarily blinds me. I blink rapidly a few times to re-focus my eyes, then scan the bedroom quickly. There's noone there, just the built-in wardrobes with their slatted doors and the chair in the corner of the room, piled with our clothes from the day before.

"Are you sure?" I ask doubtfully.

"Yes!"

I raise myself onto one arm and squint through the partly open door into the bathroom, my mind already visualizing someone hiding in the shower, a long-bladed knife held high above their head. Leo throws the covers back, startling me, and swings his legs from the bed.

"Where are you going?"

He stands naked, his body tense. "To put the light on in the hall."

He reaches through the partially open bedroom door and flips the switch on the wall. I listen for the sound of someone leaving the house in a hurry, disturbed by the light now flooding the landing and stairwell. But there's nothing.

"Shall I call the police?" I ask, grabbing my phone from its charging pod.

"Wait a moment. I want to be sure before we do anything," he says. "I'm going to check the other bedroom."

I get out of bed and grab my cotton dressing gown. I feel less vulnerable now that I'm covered, but my heart is racing as I move to the door behind him.

"I'm coming with you."

"No. Stay here, and if you hear anything, call the police."

"Wait." I hurry to the bathroom, quickly checking there's no one there, and grab a can of hairspray. I pry the lid off and hand it to him. "If you see someone, spray this in their eyes to disable them."

At any other time, he'd laugh at this, a stark-naked man with a hair product as a weapon. But he takes it, holding the can by his side, his finger on the nozzle as he moves along the landing. I watch as he searches the guest bedroom, then his study, anxiety prickling my skin, my phone primed to dial 999.

"Nothing," he calls. "I'll check downstairs."

"Be careful!" I wait a moment. "Can you see anything?" He doesn't answer, so I move to the banisters and look down to the hall below, where he's disappearing into the sitting room.

He's back in a few minutes. "The windows and doors are still locked and nothing seems to have been disturbed."

"Did you actually see someone?" I say as we go back to our bedroom.

"Yes . . . no . . . I don't know," he admits. "It was just a feeling I had, of someone being in the room."

"It could have been a dream."

He looks a bit sheepish as he puts down the can of hairspray. "It probably was. Sorry. I didn't mean to scare you. What time is it, anyway?"

I check my phone. "Three-fifteen. You'd better get some sleep, you need to be up in three hours."

We climb into bed and soon, he's asleep. But I lie awake, grateful that Leo is here beside me, remembering all the times I'd start awake in my cottage, disturbed by the noises that would echo through it at night. I love that I have him to share things with, that I no longer have to face everything alone. Leo bumping into the back of my car was the best thing that had happened to me for years.

"Do you know, that's the first time you've shown the slightest bit of interest in anyone," Debbie had said, when I told her what had happened.

She was right. I was thirty-five, and although I'd had three fairly long relationships, they'd all come to an end, not in an abrupt manner, but in a slow, I'm-not-actually-sure-where-this-is-going kind of way. I'd begun to think that I wasn't cut out for long-term relationships and although there was a slight sadness that I might not find someone to spend the rest of my life with, it had never become a serious preoccupation of mine. But once Leo was in my life, everything changed.

After six months of the weekend commute, because Leo lived at his flat in London during the week and only came down to Harlestone at weekends, we both began to want more. One evening, we went out to dinner, and when he ordered champagne, my anxiety levels quickly rose at the thought that he might be about to propose. We had never talked about getting married and I didn't want to spoil things between us by telling him that I needed time to think. As the waiter struggled to get the cork out, I wondered if maybe I should say yes. Spending the rest of my life in Harlestone with Leo suddenly seemed a lovely prospect.

"Alice, I want to ask you something," he said, once the champagne had been poured. "I want to be able to see you all the time, not just at weekends." He took a deep breath. "Will you move in with me?"

Move in with him? Did he mean in London?

"I thought for a moment that you were going to ask me to marry you," I joked to hide my confusion.

He reached for my hand. "I love you, but I've never believed in marriage and I'm not going to start now, not at my age. I've never known a happy one and it's just a piece of paper anyway. It wouldn't make us love each other more, how could it?"

"That's not what I meant," I said, taking a sip of champagne. "I'm happy not to get married. But when you say move in with you, do you mean to your flat?"

"Yes."

I couldn't give him the answer I knew he wanted. Even though I was sometimes lonely in Harlestone, it was all I knew. I'd only ever lived in Harlestone. My friends were there. My life was there.

"Can I think about it?" I asked.

"As long as you don't take too long to decide," he said, smiling. "I want us to be together all the time, not just at weekends."

I managed to avoid the subject of moving to London until six months ago, when Leo's work began to take him to the Midlands. He didn't exactly give me an ultimatum but when he asked if I would consider moving north, I knew I had to give a little if I wanted a future with him, which I did. I could do my job anywhere but he couldn't, and if we moved to London, I could still get to Harlestone relatively easily from Kings Cross. But I needed some green around me so we agreed that he would sell his flat, and I would sell my cottage, and we'd find somewhere near a park with a garden. That way he could work out his current contract in the Midlands by spending Monday to Thursday in Birmingham, and Friday to Sunday in London with me. A new home for us, a new life for me.

My mind flits to what Leo said after the party last night, about us not needing anyone else. It honestly never occurred to me that he would want us to be together twenty-four/seven. It's true that he's a very private person, and extremely good at deflecting attention away from himself when questions become too personal. When I say that people are interested, he says they're intrusive.

"Who was that?" I asked him one Friday afternoon. I'd been at the window of my cottage in Harlestone, waiting for him to arrive from London. Because of the terrible weather conditions—there had been some snow, which had turned to ice—he had left at midday, and as he got out of the car, a woman had appeared from seemingly nowhere and had begun speaking to him. Leo had tried to get away but the woman had been insistent, and I was sure I heard him telling her to leave him alone.

"Someone wanting to know what it was like to live in the village," he'd said when I asked him about her, sounding more annoyed than he should have. We were in the early stages of our relationship, and I wondered fleetingly if she was an ex-girlfriend. But Leo, I realized quickly, hated anyone invading his personal space. It's why he doesn't have any close friends, apart from Mark, who he met a couple of years ago when he did some work for his company. Which is why I feel guilty, because I don't agree that we don't need anyone else. I love Leo, but there are other people I need in my life, like Debbie and my other friends in Harlestone. They are my family and I already miss them. Luckily, here in London, I have Ginny, Mark's wife, who has become a good friend and only lives a few miles away, in Islington. And hopefully, I'll make some new friends here in The Circle.

I flip my pillow over and give it a thump to flatten it, then turn and look at Leo, his head half-buried under the covers, and realize something that I've never realized before, which is that family-wise, I'm all he's got. He's estranged from his parents and from the little he told me about them, they weren't exactly the best role models.

He murmurs restlessly in his sleep and I feel a sudden rush of love. It's not surprising he wants some stability in his life. Someone he can depend on.

FOUR

"I'll see you on Thursday," he says the next morning, lifting me off the kitchen chair and giving me a kiss. "Be careful, won't you? Make sure you lock the doors at night."

"There was no one there," I remind him, pressing my face into his shirt and breathing in the scent of him. "We checked."

He rests his chin on the top of my head for a moment. "I know. All the same, be careful."

I pull at his tie, bringing him down for a last kiss. "Love you."

In the hall, he picks up his bag and with a wave, disappears through the front door. It slams shut behind him and I listen to his footsteps receding down the drive until I can no longer hear them. For a moment, the silence is absolute and my mind flicks to the thought of someone here; a stranger watching us as we slept. It's only as I stand there, shrouded in perfect stillness that a thought slams into my head.

I don't like this house.

I'd been on holiday in Venice with Ginny when Leo called to tell me about a house he'd visited.

"It's perfect," he said, and I could hear the relief in his voice, because we had viewed at least twenty by then. "Tell Ginny she was right about Ben. He's brilliant, he's found us exactly what we need. The perfect house."

Ginny looked up from the magazine she was reading and I gave her a thumbs-up. Before we'd left for Venice, Ginny had told Leo to go and see Ben, the estate agent who had found her and Mark their dream home a few months earlier.

"In what way is it perfect?" I asked Leo, because it seemed too easy. Too good to be true.

"I took some photos, I'll send them to you now."

"It looks big," I said a couple of minutes later. And way too expensive, although I didn't say it aloud. I carried on swiping through photos of a large white house with a front garden that opened onto a private road. It was at the polar end to my little cottage in Harlestone.

"It has four bedrooms, three upstairs and one down, and two bathrooms." Leo explained.

"Four bedrooms! Leo, we don't need four bedrooms."

"Yes, but there's stuff we can do, like use the downstairs one as a second study."

I looked at the next photo. "Aren't there any fences between the houses?"

"Only at the back. Take a look at the other photos. It's a gated estate of twelve houses so it's really secure. And there's a lovely square in the middle, the houses are built around it."

I swiped through more photos, showing Ginny as she sat next to me. Each house had been built to the left of its plot, with a garage and driveway on the right separating it from its neighbor. The square, enclosed by black railings, was beautifully laid with flowerbeds, benches and paths, with a small play area in a corner for children. It looked better than anything we'd seen. But it was light years away from what I knew—and what I was comfortable with.

"I'm not sure I want to live on an estate," I said, stalling.

"It's not your ordinary estate; it's quite exclusive."

"Where is it?"

"Near Finsbury Park."

That puzzled me. We had previously excluded Finsbury as being out of our league.

"Isn't Finsbury too expensive for us?"

"That's the thing. The house has been unoccupied for a while, so Ben thinks I could get it for the same price as I'd get for my flat. It means you wouldn't have to sell your cottage in Harlestone, Alice."

"I don't mind," I protested. "I expected to."

"I know. But I also know how much it means to you. That's what I've wanted all along, to find a house that I can buy without you having to sell yours." He paused. "You could rent it out for say, six months and then if you find that you don't like living in London, you'll still have your cottage in Harlestone to go back to."

"That sounds a bit ominous," I said, moving away from Ginny and walking into the bedroom. I waited until I'd closed the door behind me. "What are you saying, Leo? That you don't think we'll last more than six months?"

"No, not at all. It's just that I know you're worried about moving to London and I thought it might make it easier for you if you knew your cottage was there, waiting in the background, in case you ended up really hating it here. A safety-net, so that we could re-think our future plans, if we had to."

Tears had filled my eyes. The thought of selling my cottage had been heartbreaking, and I'd tried desperately to keep those feelings from Leo, obviously without success. And he was right, it would make it much easier for me to move to London if I still had my cottage.

"Why are you so good to me?" I asked.

"Because I love you. So, shall I go ahead and make an offer? I'd like to get it in today."

"I'll call you back within the hour," I promised.

I took my time scrolling through the photos again. Ginny loved the house and pointed out that it wasn't far from where she and Mark lived.

"At least you won't have to cross the whole of London to come and see me," she said, reaching for her wide-brimmed sun hat and cramming it on her head. "Come on, let's go for a glass of wine to celebrate you finally moving to London."

"I haven't said yes to the house yet," I reminded her. Because there was something that was niggling me. If I didn't sell my cottage, it would be Leo's house, not our house. Did it matter, though? I thought back to what he had said about us not getting married. Would we love each other more if we co-owned a house? The answer had to be no, so I called Leo back and told him to go ahead.

I finally saw the house a week later. I realized what Leo meant by exclusive when he had to type a code into a pad to open the black wrought-iron gates that stood at the entrance to The Circle.

"Each house is linked to the entrance by video, so no unwelcome visitors can get in," Leo explained.

The first house, number 1, was on the left of the main gate and the last, number 12, was on the right. Ours—number 6—was halfway around, directly opposite the gate, with the square in between.

"What do you think?" Leo asked as we got out of the car.

I'd taken in the white walls, the red-tiled sloping roof, the neatly cut lawn, the concrete driveway, the paved path that led from the drive to the front door. It looked the same as all the other houses.

"It's like a clock of houses," I said, smiling to hide the uncertainty I felt.

There was a spacious hallway, a rather grand dining room on the left—which I earmarked at once for a library—which led, through double doors, into an open-plan kitchen that ran the length of the back of the house. To the right of the hallway, there was a spacious sitting room and behind it, a ground-floor bedroom with an en-suite shower room. A staircase to the right of the front door led upstairs to an open landing with three bedrooms, a bathroom and a study.

"I thought we could turn the downstairs bedroom into a second study, then we'd be able to have one each," Leo explained.

"Good idea, as long as I can have the one downstairs," I said, kissing him. "I love the idea of being nearer the kettle."

"No problem for me to have this one." He opened one of the doors on the other side of the landing. "This is the biggest bedroom."

"Nice," I said, looking round the bright and airy room.

"Yes, but the room next door has the en-suite. Come and have a look." I followed him in. It was a little smaller than the previous one but still large. "I thought we could knock the two bedrooms into one to make one big bedroom and an en-suite," he explained. "It would still leave us with a guest bedroom for when Debbie comes to stay."

"Sounds good," I said, moving to the window so that I could see the garden. It was early May, and a beautiful Laburnum was in bloom. There was also what looked like a cherry tree and I could see raspberry canes along the left-hand fence.

"It's beautiful," I said, captivated. "Really lovely."

He came to stand behind me and wrapped his arms around me. "I can see us sitting out there on a summer evening with a glass of wine," he murmured.

His breath was warm on my neck and I instinctively tilted my head. "Me too."

He turned me in his arms so that he could see my face. "Does that mean you like it, then?" he asked, his brown eyes searching mine.

"I love it," I said, mentally crossing my fingers, because I didn't love it, not really. But I would learn to love it, for his sake. It would grow on me.

Except that it hasn't.

FIVE

I sit cross-legged on the kitchen floor, thinking about the inner voice which had told me with such intensity, just moments ago, that I don't like this house. It's not true, not really. There are things that I love, like my downstairs study. It has the palest of pink walls, a color I never thought I'd like, but which I do, and an en-suite, because it was destined to be a bedroom. The desk that once belonged to my father stands in front of the window and in the corner, there's a sofa bed that came from Leo's flat. I also love the kitchen, with its pale marble worktops and white Bulthaup units—or at least, I will once I've finished jazzing it up a bit. It's too neat and clinical for me at the moment, all clean lines and everything hidden away in clever cupboards. So, I don't hate the house, it's more the atmosphere that I don't like.

Maybe it's just that there's no atmosphere; the house was only built five years ago, whereas the cottage where I was born and brought up, and where I lived until a few weeks ago, is two hundred years old. I'm so grateful I was able to keep it. I did as Leo suggested and it's rented for six months to a lovely couple from Manchester, who want to give country living a try.

I glance at the photographs spread on the floor in front of me. They are mostly of Debbie and my other friends back in Harlestone, but there are also some of me and Leo, taken during a week's holiday in the Yorkshire Dales. Reaching out, I pick up one of the other photos, a headshot of my sister. I stare at it for a moment, then reach for another photo, this time of my parents and sister, taken on the day of her graduation, and raise it to my lips, pressing it there, my eyes closed, remembering. I can't believe that I'm actually going to put these two precious photos on the fridge, where my eyes will automatically be drawn to them every time I open or close the door. And the eyes of other people, who might ask about my family, because then I'll have to explain. It's why I usually keep photos of them hidden away in the bedroom. But this move to London is a new start for me in more ways than one.

Moving to a kneeling position, I begin to fix the photos to the upper door of the fridge-freezer, using tiny magnets to keep them in place. When there's no space left within reach, I get to my feet and continue adding photos until the whole of the door is covered. I stand back to admire my handiwork, and the two of my sister and parents leap out at me from among the others. I look around the kitchen; it still needs more color so I fetch a pile of cookbooks from the dining room, which I've lined with bookshelves. As I pass the sitting room, I glance through the door and smile when I see that Leo has laid the "New Home" cards face down on the mantelpiece, his little joke after our conversation yesterday.

Back in the kitchen, I stack the cookbooks along the worktop. Later, I'll cut some flowers from the garden and put them on the table, in the red gold-lipped jug I found in a charity shop.

I'm still not dressed so I go upstairs, pausing when I get to our bedroom, still thrown by the size of the room. With the last of the boxes unpacked, and Leo gone, it seems sparser than usual. Overwhelmed by a sudden need to get out of the house, I look through the pile of clothes neatly folded over the back of the chair for my white sundress. The forecast for the rest of the week said to expect cooler temperatures, so today is probably the last time I'll be able to wear it. But it's not there. I know it's not in the laundry basket because I wanted to get another day's wear out of it. I must have put it back in the wardrobe.

I reach into its vast interior and look through the clothes on the rail. I still can't find my dress so I pull out some blue shorts and a vest top, noticing that my neat rows of shoes on the wardrobe floor have become jumbled up. I bend to straighten them, wondering if I could go and see Eve. She blogs for a living, mainly about beauty products, and works as much or as little as she wants each day.

"The perfect job," she told me that first day, when she came over to thank me for the invitation I'd posted on the WhatsApp group. "I'm so grateful to my sister; she's the CEO of BeautyTech and she was the one who suggested I start a blog. I write about something I love, I get to test amazing products, I'm given so many freebies that my shelves are overflowing—remind me to give you some—and I can fit it in around the rest of my life. We're lucky to be able to work from home, don't you think, Alice? I even blog from my bed sometimes!"

I could only agree. I work as a freelance translator and although I usually translate sitting at a desk, I often do the reading part of my work in bed, especially in the winter. Like Eve, I love what I do and don't miss having colleagues, or commuting. I also like that it varies in intensity. I'm in a lull at the moment, waiting for a book to come in from the Italian publisher I work with. I've enjoyed having a couple of weeks off, especially as the months leading up to the move were intense. But I need to start working again, before the boredom that I can already feel creeping up on me takes hold.

I leave the bedroom and as I walk past Leo's study, I see that his office chair has been left at an angle. I go in, lay a hand on its back and spin it around so that it sits in line with his desk. As I glance out of the window, I realize that I can see every single house in The Circle from where I'm standing. Their windows look back at me like eyes, and I give an involuntary shiver. Is that why they built the houses in a circle, so that everyone can watch each other?

Downstairs, I find my keys and slip on my sneakers. I'm not

going to disturb Eve, she's probably busy. I have legs, I can go for a walk. I explored the area just outside The Circle with Leo but we never made it to Finsbury Park.

Crossing over the road outside, I cut through the square to the main entrance, which takes me all of five minutes, and that's walking slowly. It's lovely, though. With its benches and play area, it's perfect for both children and older residents. Something for everyone; that's the beauty of the place. But the play area, complete with swings and slides, is definitely in need of a few coats of paint, which explains the messages Leo and I saw on the WhatsApp group about maintenance.

I don't know London at all, and the cacophony of car horns and sirens that hits me as soon as I leave The Circle is overwhelming. The overcrowded streets and people jostling to get past are also new to me and I realize how cocooned I've been in Harlestone, where the loudest noise are the combine-harvesters reaping crops in the surrounding fields during early summer. Still, there's something invigorating about the buzz, the feeling that I'm part of a bigger picture, and I quickly pick up my pace to match that of the Londoners. With the help of Citymapper, I make my way to Finsbury Park. By the time I arrive, I feel as if I've completed an assault course.

In Harlestone, I can walk for hours over the fields without meeting anyone. It only takes me an hour to walk around the park but I'm pleased to have somewhere I can go without fear of being run over. Also, I need to stop comparing my life before, and my life now.

I arrive back at The Circle, and as I tap the code in at the side gate, the main gate opens and Maria's people carrier drives through. She waves, so I turn right, walking past numbers 12, 11, and 10 until I get to number 9.

"Hi, Alice!" she calls, as she gets out of the car. "How are you? Have you settled in?"

"Yes, more or less. I've just been for a walk."

"It's beautiful today, isn't it? I didn't have any appointments this afternoon so I decided to leave work early and pick up the children from school." Two boys scramble from the car while she lifts out the littlest one, who must be about three years old, and slides the heavy door shut. "Go on, into the house, boys. Ask Daddy to get you some juice."

"I'm sorry you couldn't come on Saturday night," I say, walking down the drive toward her.

She gives me a rueful smile. "Me too." She has the gentlest of faces, with wide brown eyes and high cheekbones. "The babysitters we usually use deserted us."

"Yes, Tim said. It was nice that he was able to come."

"Tim?" A frown creases her forehead. "I don't think so. He was here with me and the boys. Unless he went over to yours, once I'd gone to bed."

"He must have done, because he was definitely there."

She shakes her head in amusement. "Cheeky sod. He never said anything to me about it." Grabbing her handbag from the floor of the passenger seat, she moves to the door and shouts into the hall. "Tim, you never told me you went to Alice and Leo's on Saturday!"

"Hold on!" he calls back. "I can't hear what you're saying."

"Selective hearing," Maria mouths as he comes to stand in the doorway beside her.

"Sorry, what did you say?" He looks over to where I'm standing. "Hi," he says. "Are you our new neighbor?"

And I find myself staring at a man I've never seen before.

SIX

The weirdest of feelings comes over me, a sense that something is about to happen that I'm not going to like.

"But—you're Tim?" I say, confused.

He laughs. "I was last time I looked."

"But not the Tim who came to the house on Saturday." I turn to Maria. "Well, that explains it, it was another Tim."

"I didn't think he'd have sneaked out without telling me."

"Sneaked out where?" Tim asks.

"To Alice and Leo's, on Saturday."

"I didn't."

"I know you didn't. But there was someone called Tim, and Alice assumed it was you."

I look at this Tim, registering the differences. He's not quite as tall, not quite as slim and not quite as dark-haired as the man I saw. Or quite as good-looking. And he's wearing a striped rugby shirt, which I can't imagine the other Tim wearing.

"Is there another Tim living in The Circle?" I ask. "With a wife called Maria?"

"Not that I know of," Maria says. "Unless someone new moved in over the summer. Wow, imagine having our name doubles living here!"

"She might be known as Mary rather than Maria. Maybe there's a Tim and Mary?"

Tim shakes his head. "Are you sure he introduced himself as Tim?"

"Yes." I laugh to hide my uneasiness, because it's just occurred to me that the man never actually said his name was Tim. I'd said "you must be Tim" and had let him in without waiting for him to say whether he was or not. And what about him calling his wife Mary rather than Maria? Was that because he'd misunderstood what I'd said and had looked for something to cover the slip he'd made?

"How old was he?" Maria asks.

"It's difficult to say—early forties, maybe?"

I tell them as much as I can about the other Tim but they can't come up with anyone who fits his description.

There's a crash from inside the house. "Better get back to the boys," Tim says hastily.

"It'll be someone's brother, or someone who just happened to walk in off the road and slip through the gate behind someone," Maria says. "Since Will was in that television series, there've been a couple of instances where fans have got in."

"He didn't look like a fan."

Realizing I'm being boring, I decide to stop talking about the man who gate-crashed the party. But I can't get him out of my mind, so during my fifty-yard walk home, past numbers 8 and 7, I call Leo.

"Did you speak to someone called Tim on Saturday evening?" I say, after I've asked him about his day.

"I don't think so."

"Could you try and remember whether you did or not? It's important."

There's a pause. "I don't remember a Tim. Why?"

I see Geoff coming across the square with two bags of heavy shopping and give him a wave. "Because a man called Tim came along and I thought it was Maria's husband from—"

"It couldn't have been," Leo interrupts. "I saw him this morning as I was leaving and he apologized for not being able to come."

"I know, I was just talking to him." I stop at the bottom of our drive and dig in my pocket for my keys. "The thing is, there doesn't seem to be another Tim living here." Tucking my phone under my chin to unlock the front door, I launch in to an explanation of the conversation I'd had with the stranger.

"Wait a minute," Leo says when I get to the end. "He didn't actually say his name was Tim? You said 'you must be Tim' and that was it? He never actually said that he was?"

"He didn't say that he wasn't," I say defensively, stepping into the hall and kicking off my trainers.

"And the thing about his wife—you said Maria and he said Mary?"

"Yes."

"What did he look like?"

"Tall, dark hair, gray eyes, smartly dressed," I recite, padding to the kitchen in my bare feet, the wooden floor deliciously cool beneath my feet. "Does it ring any bells?"

"None at all. Maybe you should ask around. He must have spoken to someone at the party. How long did he stay?"

I take a carton of juice from the fridge, pausing a moment to acknowledge the photo of my sister and parents. "I don't know. I left him to get a drink while I closed the front door. I saw him in the kitchen but I didn't see him after that. Are you sure you didn't see him in the garden?"

"Yes, I'm sure. I hope he didn't go upstairs. There's a lot of confidential stuff in my office."

I want to lie but I can't. "Not by himself, no."

"What do you mean?"

I reach into the cupboard for a glass and pour juice into it. "Just that I showed a few people around."

"What! Why?"

"Because they were curious to see the work we'd had done."

"For God's sake, Alice, I can't believe that you showed a bunch of strangers around our house!" He can't hide his exasperation and I can picture him running a hand through his hair, almost as if he wants to tear it out in frustration at my naïvety. "How do you know that this man didn't go snooping around once he was on his own?"

"He didn't," I protest.

"You said you didn't see him again. Maybe that's because he was upstairs, having a good look through everything."

"He wasn't the type. He looked—I don't know . . ."

"There isn't a type! Have you checked if anything is missing?"

"No—"

"Well, maybe you should make sure your jewelry and credit cards are still there."

Worry starts to take hold. "I'm sure everything's fine," I say, making an effort to sound upbeat to de-stress him. "He's probably a friend of someone who lives here. Maybe he was staying with them or something."

"Wouldn't he have said?"

"I'll ask around," I tell him, wanting to be off the phone.

"Call me later. If you don't find out who it was, we should probably tell the police."

I hang up and run upstairs, propelled by the thought of the man being in the bedroom. Hurrying over to the dressing table, I check that my jewelry is there—it is—and that my credit cards are still in my bag, which has been on the shelf in the wardrobe since I put it there on Saturday evening; they are. Everything is exactly as it should be. But I can't relax and I know I won't be able to until I find out who the man is and why he gate-crashed our party.

It's seven in the evening when I decide to go and see Eve and Will. Someone must know who the man was, if anything he would have needed a code to get into The Circle. But Eve's car isn't in the drive and when I knock on their door, there's no answer, so I carry on walking around The Circle anti-clockwise, disrupting people's dinners and television programs. Some kindly invite me in but I stay on the doorstep and quickly explain about the man who turned up uninvited on Saturday, asking if anyone spoke to him. But nobody has.

"Are you sure he wasn't a figment of your imagination?" Connor asks with a slow drawl when I get to number 11 and describe the tall, dark, good-looking stranger that I'm trying to trace. Tamsin, standing next to him, doesn't exactly smirk but a half-smile plays on her lips and my cheeks heat with embarrassment.

The people at number 10 don't remember seeing our gatecrasher, neither does Geoff at number 8, and I'm halfway up Lorna and Edward's drive when I remember that they didn't come on Saturday. But worried that they'll have seen me from their window, I ring on their doorbell anyway.

"I hope you don't mind if I don't invite you in," Edward says, when he opens the door. With his shock of white hair neatly parted to one side and blue eyes undimmed by age, he is still a handsome man. "We haven't been well and we wouldn't like you to catch anything."

"Oh, I'm sorry," I say, feeling bad for disturbing them. "Can I do anything to help?"

Edward shakes his head. "We'll be right as rain in a couple of days. It's just a touch of flu."

"We're sorry we couldn't make your party," Lorna says, appearing behind him, patting her neat bob—the same white as her husband's—self-consciously into place. "Did you enjoy it?"

"Yes, very much, thank you." I pause and they both smile at me expectantly. "There was something strange though," I say. "I discovered earlier that one of the men who turned up shouldn't have been there."

"Oh?" Edward says.

"I thought he was Tim from number 9," I explain. "But I saw Tim earlier and realized my mistake. So now I'm curious as to who he was . . . Leo is worried and wondering if we should call the police. But I'm sure there's a simple explanation," I say hurriedly, because Lorna's face has bleached almost as white as her hair.

She raises a hand and clutches at the string of pearls looped around her neck.

"He said he was a friend of yours," she says. Her voice is strangely strangled, and I worry for a moment that she's pulling too tightly on the pearls. "And that you weren't answering the intercom. That's why I let him in."

The confusion on Edward's face quickly turns to shock. He stares at his wife, as if he can't quite believe what she did. Now Lorna's face floods with color. "I'm so sorry, I didn't realize you'd only invited residents."

"It's fine," I reassure her quickly. "It's actually a relief to know how he got in. But could you tell me exactly what he said?"

"He said he'd been invited for drinks at number 6 but that you probably couldn't hear the intercom because of the noise."

"Did he mention us by name?"

She takes a moment to think about it. "No, he just said for drinks at number 6. I've never let anyone in before, not without checking first. I can't imagine why I did this time." She looks guiltily at Edward and he nods, agreeing that it's the first time she's ever acted so imprudently.

"I'm sure it's all fine," I say again.

"Let us know if you find out who he was," Edward says, already closing the door.

"I will."

But there's only Eve and Will left to ask. I check their drive; Eve's car is there, so I go straight round.

SEVEN

Eve stops chopping a bunch of leafy coriander and turns to me, the knife in her hand.

"Nobody remembers him at all?"

I shake my head in frustration. "I've been all the way around The Circle. You and Will are my last hope."

"You said he was tall?"

"Yes, taller than Tim."

"And he said he was Tim?"

"He didn't say that he was or wasn't. I presumed he was, because we'd been talking about either him or Maria coming. The only thing I know is that he's not from The Circle."

Eve puts down the knife and wipes her hands on a towel. "Sounds like a gate-crasher to me," she says, laughing.

"You don't have to sound so cheerful about it."

"Sorry. It's just that I kind of admire gate-crashers, especially if they manage to get away with something big. As long as they don't do any damage, or steal anything." She looks at me. "Did he?"

"No, but that's not the point. We didn't invite him so he shouldn't have been there."

"Me and Will gate-crashed a wedding once," she says. "It was amazing. We were having a drink at a hotel and we were surrounded by this huge wedding party—there must have been at least two hundred guests. Then someone came in and called everyone through to help themselves to an enormous buffet. It was the summer and we could see people carrying their plates out to these white-clothed tables which had been set up outside. We watched for a while and it seemed to be very casual; there were no set places, people just sat where they wanted. So we tagged onto the end of the line, filled our plates high with food and plonked ourselves down on a table where there were three older couples."

"You didn't!"

"We did. We didn't feel bad as they seemed relieved to have us making up the numbers at their table. When they asked us how well we knew the bride and groom, we said, almost truthfully, not very well at all. It turned out that they didn't either. They were neighbors of the bride's parents and they sort of hinted that they'd only been invited out of politeness, because they were neighbors, not because they were good friends. And we definitely livened up their evening so didn't feel we'd done any harm. Besides we were hungry, and very young. We probably wouldn't do it now."

"I'd never be brave enough," I say. "But, our mystery man—what would his motive have been for gate-crashing a drinks evening? He would only have got a sausage roll and a few crisps out of it, and he didn't even get those because no one remembers seeing him in the garden. I saw him getting a drink of water from the tap in the kitchen but I doubt that thirst was his motive for turning up uninvited."

"Are you sure nothing was taken?"

"Pretty sure. Nothing major anyway. My jewelry and credit cards were still there when I checked and there doesn't seem to be anything missing from the house. We don't have anything valuable anyway."

"Did he go upstairs?"

"Yes, but only because I offered to show him the work we had done."

Eve pauses at this and rubs her hand across her forehead. "Did you stay with him all the time?"

"Yes—but I suppose he could have gone back up when I was outside. Leo is really annoyed because he has sensitive work-related stuff in his office."

Eve picks up the knife and goes back to the coriander. "I'll ask Will if he remembers a stranger at your party. He'll be here in a minute. Have you eaten? Would you like to stay for dinner?"

I get reluctantly to my feet. "That's lovely of you, it smells delicious. But I'd better phone Leo back. And go through the house again, just to make sure nothing is missing."

I check that our computers, tablets, and valuables are where they should be, but before I can call Leo, Ginny calls me.

"How did your drinks evening go?" she asks.

"Really well. I managed to meet just about everyone who lives in The Circle. The best thing is, there are quite a few couples who seem to be the same age as us. Eve and Will are younger, but the others seem to be in their late thirties, early forties. Next time you and Mark come over, I'll invite them round so that you can meet them." I pause. "I managed to make an enemy, though."

"Oh?"

"Not really an enemy but she didn't seem to like me very much. A beautiful redhead called Tamsin. I think she thinks I'm going to muscle in on her friendship group. She's friends with Eve, and as Eve lives next door, maybe she's worried we're going to be popping in and out of each other's houses all day long."

"I suppose you're going to have to be a bit careful about already established friendships," Ginny says. "Especially in a small community like The Circle."

"You make it sound like a sect."

"Maybe it is," she whispers dramatically.

She's joking, but it doesn't stop a shiver running through me.

"Everyone seemed really interested in the work we had done upstairs," I say.

"I'm not surprised. It's lovely. Leo did a really good job."

"What about you, did you have a good weekend?"

"Mark had a round of golf with Ben, so it was very good."

I laugh. Ginny and Mark work together, so are pretty much together twenty-four/seven and Ginny has been trying to get Mark to play golf each weekend so that she can have some "me-time." She's roped in the services of Ben, who, as well as being an amazing estate agent, is also an amazing golfer.

"And will that now become a weekly thing?" I ask.

"I hope so," Ginny says fervently. "You can't believe how good it was to have some time alone in the house."

"I've got a bit too much of that at the moment."

"You'll be fine once you've settled in."

"I hope so."

I don't mean to sound despondent but Ginny picks up on it straightaway. "Is everything all right?"

"It's just that I really want to start making friends here but Leo thinks we should take our time. He wasn't too pleased when I went ahead and invited people over for drinks. And then I let a gate-crasher in so he's even less happy with me now."

"Ooh, tell me more. I'm intrigued!"

I tell her about the man who nobody remembers speaking to, and the more I talk about him, the more uneasy I feel.

"Sorry, Ginny, but I really need to call Leo," I say. "At least I'll be able to tell him how our gate-crasher got in."

"No problem. Give him my love."

I call Leo and tell him what Lorna told me.

"Well, that's one part of the mystery solved," he says. "Although we still don't know why he turned up." He gives a sigh of irritation. "I really can't believe you showed people around the house."

"Sorry," I say guiltily. "But all your client files are locked away in the filing cabinet, aren't they?" I add, wondering if that's why he won't let it go.

"That's not the point."

"Do you think it might have been something to do with your work, then?"

"I'm a consultant, not a spy." His voice has an edge to it. "Look, I don't want to worry you, but have you got your keys?"

"They're in my bag. Why?"

"It's just that—well, you know I heard someone in the house last night? I was wondering if it might be linked to our uninvited guest."

I feel a prickle of alarm. "I thought we agreed that there was no one there."

"I know. And if you have your keys, it's fine. I've got mine and they're the only two sets that were in the house during the party, so it's not as if one of them has gone missing."

"And we have a mortice lock on the inside of the front door, so nobody can get in anyway," I point out. "Unless you to forgot to lock it before we went to bed?"

"No, I don't think I did. But make sure you lock it tonight, Alice. And carry on asking around, will you? We need to find out who that man was."

"Will do."

But there isn't anyone else to ask. The mystery man has slipped away as easily as he slipped in.

EIGHT

I gather my pillows and quilt together and carry them upstairs, slightly embarrassed at having slept in my study for the last two nights. But when it came to going to bed on Monday evening, I couldn't bring myself to sleep in the bedroom alone. It wasn't just that Leo had thought there was someone in the house the previous night, it was also the knowledge that we'd had an uninvited guest. Feeling safer downstairs, I pulled out the sofa bed and slept there.

I re-make our bed, because I can't sleep downstairs forever, and go to my wardrobe for a pair of jeans. As I take them from the shelf, I see my white sundress, the one I'd wanted to wear on Monday, wedged between two other dresses. I take it out, glad to have found it. If I add a cardigan, I'll be able to wear it today. As I slip it over my head, the slight scent of washing powder tickles my nose; despite having worn it at the party, it still feels fresh and clean.

The mail comes as I'm having breakfast, bringing a copy of the novel I've been commissioned to translate from Italian into English. I like to read books through twice before I start translating, making notes as I go, so I take it through to the study and curl up on the sofa, glad that I'm going to be able to get back into my usual routine of working from nine to seven, four days a week. Until now, I've given myself Fridays off so that I could have three-day weekends, but with Leo working from home on Fridays, I'm going to take Thursdays off instead.

It's hard to concentrate at first, because my mind is still preoccupied by our gate-crasher, wondering if we'll ever be able to find out who he was. And more importantly, why he turned up, because that's what's bothering me most.

Toward the end of the morning, when I'm quite a few chapters in, I hear voices in the road outside. Closing my book, I go through to the sitting room and from the window, see Eve standing in front of the small black wrought-iron gate that leads into the square, chatting to Tamsin and Maria who, judging by the numerous bags they're carrying, look as if they're on their way back from the local shops. I watch enviously as they laugh together at something Eve has said. A wave of loneliness hits; I want so much to be part of their group that before I can stop myself, I'm heading out to join them.

I walk down the drive and wait to let a supermarket van pass. It stops in front of Lorna and Edward's and I cross the road behind it, giving a wave to Edward as he comes out of his house. The three women are no longer laughing but are huddled together, the way people do when they're talking about something serious, something secret. I curse my bad timing. I don't want to interrupt them—but it's too late. Maria has seen me.

"It's amazing that it doesn't seem to bother her," Tamsin is saying as I approach.

"I'm beginning to wonder if she actually knows," Eve replies.

"Of course she does," Tamsin scoffs.

Maria looks up brightly and I realize that they were talking about me.

"Hi, Alice, how are you?"

"Fine, thanks," I say, smiling at her.

Eve and Tamsin turn quickly. They're both wearing dark sunglasses and I feel even more intimidated at this visual barrier between me and them.

"Alice!" Eve cries, as if she hasn't seen me for months. She pushes her sunglasses on top of her head and her pixie cut splays out on each side. "What have you been up to?"

"Reading. I heard voices and thought I'd take a break."

"What are you reading?"

"A book I have to translate."

"Into which language?" Maria asks.

"English, from Italian."

"Impressive."

"Will's grandmother is Italian and he's trying to teach me so that I can speak to her, as she doesn't speak any English," Eve says. "I'm not managing very well."

"You should try Russian. It took me ages to be able to hold a conversation."

Eve looks at Maria in awe. "I didn't know you spoke Russian."

"I do, but not very well. I'm not fluent or anything."

I turn to Tamsin, aware that she's been silent. Today she's wearing pale blue jeans and an orange T-shirt, which on any other redhead would look weird. On her, it looks great. "How about you? Do you speak any languages?"

"No." Her voice is curt.

"Right." She might not like me but she's bordering on rude. I look at her appraisingly. She's stunningly pretty but there's an air of sadness about her. Suddenly, I want to find out more about these three women.

"I was wondering—would you like to come in for a coffee instead of standing in the road?" I ask. "Unless you have work to do?"

"I don't!" Eve says. "Not today."

Maria smiles. "Me neither, so that would be lovely."

"I can't." Tamsin lifts her arms to show her bags of shopping. "I need to go and put this away. But I'll see you two later."

I know I shouldn't take it personally. But I do.

By the time we're halfway through a pot of coffee, I'm getting a real picture of who my new neighbors are. Eve and Will have known each other for twenty years and they're thirty-one now.

"We got together at our school's theater club," Eve explains. "He didn't want to join at first because it was mainly girls. But as we were friends, he began to tag along with me and suddenly everyone realized that he had this amazing talent. Except he wouldn't do anything about it until I persuaded him to audition for RADA—and he only agreed because I refused to go out with him unless he did."

"I love that story," Maria says. "Tim and I met taking our rubbish bins out at uni."

Maria and Tim are in their late thirties. Tim is a qualified psychologist, working part-time while he undergoes further specialist training in psychotherapy, and Maria is a speech therapist, working four days a week until Luke, their youngest son, starts at nursery.

"I work every day except Wednesday," she explains. "It's lovely to have a day off in the middle of the week. It means I can go to yoga with Eve and Tamsin, and pick the boys up from school afterward. Tim does the school runs otherwise."

"I never work Wednesdays either," Eve says. "If I did, I'd never see Maria."

I mentally move my day off from Thursday to Wednesday. The yoga class sounds fun.

"That's funny, Wednesday is my day off too," I say with a smile.

I ask about Tamsin and Connor. They're the same age as Maria and Tim and, as I already knew from Leo, Connor is in whiskey, selling high-end brands to rich clients. Tamsin, who used to be a model—no surprise there—is now a stay-at-home mom.

"She's also a mathematical genius," Maria says. She's dressed from top to toe in black and with her dark hair, she looks amazingly dramatic. "She does all these online courses and once she's passed her exams, she's going to set herself up as an accountant."

"Wow," I say, impressed. "I'd love to have a mathematical brain."

"So, have you found out any more about the mystery man?" Eve asks, reaching for a biscuit.

"No. I'm trying not to let it bother me but what I regret most is the effect it's had on Lorna, because she was the one who let him in. It's really shaken her."

"That's a shame." Worry chases Eve's smile away. "She and Edward don't need any more stress in their lives. Do you know about their son? He was killed in Iraq. He was their only child, which makes it somehow worse."

"How awful," I say, shocked. "It must have been terrible for them."

"They lived on the coast—Bournemouth, I think—but they moved here three years ago," Maria says, taking up the story. "Lorna told me that as time passed, the memories dragged them down more, and they wanted a fresh start. They chose London because they loved going to the theater and visiting museums and, because of their advancing age, they'd found the traveling up and down from Bournemouth more difficult. And they were fine for a while, they were really sociable and went out quite a bit, just as they'd planned. But then the whole thing of losing their son caught up with them and they've become near recluses. It's sad really, because they never go anywhere now, not even shopping. They get everything delivered, even their clothes. It's as if they've lost all their confidence."

"Or their will to live," I say quietly. I catch them exchanging uneasy glances and decide to get it out there. "It's just that I know what it's like to lose someone you love. My parents and sister were killed in a car accident when I was nineteen. I kind of lost the will to live for a while afterward."

"Oh Alice, that's awful," Eve says, reaching for my hand. "I'm so sorry."

"My sister was only twenty-two. She'd been on vacation in Greece with her boyfriend, and my parents had gone to fetch her at the airport."

"I can't imagine what it must have been like." Maria's eyes are full of sympathy. "How did you cope?"

"I had my grandparents to think about. I had to be strong for them, and they had to be strong for me. We pulled each other through."

As I refill their mugs, I'm secretly glad Tamsin didn't join us. It's why, when Maria mentioned the yoga class, I didn't say anything to make her think I was fishing for an invitation to join them, even though I'd like to. I don't want to get Tamsin's back up even more. Anyway, didn't Leo warn me not to rush headlong into friendships?

"Sorry, Alice, but I have to go," Maria says, bringing me back to the present. "Yoga is at two o'clock and I need to run home and grab my leggings. Eve, I'll meet you outside."

"It's our Wednesday ritual," Eve explains, once Maria has left. "We have our yoga class and then I go with Tamsin and Maria to fetch their children from school. If the weather's nice, we stop in the square so that the kids can have a play. Then we go back to someone's for tea."

"It sounds lovely," I say wistfully.

Eve opens her mouth and I think for a moment that she's going to ask me to join them. "Have you ever done yoga before?" she asks instead.

"Never." I give her a tentative smile. "Maybe I'll join you when the new term starts in January."

Eve leaves, and I watch from Leo's study as she and Maria walk across the square to meet Tamsin. It was a lovely break and I'm happy to get back to reading my book. I'm so engrossed in the story that when there's a ring on the doorbell, I jump in alarm. I close my book quickly, hoping it's Eve, asking me to join them in the square. I glance at the time on my cell phone; it can't be Eve, it's just before three so they won't have finished their yoga session yet. Maybe it's Lorna, or Edward.

I push my phone into my back pocket and open the door.

He has his head turned away from me, looking toward the square, but there's no mistaking him. Instinct has me quickly slamming the door, but not so quickly that I miss his look of surprise as he turns to face me. I back away, my heart racing. Why has he come back?

The doorbell rings again. I leap forward and latch the chain into place.

"Ms. Dawson?" His voice comes through the door.

"If you don't go away, I'll call the police," I say tersely.

"I really hope you won't. Ms. Dawson, my name is Thomas Grainger and I'm a private investigator looking into a miscarriage of justice. My client's brother was accused of a murder he didn't commit."

"I don't care, I'm still going to call the police. You entered my house illegally last Saturday!"

"Actually, you invited me in."

"Only because I presumed you were someone I'd invited!"

"You asked me if I was Tom, which I am, except nobody really calls me that."

"I said Tim!"

"I'm not sure you'd be able to prove that in a court of law." There's a smile in his voice and I feel my guard lowering a little. "Could I ask you to open the door? I really do need to speak to you and I can't have a conversation through a block of wood."

Reluctantly, I open the door but keep the chain in place. He peers at me through the gap, bending his knees slightly so that I can see his face. Behind him, the road is empty.

"Thank you." He takes a card from the inside pocket of his jacket and holds it out to me. "As I said, I'm a private investigator and I'm looking into the murder of Nina Maxwell."

I don't take the card, I can't. Just hearing the name sends my mind spinning. It might have happened over a year ago, but I'll never forget the murder, because my sister was called Nina.

It's always the same. If I meet someone called Nina, I automatically want to be their friend. If I read something about someone called Nina, I'll take their story to my heart. That's how the death of my big sister, who I idolized, affects me. She lives on in the lives of other women called Nina.

It takes me a moment to let go of the memories that crowd my brain.

"Nina Maxwell?" I say. "I don't understand. What has her murder got to do with me?"

A slight frown crosses his face. "Nothing, other than this is where it happened."

I stare at him through the gap. "What—here, in The Circle?"

His frown deepens. "No, here in this house."

I shake my head. "No. There must be some mistake. She didn't live here, not in this house. We would have known if she had, the estate agent would have told us."

"I'm not sure—"

"I'm sorry," I say, cutting him off, hating the way he's making me feel. "You've made a mistake. Maybe Nina Maxwell did live somewhere in The Circle but it couldn't have been here. We wouldn't have bought the house if there'd been a murder here. And we would have known, because the estate agent would have told us."

I begin to push the door shut but he holds my gaze.

"I'm afraid there's no mistake, Ms. Dawson. This is where Nina Maxwell lived." He pauses. "And where she died."

NINE

For the second time in the space of a few minutes, I slam the door in the man's face. My legs shaking, I sit down on the stairs.

"I'm sorry." I jump at the sound of his voice coming through the door. I thought he'd gone. "I know this must have come as a shock."

"Go away, or I really will call the police," I say angrily.

"All right, I'm leaving now. But could I ask you to do something? First of all, google the murder. And secondly, call your estate agent and ask him why he didn't disclose details of it when you bought the house." There's a sliding noise as his card is pushed through the letter box. "If you feel able to speak to me again, please contact me at this number. Both I, and my client, would be very grateful."

His footsteps retreat down the path. Nailed to the stairs by a creeping dread, I can't move. What if it's true? I take my cell phone from my pocket and type "Nina Maxwell murder" into my search engine. I look at my screen, where several links to news reports have come up. I open the first one, dated 21st February 2018, and see a photo of a pretty, blond-haired woman with laughing brown eyes, a gold chain just visible around her neck. I recognize the photo; it was all over the media in the weeks following the murder. My heart in my mouth, I scroll to the article underneath.

A thirty-eight-year-old woman has been found murdered in London. Police were called to a house in The Circle, an exclusive residence in Finsbury Park, at approximately 9.30 p.m. last night, where they discovered the body of Nina Maxwell.

Nausea swirls in my stomach. I force myself to read the article again, my eyes sticking on the words "The Circle," hoping that if I stare at them long enough, they'll disappear. But they don't, and although there's no mention of the house number, the possibility that Nina Maxwell was murdered here, in the house where I'm living, is terrifying. A memory from the time of the murder comes to me—a cordoned-off house with bouquets of flowers placed respectfully on the pavement outside. Was it this one?

I push myself up from the stairs, grab my keys and open the front door, half afraid I'll find the private investigator on the doorstep. Thankfully, there's no sign of him. Or of anyone else. I step outside, feeling horribly exposed. But I can't stay in the house, not now.

I cross over the road, push open the gate to the square and sink onto the nearest bench, my mind still reeling. I don't know why I feel threatened. Thomas Grainger has been perfectly pleasant on the two occasions I've spoken to him. It's not *who* he is that frightens me, I realize, but what he said. How come he knows a murder was committed in the house where Leo and I are living, and we don't? How come Ben didn't tell Leo?

I find the contact details of Redwoods, the estate agents, and call them.

"Can I speak to Ben, please?" I ask, when a woman answers, trying to hide my agitation.

"I'm afraid he's away for a few days." She sounds bored rather than sorry.

My heart sinks. "When will he be back?"

"Monday. Can I help? I'm Becky, I work with Ben."

I hesitate, tempted ask her if she knows anything about a murder in the house that Leo bought through them. Surely everyone who works in the agency would have to know its history, if it included a recent death?

"My name is Alice Dawson," I say, deciding to go for it. "My partner, Leo Curtis, recently bought a house in Finsbury through Ben—number 6, The Circle. I was wondering—I heard a rumor that something happened in the house back in February last year. Someone said a woman died there?" I can't bring myself to say the word murdered.

There's a long pause, which I don't like. "I'm afraid you'll have to speak to Ben, Ms. Dawson."

"That's exactly what I want to do. Can you give me his cell number, please?"

"I'm sorry, I can't do that. But I can ask him to call you as soon as he gets back on Monday."

"Yes, please do."

I cut the call, feeling stupidly close to tears. I rub my eyes angrily, but I can't stop my increasing horror at the thought of our house being the scene of a murder. Becky might not have confirmed it but she hadn't denied it. Rage begins to build up inside me. How could Ben have kept it from us? He told Leo that the house was cheaper than its market price because it had been standing empty for over a year. Leo would have asked why, and Ben must have lied, or avoided giving him an answer. Leo is going to be devastated. If it's true, we're going to have to start house-hunting all over again.

My mind races ahead—Leo will put the house back on the market and we'll move into temporary accommodation while we find somewhere else to live. Or, better still, move back to my cottage. I quickly extinguish the tiny spark of happiness that the thought of going back to Harlestone brings. It seems misplaced among the reality of the murder and anyway, my cottage is rented out for another five months.

I want—need—to speak to Leo, but when I call his number, it goes through to voicemail. I wait a few minutes, then try again, but he still doesn't pick up. I want so much to get to the bottom of it that I decide to call the estate agents back and insist on having Ben's cell number. But something occurs to me. What if he wasn't obliged to tell Leo about the murder? Bringing up my search engine again, I type *Do estate agents have to disclose murder at a property?* A helpful article came up but as I start to read it, my gratitude turns to dismay. It seems that although most estate agents would mention it, there's no obligation to do so.

Stunned, I lean back against the bench. I can't believe that Ben was so unscrupulous. Even if he wasn't obliged by law to tell Leo, what about his moral obligation? He was recommended to us by Ginny and Mark, he and Mark have become friends. I need to warn them about him.

I send Ginny a message **Can you talk?** Ginny, being Ginny, is able to tell from those few words that something is wrong and calls straightaway.

"Alice, what's up? Are you all right, is Leo all right?"

"Yes, we're both fine. But Ginny, I need your advice. Actually, I need to speak to Ben. Do you have his cell number, by any chance?"

"Mark does. Why—is there a problem with the house or something?"

Surprise jolts through me. "How do you know?"

"I don't." Ginny sounds puzzled. "But if you want Ben's number, it must be to do with the house, because why else would you want to talk to him?"

"Yes, it is about the house. I've just found out that a woman was murdered here, at number 6." Just saying it makes the horror come back and I grip the wooden bench with my free hand, grounding myself.

"What?" I can hear the shock in Ginny's voice. "Did you say a woman was murdered in your house, the house Leo just bought?"

"Yes."

"Are you sure?"

"Yes, I checked. Do you remember the Nina Maxwell murder? The woman who was killed by her husband?"

"Didn't he commit suicide?"

"Yes, I think so. This was their house, Ginny, this is where it happened. I checked the news reports, they mention The Circle, they don't say what number but it was here, I know it was."

"Alice, that's awful, I'm so sorry!"

"It must be why the house was empty for so long, why nobody wanted to buy it. I don't blame them, I don't want to stay here now, I can't bear to be in the house. I'm sitting in the square and even that's too close. Ben should have told Leo, but he didn't."

"But—I don't understand. Wouldn't he have been obliged to?"

"Apparently not, I checked."

"Perhaps he didn't know."

"I think he must have."

The gate clangs open and looking up, I see Geoff closing it behind him as he comes into the square. He's wearing his usual outfit of shorts and a baggy shirt, except that he's added a peaked cap to protect his balding head from the sun. He gives me a cheery smile and for a moment, I'm tempted to jump up and ask him if he knows anything about the murder. Instead, I smile back, keeping my head bent low over my phone so that he'll realize I'm on a call.

"I can't believe Ben wouldn't have told you," Ginny is saying. "I don't know him that well—Mark knows him better than I do—but I can't imagine he would be so dishonest."

"That's why I need to speak to him," I say as Geoff walks past. "I called his office and they told me he's away for a few days. But this is important. Could you get his number from Mark?"

"I'll call him now. Do you want me to call Ben for you?"

"Would you?" My voice breaks. "It's just that she was called Nina. If you could find out if he knew, I'll take it from there."

"Of course." Ginny's voice is full of sympathy. She never knew Nina but she understands why I'm extra upset. "I'll call you back."

It seems an eternity before my phone rings again, an eternity where I feel completely alone, because Geoff has long since gone and there's no one else around. Then, just as my phone starts ringing, I see Eve, Tamsin, and Maria come through the gate at the other end of the square with a group of chattering children. About to take the call, I shift quickly on the bench, turning my back to them, hoping they won't see me and decide to come over. But when I check the number, it's not one that I know. I stare at the screen, hating the effect it's having on me, the way it's making my heart race. What if it's the private investigator?

I press the green icon, accepting the call.

"Ms. Dawson?" It's a man's voice and I'm about to cut him off when I realize it isn't Thomas Grainger.

"Yes," I say curtly, because it has to be Ben.

"Ms. Dawson, it's Ben Forbes, from Redwoods. I've just had Ginny on the phone and I wanted to call you myself. I hope that's all right?"

"Yes, it's fine, I just want to get to the bottom of this, I want to know how we've ended up living in a house where a woman was murdered."

"I know it must have come as a shock to you," he says, echoing Thomas Grainger's words.

"You can say that again," I say fiercely, because it's obvious he knew. "Surely you should have told Leo, even if you weren't legally obliged to?"

"Can I ask how you found out?"

"A neighbor told me," I invent, because he doesn't need to know about the private investigator. "Anyway, why does it matter how I found out? We should have found out from you."

"Can I ask—have you spoken to Mr. Curtis?"

"No, he's at work. He's going to be devastated, because there's no way we can live here now. I hope you realize that."

"I think you should call Mr. Curtis, Ms. Dawson."

"I will, once I know why you didn't tell him about the murder."

"I'm sorry, Ms. Dawson, but Mr. Curtis already has the facts. He knew the history of the house before he made his offer. He knew why it had stood empty for over a year, why it was cheaper than it should have been." He pauses, giving me time to absorb what he's saying. "When he came back with his offer, I asked him if he was sure you were all right with it, because although we had a few couples who agreed to view the house, they said they wouldn't feel comfortable living there. Mr. Curtis assured me that you were fine with it, that you were willing to overlook its history because it meant you'd be able to keep your cottage—in Sussex, I believe?" Another pause. "I'm sorry, Ms. Dawson, but you really need to talk to Mr. Curtis."

TEN

I'm so numb with shock that I barely hear my cell phone ringing. It's Ginny. I don't take the call, I can't. My mind is too busy stumbling over what Ben told me.

I can't believe it. I can't believe that Leo went ahead and bought the house despite knowing about the murder, it seems too incredible. How could he be all right with it? How could he think, even for a minute, that I'd be all right with it? He knows how squeamish I am, how I can't watch a film without leaving the room as soon as I sense something bad is going to happen. Which must be why he didn't tell me, because he knew I'd refuse to live there. What makes it worse is that he lied to Ben about having told me. And what makes *that* worse is he told Ben that the reason I didn't mind living there was because I wouldn't have to sell my cottage. How could he? He's made me out to be both insensitive and mercenary, and I hate him for it. At least Ben knows the truth now. But it only makes me feel marginally better.

I can't understand Leo's motivation for not telling me. He must have known I'd find out eventually. Is that why he didn't want to have people over for drinks, in case someone mentioned the murder? And why had no one mentioned it, why had neither Eve or Maria, or anyone else at the party said anything?

Because they couldn't, I realize dully. They presumed that I knew, that I was fine about it. They were hardly going to introduce it into the conversation—*So, Alice, what's it like living in a house where a murder took place?* I remember Tamsin's comment at the party about me being brave. She hadn't been referring to my move from the country to London, but my move into a house with a terrible past. And then, this morning, the conversation I overheard when I went to join them. What had Tamsin said? I close my eyes and her voice comes back to me. *"It's amazing that it doesn't seem to bother her."* And Eve's reply—*"I'm beginning to wonder if she actually knows."*

I feel a rush of gratitude toward Eve, for realizing that maybe I'm not as heartless as everyone must think. I'm surprised she's been so friendly, surprised the people here have been generally welcoming. Maybe some of them were secretly judging us for buying the house but the majority had seemed interested—

Oh God. I lean forward, my head heavy in my hands. I had paraded people through the house, I had taken them upstairs. What must people have thought? The ones who had been eager to see the bedroom—was that because the murder had taken place there?

My phone is still in my hand so I google the murder again and find an article written four days after Nina Maxwell's death. There are more details: her body was found in her bedroom, tied to a chair. Her hair had been cut off and she had been strangled. *A man has been arrested and is helping the police with their inquiries,* the article finishes.

Bile surges in my throat. I knew how Nina Maxwell had died, it had haunted me for months after. But to see it written in black and white—I fight down the nausea, channeling it instead into anger at the people who had wanted to see the bedroom where it had taken place. Tamsin and most of the women hadn't accepted my invitation to show them the renovations, it was mainly the men who'd been interested. Eve had already been upstairs, not at the party, but the day she came over to introduce herself, and I'd dragged her to the bedroom to show her our huge wardrobe. She had held back at first and I'd put her hesitation down to a desire not to appear nosey.

"Alice?" Lifting my head, I see Eve walking down the path

toward me. "What are you doing sitting here?" A frown furrows her brow. "You're shivering! Is everything all right?"

"No, not really."

"Are you ill, do you need me to call someone?"

"No, I'm fine. Well, I'm not fine, obviously," I say, trying to joke. "But I'm not ill. I just feel so humiliated, so angry!"

"Angry is good," Eve says, coming to sit next to me. The smell of her perfume—Sì, by Armani—is oddly comforting. "Much better than ill, or sad. Why don't you tell me what's happened?"

"I've just found out that our house," I thrust my hand toward it, "was the scene of a brutal murder." I look at her in anguish. "I didn't know, Eve. Leo knew but he didn't tell me."

"Oh, Alice." The sympathy in Eve's eyes is also comforting. "I was beginning to think that you might not know. At first, I thought you were one of those people who are able to compartmentalize things, who are able to say 'that was then, but this is now.'"

"I could never be that insensitive. I'm surprised you could bring yourself to talk to me. I'm surprised anyone could talk to me when I didn't acknowledge the murder, not even to say how sorry I was that you had all lost your neighbor."

"No one was judging you, Alice."

"I think Tamsin might have been."

"Well, maybe. A bit. Nina was her best friend, so it's under-standable." She pauses a moment. "The first time she saw you, she thought for a moment that you *were* Nina. She was standing at her bedroom window and she saw you crossing the square. You're about the same build as Nina was and from that distance, she could only see your long blond hair. It gave her a bit of a shock."

I nod distractedly. "But why weren't people judging me?" I ask. "Shouldn't they have been?"

Eve pushes her hand through her hair. "I think everyone was just relieved that the house had been sold, that it was going to be lived in and not standing empty. It had become a bit of a shrine, I suppose, and some of the children began to say it must be haunted, and their parents didn't want them believing that it was. When we heard that someone had bought it, it was as if a breath of fresh air was coming to The Circle. At last, we were going to be able to move on." She looks at me earnestly. "People are grateful, Alice. We see it as a new beginning."

"Maybe, but we're not going to be able to stay here now. At least, I'm not. It obviously doesn't bother Leo."

"He told Will it was why he wanted to change it around upstairs, get rid of the room where it happened. He said he wanted to make it easier for you to live there."

"Insinuating that I knew about it," I say, digging in my pocket for a tissue. "And of course, nobody dared mention the murder on Saturday, even though there were plenty who were eager to see where it had taken place. You'd have thought at least one person would have asked me if I was OK living with the ghost of a murdered woman."

Eve looks uncomfortable. "I might have had something to do with that. Leo told Will he'd appreciate it if no one mentioned the house's history in front of you as you were obviously sensitive about it. Will told me and I sort of spread the word."

A memory comes back, of Leo going to see Will, the day after I told him I'd invited people for drinks. "I can't believe it!" I say, my anger coming back. "He really didn't want me to find out, did he?" I look at her, hoping she'll be able to give me an answer. "I can't understand it, Eve. He's never done anything like this before, he's never kept anything back, he's never not told me the truth. And he must have known that I'd find out eventually. It's not the sort of thing that can be kept a secret."

"How did you find out?" Eve asks, reaching into her bag and bringing out a peaked cap, and using it to fan herself.

"I got a phone call," I say, hoping she didn't notice my slight hesitation. "From a reporter." I'm not lying to her because I'm almost sure that Thomas Grainger is a journalist, and changed his job description to private investigator to make it sound more palatable.

She jams the cap on her head, not caring that her sunglasses are caught under it. "What did they say?"

"She asked me how it felt to be living at the scene of a brutal murder," I improvise, changing the pronoun to move further away from the truth. "When I said that I didn't know what she was talking about, she told me to google Nina Maxwell." That part at least is true. "So, I did."

"What an awful way to find out."

I shake my head slowly. "I can't believe Leo knew." The memory of how I accused Ben of not telling Leo makes me flinch internally. "Leo told the estate agent that I was fine with it because, with the house being cheaper, it meant I could keep my cottage in Harlestone. He made me sound completely heartless."

She tries to hug me but because of the way we're sitting on the bench, it's awkward, and I realize that I don't know Eve, not really. Do I even know Leo?

"What are you going to do?" she asks.

"I need to speak to Leo but I don't want to call him, I need to see his face. He's back tomorrow evening so I'll have to wait until then. But I can't stay in the house, so I'll go to a hotel." I turn to her. "Can I ask you a favor, Eve? I need to get a couple of things from the house, would you come with me? I know it's stupid but I feel a bit funny going in there now."

"It's not stupid and of course I'll come with you. And you don't need to go to a hotel, you can stay with me and Will."

I falter at this, suddenly unsure of what I want. "Are you sure?"

"Sure I'm sure!"

"I don't need much, just some pajamas, a toothbrush and a change of clothes. And my book and laptop."

"Come on then."

On the doorstep, I hand my keys to Eve. She unlocks the door and goes into the house, while I wait on the doorstep, dread cramping my stomach. I don't know what I'm expecting. For it to be different, I suppose. At least to feel different. But it doesn't, it feels just the same, so I go in.

Eve stoops to pick up something.

"Someone's card," she says, handing it to me without looking at it.

"Thanks." I tuck it in my pocket and wait while she takes off her cap, shoves it into her bag, then kicks off her trainers. I slip mine off and follow her upstairs to the bedroom. She walks straight in but I stop in the doorway.

She holds out her hand to me. "It's just the same as before, Alice. Nothing has changed."

I take a steadying breath and look around the room. She's right, it is the same. The patterned curtains are still billowing in the breeze, just as they were this morning. My hairbrush is still on the dressing table, the clothes I wore yesterday are still draped over the chair. But—

"I can't be here," I say, overwhelmed by a feeling of mounting panic. Going over to the chest of drawers, I grab a pair of pajamas and some underwear then run out of the room, away from the evil I can feel seeping into my pores.

ELEVEN

"Here." Eve holds out a mug of tea. "Drink this, and then we'll open a bottle of wine."

"Sorry. I don't know why I made so much fuss about being in the bedroom." Curled up on the pale leather sofa in her sitting room, my feet tucked under me, I realize she deserves the truth. "Actually, I do. My sister's name was Nina, so anything to do with anyone called Nina always affects me more."

She gives me a hug. "Oh, Alice, I'm so sorry."

"If my sister had lived, she would have been the same age as Nina Maxwell. I know it sounds horribly dramatic but it makes me feel as if my sister has been killed twice over."

"That, coupled with Leo not telling you about the murder, would be enough to make anyone freak out," she says. "It's a lot for you to cope with."

A glass of Chablis later, I'm beginning to feel better. "What was she like?" I ask.

"Nina?" Eve takes a sip of wine. "I didn't get the chance to know her well because we only moved here five months before she died. She was lovely, quite spiritual. As well as being a therapist, she was also a qualified yoga instructor." She smiles. "She started our yoga group and after she died, we carried on with it, in her memory."

I like that Nina Maxwell enjoyed yoga, because my sister had too. She had tried several times to get me to go to her class with her, but I'd always had something to do. After, I wished so much that I'd gone, even once. I also like that Nina Maxwell was a therapist; it seems she was a caring person.

"And her husband?"

"The nicest man you could hope to meet. From what I knew of him, anyway. But you never really know, do you?"

"You must have been shocked when he was arrested for her murder."

Eve reaches toward the low glass table that is neither round nor square but an indeterminate shape, and picks up her glass. "Everyone was." She takes a sip of wine. "We couldn't believe it, we thought it was a case of 'it's always the husband until they find the real culprit.' But then we heard he'd committed suicide."

I remember what the investigator said about a miscarriage of justice. "And that made you think he must have killed her?"

"Yes."

"But why?" Eve looks suddenly uncomfortable. "I'm sorry to ask all these questions," I say. "I'm just trying to understand. But if you prefer me not to ask, that's fine."

"No, it's OK. It's actually a relief to be able to talk about it to someone who wasn't here at the time. It's sort of become a taboo subject." She pauses, thinking about my question. "Apart from there being no signs of a break-in, there were several reasons why we believed Oliver must have killed her. First, the fact that he committed suicide made us think that he couldn't come to terms with what he'd done, because he truly loved Nina—that's what's so tragic. And other things came to light which made us think it was not just possible, but probable."

"What things?"

"The first was that he lied about the time he got home that

night." She frowns, catching herself, then looks at me apologetically. "Actually, it doesn't feel good to be repeating things I only heard second or third hand. As I said, I didn't know Nina that well. Tamsin knew her better than I did. And Lorna was the one who witnessed everything." Putting her glass back down, she reaches for the bottle of wine. "Here, let me top up your glass for you."

Although I'm curious, I'm happy not to talk about the murder. I also respect her for not wanting to gossip.

"Shall we watch a film?" Eve suggests. "Something light to take your mind off things for a while?"

"Good idea," I say.

"I don't suppose you want to watch *When Harry Met Sally,* do you? I've only ever seen it once."

I laugh. "Why not? I could do with something light-hearted."

Although my mind keeps wandering back to the murder, the film keeps us occupied until Will comes home.

"Please tell me you're not hungry," Eve says, jumping to her feet and giving him a kiss. "Alice and I have been chatting. She's going to stay the night, isn't that nice?"

I can see her signaling to Will with her eyes to make him understand that there's been a bit of a crisis.

Will shrugs off his backpack and puts it down on the floor "Very," he says, smiling at me. "And yes, I'm hungry, I always am after rehearsing all day. Have you two eaten?"

"No," Eve says mournfully. "Not even a bag of crisps."

"Then how about I make a big bowl of pasta?"

She flings her arms around him. "I was hoping you'd say that." She turns to me. "Will makes the best pasta in the world. His great-grandmother passed down her recipe for the most delicious sauce. You're going to love it!"

"Except that if I make it from scratch, it will take two hours," Will points out.

"Oh yes, I forgot about that." Eve looks so crestfallen that I laugh. "All that simmering to reduce down the tomatoes."

"Exactly. So, I'll make a carbonara, if we have bacon."

Eve beams at him. "We do. Would you like a glass of wine to drink while you're cooking?"

"No, don't worry, I'll get myself a beer." He heads to the kitchen. "See you in about twenty minutes."

The sound of my cell phone ringing sends me into a panic.

"It's Leo. I can't speak to him, not yet."

"Then don't," Eve says. "Send him a text and tell him you're having dinner with us and that you'll speak to him later. That will give you time to work out what you're going to say."

"Good idea," I say, immediately feeling calmer.

Eve gets to her feet. "I'll lay the table while you do that," she says, giving me space. "Come when you're ready."

I message Leo and when he sends back a cheery OK, have fun! I immediately feel guilty that he has no idea of what I'm going to be saying to him when we speak. I remind myself that it's not my fault, that he's the one who hasn't been upfront but it only makes me feel slightly better.

The good thing about the houses in The Circle being built to the same model is that I know exactly where Eve and Will's kitchen is. As I walk down the hall toward it, I can hear them talking quietly together and guess that Eve is telling Will why I'm there.

"Can I help?" I ask, pushing the door open.

"Only by joining me in another glass of wine," Eve says, taking a fresh bottle from the fridge.

They've made a breakfast bar where we have our table. I heave myself onto a steel bistro-style bar-stool, watching as they move around the kitchen together, Will nudging Eve every now and then, pretending that she's getting in his way. I smile, thinking how good they are together, and then think about me and Leo. Are we good together? I used to think so. Now, I'm not so sure.

We move to the table and while we eat steaming bowls of delicious pasta, I wait for Will to say something about what has happened, and I wouldn't mind, because maybe he'd have some insight into Leo's psyche, come up with an explanation as to why he decided to keep something so major from me. But although I've relaxed a bit, because Will is brilliant at making me laugh, he doesn't mention Leo or the murder at all.

Later, as I lie in their pretty guest room, I remember, not long ago, talking to Leo about one of my friends, who had just found out that her husband had gambled all their money away.

"You should have seen her, Leo, she's so broken. She doesn't know what to do, whether to stay with him or leave him. She says all the trust has gone."

"What would you do if you were in her place?"

"If I couldn't trust you, I couldn't be with you. And if I couldn't be with you, life wouldn't be worth living." I had stared deep into his eyes. "Do you see how much I love you?"

Back then, I never imagined those words would come back to haunt me. But they have, and worried about the conversation I'm going to have to have with Leo, I'm unable to sleep. He must have thought it strange that I hadn't called him back but maybe he fell asleep before he realized. Remembering that Ginny called several times, I scrabble on the floor for my phone and send her a holding message:

Leo knew about the murder, Ben told him. I'm with Eve and Will next door. I'll call you tomorrow xx

I manage to chase Leo from my mind but he's replaced by Nina Maxwell. It's hard to stop myself from thinking about what she must have endured but I eventually manage to force my thoughts away from her death, toward her life, and fall asleep wondering what sort of person she was.

PAST

"How are you?" I ask, smiling. This is her eighth session and we've been making excellent progress.

"I'm good," she says. "I'm feeling much more positive about everything."

It's true that this is the most relaxed I've seen her. She was still wearing classic skirts and formal shirts at her fourth session. Today she's wearing a pleated skirt that comes to just above her knee. Her hair is tied back, as usual, but if the last few sessions are anything to go by, it will soon be loose around her shoulders.

"Excellent," I tell her. "I take it you've had a good couple of weeks?"

"Yes." She raises a hand and pulls the elastic from her ponytail. "I've spent a lot of time thinking about what we talked about last time," she says, swishing her head from side to side, settling her newly released hair around her shoulders.

I nod approvingly. It's taken a while, but at our last session, she finally accepted that her husband is at the root of her problems and that the only way forward, if she is to gain some inner peace, is to leave him. I wait for her to expand.

"You were going to speak to your husband," I prompt, when she doesn't say anything. "Could that be the reason you're feeling better?"

She nods. "We had a long discussion, and it made me realize something. He's not the reason for my unhappiness."

I stifle a sigh. It is not my place to show disappointment, but it's there, nonetheless. I draw my notepad toward me. "During our last session, you had concluded that he is," I say, consulting the notes I'd made. I pause. "You had also made the decision to leave him."

"I know. But everything's different now. I'm not unhappy anymore. I don't think I ever was, really."

The sun is bright today, despite it being cold outside, and through the blinds, lines of light run across her face in perfect blocks.

"I think we need to explore the reason for your change of heart."

"I think it's just that I came to my senses." She smiles across at me. "And I have you to thank for that."

"Oh?"

"Yes. You said honesty was the best policy so I told Daniel how I felt—not that I wanted to leave him, but that I was unhappy—and he said that I wasn't unhappy, I was bored. And I realized that he was right." She fiddles with the tiny silver J, which hangs from the clasp of the white-gold Omega watch on her wrist. "I've never thought about getting a job because financially, I haven't needed to. It means I have too much time on my hands—too much time to think, too much time to focus on myself when I should be looking outward, channeling my energy into helping others. Daniel suggested that I do some voluntary work and he's already put me in touch with a couple of organizations." She laughs. "I told you he was perfect."

"That's progress indeed," I say, smiling.

"I guess I'm going to have to stop these sessions," she says. "I feel guilty for never having told Daniel about them and I'm not sure I really need them now. On the other hand, I don't want to undo all the good work we've been doing by stopping abruptly." She looks at me anxiously. "What do you think?"

"I think a few sessions of the relaxation therapy we discussed during our first session would be a good way of transitioning out of therapy. Is that something you think you'd like to consider?"

She nods happily. "Definitely. Relaxation therapy is something that Daniel will understand."

"Good." I hate losing clients when I've put so much work into them. I check the time on my watch and stand up. "We have time for one now, if you like."

TWELVE

"Stay as long as you like," Will says the next morning, taking his plate and coffee cup from the breakfast bar and putting them into the dishwasher. "Just pull the door behind you when you leave."

"Thanks," I say gratefully.

"Are we leaving together, Eve?" he asks, pushing his shirt, which he'd been wearing loose for breakfast, into the waistband of his jeans. "Because I need to go now."

Eve slides off her bar-stool and looks anxiously at me. "Are you sure you don't want me to cancel my mum? She won't mind."

"No, it's fine, I need to think about what I'm going to say to Leo."

"Then yes, Will, I'm coming with you." She gives me a quick hug. "If you need me at all, just call. You have my cell phone."

"And we're both here this evening," Will adds, picking up his backpack.

"Thank you. You've both been so kind."

Eve hovers. "Will you be all right?"

"I'll be fine. I have work to do."

But I'm too wound up to concentrate on the book I'm meant to be reading. And hurt. And insecure. For Leo to have lied to me, and about me, makes me wonder what else he might have hidden from me. I actually know very little of his life before we met. I know that he left home at eighteen because of his difficult family background and drifted from one low-paid job to another, until he realized that education was the answer to his problems. He studied hard and worked for a couple of investment management companies before setting himself up as a freelance consultant in risk management.

Needing something to do, I open my laptop and then pull out the business card Eve passed to me when she took me back to the house last night. I hold it tightly along the edges; the font is black in a block print: THOMAS GRAINGER. I type "Thomas Grainger, Private Investigator" into my search engine, to see if he's legit. To my surprise, he is. His website is professional and discreet and his offices are in Wimbledon. I put the address into my phone. With new motivation, I begin to research Nina Maxwell's murder. I want to know everything there is to know although I'm not sure why. Maybe it's my subconscious telling me I'll feel better if I have all the facts. Something to do with feeling in control, instead of completely out of control.

I read article after article, making notes as I go, but I don't learn much more. She was killed at around 9 p.m. Her husband called 999 at approximately 9:20 p.m. to say that he'd come home from work and had found her dead in the bedroom.

My stomach churns when I remember Leo's insistence on knocking the two bedrooms into one. "I want to change things around a bit up here," he'd said. *I bet you did*, I think resentfully. *I bet you wanted to change things around so that when I eventually found out about the murder, I wouldn't be able to freak out about sleeping in the same bedroom, because essentially, it wouldn't be the same.* Except that essentially, it is.

According to one of the more detailed reports, there had been a struggle during which Nina Maxwell had put up a valiant fight before being rendered unconscious, then tied to a chair with belts from bathrobes belonging to her and her husband. As far as I could see, everything pointed to her husband being the killer.

A text arrives: **Hope to be home by 7. I've got the Residents' Association meeting tonight so I'll only have time for a quick dinner. Can't wait to see you xx**

I text back: **Message me when you arrive at Euston.**

Had he noticed that I didn't put my usual two kisses? When he texts from Euston at six forty-five, I take my courage, laptop, book and bag in my hands, and go home.

Home. *This is my home now*, I remind myself as I put the key in the door. In the few weeks that I've been here, I've made it our home, mine and Leo's. What's going to happen if I can't bring myself to stay here?

In the hall, I try to think about the happy times Nina Maxwell must have had in this house. Because she must have been happy; she'd had friends and from what Eve had said, her husband was lovely. Except that he had ended up killing her. From the photos I've seen of him during my research and the testimonies I've read, he didn't seem capable of murder. But then, not many people do.

Determined to think of them as Nina and Oliver, rather than victim and perpetrator, I walk around the house using memories of my sister and her boyfriend to picture their life together. I imagine them in the kitchen, chatting as they made dinner, then curled up on the sofa in the sitting room, watching a film, Nina's legs hooked over Oliver's, living a perfectly normal life until something terrible had changed their lives forever. Just as it had my sister's.

By focusing on Nina and Oliver as people, I manage to lose some of the anxiety that has gripped me since yesterday. Wanting to test myself, I move toward the stairs. I'm fine when I get to the landing, fine when I go into the spare bedroom; it's just a bedroom. But when I push open the door on the other side of the landing and peer into the room beyond, all I can see is what I've tried to block from my mind—Nina's lifeless body tied to a chair, her long blond hair strewn on the floor around her. The image is so vivid I can hardly breathe. Slamming the door behind me, I hurry downstairs, clutching dizzily onto the handrail. Aware that Leo will be arriving at any moment,

I go to the kitchen and scoop water from the tap onto my face, then sit down at the table, waiting to find out how it is that I'm living in a house where a woman was murdered.

I don't have long to wait before I hear Leo's key in the door, his footsteps in the hall, the thump of his bag as he lets it drop to the floor.

"I'm home!"

The soft brush of material as he slips his jacket from his shoulders, the chink of coins as he hangs it over the newel post, the whip of his tie as he pulls it from under his collar, the sigh as he eases his neck—I hear them all.

"Alice, where are you?" he calls.

I can't see the frown that crosses his face at the silence that greets him, I can only imagine it. He walks across the hall and into the kitchen, his shoes still on his feet, the frown still on his face, which quickly turns to relief when he sees me sitting at the table.

"There you are," he says, a smile in his voice. He bends to kiss me and I twist away from him.

"What's the matter?" he asks, alarmed.

"Who are you, Leo?"

The color drains from his face so fast that my instinct is to jump up and make him sit down. But I stay where I am and watch dispassionately as he grabs hold of a chair, leaning heavily on it as he tries desperately to recover his composure.

"How could you? How could you keep something so—so terrible, so horrible, from me?" I say, frustrated that I can't find anything better than "terrible" or "horrible" to describe what happened upstairs. "How did you think I wouldn't find out?"

"Who told you?" he asks, his voice so low I have trouble hearing him.

"A neighbor." I don't care that I'm lying. I'll tell him about Thomas Grainger once I've got to the bottom of his deception.

He looks up, shock visible beneath the anguish on his face.

"A *neighbor* told you?"

I hold his gaze. "Yes."

"But—" He runs a hand through his hair, keeping hold of the chair with the other. "Which neighbor?"

"What does it matter who it was?" I say impatiently. "How could you lie to me, Leo?"

"I-I—" He sounds close to tears and I feel a twinge of alarm, and also a little ashamed. He must have been living in dread of me finding out. But I can't forgive him, not yet.

"What's almost worse is that you lied *about* me, not just to me."

"What do you mean?" he mumbles.

"You insinuated to Ben that I was fine about living here, because it meant that I could keep my cottage in Harlestone."

He stares at me for so long that I think he's going to deny it, or tell me that Ben misunderstood. After what seems an eternity, he pulls out the chair he's been holding onto, and sinks onto it.

"I'm sorry." The relief on his face tells me he's glad it's out in the open.

"What were you thinking? Were you hoping that I wouldn't find out?"

He studies his hands. "No, I knew you would. I was hoping that you wouldn't before I could tell you."

"And when were you going to tell me?"

"I—I just wanted you to be a bit more settled here."

"Why?"

"So that you'd find it harder to leave. It's why I didn't tell you before I bought the house. I knew you would refuse to live here and—" he raises his eyes to mine, "I really wanted to."

"So much that you were willing to overlook that a woman had died here?"

"It's not the same house, Alice. It's been redecorated and renovated, and I've changed the layout upstairs."

I slam my hand down on the table. "It's exactly the same house! I don't understand how you can't see that! It's still the house where a murder took place!"

He gives a helpless shrug, which does nothing to calm me. "Then maybe it's just that I'm able to live with that. I know it might sound callous, but it doesn't really bother me. And I remember you saying once, when someone pointed out that people must have died in your cottage, given that it's two hundred years old, that it wouldn't bother you if they had."

"There's a huge difference between someone dying peacefully in their bed of old age and being brutally murdered at thirty-eight years old!"

"We can't always know the history of the houses we live in. Somebody might have been murdered in the cottage in Harlestone."

I hate that he has a point.

"I mean, if somebody called you tomorrow, and said, 'Hey, I've just discovered that fifty years ago, somebody was murdered in your cottage,' would you leave immediately and never spend another day there?"

I hesitate. I love my cottage. Noticing, he leans forward.

"You would still stay there, wouldn't you? You wouldn't sell up."

"Yes, actually, I would. I'd put it on the market. Even fifty years is too close."

"I don't believe you," he says, rubbing his face with his hands.

My anger flares again. "Since when has this become about me? And since when have you started not believing me? I'm not the one in the wrong, Leo, you are!"

"I know, and I'm sorry." He reaches for my hand but I move it away.

"What must people have thought on Saturday, when I offered to take them upstairs to see the changes we'd made? They thought I knew about the murder."

"I never expected you to show people around."

"That's why you didn't want to have people over, isn't it?" I stand up, needing to put distance between us. "You were worried someone would mention what had happened here." I move to the other side of the kitchen and lean against the worktop. "I don't understand, I don't understand how you thought you could get away with it."

He opens his hands, pleading with me to understand. "I wasn't trying to get away with it. I was going to tell you, as soon as the time was right."

"And until then, you didn't mind people thinking I was a callous bitch."

"I'm sure no one thought that."

"Tamsin did."

"The redhead?"

"Yes. I overheard her say that she couldn't believe it didn't bother me. I had no idea what she was talking about. Now I do."

He sighs. "What do you want to do?"

I grab a cloth and start wiping the worktop, which is already clean. "I can't stay here, not now."

"We could go and stay in a hotel for few days."

"And then what? Come back here and pretend the murder never happened?"

He flinches. "Not that it never happened, no. But maybe accept that it happened, and move on. I think you should give the house a chance, Alice."

I stop wiping and turn to look at him. "What do you mean?"

He leans forward, fixing me with his eyes. "Make new memories for it. Be happy here."

Resentment bursts out of me. "Be happy here? How can I?" I throw the cloth angrily into the white enamel sink. "She was called Nina, Leo!"

"I know, and that's another reason I hesitated about telling you." His voice, quiet and reasonable, is designed to calm me. "I was worried that, just when you'd decided to try and let go of the past by leaving Harlestone, it would bring everything back. You've done so well by actually agreeing to move here. Can't we build on that?" He waits for me to speak but I can't because what he said about making new memories for the house has struck a chord. He rubs at his face again. "What do you want to do? Do you want to go back to Harlestone? Do you want me to put this house up for sale and rent a flat in London while I wait for it to be sold? Because that's what I'd have to do. I couldn't take all that traveling from Harlestone to Birmingham each day so I'd have to live in London during the week and see you at the weekends—sometimes, occasionally, just like we did before we moved here. Is that what you want?"

He sits there, waiting for my answer, the fine lines around his eyes deeper than before. But I can't give him one. I want everything he suggested and none of what he suggested. I don't want to stay—but I don't want to go. I want him to leave—but if I'm going to stay here in the house, at least tonight, I don't want to be alone. The only thing I'm sure about is that, for the moment, I don't want to be anywhere near him. Or anywhere near the room upstairs.

I move toward the door. "I don't know what I want," I say, my voice tight. "And until I do, I'll be sleeping in my study."

It's only when I'm making up the sofa bed that I realize I didn't ask him why he wanted the house so much.

THIRTEEN

"Why did you want this house so much?" I ask Leo the next morning. We're standing in the kitchen. It's spotless, because neither of us bothered to eat last night and the early morning light is bouncing off the pale marble surfaces.

"Sorry?" He looks tired, but not as tired as I do.

"Yesterday, you said that the reason you didn't tell me about the murder before moving in was because you knew I'd refuse to live here and you really wanted this house. I'm asking you why you really wanted this house. It's a nice house but not so nice that anyone with a conscience would overlook a murder." I know I'm being harsh but I barely slept and fatigue is dragging me down.

He walks over to the black and chrome coffee machine.

"Coffee?"

I'm dying for one. "No thanks."

He makes his coffee before answering my question, as if he's hoping I'll tire of waiting. But I'm prepared to give him as much time as it takes.

"I wanted this house because it's in a secure environment," he says eventually. "I like that nobody can get in unless they live here, or they're let in by someone who lives here. It makes it safer. And because I could afford it. I'd never have been able to afford it if it didn't have a past."

"Since when have you become security conscious?"

"Since I started getting harassed by clients."

"I wasn't aware you'd been harassed by clients."

He glances at me. "That's because I chose not to tell you."

"I know you had unwanted calls," I say, remembering the times he answered his phone only to hang up straightaway, and the way he sometimes stared at the screen before deciding not to answer, then telling me it was a wrong number. "I didn't realize they were from clients. But nobody actually came to the door, did they?" I pause as a memory resurfaces. "Except that woman, the blond one, in Harlestone. I asked you about her at the time and you told me she wanted to know what it was like to live in the village. Was she one of your clients?"

"No," he says. "The point is, if a client had wanted to find out where I was, they could have. I've never given anybody your address but if somebody had turned up in Harlestone looking for me, every single person in the village would have taken them right to your front door and on the way, told them what I'd had for dinner the previous evening."

There's something about his reasoning that doesn't ring quite true. He's not telling me everything—but what is it that he's holding back?

"But this—The Circle—is a small community in the same way that Harlestone is," I say, perplexed.

He gives a tired sigh. "That's exactly why I chose it. I would have preferred an anonymous block of flats with a built-in security system, something like I had before. But you made it clear you weren't going to live somewhere like that so I looked for a way to keep both of us happy. Here we have the intimate set-up that you prefer and the security that I need. It's a compromise, Alice, another damn compromise."

"Isn't that what relationships are about?" I say, stung. "Compromise?"

He takes his cup from the machine. "I'll let you have your breakfast in peace. If you want to talk, I'll be in my study."

Tears sting my eyes. I'd lain awake most of the night and I still don't know what to do. I'm tempted to go back to Harlestone but if I do, I'll have to ask Debbie if I can stay with her for the next few months, because I can't move my tenants out without notice. But where will that leave me and Leo? He's right, we'd have to go back to how we'd managed before, only seeing each other at weekends when the whole point of moving to London was so that we could spend more time together. And I can't get what he said about making new memories for the house out of my mind. It's created a feeling of obligation that I resent, because if I don't take up the challenge, I'll feel as if I'm turning my back, not just on Nina Maxwell, who I feel bound to in some inexplicable way, but also my sister.

"I meant to ask." His voice comes from behind me and turning, I see him standing in the doorway. "You said a neighbor told you about the murder. Was it Eve?"

"No."

"Who was it, then?"

I have no choice. I have to tell him what I told Eve.

"It wasn't a neighbor, it was a reporter," I say, horribly aware that there are too many lies creeping into our relationship.

"A reporter? You mean, a journalist?"

"Yes."

"Did they come here?"

"No, it was a phone call."

"A man or a woman?"

"A woman."

He rakes his hair, a sign that he's riled. "Did she say which newspaper she was with?"

I turn to the coffee machine and start pressing buttons. "No."

"Didn't you ask?"

"No, I was in too much shock to care."

"Did you get her name?"

"No."

"What did she say, exactly?"

"She wanted to know what it was like to live in a house where someone had been murdered." I stop abruptly, wondering if he's noticed that I used almost the same phrase as he did when he told me about the woman who came to Harlestone—*She wanted to know what it was like to live in the village.* Which means we're both lying.

"Did she say anything else?"

"No." I look at him curiously. "Why?"

"No reason."

He leaves and I sit down at the table. Something isn't adding up. Leo seems paranoid about my fictitious reporter. And his behavior yesterday when I first confronted him had been over the top. He'd looked as if he'd been about to pass out. But his reason for not telling me—that he wanted this house because it provided him with security—doesn't stand up.

I go to my study, closing the door behind me. Since last night, it has become not just my workplace, but my haven. The bed is now a sofa again, the quilt folded neatly into the bottom of the cupboard, because I can't work in a mess. I sit down at my desk. I need to call Ginny, and a message has come in from Eve, checking that I'm all right. I text Eve back and tell her I'm fine, and that I'll see her after the weekend. **If you need me before then, just let me know xx** she replies and I feel lucky to have made a friend so close to home. Home. Again, the word resonates in my brain. Can it ever be my home now?

I call Ginny.

"How are you?" she asks.

"Not good."

"Did you speak to Leo?"

"Yes, he said he didn't tell me because he really wanted the house and he knew I wouldn't want to live here once I knew about the murder. He was right about that." I pause. "It's the reason he gave for wanting the house that doesn't ring true. He told me it was because it's in a gated residence and nobody can get in unless they are let in by a resident. He said he'd been harassed by some of his clients."

"Do you mean he's received threats of some sort?" Ginny asks.

"I don't know. He's never mentioned being harassed to me. I know there were some phone calls that he didn't answer, or where he hung up straightaway. And once he got annoyed with a woman who tried to speak to him outside the cottage in Harlestone. He said she wasn't a client, but he was more annoyed about it than he should have been."

"How have you left it with him?"

"Well, I slept on the sofa bed in the study and I'll be sleeping there again tonight."

"I'm really sorry, Alice."

"Thank you, but it's fine. Or it will be."

I hang up, wondering if it will ever be fine between me and Leo. I know I'll never be able to sleep in the bedroom again, not now that I know what happened there. That in itself isn't a problem as we can move into the guest bedroom, and Leo can put his gym equipment in our bedroom instead of in the garage, where he usually works out. But for the moment, I can't think about sharing a bed with him. And why is Thomas Grainger investigating the murder, anyway? He said he was working on behalf of his client, and then something about their brother being accused of a murder he didn't commit. His client must be Oliver's brother or sister, which makes me slightly dismissive about his miscarriage of justice claim. It's normal for close family members not to believe their loved ones are capable of murder. It doesn't mean they didn't do it.

I search on my phone for the screenshot I took of Nina's photo. Her long blond hair is gathered into a messy bun and thin gold hoops hang from her ears. She looks happy and carefree and I'm hit by a familiar wave of sadness.

"Who killed you, Nina?" I murmur. "Was it Oliver?"

She stares back at me, a smile at the corner of her mouth. *That's for you to find out*, she seems to be saying.

I study her photograph, looking for a trace of my sister. There isn't; my Nina was darker than this Nina, darker than me. My sister who wanted me to be called Nina like her. She was three when I was born and very insistent, so my parents told her she could choose my name. She chose it from her favorite book, *Alice in Wonderland*.

The rest of the weekend passes with me and Leo avoiding each other, moving to different areas of the kitchen if we happen to be there at the same time and being extra polite, like two almost-strangers. When he tells me that he's off to play tennis with Paul, I have to hide my surprise. In his place, I'd be too embarrassed to show my face. But then I realize that apart from Eve and Will, no one from The Circle knows that he didn't tell me about the murder.

I use the time to catch up on the work I didn't do on Thursday and Friday, and by the time Sunday evening comes around, I've finished the first read-through of the book.

I'm pulling out the sofa bed when Leo knocks on the door.

"Thank you for not leaving," he says, helping me move the cushions.

"I still might. I haven't decided what to do yet."

He nods. "I'm going to commute to Birmingham this week, so that you won't be alone in the house at night—if you decide to stay," he adds.

"Thanks," I say, because I'd forgotten that I was meant to be by myself until Thursday. We make up the bed and I close the door behind him, struck by the irony of the situation. This was meant to be a new start, a chance—once his current contract was finished—for us to live as a normal couple where, after a day's work, we would meet again in the evenings—every evening—to chat about our day face to face. Even if we can get over this, what if it doesn't work out? What if we find we can't live together day after day? Maybe our relationship only worked until now because we lived apart for most of the time.

I'm almost asleep when I remember I need clothes for the morning. Since Friday, I've lived in clothes pulled from the ironing basket but they're now back in the wash. My clean ones are in the bedroom, where I don't want to go.

I text Leo.

Before you leave, please get me some clothes from the bedroom and leave them on the chair in the hall. My white
shorts, my red dress, a pair of jeans, two white T-shirts, two
navy T-shirts and four sets of underwear. My white sneakers
and the blue sandals with the gold bar. And socks. Thanks.

I turn off my phone and go back to sleep.

FOURTEEN

I wake in the night, my heartbeating hard against my ribs. Something woke me, I don't know what. I lie without moving, holding my breath, my body tensed, trying to work it out. And then it comes to me. There's someone in the room and I know instinctively that it isn't Leo.

There's no light near me, the nearest lamp is on my desk. I'm too scared to move, too scared to open my eyes. My eyes dart around under my closed lids. Where are they? Shouldn't I be able to hear them breathing, detect some sort of movement? There's nothing, just a feeling that someone is watching me. Then, when the effort of not moving, not breathing, becomes too much, the sense of someone being there leaves me.

My held-in breath whooshes from me, a shuddering gasp in the suffocating silence of the night. I wait for my heartrate to slow, then move my legs from under the covers. I feel too vulnerable to leave my bed so I stretch my arm toward my desk and turn on the lamp. The weak yellow light doesn't reach into the corners of the study but I'm able to see that there isn't anyone there. The door is slightly ajar, and I can't remember whether or not I closed it before going to sleep.

I get out of bed, about to call for Leo, then stop. I can do this myself. My heart in my mouth, I switch on the light in the hall. Taking a deep breath, I walk through the downstairs rooms with pretend confidence, giving myself courage, turning on lights as I go. There's a neat pile of clothes on the chair in the hall; Leo must have brought them down once I was asleep to save him doing it in the morning. I continue upstairs, checking his study and the guest bedroom. The door to our bedroom is shut. I put my hand gently on the handle and push it open. It creaks slightly and I hold my breath, expecting Leo to wake up, ask who's there. But there's no sound. I peep in; he's sleeping soundly, his breathing deep and regular.

I'm going back downstairs when I see it, a white rose cut from the garden lying on the window sill next to the front door. I smile grimly to myself, amazed that he thinks I can be won over so easily. I carry it through to the kitchen, open the bin and dump it inside.

Back in bed, I leave the light on and my door half-open so I'm not in complete darkness. I expect to have trouble getting to sleep but suddenly, it's morning and Leo has already left for Birmingham.

The next morning, a text comes in from Eve—**Coffee?** I check the time; it's already nine o'clock but I can start work a bit later today. I go straight over. She comes to the door dressed in white running gear, eating toast spread thickly with peanut butter.

"I did a five-mile run this morning, so I'm allowed," she says, offering me her plate. "And you're allowed, because you had a crap weekend. Or maybe you didn't?"

I take a piece of toast and follow her to the kitchen. "It was crap on the Leo front but the upside was that I managed to get a lot of work done. It took my mind off everything, which was good."

"You were able to stay in the house, then?"

"Yes, but I slept downstairs, in my study."

Eve puts her plate down, hoists herself onto the worktop, then picks up her plate again.

"How did it go with Leo?"

"We're keeping our distance while I try and work out how I'm feeling. I'm so confused about everything. I feel I should be running away from the house, maybe even running away from Leo. But he said we should create new memories."

She tilts her head to one side, looking at me. "How do you feel about that?"

"I'm not sure. This might sound strange, but since Leo said that, I've begun to feel as if I owe it to Nina to stay. I feel drawn to her in some way. When I went back to the house on Thursday, I could almost sense her presence, I could see her in the sitting room with Oliver, see them together in the kitchen. And when I think how she must have suffered," I add quietly, "any hardship that I might be feeling is nothing in comparison. Maybe Leo is right, maybe the only way to rid the house of the evil that happened there is to create new memories."

"Good vibes chasing away bad ones doesn't sound strange at all," Eve says. "Don't you want to sit down?"

"Sorry," I say, realizing I've been pacing the kitchen. I pull out a chair. "Leo should be staying in Birmingham until Thursday, like he usually does, but he's going to come home every evening so that I won't be alone at night."

"That's good of him."

"What would you do, Eve, if you were in my place?"

"I think if I was kind of managing, which you seem to be, I'd stay for a while, see how things pan out."

"I'd feel much better if I could go and see everyone here and explain that I didn't know about the murder before moving in. But I suppose that would be kind of weird."

"If you really want it out there, I could tell Tamsin and Maria and they could tell their neighbors, who would tell theirs, and before you know it, it will be common knowledge," she says. "Would you like me to do that?"

"Yes, please. I really need people to know I'm not callous." A new thought comes to worry me. "But what will people think when they know that I know about the murder and am able to carry on living in the house, at least for the moment?"

"They already thought that you knew, and the only thing they thought was that you were incredibly brave. So that's what they'll continue to think, that you're brave. And not many people would be able to afford to move out and rent somewhere else to live while the house is being resold, so they'll understand that too. Your cottage is rented out, it's not as if you can go back there. Anyway, why do you care what people think?"

"I don't want to be shunned when I've only just arrived here."

Eve bursts out laughing. "You're not going to be shunned!"

"So, if I invite you, Tamsin and Maria to lunch on Wednesday, before you go to your yoga class, will you come?" I say, surprising myself, because I hadn't actively thought about inviting them over.

"Sure we will! We came to your drinks evening, didn't we?"

"I'd like to invite Cara but I don't think she's around during the day. Did she say she works for Google?"

"Yes, she's a software engineer. She works crazy hours so you'll only be able to get hold of her at weekends."

"Just the four of us, then."

I leave soon after. Eve told me I could work at hers but if I'm to stay here, in this house, I need to get used to being alone. "What would you do, Nina?" I murmur to the photo of my sister pinned to the fridge. "Would you stay or would you go?" But there's no answer, just the absolute stillness of an empty house.

Instead of doing a second read of my book, I decided to start translating straightaway. Translating requires focus and right now, I need to be able to concentrate on something other than the murder.

The day passes surprisingly quickly. When Leo arrives home, he goes out of his way to apologize, to try and make good the harm he's done.

"Your hair looks nice," he says, referring to the way I've plaited it to keep it out of my way while I'm working.

"Thanks."

He sighs. "Tell me how I can make it up to you."

"I don't know, I don't even know if you can. How can I trust you if you're able to keep something so momentous from me?"

What I hate most is that I feel I'm being unfair. But expecting me to fall into his arms, say I forgive him, is too much. He offers to make me dinner and when I refuse, he eats quickly and disappears to his study. He doesn't mention the rose I threw in the bin so maybe he didn't see it.

The house is quiet, too quiet. Realizing I didn't tell Leo that I thought there was someone in the house last night, I'm tempted to go after him. But I don't want him to think that I'm using it as an excuse to start a conversation. Anyway, there wasn't anyone there, it was just the murder playing on my mind.

FIFTEEN

I leave it to Eve to invite Maria and Tamsin to lunch and the three of them arrive together, turning up at twelve with flowers from Maria's garden and a bottle of wine. They're all wearing shorts and T-shirts, which makes me feel overdressed in my mid-length flowing skirt.

"Come in," I say, moving back to let them past.

Eve and Maria walk straight in but Tamsin hovers uncertainly outside the door and for a confused moment, I think she's having reservations about having lunch with me.

"Sorry," she says. "It's just that this house always reminds me of Nina."

"Of course." I nod sympathetically, wanting to reach out and hug her. But she steps quickly inside.

"How are you?" Maria asks, giving me a hug. "It must have been such a shock, finding out about Nina like that. I can't imagine how you must have felt."

"Angry and scared," I say, leading them out to the garden. "I wanted to leave, I didn't think I'd be able to stay."

"But you're still here," Tamsin says pointedly.

If anyone is going to judge me, it's Tamsin.

I turn to her. "Yes, I'm still here. For the moment." I smile tentatively. "I was hoping you might tell me about Nina. I'll never be able to sleep in the bedroom upstairs again but if I knew she'd had some happy times here, it might help me feel less anxious."

Tamsin's face softens. "She had lots of happy times here."

"Shall we chat over lunch?" Eve says. "It's just that we need to leave here by twenty to two for our yoga class."

"Yes, I know," I say. "I've made a salmon quiche and salad, and there's strawberries for dessert. I hope that's OK?"

Maria smiles. "Sounds perfect to me!"

It's one of those beautiful mid-September days, with the sun warming the garden. A gentle breeze carries the heavenly scent of brightly colored phlox to where we're eating on the terrace, adding to the impression that we're still in summer. There's so much I want to ask them about Nina but I curb my impatience and ask instead about Maria's children, and Tamsin's two little daughters, Amber and Pearl.

"I love their names," I tell her.

She smiles. "Thanks. You'll have to join us on a Wednesday afternoon, then you can meet them in person."

"I'd like that," I say, pleased that the invite has come from her. "I've only ever seen them from afar."

I wait until they sit back, their empty plates in front of them.

"I know Nina was thirty-eight and Eve told me that she was a therapist, but that's all I really know about her," I say.

Tamsin brushes a couple of crumbs off her immaculate white T-shirt. "She loved her job, she loved helping people. She had time for everyone, you could always go and see her if you had a problem. She helped me so much."

"And Oliver? What did he do?

"He worked for a shipping company," Maria says. "I'm not sure what his actual job was but he traveled abroad quite a bit."

"And they were happy together?"

"Yes, very."

"Except—" I hesitate. "He killed her."

Tamsin glares at me from across the table. "Who have you been talking to?"

"No one," I say hastily. "I only know what I read in news articles."

"Isn't that enough?"

I flush, embarrassed at the sudden change in atmosphere, as if the temperature has suddenly dropped ten degrees.

"I'm just trying to understand the sort of person she was," I say, trying to get things back to how they were. "Eve mentioned that she was quite spiritual and that she started your yoga group. Did she have any hobbies?"

It doesn't work. "Why does it matter?" Tamsin says coldly. "It's hardly important now."

I hate playing the sister card but I can't think of any other way to get her on my side. I push back my chair. Eve turns worried eyes on me.

"It's OK," I say. "I'm just going to get the strawberries. I'll take the plates through at the same time."

In the kitchen, I deal with the plates, take the strawberries from the fridge, and the photo of Nina from the door.

"Did Eve tell you about my sister?" I ask Tamsin, putting the strawberries down in front of her and going back to my seat.

She shifts awkwardly. "Yes, she did. I'm sorry."

"This is a photograph of her," I say, holding it out.

Maria reaches over and takes it. "She was beautiful."

"Can I see?" Eve asks. She looks at the photo then looks up at me. "She has the same eyes as you."

"Yes," I say. I turn to Tamsin and Maria. "Eve probably told you that my sister was called Nina. I know it's stupid, but since she died, I have this need to know about other Ninas."

"It's not stupid," Maria says. She smiles. "I don't know about your Nina but our Nina loved taking impromptu photographs. It could be quite annoying sometimes because she would get you at your worst moment, when you were eating, so your mouth was open, or full of food."

"Or when you'd had a bit too much to drink, so you'd have that glazed look in your eyes and a red nose," Eve says, miming the pose and making me laugh.

"But she also took some beautiful photos." Maria looks across the table at Tamsin. "I have some lovely ones of the children, you do too, don't you, Tamsin?"

"Yes." To my dismay, Tamsin's eyes fill with tears. "I still miss her."

"I'm sorry," I say guiltily. "I shouldn't be asking you about her. It's just that I want—I don't know—to make her real, to have a sense of who she was, I suppose. It might help me decide whether to stay or not."

Tamsin fishes for a tissue and blows her nose. "I hope you do. It's nice to have the house lived in again instead of it being like a mausoleum."

"Thank you," I say, because it had sounded genuine.

"Eve said you found out about the murder from a reporter?" Tamsin adds.

"Yes, that's right."

She picks up her bag and rummages inside, drawing out a new packet of tissues. "What did she say, exactly?"

"She asked me how it felt to be living at the scene of a brutal murder," I say, remembering what I told Eve, because I don't want my lie to come back to bite me.

"And that's all she said?"

"Yes. I told her that I didn't know what she was talking about and she advised me to google the Nina Maxwell murder."

"Did she give you her name, or tell you which publication she was with?"

"No." Tamsin's questions make me uncomfortable. Does she know I'm lying?

"So how do you know she was a reporter?"

She does know I'm lying. "I—I don't know, I just presumed that she was. Who else could she have been?"

"Tam," Maria says gently. "Stop. You're making Alice uncomfortable."

"Sorry. It's just that I hate the thought of someone poking their nose in, dragging it up again when we've only just managed to put it to rest."

"Let's talk about something else," Eve says brightly. "Like Christmas, or Halloween, or Maria inviting us to supper on Friday." She looks over at her. "Isn't that right, Maria?"

Maria laughs. "Thanks for reminding me. Tamsin, Alice, are you free Friday evening? I mentioned supper to Eve yesterday and she and Will can make it, so I hope you can too." There's no reply from Tamsin; she's staring out of the window, lost in thought. "Tamsin, are you and Connor free on Friday?" Maria says again, more loudly this time.

"What?" Tamsin shakes her head quickly as if to clear it. "Yes, why?"

"For supper at mine."

"That will be lovely, thank you."

"What about you, Alice, are you and Leo free?"

"I think so."

"Why don't you let me know once you've spoken to him?"

"I'll ask him tonight," I promise.

They leave soon after and while I tidy up, I think about Maria's invitation. I'd love to go because I don't want to miss the chance to see the friendship group that Nina and Oliver were part of in action. I want to observe the dynamics between the couples, see how they interact with each other, get to know them a little better. There are things I don't fully understand, like their insistence that Nina and Oliver were blissfully happy. If they were, why did he kill her? Remembering what Eve had said about Lorna witnessing everything, I decide to go and see her.

In the study, I swap my T-shirt, which I managed to spatter with dressing, for a clean one, grab my keys from the table in the hall, throw open the front door—and find myself looking straight at Thomas Grainger.

SIXTEEN

I've startled him as much as he's startled me. His arm, which he'd raised to ring the doorbell, drops quickly to his side. He takes a step back, as if he's expecting me to verbally attack him.

"Ms. Dawson, I'm sorry." He raises his hands in a backing-off gesture. "I'll leave, it's fine."

"Wait a minute." He stops, his body half-twisted toward the drive. "You said you were investigating Nina Maxwell's murder."

He turns back to face me. "That's right."

"Why now, more than a year after she died?"

"I've been investigating it since her husband committed suicide. But I had to put it to one side because I couldn't get the information I wanted. I'm a private investigator, so persona non grata as far as the police are concerned."

"What information do you want?"

He finds my eyes, holds my gaze. He had done exactly the same thing last time, I remember. I want to look away but I can't. There's something mesmerizing about them.

"I'm afraid I'm not prepared to discuss anything on the doorstep."

It's now or never. If I don't invite him in, he won't come back. I open the door wider.

"Thank you." He steps into the hallway. "I really appreciate you agreeing to let me talk to you." I take him through to the sitting room, wondering what I'm doing letting a stranger into my house. He might be dressed smartly—a casual, lightweight suit and open-necked pale blue shirt—but he could still be a murderer. He could be Nina's murderer. I take my phone from my pocket, hold it in my hand. I offer him a chair but I stay standing by the door. If I need to make a quick exit, I can.

"I'd like to apologize again for the shock you must have got last week when I told you about the murder," Thomas Grainger says. "I had no idea you didn't know."

"I realize that."

"I hope it didn't cause any trouble."

"None at all." I'm not about to tell him that Leo kept it from me and that we're barely speaking. "My husband and I are deciding what to do." He doesn't need to know that we're not married either. "We're not sure how we feel about living here now."

"I can understand that."

"I think you should start at the beginning. How did you know we were having drinks here?"

"I'm afraid I can't tell you that."

"Why not?" He looks steadily back at me. "Are you in touch with someone from here?"

"No, absolutely not." He waits for me to move on and when I don't, he nods. "Let's just say that I found out through the invitation you posted."

It takes me a while. "You've hacked the WhatsApp group?" He doesn't confirm or deny it and I'm not even sure a WhatsApp group can be hacked. I don't press him any further because he wouldn't tell me anyway. "So why did you decide to crash it?" I say instead.

"It was unethical of me, I know. But I've been trying to gain access to the house for over a year now. I posed as a potential buyer once but the estate agent stayed with me the whole time, so I was unable to do what I'd hoped to do, which was take a look at the room where the murder took place. Without a general idea of the layout of the place where a victim died, it's hard to offer an alternative version as to what might have happened that night." He gives a slight smile. "The fact that I was shadowed during my visit only strengthened my belief that my client's brother wasn't responsible for Nina Maxwell's murder. I'm convinced the agency had instructions from the police to keep a close eye on anyone who showed an interest in the house."

My curiosity aroused, I move to the chair nearest the door and perch on it. "Why would they do that?"

"Perhaps they were hoping the real killer would return to the crime scene and somehow give himself away."

"But the police believe that the killer is dead, don't they? That it's a closed case."

"Not according to my source." He sees my frown. "Yes, it's true, every private investigator has a source somewhere in the police, just as a journalist does. Often the same one. And my source tells me that the investigation is still ongoing." He pauses. "Can I ask if your experience was the same when you visited the house?"

"My husband visited it without me. I only saw it after he bought it." He tries to hide his surprise but he's not quick enough. "So, our drinks evening?"

"I thought I'd be able to pass unnoticed." He gives a slight smile. "It didn't occur to me that you had only invited people from here. Once I realized, I left."

"Well, my next-door neighbor, the lady who let you in, is elderly and she's been badly affected by all this. She was very upset when she learned that you weren't a friend of mine."

"I'm sorry. Again, I'd imagined a big party and thought I'd be able to slip in through the gate behind someone."

"How did you get in? Just now? You didn't disturb my neighbor again, did you?"

He shakes his head. "I intended to ring your intercom in the hope that you would agree to listen to what I had to say. But there was someone in front of me and he let me in. I wanted to tell him that he should be more careful but I suppose that if he'd been playing by the rules, he would have had to slam the gate in my face, and most people aren't like that, they're too polite. Last time I came to see you I walked in through the main gate after a car." Another pause. "I don't know if you or your husband are on a residents' committee or anything but perhaps you should mention it, and maybe change the code. I was able to see the code he typed in over his shoulder."

"I'm sorry, but I still don't understand what you're doing here."

He shifts on his seat. "Believe me, I wouldn't be troubling you if time wasn't running out."

"What do you mean?"

A shadow clouds his face. "My client isn't in good health. She's determined to clear her brother's name while she can." He stops and I can see that he's having some kind of internal struggle. "I was at university with Helen," he says, giving up the struggle. "I never really knew Oliver because he was five years younger than us, but even back then I knew how much he meant to her. When she said she didn't believe Oliver was responsible for Nina's murder, and asked me to help her, I felt I couldn't refuse."

I nod sympathetically, desperately sorry for Oliver's sister.

"Why is Oliver's sister persuaded that it wasn't him who killed Nina?" I ask. "Nobody wants to think the worst of someone they love. Maybe she just doesn't want to believe that her brother was capable of murder."

"That's what I thought at first. I hate to say it but I was—and this sounds awful—humoring Helen by agreeing to look into the murder, because in my experience, it bore all the hallmarks of a typical crime of passion. But many people have testified that Oliver Maxwell was the gentlest, kindest of men and that he adored Nina. The cynics point to his suicide and say that he killed himself because he couldn't cope with what he'd done. Those that knew him take it as a testimony of his broken heart. Not only couldn't he bear to live without her, he also couldn't bear to live with the violence of her death."

So which camp did that put Eve, Tamsin, and Maria in, I wonder? They had known Oliver, they had told me he was the loveliest of men. Yet they believed that he killed Nina. Why was that?

"Wait a minute—did you say 'crime of passion'?" I say, realizing.

"Yes." He pauses. "Apparently, Nina had been having an affair."

I stare at him. "An affair?"

He leans forward in his seat. His skin is pale, almost translucent, providing a marked contrast with his dark hair.

"Yes."

"But—who with?"

"That's what I'm trying to find out."

"Why?"

"Because I think he might be responsible for her murder."

My mind reels. "Did the police know she was having an affair?"

"Yes."

"Then they must have found out who he was and eliminated him from their inquiries."

"That's what you would have thought," he agrees.

"I suppose if Oliver knew Nina was having an affair, he had a motive to kill her."

"Except that, according to the people who knew him best, he would never have harmed Nina."

"I'm not sure why you think I can help you. I've only just moved here—as you know," I add pointedly.

"It's exactly for that reason that I'm asking for your help," he says earnestly. "When Helen first asked me to look into the murder, I tried to speak to people here myself. But I came up against a lot of—not hostility, exactly, but tight lips. It's why I didn't hang around at your drinks evening. When I looked through the kitchen window and saw that the people you'd invited were the people I had tried to talk to, I thought it wiser to leave before someone recognized me." He pauses. "You didn't know Nina, you don't really know anyone here yet, which makes you impartial. I know this is a lot to ask but—if you happen to hear anything—you know, in conversations with the neighbors—perhaps you could let me know?"

I stand up. "I'm sorry, I couldn't do that."

He gives a small smile. "Of course." He gets to his feet, holds out his hand. "Thank you for your time. Goodbye, Ms. Dawson."

His handshake is strong, dependable. It makes me feel that I can trust him but, at the same time, I'm disappointed that he wanted me to betray the confidences of the people I'm hoping will be my friends. Given the circumstances, I suppose it's understandable that he wants to get closure for Oliver's sister before it's too late. He strikes me as the sort of man who would do a lot for a friend—but not someone who would give that friend false hope, or take on a lost cause. He admitted that at the beginning, he was only humoring Oliver's sister.

What made him change his mind?

SEVENTEEN

I've barely begun working when the highlighter I'm using dries up on me. I know Leo has some in his study so I force myself upstairs. Living with Nina's ghost isn't easy. I pause, one foot on the next step. *Living with Nina's ghost.*

After my sister died, there were times when I felt she was with me, times when I could feel her presence, especially in the quiet of the night or when I was feeling particularly low. It was as if she was letting me know that I wasn't alone. I hadn't been particularly spiritual before but, intrigued, I began to read about life after death and, because of what I had experienced in relation to my sister, I came to accept that sometimes, our spirit lives on, particularly when a person dies unexpectedly before their time. One of the things I read was the belief that if a death was violent, the spirit of that person might wait around until their murderer was brought to justice. It had particularly marked me because I hadn't sensed my sister's presence since the day her case was brought to court, and although I hadn't been satisfied with the outcome, maybe my sister had been, which was why she had left. What if Nina Maxwell's spirit is living on, here in the house, waiting for justice to be done?

The study on the first floor is Leo's space and I'm always surprised at how tidy it is. There's nothing on the desk apart from a wooden ruler and a couple of pens. I pull open the drawers that run down each side of the desk. The bottom one on the left-hand side is jammed full of pens, pencils and highlighters. I choose a yellow one and, as I take it out, the back of my hand brushes against something taped to the underside of the drawer above. Curious, I push the jumble of pens and pencils to one side and unpick the tape with my fingers. There's something metal underneath. I let it fall into my hand and see a tiny key, which I recognize as coming from one of those metal cash boxes that I used to save money in as a teenager. I turn it over, inspecting it. If Leo has gone to the trouble of hiding it, there must be something he doesn't want anyone, including me, to find. Was that why he was so jittery when I told him I'd taken people upstairs to see the work we'd had done?

I turn to the gray metal filing cabinet that stands in the corner, where Leo keeps his client files. I tug at the top drawer but it doesn't open. Neither do the other three; all the drawers are centrally locked. Puzzled, I go back to the desk, looking for another key, running my hand along the underside of each drawer in case Leo has hidden that one too. When I don't find anything, I search the rest of the study.

I empty the pen holder on the desk, run my fingers over the little ridge above the doorway and come away with nothing but dust. I get down on my hands and knees and look under the desk, hoping to find the key to the filing cabinet taped somewhere on its underside. I turn Leo's chair upside down, check behind his computer, under the keyboard and then repeat the whole process. But I can't find the key. Frustrated, I stick the tiny key back where I found it and go back to work.

While I'm on my lunch break, I remember that before Thomas Grainger turned up yesterday, I'd been on my way to see Lorna. It's early afternoon, so I'm not worried about her and Edward being in the middle of lunch. But no one answers my knock and I don't like to insist, because they might be having a nap. I turn to go home and see Will standing at the bottom of the drive, on his way out.

"Hi, Alice!" he calls. "How are things?"

"Oh—you know. I was hoping to see Lorna but she doesn't seem to be in."

"I'd suggest going to see Eve but she's at her mum's. She'll be back around five, if you're looking for company."

"Thanks, Will."

He gives me a wave and I turn back to the door, because I can hear a lock being turned. The door opens, the chain still in place. Lorna peeps at me timidly through the gap.

"It's only me," I say cautiously. "I didn't mean to disturb you."

"I wasn't going to answer but I heard your voice." She stares for a moment, as if deciding whether or not to let me in. She doesn't seem to want to and I'm about to apologize and tell her I'll call back another day when she begins removing the chain, slowly, as if she's hoping I'll get fed up waiting and go away.

"Are you sure?" I ask doubtfully, when she finally opens the door.

"Yes, come in. It's just that Edward isn't here and I'm always more careful when I'm on my own."

"That's very wise. How is he?"

"Much better, thank you." She opens a door to the right and I follow her in to a cozy sitting room.

"This is lovely," I say, admiring the delicate pastel tones. There's the beautiful scent of lavender and I trace it to a crystal vase, sitting on a low table. Like ours, her sitting room looks onto the square and from the window, I can see our driveway perfectly.

We sit down.

Lorna gives me a nervous smile. "Would you like a cup of tea?"

"No, thank you. I just wanted to ask you something."

"It's not about letting that man into your party, is it? I don't know what came over me. I'm usually so careful."

"No, it's not about that," I reassure her, sad at how much it has knocked her confidence, because she doesn't seem quite as sharp as when I first met her, nor quite as smartly dressed. Although she's wearing her pearls, her clothes—a camel skirt and blue patterned shirt—seem hastily put together, and her hair isn't the same neat bob.

"Have you managed to find out who it was?" she asks.

I hesitate, because I know that if I tell her the truth, that the man is a private detective, she'll feel better about having let him in. On the other hand, I'd have to tell her that he's investigating Nina's murder. She would ask why, and I'd have to admit that Thomas Grainger believes Oliver was innocent. I don't want to open old wounds.

"Not yet," I say, making a quick decision. "But I'm not worried about him and I hope you aren't either. I know how upsetting it must be after what happened to Nina," I add, pleased to have found the perfect lead into the conversation I want to have with her.

Lorna raises her hand to her pearls.

"It was terrible," she says, her voice barely a whisper. "Truly terrible."

"I didn't know about it, I only found out a few days ago."

Lorna looks shocked. "Oh Alice, that's awful. But—I don't understand. Why didn't you know?"

"Because Leo chose to keep it from me. He *was* going to tell me, but he hoped that by the time he did, I'd have grown to love the house as much as he does and wouldn't want to leave."

"Do you want to leave?"

"It's so difficult. I'm not sure how I feel about the house, but I love The Circle, everyone has been so welcoming and I know I'd make friends here. I wanted to leave, but then Leo said something that I can't get out of my mind. He said that the house deserved to have new memories, happy memories." I pause, working my way through my feelings. "It's not that simple, though. Leo and I aren't really speaking at the moment because I can't forgive him for not being upfront with me before we moved in. It's all a bit of a mess, to be honest."

"I can see that," Lorna says, and I smile gratefully at her. It's a relief to be able to pour out my heart to someone with life experience who, like me, has lost someone she loved.

"I don't have any family apart from Leo," I say, on impulse. "My parents and sister were killed in a car crash when I was nineteen years old."

Lorna's hand moves to her heart.

"You lost your sister and your parents? Your poor thing, how did you cope? To lose three loved ones—it doesn't bear thinking about."

"If it hadn't been for my grandparents, I'm not sure I would have coped. They were so strong; they'd lost their only son, their only child—" I stop, halted by the look of desolation clouding her face. "I'm so sorry, Lorna, that was clumsy of me. I know you lost your son too." Lorna doesn't say anything; her fingers pluck at the material of her skirt and I hate that I've upset her. "It must have been so hard for you."

"Yes, it was," she says, her voice almost a whisper. "Any loss is terrible, however it happens."

We sit in silence for a moment. I wonder if I should leave her in peace but I want to find out what I can. "I was wondering—would you be able to tell me about Nina? Maybe if I knew a little about her, if I could make her real to me, it would help."

Lorna eyes dart, as if she's looking for a way out. Then she nods and squares her shoulders in acceptance of my request.

"She was lovely," she says. "So was Oliver. He was like a son to us, he would help us in the garden, cut the hedges, mow the lawn, that sort of thing. That's why I still don't understand what happened, why it all went so wrong between them. One minute they were the happiest couple in the world and the next—we heard them arguing one evening, it was awful. Oliver sounded so angry, which was strange, because I'd never seen him get cross about anything. But they say that, don't they, that sometimes, when easy-going people explode—well, they really explode. Edward and I didn't know if we should go over, or call the police. We were so worried for them."

"And did you? Call the police?"

"No, because everything calmed down. Oliver was still angry but he wasn't shouting."

"Did you hear what they were arguing about?"

A frown comes over her face and I realize that, like with Tamsin, I've crossed some sort of invisible line.

"I'm sorry," I say hastily. "I don't mean to pry."

Lorna's internal struggle is visible on her face as she tries to work out how much she should tell me. Her shoulders sag.

"Edward said I shouldn't talk about it, but nobody does and somehow, it makes everything worse."

"I can understand that," I say gently. "When my sister died, people stopped talking about her, they thought it would upset me. But it upset me more when nobody mentioned her at all, as if she'd never existed for them."

"I'm not allowed to talk about our son, or have photos of him anywhere in the house."

"That must be hard."

"It is." Tears fill her eyes but before I can say anything, she blinks them away. "But back to Nina and Oliver," she says, giving me a wobbly smile. She pauses a moment to recall everything. "I went to see Nina the next day, the day after we'd heard them arguing. I waited until Oliver had gone to work. She was in a dreadful state, very tearful. She was mortified that Edward and I had heard them fighting. She said it was her fault, that she'd been having an affair and that Oliver had found out."

"Did she say who she'd been having an affair with?" Appalled that I've been so brusque, I rush to apologize. But she takes my question at face value and carries on talking.

"No, but she said she was going to break it off with him. And then, that night, just hours later, Oliver—" She stops. "I still can't believe it."

"Maybe it wasn't Oliver," I suggest carefully. "Maybe it was the man Nina was involved with. You said she told you she was going to tell him it was over. I'm sorry, but why couldn't he have been the one to have killed her?"

She fishes a tissue from her sleeve. "Because Oliver lied to the police and that proved his guilt," she says, wiping her eyes. "I wish I'd known, I wish I'd known what he was going to tell them because—I know I shouldn't say this—I would have lied—not lied exactly, but I would have told the police I hadn't seen anything. But when they came to see us that evening, I had no idea that Nina had been murdered and they didn't tell us. They wanted to know if we had seen or heard anything and I answered truthfully, that I saw Oliver come back just after nine o'clock and go into the house. I knew it was just after nine because we'd sat down to watch the news on the BBC news channel, like we always do at nine o'clock—they say old habits die hard, don't they, and anyway the *News at Ten* is on too late for us now—and when we heard Oliver's car, I got up and looked out of the window. I wouldn't normally have done that, not in the winter when the curtains are already drawn, but we were anxious because of the argument we'd heard the night before. I waited a moment, hoping they wouldn't start arguing again. But I didn't hear anything so I went back to the news." She stops a moment. "It must have been about half an hour later, because the news was ending, that we heard a lot of cars pull up and when I looked out, I saw it was the police. We thought that Oliver and Nina had been arguing again and that one of them, or maybe another neighbor, had called for help. To tell you the truth, we were relieved that the matter had been taken out of our hands because if we *had* heard them arguing again, like the previous night, I think that this time, we might have called the police—or at least gone round to try and calm things." She twists the tissue in her hands. "The next thing we knew, the police were knocking on the door, asking their questions. We only found out the next morning that Nina had been murdered."

"It must have been such a shock," I say gently. But lost in the past, I'm not sure Lorna hears me.

"Oliver told the police that he hadn't gone into the house, that he'd gone to sit in the square for a while. But it wasn't true."

"Could he have gone into the house and then gone straight back out again, to sit in the square?" I suggest.

Lorna shakes her head again. "If he had, he would have told the police. If I'd known he was going to say he'd gone to sit in the square, I wouldn't have mentioned seeing him go into the house. But I didn't know, I didn't know he was going to lie. And why would he have gone to sit in the square at nine o'clock at night, when it was cold and dark?"

"Did you tell the police about the conversation you had with Nina, when she told you she'd had an affair with someone?"

"Yes, and they were very interested, because it gave Oliver a motive for killing Nina."

"Didn't they consider that maybe it was the man she was having an affair with who killed her?"

She looks sadly at me. "Why would they? It was Oliver who killed her."

I nod. "I won't take up any more of your time. Thank you for talking to me."

"Do you think you'll be able to stay?" she asks. "Now that you know about the murder?"

"I don't know. My sister was called Nina and it's hard to explain, but if I leave, it will be as if I'm abandoning her too. I know it's not healthy but I haven't let her go yet, not really."

"That's understandable."

"After almost twenty years?"

"I think time has no meaning when it comes to grief."

The gentleness in her voice brings sudden tears to my eyes and I nod, grateful that she understands.

"I'll let you know what I decide," I promise. "Everyone here has been so kind—Eve and Will have been amazing, and Maria and Tamsin are lovely too. And I still love Leo, despite everything."

"Yes—well, it's been lovely talking to you, thank you for coming by," she says. She leans in to give me a kiss, and I hear the whisper of her voice in my ear.

Startled, I pull back. "Sorry?"

Again, Lorna's hand flies to the pearls at her neck. "I was just saying goodbye." She seems flustered. "Perhaps I shouldn't have embraced you but after what you told me about your parents and sister—" Her voice trails off.

"No, no, it's fine, I thought—"

Moving back, Lorna opens the door. "Goodbye, Alice."

EIGHTEEN

Anxiety presses down as I close the front door behind me. Had Lorna really whispered *Don't trust anyone* when she'd leaned into me, or had I imagined it?

I must have imagined it because why would she have felt the need to whisper when she was alone in the house? She had told me that Edward was out. I try and recall what I was saying before she whispered in my ear. I'd been talking about Will and Eve, and I think I mentioned Maria and Tamsin, and then Leo. She couldn't have been warning me about Leo, she doesn't even know him. Had she meant Will and Eve? Maybe she had heard me chatting to Will before she opened the door. Unless she meant Maria, or Tamsin. Or no one at all, because she hadn't whispered anything.

I'm on my way up to Leo's study to watch for Edward walking back across the square, because I can't believe that Lorna would have lied to me about being on her own in the house, when there's a ring on the bell. Retracing my steps, I open the door and see Tamsin standing there, her hands pushed into the pockets of a brown leather jacket.

"Oh, hi Tamsin," I say, surprised. "How are you? Do you want to come in?"

She shakes her head. "No thanks. I just want to say that I don't think you should be upsetting Lorna by bringing up the murder again."

My cheeks burn. "I was only trying to find out a little more about Nina."

"Why?"

"Well, I—"

"Why do you want to know more about Nina?" she interrupts. "Didn't we tell you enough yesterday at lunch? What more could Lorna tell you about her than we, her friends, already have?"

"I—I was just trying to help," I stammer. "Lorna said she was glad to be able to talk about Nina."

"Bullshit." I flinch at the animosity in her voice. "Look, I understand that it must have been a shock to find out about the murder," she goes on. "And I have no idea what that reporter's motive was in contacting you. But you're going to do more harm than good if you start sticking your nose into things that don't concern you. You don't want to start alienating yourself, especially if you decide to stay here." Turning her back on me, she walks down the drive without saying goodbye.

My face burning at Tamsin's unjustified aggressiveness, I run upstairs to Leo's study and watch from the window as she walks across the square to her house. Maybe it's the truth behind her words that stings. I had upset Lorna. Losing Oliver must have been like losing her son all over again, but somehow worse, because she had been the one to pull the trigger. As she'd sat there, twisting her hands in her lap, I'd felt the weight of her guilt. But I don't like being threatened and Tamsin's visit had felt like a threat. How did she know I was asking Lorna about Nina anyway? Did she see me coming out of her house and make an educated guess?

There's still no sign of Edward. I scan the other houses and see Tim standing at the upstairs window of number 9, also watching the square. Even though I'm doing the same thing, it makes me uncomfortable to see him there. Ten minutes pass, then fifteen. A movement to the left catches my eye—Lorna and Edward's garage door swinging upward and outward. I look down and see Edward, his green gardening shoes on his feet, walking down the drive toward their wheelie bin. I watch as he takes hold of the handle and pulls it slowly back up the drive and into the garage. So, he wasn't out, as Lorna had said.

Unless—her actual words had been "Edward isn't here." I had taken that to mean he was out; but maybe all she had meant was that he wasn't there in the house with her, but in the garden.

When Leo comes home, he asks me if I want something to eat. Still upset by Tamsin's visit, and worried about Lorna's warning—if that's what it was—I'm not hungry. I sit at the table and follow him with my eyes as he walks from cooker to fridge and back again, silently asking *Who are you really, Leo? How come I didn't know that you would ever lie to me?* And more importantly—*why have you got a key taped to the underside of your drawer? What is it that you're hiding from me?*

"We've been invited to Maria's tomorrow evening for supper," I say, breaking the silence.

He turns from the cooker. "Are you sure you want me to come?" He sounds as if he wants the answer to be no.

"It will look strange if you don't."

"If you prefer to go without me, I can always say I'm ill."

For a moment, I wonder if I should tell Maria we can't go. I can barely act normally around Leo and I don't want the awkwardness between us to spoil the evening. Also, Tamsin will be there. But I want to get to know the other couples—and I'll be doing Leo a favor if I cancel. Everyone will understand if things are a bit fraught, given that he didn't tell me about the murder.

I take out my phone. "I'll call Maria and tell her to expect both of us."

"Lovely," Maria says, when I tell her we're free.

"Can I bring anything?" I ask.

"Not at all. Is 7 p.m. all right for you?"

"It's perfect."

I hang up. "It's at seven," I tell Leo.

"Great," he says, trying to inject enthusiasm into his voice.

He doesn't try to make small-talk while he eats his dinner, just reads the news on his phone, a glass of full-bodied red wine in his hand. I don't know whether to be offended or relieved.

"I saw Lorna today," I say.

"How is she?"

"Still upset about letting someone in to The Circle on Saturday evening. I told her that I'd only just found out about Nina," I add, unable to stop myself from having a dig.

He takes a sip of wine. "Right."

"We talked about Nina and she told me that Nina had had an affair. So now I'm thinking that maybe it wasn't her husband who killed her but the person she was having an affair with."

His glass slips from his hand and crashes onto the table. Wine seeps across the wood, like blood from a wound. For a moment, we both stare at it, seemingly mesmerized. Then he leaps to his feet, grabs a tea-towel from the side and begins dabbing at the table while I move the glass out of the way.

"Sorry," he says. "My hand slipped."

I frown at the mess the wine has made, then pick up his glass and stand it on its base again. "No harm done."

"I don't think it's a good idea to gossip about the dead," he says, kneeling to mop up the wine that has spilled onto the floor. I stare at the back of his head, noticing for the first time that his hair is thinning on top. Flashes of pink skin show through as he begins to rub vigorously at the floorboards.

"Lorna wasn't gossiping, I asked her to tell me about Nina," I say.

He balls the tea-towel, walks over to the sink and puts it down on the side. Turning on the tap, he rinses his hands. "Why?"

"Because I want to know about the woman whose house I'm living in."

"Only because she was murdered," he says. "If she hadn't been, you wouldn't have been curious about her."

I glare at his back. "So, Leo, how was it for you when Ben told you that a young woman had been murdered in the house you wanted to buy? Weren't you curious? Didn't you ask any questions about her, not even ask who she was?"

He reaches for a clean towel and turns. "No, I don't think I did," he says, drying his hands carefully. "If I remember rightly, it was Ben who volunteered her name."

"And you didn't google her to find out what had happened? You were that disinterested?"

"I wasn't disinterested. I recognized her name and I knew what had happened, I remembered the case. Anyone would have remembered it, it was well-documented at the time, in the press, in the papers."

"Yet there was never any mention of her having an affair."

He puts the towel down, comes back to the table. "Maybe she didn't have one. Maybe it was just a rumor."

"No," I say. "She admitted it to Lorna." I go to refill his glass but he shakes his head.

"That must be why her husband murdered her, then. He found out she'd been cheating on him and killed her in a fit of jealousy."

"Maybe. Unless it was the other man who killed her."

He frowns. He seems on edge, but then he's never enjoyed listening to gossip. "Why do you say that?"

"Because, according to Lorna, Nina was going to tell him that it was over. And because everyone says that Oliver was the nicest man you could ever wish to meet."

"Everyone?" He pounces on the word.

"The people here! His friends and neighbors."

Leo picks up his near-empty wine glass and drains it. "If there had been anything suspicious to find, I think the police would have found it." He pushes away from the table. "I've got work to do. I'll see you later."

I listen as he goes upstairs and into his study. A moment later, I hear the screech of metal on metal and I know that sound, it's one of the drawers in the filing cabinet being pulled open. So, the key to unlock it was up there somewhere. Unless—I go out to the hall. His bag is no longer by the front door and his jacket has gone from where he usually hangs it on the newel post. Maybe he carries the key around with him. But why would he do that? His client files can't be that confidential, can they?

NINETEEN

When morning comes, I know I can't do it. I can't go to Maria's. I don't want to have to pretend that everything is all right between me and Leo and I don't want to have to face Tamsin. What if she tells everyone I've been upsetting Lorna?

"I'm going to Harlestone for the weekend," I tell Leo. "I'll be back Sunday evening."

He looks at me, surprised. "Right, OK. Are you staying with Debbie?"

"Yes. I need to get away from The Circle for a while."

"What about supper at Maria's?"

"You can go by yourself, if you like," I say, knowing that he won't.

I call Debbie.

"Are you busy this weekend?"

"Why, are you coming down? Oh God, I'm so happy, you don't know how much I've missed you! Is Leo coming? Do you want to stay here? There's plenty of room!"

I laugh, immediately feeling better. Debbie lives on her own in a large four-bedroom farmhouse. She's never married but has had several men in her life, although she's now happily single.

"No, I'm coming on my own and yes, I'd love to stay with you."

"Even better! Not that I don't love Leo, but it means we can really chat and you can tell me all about living in London."

She makes it sound as if it's the other side of the world. But like me, Debbie was born and bred in Harlestone. She's never even been to London, preferring to stay with her horses, running her riding school.

"Is it all right if I arrive today?"

"Of course. Are you driving down?

"Yes, I'll aim to arrive around lunchtime."

"Great!"

I call Maria and am relieved when my call goes through to her voicemail. I leave a message, apologizing profusely, telling her I need a break and have decided to go away for a couple of days. She texts back ten minutes later, saying that she understands, which puts my mind at rest.

Being back in Harlestone is bittersweet. As I drive through the village, the brightly colored hollyhocks standing tall and proud like sentinels against heat-soaked walls and the huge domes of white hydrangeas peeping their heads over garden fences makes me realize how much I've missed it. So much has changed in the month I've been away. The field of yellow rape that I loved to walk through on my way to the village store has since been plowed, and I wonder who was the first to tread a new path through the heavy clods of earth.

Debbie, back from a ride on her fearsome horse Lucifer, senses my low mood. While she cleans her riding boots over a sheet of newspaper, I tell her about Leo and how he hadn't told me the truth about the house he bought.

"I can't understand it," Debbie says, her forehead creased in bewilderment. "What a thing to keep from you. No wonder you don't particularly want to go back. Even I'd feel uneasy living in a house where someone has been murdered and I've got a strong stomach." Her boots clean, she goes to the sink to wash her hands.

"And now I've started putting people's backs up by trying to find out more about the murder," I say.

Debbie turns, water dripping from her elbows. "Why?" she asks, reaching for a checkred towel.

"Because they don't like me asking questions."

"No, I meant—why do you want to know more about the murder?"

"Because it isn't as straightforward as people make out. There are rumors that there was a miscarriage of justice, that it wasn't her husband who killed her."

"Have the police re-opened the investigation, then?" she asks, checking her reflection in the pine-framed mirror that hangs on the wall. Usually wild and unruly, her auburn hair has been flattened by her riding hat, and she remedies this, using her fingers as combs.

"I don't think it was ever closed," I say.

She frowns. "But why are you getting involved? Sorry, Alice, but I can kind of understand that people don't want to talk about it. You should leave it alone, let sleeping dogs lie."

"I can't."

"Why not?"

I look away. "She was called Nina."

"Oh Alice." She comes over and sits beside me, puts an arm round my shoulder, and gives me a hug. "You need to let go."

I lower my head, ashamed. Debbie was there to witness my obsession with a mutual friend's daughter here in Harlestone, born long before my sister died, who happened to be called Nina. Although I was always fond of her, I became a little obsessed after my sister's death, buying her expensive presents and generally doting on her until her mum gently told me that I needed to stop, because it was too much. Stupidly, I had felt hurt and it had ended up spoiling our friendship.

"I'm trying," I say quietly.

"But even if there was a miscarriage of justice," Debbie points out, "it's not your place to go around asking questions, especially on the basis of a rumor."

"It's not just a rumor. I had a visit from a private investigator.

He's looking into the case for Nina's sister-in-law, who is convinced that her brother was innocent."

"Well, of course she is."

"But my neighbor told me that Nina admitted to her that she was having an affair with someone. So why couldn't it have been him who killed her?"

"Didn't the police investigate him?"

"I don't know." I hesitate. "The private investigator asked me to keep my eyes and ears open, let him know if I heard anything."

Debbie's mouth drops open. "He asked you to spy on your neighbors?"

"I refused," I say quickly.

"I hope so. If you decide to stay in The Circle, and want to be accepted—to belong—you need to keep your head down. And really, you should be focusing on you and Leo, not on the murder of someone you didn't even know," she adds gently.

We spend the rest of the weekend catching up with friends from the village, our plans for a long walk scuppered by a blast of rain and cold air that comes in from the east. It matches my mood as I drive back to London on Sunday afternoon but as I get nearer, I give myself a mental shake. Being in Harlestone, away from The Circle, has allowed me to get some perspective. If Leo and I are to get over what he did, I need to make the first move.

I park the car on the drive and go into the house. I thought Leo might have come to the door when he heard me arrive but he's nowhere in sight. I find him in the kitchen, sitting at the table, a glass of wine in his hand, his phone open on one of his news apps.

I clear my throat. "Hello."

He looks up. "Hi. Did you have a nice time with Debbie?"

"Yes, thanks. What about you, did you have a good weekend?"

"Yes, great." He raises his hands above his head, stretching, then links them behind his neck. "I played tennis with Paul and then I spent the rest of the time watching stuff on Netflix."

He looks carefree and relaxed, and a wave of jealousy hits. I swallow it down.

"Shall I make dinner?" I ask.

"I've been snacking all day so I'm not hungry. But go ahead if you want something."

He goes back to the news, oblivious of my eyes on him, oblivious to the frustration building inside me. I'd been about to ask if I could have a glass of wine with him but suddenly, I'm furious. How dare he sit there as if he doesn't have a care in the world when he screwed up so badly?

"I'm going to my study," I say.

"Don't you want a glass of wine?"

"No thanks."

"OK."

He returns to his screen, seemingly unconcerned. I watch him dispassionately for a moment.

"You can stay in Birmingham this week," I say.

His head jerks up. I've got his attention now. "Sorry?"

"You don't need to come home each evening, you can stay in Birmingham."

"But—where are you going?"

"Nowhere."

"What, you're going to stay here by yourself?"

"Yes."

He stares at me like he doesn't know me. "What about Thursday? Do I come home?"

"I'll let you know on Wednesday."

In my study, I go over everything I've learned about Nina's murder. Lorna and Edward heard Nina and Oliver arguing; the next day, Nina admitted to Lorna that she had been having an affair. That evening, according to Lorna, Oliver had come home at 9 p.m. and had gone straight into the house. Twenty minutes later, Nina was dead. That evening, according to Oliver, he had arrived at the house at 9 p.m., had gone to sit in the square for a while, and only then had gone into the house. And had found Nina dead. Which was it? Lorna was adamant about what she'd seen. So why had Oliver said he'd gone to sit in the square when he so obviously hadn't? Had he panicked and said the first thing that had come into his head? Or had he planned it out beforehand, hoping that nobody would be able to say that he *hadn't* been in the square, because nobody would be watching from their window at that time of night?

TWENTY

Leo takes a while getting ready for work the next morning, giving me time to change my mind about staying on my own. His footsteps are heavier than usual as he moves around upstairs. He's making his presence felt, showing me how empty the house is going to be without him.

He comes downstairs and drops his bag in the hall with an exaggerated thud. It's irritating, this over-the-top reminder that he's leaving for several days. It was how we were meant to be living until his Birmingham contract finished, him leaving on Monday mornings and not coming back until Thursday. Now he's perceiving it as a punishment.

I stay in bed long after he's left for work, overwhelmed by a lethargy I can't shake. The uncertainty of our situation has hit me hard. I'd been so full of hope coming here; a little nervous as to how I was going to adapt to living in London, but looking forward to being with Leo on a more regular basis. Now our relationship seems to be falling apart. Even in the aftermath of my parents' and sister's deaths, I hadn't felt this alone.

It's the need of a coffee that gets me to my feet. I carry it through to the sitting room and drink it standing by the window, watching the trees start a slow shed of their leaves. It's gone nine o'clock, I'm late at my desk. A movement catches my eye, Eve coming out of her house. She's dressed in her running gear and I'm about to knock on the window and wave when Tamsin appears behind her. I step back quickly, but I can still see them. They exchange a few words, then Eve runs across the road and into the square, leaving Tamsin standing on the drive.

Needing breakfast, I go to the kitchen, put some bread in the toaster and search the fridge for honey. A ring at the doorbell startles me; the jar slips from my hand and smashes on the floor, right by my bare feet. I stare at the shards of glass sticking to the bottom of my blue pajamas, wondering where to begin cleaning up the mess, and the doorbell rings again. Whoever it is isn't going to go away.

Stepping carefully over the broken jar, I go into the hall, open the door and come face to face with the one person I could do without seeing. Tamsin.

"Hi, Alice." In deference to the colder weather, she's wearing a white padded jacket and white suede ankle boots. She looks perfect.

"Sorry," I say, conscious of being in my pajamas. "I'm not feeling good. So, if you're here to have another go at me, I'd rather you come back another day."

She shuffles from one foot to the other. "No, I'm not, I'm here to apologize. I shouldn't have been so aggressive. I was having a bad week."

"It's fine. But as I told you, I didn't upset Lorna, she said it was a relief to talk about Nina because nobody did anymore."

Tamsin nods, and I ignore the image that comes to mind, of Lorna playing with her pearls.

"I wondered if you'd like to come for coffee on Friday," she says. "In the morning, around ten-thirty. I know you work but would that be OK? Eve will be there," she adds, as if she thinks I might not go if it's just the two of us.

I'm not keen on interrupting my working day but I can always work through lunch to make up for taking time off in the morning. "Thank you, that would be lovely," I say.

She looks both pleased and relieved. "Great! Well, goodbye, Alice, I hope you feel better soon."

I watch her as she walks down the drive.

"You look beautiful, by the way!" I call.

She turns and gives me a little wave but there's sadness on her face, as if she doesn't really believe me.

In the kitchen, I clean up the mess from the broken jar with renewed energy. It's the house that's stifling me, I realize. What I need is a blast of cold air. Half-an-hour in the garden will help. I can do some weeding. I enjoy weeding, it's the kind of task I can do on autopilot, leaving my mind free to wander.

The previous day's rain makes the weeding easier. I'm halfway up the left-hand side of the garden when I discover a panel missing in the fence between our house and Eve and Will's. It's not a problem because the gap is partly covered by thick green foliage. I push it aside and realize that I could walk straight into their garden if I wanted to. Maybe Eve and Nina used it as a shortcut instead of walking across the driveway when they wanted to see each other. I make a mental note to ask her about it when I next see her.

My cell phone rings. I straighten up, ease my back. It's Ginny.

"Hi, Alice. I'm calling to see how you are. Am I disturbing you?"

"No, it's fine, I'm taking a break in the garden. It's lovely to be outside. How are you? Did you have a good weekend?"

"Well, I'm fast becoming a golf widow, which suits me fine. Mark and Ben spent the whole day yesterday on the golf course. Ben came back for a drink afterward, he was asking about you."

"That was nice of him."

There's a pause. "I'm actually calling because Leo called me this morning."

"Leo?"

"Yes. He said that you don't want him coming home this week, that you told him he could stay in Birmingham. He wanted me to check that you'll be all right on your own."

"I'll be fine," I say, sounding braver than I feel, because I do have a niggling apprehension about being on my own tonight.

"Would you like me to come and stay?"

"That's lovely of you, but honestly, it's fine. I need to do this, Ginny, I need to see if I can stay here. We've only been here a month, I don't want to give up yet."

"I think Leo's afraid you might give up on him."

I sigh. "To be honest, I don't know how I feel about him anymore. I still can't get my head around him lying to me."

"How about we have lunch this week? I'll take a longer lunch hour."

"That will be lovely. When were you thinking?"

"Either tomorrow or Friday."

"Tomorrow," I say, remembering coffee at Tamsin's on Friday morning. "Shall we go to the restaurant in Covent Garden where they serve that delicious monkfish? It's not too far for you, is it?"

"Neptune? I can walk there in ten minutes. I'll call and make a reservation for twelve thirty."

"Great, see you there."

The two invitations, plus the weeding, make it easier for me to get back to work. I love the story I'm translating and I become so absorbed in it that it's three o'clock before I stop for something to eat. The sun has come out and rather than head straight back to work after a sandwich, I decide to go for a walk in Finsbury Park and translate this evening instead. With Leo not coming home, I'll need something to take my mind off being alone in the house.

Half an hour later, I'm on my way, glad to be away from The Circle, from its cloying, claustrophobic atmosphere. It's the gates, I decide. They make it feel a bit like a prison. If they weren't there, The Circle would be just another street in London.

The park is glorious in its new autumn colors. I walk for an hour, trying not to think of anything much, then sit down on a bench and watch the world go by. A few people stride along, in a hurry to be somewhere, but most stroll leisurely, especially the mums with young children, or the older couples, some hand in hand. I smile, then feel a pang of melancholy. Will Leo and I ever have children, grow old together? Is it strange that we have never talked about having children? Or was it a conversation we were waiting to have once we'd settled into our new life in London?

"Alice!"

I look up and see Eve jogging toward me.

"You're not still running, are you?" I ask in pretend alarm. "I saw you leave at nine this morning."

She laughs and sits down on the bench, taking a moment to catch her breath.

"No, I ran with a friend, then went to hers for lunch. Now I'm jogging back to blog. What about you? Did you have a good weekend? Leo said you were away."

"Yes, I went back to Harlestone and caught up with some of my friends there. I felt bad about canceling on Maria at the last minute, but I needed a change of scene."

"Don't worry, she understood."

"Also, I had a bit of a run-in with Tamsin so I thought it better to keep my distance."

Eve wrinkles her nose. "Yes, she told me. If it helps, she's feeling bad about it."

"I know, she came and apologized this morning, which was nice of her. And invited me for coffee on Friday."

"Oh, good, she said she was going to. Don't think too harshly of her, Alice. Nina's death hit her hard."

"It must be dreadful to lose your best friend in such a terrible way," I say, watching a little dachshund sniffing around a pile of leaves.

"It was all the harder for her because—well, there wasn't a row, or anything like that, but I think that when we moved in next door, Tamsin felt a bit pushed out."

"In what way?"

"The thing is, I only knew that Tamsin and Nina were best friends, or had been best friends, after Nina died, when Tamsin came to see me. She was distraught, she wanted to know if she had upset Nina in any way. I asked her what she meant and she said that until a few months before her death, she and Nina had been best friends, always popping in and out of each other's houses, having supper together at weekends. Then, suddenly, everything changed. She said she'd go past Nina's house and see me chatting to her through the window, and wonder why Nina hadn't invited her to join us. I told her they were usually spur-of-the-moment coffees—you know, Nina would see me coming back from a run and shout 'want a coffee?' But there were the suppers too. We went around to Nina and Oliver's a few times with Maria and Tim, but Tamsin and Connor were never there, which was why I didn't know she and Nina were supposedly best friends. I asked Maria about it recently, asked if she knew what had happened between them and she said that she didn't. Nina had stopped coming to yoga too, and Tamsin suspected it was because she didn't want to see her." She pauses. "I really liked Nina but it bothered me afterward, to think that she was being—well, maybe a bit mean."

I nod slowly. "Was it common knowledge that Nina was having an affair?"

"Who told you that?"

Was there a slight edge to her voice or had I imagined it? "Lorna."

Eve shakes her head. "No. We only found out after." She turns to look at me. "You can understand now why we were able to accept that Oliver killed her."

Just like that, I want to ask, *without question?* "But why couldn't it have been the man she was having an affair with who killed her?" I ask instead.

Eve bends to tie her lace. "I'm sure the police looked into it," she says, straightening up again. "And if they didn't think there was anything to investigate, well, who were we to argue?"

Oliver's friends, I want to say. *You were Oliver's friends.*

"You said Tamsin was Nina's best friend. Did she know about her affair?"

"No, not back then. Nina never spoke to her about it."

"I remember Tamsin saying at lunch last week that Nina had really helped her. Did she see her in a professional capacity?"

"No, Nina wouldn't have been allowed to be her therapist, given that they were friends. Tamsin suffers from depression—I don't think she'll mind me telling you that—and I think Nina gave her advice on natural remedies, as Tamsin didn't want to take anti-depressants. Which is why it was doubly hard for her when Nina began distancing herself. Tamsin felt abandoned, and not just physically."

"Did Nina work from home?"

"No, she had an office about twenty minutes from here."

"What about Connor, what's he like?"

"Connor is Connor. He's actually all right when you get to know him. But he can be a bit insensitive, especially to Tamsin."

I don't want to pry but I'm curious. Luckily, after a drink from her water bottle, she carries on without any prompting.

"For example," Eve goes on. "After the murder, Tamsin wanted to move away. We all did; it was a natural knee-jerk reaction. A violent murder had happened in close proximity to where we were living and we were all scared. But Connor insisted they were staying and refused to even consider a possible move. If he had tried to find a middle ground, told Tamsin that yes, they could think about moving away if that was what she really wanted, she wouldn't have broken so completely. Will was brilliant, he said that we could put the house back on the market even though we'd only been here five months. Lorna especially was in a terrible state. She wanted to go and stay with her sister in Dorset, at least for a while, and Will offered to drive her and Edward there. But the next day, Edward was taken to hospital with a heart attack, brought on by the stress of the murder next door, so they hadn't been able to leave. Anyway, before anyone could do anything, Oliver was arrested, then he killed himself. And everyone began to feel safe again. The only people that did actually move away were the Tinsleys, who lived at number 3."

"Hm," I say, because my mind is still stuck on Tamsin and Nina's falling out. I don't want Eve to know that she's given me lots to think about so I look for a way to change the subject.

"By the way, I was in the garden this morning and I found a gap in the fence between our two properties."

"Gosh, I'd forgotten about that! Oliver used to lend Will his lawnmower because it was a new state-of-the-art one and they opened up the fence so they could push it through instead of having to take it around the front. You'll probably find a gap on the other side too, because Oliver used to cut Lorna and Edward's grass for them. Geoff does it now."

"He lives on the other side of them, doesn't he?"

"Yes."

"Does he live there on his own? Someone mentioned that he's divorced."

"Yes, for a few years now. I never knew his wife but Maria did, because they were neighbors. She met someone at work and that was it, marriage over." She stands up and stretches her arms above her head, easing her muscles. "Sorry, but I need to go. Do you want me to ask Will to put the panel back up?"

"No, don't, it's fine. The gap has grown over anyway. And you never know, it might come in useful," I add with a smile.

"Is Leo coming back each evening, like he did last week?"

"No, I told him not to. It's a long journey to have to make twice a day."

"Then do you want to come and sleep at ours?"

"That's lovely of you. But if I'm to stay here, I need to get used to being in the house on my own."

"If you change your mind, just let us know. Do you want to jog back with me?"

"No, thanks, I'm not really the jogging kind."

She laughs. "Bye, Alice. It was nice talking to you. See you at Tamsin's on Friday, if not before."

I watch her thoughtfully as she runs off. I'm grateful for everything she told me but it was a huge amount of information to dump on me in one sitting. Maybe it's Eve I'm not meant to trust. And from what I'm beginning to learn about Nina—her affair, her rejection of Tamsin—maybe she wasn't as lovely as I thought.

PAST

*I have a new client and a new office. It's on the first floor of an old, **rickety** building and I hear her running up the stairs, her feet hammering **on the** wooden steps. She's late.*

*"I'm sorry," she says, flustered. "I got lost. I haven't been living **here** long and I don't know my way around yet."*

*"It's fine," I say, giving her a smile. "You really shouldn't have run." **I** mean it; her cheeks are flushed and she looks slightly sweaty. Her **hair is a** mess, half of it still tied up, the other half falling in strands around **her face.***

*I wait while she takes off her coat and extra-long scarf, both of **them** black. The dress she's wearing is also black, as are her boots. **She sees me** looking and gives a self-conscious laugh.*

*"Trying to fit in," she explains. "Most of the women here seem to **wear** black."*

*I smile non-committally and tell her to make herself comfortable, al-though it may be difficult in the angular chair I've chosen for this office. **I ask** her if she's warm enough; it's cold outside, the temperature is **almost zero.***

"Yes, thank you," she says.

*I move my eyes to the window, giving her time to settle. The **street** outside is busy with the sounds of people going home after their **working day.***

"How are you?" I ask, once she's sitting down.

*She shifts in the chair. "To be honest, I'm not really sure why **I'm here.***

I mean, there isn't really anything wrong. I just need to talk to someone, I guess."

"That's what I'm here for," I say, putting her at ease.

She nods. "I'm not sure where to begin."

"Why don't I ask you a few questions first?"

Another nod. "Yes, of course."

I pull my pad toward me. "Before we begin, I want you to know, and remember, that anything you say in this room is confidential."

She gives a little laugh. "Good. Not that I'm going to tell you anything amazing. As I said, I don't really know why I'm here. My life is perfect. But I'm not happy. I feel terrible for saying that but it's true."

The tension in her vibrates around the room. I pick up my pen and jot down the words—"perfect" and "unhappy" then lean forward in my chair.

"Do you know what Henry David Thoreau believed? 'Happiness is like a butterfly; the more you chase it, the more it will elude you. But if you turn your attention to other things, it will come and sit softly on your shoulder.'"

She smiles, relaxes. It always works.

TWENTY-ONE

I start awake. I'm about to open my eyes but some primal instinct tells me that I need to pretend I'm still asleep. My mind darts, trying to work it out. And then I realize; there's someone in the room.

Adrenaline surges through my body, whipping my heartrate to a frenzy. It hammers in my chest and I tell myself frantically that I'm imagining it, remind myself that last time this happened, there was no one there. But I know, with a horrible, terrible certainty, that someone is standing at the foot of my bed. I lie in a state of near-paralysis, not daring to breathe, waiting for the crush of their body on mine, the tightening of their hands around my throat. The tension is unbearable; I try to hold on to my fear but I can't.

"Go away!" The words tear out of me and I push myself up forcibly, ready to face whoever is there. The room is in darkness, panicking me further, because I had left the lamp on. I reach down, fumbling for the switch, steeling myself for a hand seizing my bare arm and pulling me from the bed. I snap the light on and scan the room, my breath coming in shallow gasps as I peer into the shadows. There's no one there. I wait, listening to every noise the house is making. But nothing sounds wrong.

I slump back against my pillow, cold sweat on my forehead,

trying to slow my pounding heart. *It's all right, it's all right. Nothing happened.*

But there was someone there, I know there was. I slide my cell phone from under my pillow, tap 999, then change my mind and find Leo's number. I need to hear someone's voice and he's the only person I feel I can call at—I check the time, and when I see that it's only two o'clock, the knowledge that I still have the rest of the night to get through is devastating. It won't be light for another five hours and I'm not going to be able to go back to sleep, not now. I force myself to be calm. I'm not going to call Leo. Nothing has happened to me, nothing will happen to me now. But why would someone break into the house to do absolutely nothing? And how did they get in?

Reluctantly, I get out of bed and make the same journey through the house that I made a week ago, but with less bravado because this time, Leo isn't asleep upstairs. In the kitchen, I check the French windows. There's no broken glass, no sign of forced entry. Moving to the worktop, I grab a knife from the drawer. The knife, black-handled with a serrated edge, used for cutting lemons, will only be dangerous if I plunge it deep into someone. Which I could never do. Nevertheless, it gives me a weak kind of courage.

The windows in the downstairs rooms are intact, nothing has been disturbed. The front door is still locked from the inside. I continue slowly up the stairs, my heartbeat increasing with each step I take. I try not to think about someone leaping out at me from the guest bedroom or the study. With those lights now on, the whole house is ablaze, except for our bedroom, the one Leo and I used to sleep in. The one where Nina was murdered. I push open the door, snap on the light and peer in. Like the other rooms, it's empty. And yet. I stand still, trying to work it out. There's a sort of presence, not a physical one, but something invisible, intangible. Something I can sense, but can't name. Slamming the door behind me, I hurry downstairs.

Somehow, I make it through the next few hours. To pass the

time, I make several cups of tea and drink them in the sitting room, feeling safer at the front of the house. I want to check the street outside but the thought of seeing someone standing there, watching the house, watching me, is almost more terrifying than thinking they're inside, so I keep the curtains closed. At five, I crawl back into bed. Dawn will be breaking soon, people will be waking up, getting ready to start the day ahead. Nobody will come now.

When I wake, and think about the previous night, it's impossible to believe that it was anything but my imagination. Maybe I turned off the lamp myself, without realizing, as I descended into sleep? I walk through the house again, checking the windows and doors for the slightest trace that someone had somehow managed to get in. But there's nothing out of the ordinary.

My positivity takes a knock when I find strands of my hair on the worktop in the kitchen. Added to the ones I found in the bathroom this morning, it points to the thing I fear most, losing my hair again. Some months after my parents and sister died, my hair became noticeably thinner and when Debbie persuaded me to see a doctor, I was diagnosed with Telogen effluvium, brought on by the stress of what had happened. Barely able to eat since the accident, I'd lost a lot of weight. If I didn't want to aggravate the condition, the doctor told me, I needed to start eating healthy, balanced meals again. My hair eventually recovered, but it was a long process and, at nineteen years of age, hugely distressing.

The stress I'm feeling now, because of what happened in this house, and Leo not telling me, is nothing to the stress I felt back then. But I'm older now, my hair naturally more fragile. I twist it into a loose knot, secure it with a clip. If it's not hanging around my shoulders, I won't be constantly thinking about it.

In the fridge, I look for something for breakfast and find in the vegetable drawer, along with an overripe avocado, a bottle of expensive champagne, which Leo must have put there before he left yesterday. I'm not sure if it's for me—if, like the white rose he left me in the hall, he's trying to make up for everything—or if he put it there to drink when he's next home.

There's a message from him on my phone—**Everything OK?**—to which I reply **Everything fine.**

I go back to my breakfast but my appetite has gone, chased away by my worry over the state of our relationship. I'm glad I'm meeting Ginny for lunch, I desperately need someone to talk to.

I work for a couple of hours, then leave the house. Edward is in their front garden, tending his roses and, remembering what Tamsin said about me upsetting Lorna with my questions about Nina, I feel suddenly awkward.

"Hello!" I call, testing the water.

The smile Edward gives me puts my mind at rest. "Alice! How are you?"

I walk over the drive toward him. "I'm fine, thank you, I hope you are too?"

"Yes, yes, I can't complain. Are you going shopping?"

"No, I'm meeting a friend for lunch. How is Lorna?"

"She's very well. It was nice of you to call by the other day. She gets a bit lonely sometimes."

"I hope I didn't upset her."

"Upset her? Why would you have upset her?"

"I'm afraid I was asking about Nina and Oliver."

"Don't you worry your head. If she was upset, it was about you. She told me you lost your parents and sister?"

"Yes, that's right."

"What a shocking thing to happen. A drunk driver, was it?"

"No, just a young driver without much experience."

"Absolutely terrible for you," he says, shaking his head.

"Yes, it was. But it's in the past now."

"It doesn't do any good to dwell on the past," he growls and I know, from the fierce look on his face that he's thinking about his son. He's of the generation where people don't talk about their emotions.

"You're probably right," I say.

He turns away. "Well, I'd best get on."

"If you need shopping or anything, I hope you'll let me know."

"Thank you, but we get everything delivered. We don't really go out anymore."

Except that he was meant to be out the other day.

I nod. "Well, goodbye, Edward. Tell Lorna I'll see her soon."

TWENTY-TWO

Ginny is already at Neptune when I arrive. She's beautifully dressed in a chocolate-brown leather skirt and jacket that I've never seen before.

"Mark's birthday present to me," she says, when I mention it.

"That's the problem with working from home," I say. "It doesn't matter what I put on in the mornings. I'd love something like that but I'd never get any wear out of it."

We have a quick catch-up while we study the menus but once we've ordered, I find myself confiding my worries to her.

"I can't work out if the reason I'm finding it hard to forgive Leo is because our relationship was already doomed before he lied to me," I say, turning my fork over and over on the white cloth. "When we only saw each other at weekends, we were on our best behavior, not wanting to spoil the time we had together. We didn't really know each other. It's only now that we're discovering each other's faults and weaknesses."

"But you love him," Ginny says.

"Yes. But I'm not sure that the love I feel for him is strong enough to overcome the negatives." I look guiltily at her. "That makes me sound horrible, I know."

"Not horrible, just honest."

"I don't want to give up on our relationship so I need to find a way forward. It's just that, for the moment, I seem unable to." I give her a smile. "Come on, let's talk about something else."

We're interrupted by the waiter bringing our food over.

"Something weird happened the other day," I say, when we've finished eating. "You know I told you that Nina admitted to Lorna, the lady who lives next door, that she'd been having an affair? When I mentioned it to Leo, he almost jumped out of his skin."

"Even I was surprised when you told me." Ginny sits back in her chair and places a hand on her stomach. "That was delicious."

"Yes, but it was more than surprise. He dropped his glass of wine, it went everywhere and—I don't know—he just seemed overly flustered."

"Strange." She laughs. "Unless he was the one having an affair with her."

"What?" I stare at her and she sits up quickly and reaches across the table for my hand, her two silver bangles jangling together. "Alice, I'm joking! Leo didn't even know Nina."

It's too late, I can't stop the thought from flying through my mind. "What if he did? What if he did know her?"

"Stop it." She gives my hand a shake. "Don't start imagining something that didn't happen. How could he have known her?"

"I don't know. She was a therapist, maybe he was a client."

Ginny groans. "I wish I hadn't said anything. It was a joke, Alice, seriously." She picks up her menu. "Do you want dessert?"

"Sorry. No, just a coffee." I close my menu and put it down on the table. "Tamsin has invited me to hers on Friday."

"Tamsin? Your archenemy? How come? Tell me, I want to know everything."

I launch into an account of my latest conflict with Tamsin and her subsequent apology and by the time we leave the restaurant half an hour later, I can tell Ginny's relieved that I've forgotten what she said about Leo having known Nina. But I haven't, it's lodged right there in the back of my mind.

It's a direct tube ride from Covent Garden back to Finsbury Park. It's the way I came, on the Piccadilly line, but I go to the map on the wall in the Underground station, wanting to see where else I could get to. My eyes fall on Leicester Square—theaterland—and Knightsbridge, where I know Harrods is. It's also home to the Natural History Museum, another place I'm keen to visit. I follow the dark blue line past Earl's Court right to the end, amazed that I can get all the way to Heathrow Airport from practically my front door. The Piccadilly line is certainly a good line to live on. And if I change at Earl's Court, I could go to Kew Gardens and—I follow another branch of the line—to Wimbledon. Leo and I both love watching tennis and I wonder how difficult it is to get tickets for a match there. And then I wonder if Leo and I will even last until next summer.

I'm about to turn away when I remember that Thomas Grainger's offices are in Wimbledon. I take my cell phone from my bag and find the address—26 William Street. I stand for a moment. A part of me wants to go and check out the address, just to make sure he is who he says he is, in case I ever need to call him. I don't know why I'm thinking I might need to call him—except that if there *was* a miscarriage of justice and I do hear something which could put the real perpetrator away, wouldn't it be my duty to tell him? There's something off about the way everyone was so quick to accept that Oliver killed Nina. Maybe they're protecting someone, someone from The Circle who they suspect of having had an affair with Nina. But who?

I go through the barriers and instead of heading north on the Piccadilly line, I head south toward Earl's Court, then change to the District line. I've never traveled so far on the tube by myself and when I get off at Wimbledon, I'm so out of my comfort zone that I'm tempted to go straight back home. Everyone seems to know where they're going except me.

I move to the side and use Citymapper to locate William Street.

It's quite a long walk and the further I go, the more I wonder what I'm doing here. William Street is a long road of smart townhouses, most of which seem to have been turned into offices. I approach number 26; there's a discreet gold plaque on the wall and I have to go up the first two of four stone steps to read the words *Thomas Grainger, Private Investigator.* Behind the dark blue door, I can hear a murmur of voices and when they get steadily louder, I realize that someone is coming along the corridor. The thought of him discovering me on the doorstep sends me scooting back to the pavement. I just have time to hide myself in the doorway of a house two doors down when the sound of someone saying goodbye—a woman—and a man's voice answering her, reaches my ears. I bend my head over my phone, pretending to search for something, praying that the door in front of me won't suddenly open. My back is to the road and when I hear the light click of heels on the pavement, I breathe a sigh of relief. Turning my head slowly, I check number 26 to make sure Thomas Grainger isn't still there. He isn't, so I leave the doorway and see a woman, smartly dressed in a camel-colored coat, walking down the road. I need to go back that way anyway, so I follow her to the tube station, wondering what business she had with a private investigator. The majority of his cases are probably people wanting to know what their partners are up to. *Maybe I should get him to check out Leo for me,* I think, and then feel guilty.

I get home and even as I'm dialing Thomas Grainger's number, I'm wondering what I'm doing. What's the point of calling him when I have absolutely nothing to tell him? But it's too late; my call connects before I can hang up.

"It's Alice Dawson," I say, instantly recognizing his voice.

"Ms. Dawson, thank you for calling." He can't quite hide his surprise, which is understandable after I told him that I wouldn't help.

It sounds too formal. "Alice," I say. "You can call me Alice."

"And I'm Thomas."

"I'm sorry, I'm not really sure why I am—calling you, I mean." I hate that I sound flustered. "I don't have any news. I did go and see my neighbor, but she didn't tell me anything that I'm sure you don't already know. She was the one who saw Oliver arrive home on the night of the murder and—"

"I could come by tomorrow afternoon," he says, interrupting me.

My heart misses a beat. "But there's nothing really to tell. I can go over it now, if you like."

"I prefer not to talk on the phone. I'm going to be in your area anyway, so it's no trouble. Would 2 p.m. suit you?"

"Yes, but I'm not sure—"

"Thank you, Alice, I'll see you tomorrow."

I try to concentrate on my work for the rest of the day but the guilty feeling in the pit of my stomach has me constantly reaching for my phone, wanting to call Thomas Grainger and tell him not to bother coming over. Even though I'm not going to be telling him anything he doesn't already know, it feels wrong to be speaking to him. I wish I could run it by someone but I already know what Debbie would say. And I can't ask Ginny for advice, because I still haven't told Leo that the man who gate-crashed our party is a private investigator. If Ginny knows, she might tell Mark, who would tell Leo. And I need to be the one to tell him. The reason I haven't told him yet is that I know he'll call the police, and Thomas will get into trouble if they find out he's investigating Nina's murder. And I don't want that to happen.

I work late into the evening to make up for taking most of the afternoon off and when it gets dark, still traumatized by my experience last night, I read in the sitting room with the curtains open, getting up occasionally to check what the other residents of The Circle are doing. It's comforting to see lights on, to know that even though it's late, not everyone is in bed.

By the time one o'clock comes, most of the lights have gone out and I feel nervous standing at the window in full view. There could be someone waiting in the shadows, someone who can see me even if I can't see them. Of the few lights that are still on, one comes from Tamsin's house and I like to think that she might be awake too.

When I go to bed, I leave the light on in the stairwell so that the house isn't in complete darkness. But I'm unable to relax and I know that I've been fooling myself in thinking that I can ever feel comfortable living here. Ginny had been appalled when I told her that I'd thought there was someone in the house the previous night, and had urged me to move in with her and Mark while I sort things out with Leo. I should have taken her up on her offer—and tomorrow I will. I don't know what will happen between me and Leo, the only thing I know is that I can't go on living in The Circle.

TWENTY-THREE

Thomas arrives at precisely two o'clock. I was expecting him to ring on the intercom, so it's a shock to find him at the front door.

"I thought I'd check if the entry code had been changed. It hasn't," he says, by way of explanation. He sounds disapproving.

"I'll speak to someone about it." I close the door on the cold wind that followed him in and lead him through to the sitting room. It feels rude not to offer him a coffee but I want to get rid of him as quickly as possible. Even though I managed to get through the night unscathed, I still don't want to be here. The only thing I'm hesitating about is whether to go to Ginny's, or to Debbie's in Harlestone.

"I don't have very long, I'm afraid," he says, as if he's read my mind and is putting me at ease.

"Yes, of course." I wait until he's sitting down, his phone on the table beside him. "How is Oliver's sister?"

"Health-wise, not so good. But it's done wonders for her morale knowing that we might be able to make some progress in clearing Oliver's name. She's very grateful to you, Alice."

I frown. "As I said on the phone yesterday, I don't think I'm going to be telling you anything you don't already know. I'd hate for you, or Oliver's sister, to have false hope."

"Believe me, false hope is the last thing I want to give Helen."

I tell him quickly about my visit to Lorna.

"Did Helen—Oliver's sister—know that Nina was having an affair?" I ask.

"Not until my police source told me about your neighbors' testimony."

"Was she aware there were problems in the marriage?"

"No, but she said that Oliver probably wouldn't have told her if there had been."

"My neighbor was adamant that she saw Oliver go into the house," I say. "But what if he went in, then went out again? Maybe he heard Nina breaking things off with the man she was having an affair with, and decided to leave them to it. And then, while he was in the square, that person killed her."

"You don't know how much I'd like that to be true. But if that was the case, wouldn't Oliver have said as much to the police? He maintained that he didn't go into the house at all, even when his lawyer suggested to him that it might have been the case."

"What do you think happened?" I ask.

"I believe Oliver, because he had no need to lie. But I also believe your next-door neighbor—Mrs. Beaumont." He leans forward, fixing me with his eyes. "Think about it for a minute; she sees Oliver arrive, she sees him getting out of the car. At that moment, someone sneaks past the car and goes into the house. Oliver, about to head to the square, doesn't see that person because he's going in the other direction. Your neighbor, thinking that she's seen Oliver go inside, has stopped watching because she's anxious that he and Nina might start arguing again. It's why she doesn't see Oliver walk into the square. And as nobody else came forward to say that they saw him there—well, in the police's eyes, without an alibi, he has to be lying."

I nod slowly, realizing that what Thomas said is not possibly what happened, but probably what happened. I like that he believes both Oliver and Lorna.

"So, what we need to find out is who could have sneaked past Oliver into the house." I flush, realizing I said "we" and not "you." "The person Nina might have been having an affair with."

"Exactly."

"What I don't understand is why everyone was so quick to condemn Oliver, and why nobody wants to believe that someone else could have killed her. Do you think they're protecting somebody?"

"Yes," he says softly. "I do."

"Someone from here—from The Circle?"

"Why else would they close ranks?"

"It's true that they don't seem to like me asking questions about Nina," I say. "Tamsin especially. She was Nina's best friend and she really didn't like me going to see Lorna." I stop, realizing I've said too much.

"It's understandable, if she was Nina's best friend. Does Tamsin have red hair, by any chance?"

"Yes, how do you know?"

"Because Nina often spoke about her to Helen, but Helen couldn't remember her name and I wasn't sure which one of Nina's friends she was." He consults his phone. "There was another friend who used to go to yoga with them."

"That would be Eve, my immediate neighbor."

He nods. "Eve Jackman. Does she have a partner?"

"Yes, her husband, Will."

"I've got here that they moved in about five months before Nina was murdered."

"That's right."

He looks up. "There's another friend then, someone Nina had known for longer."

"That would be Maria. You know, married to Tim, except that he calls her Mary because she went to a convent school," I say dryly.

He gives a slight smile. "Ah yes, that Maria. Maria Conway and her husband Tim."

"Yes."

He finishes tapping into his phone and slides it into his pocket. "Thank you," he says, getting to his feet. "And once again, please don't do anything that you don't feel comfortable with. The last thing I want is to put pressure on you, so I won't be contacting you. If anything comes up and you feel able to tell me, you have my cell."

I don't bother telling him that I'm not going to be around much longer. "Give my best wishes to Helen," I say.

"I will, thank you."

I close the door behind him and lean against it, aware that the thought of not seeing him again is bothering me more than it should. There's something about him that I find reassuring. He's solid, the sort of person you could rely on if things got tough, and I wonder if his relationship with Oliver's sister is more than platonic. I go over what I told him, wanting to make sure that I hadn't said anything to feel guilty about. I hadn't repeated what Eve told me yesterday, about the falling out between Nina and Tamsin, because I'm not sure why she told me, and with Lorna's warning stuck in my mind, I prefer to be cautious. I wish I knew if she actually whispered anything. It doesn't matter, I realize, I'm leaving. But there are still a few personal ends that I want to tie up before I go.

I call Leo. He picks up straightaway.

"Alice, thank you for calling." His relief whooshes down the line and I remember that I'm meant to be letting him know if he can come home tomorrow. He's going to be pleased when I tell him that he can—but maybe not so pleased when I tell him that I won't be here.

"Why did you jump when I mentioned Nina having an affair?" I ask.

I can hear his mind adjusting itself away from what he thought I was phoning about, to why I'm actually calling.

"Because you insinuated that maybe he was responsible for Nina's murder."

"So?"

"It's just that when I played tennis with Paul on Saturday, he told me that Nina used to see quite a few of the men from The Circle."

I frown. "Do you mean in her role as a therapist? Because I don't think she'd have been able to see them in that capacity, if they were friends or neighbors."

"No, not as a therapist. She helped them out with other stuff, Will with his lines, Connor with his whiskies, that sort of thing."

"That doesn't mean she was having an affair with either of them."

"I never said she was."

"How did you come to have this conversation with Paul, any-way?"

"I just happened to ask him what Nina and Oliver were like. He said that they were both really nice people, always helping others out. Oliver used to help the older residents with their gardens, do odd jobs for them." He pauses. "All I'm saying is that a lot of people here were close to Nina, men as well as women, which is why I don't think you should be going around talking about her having an affair and then saying you think he might have murdered her, like you said to me."

"But if it was someone else who murdered her, don't you think he deserves to be brought to justice?"

"Well, yes, of course."

"Even if it turns out to be someone from The Circle?"

There's a pause and I can almost see the two deep lines between his eyes that appear whenever he frowns. "Is there something you're not telling me?"

"Just that not everyone thinks Oliver is guilty."

"What do you mean?"

I'm pacing the floor now, wondering if I should tell him about Thomas, how he's an investigator and not a reporter, and how he thinks that Oliver is innocent. But if I tell him that he's a friend of Oliver's sister, Leo will say he has a vested interest. Besides, if he asks how I met him, I'll have to tell him he's the man who gate-crashed our drinks evening, and Thomas's credibility will be less than zero, private investigator or not. And, I remind myself, it's no longer my business.

"I'm finding it hard to reconcile this image of Oliver as a par-agon of virtue but also a killer," I tell him, coming to a stop by the window. Maria and Tim, on the way into the square with their boys, are chatting to Geoff at the gate. I watch for a moment. Did

Nina help Tim and Geoff in some capacity too, as well as Will and Connor?

"Maybe. But I don't understand why you're getting involved." Leo interrupts my train of thought. "Unless it's because of your sister. Because if that is the reason, you need to let it go. It isn't healthy, Alice."

I hang up before he can say anything more and remind me what my therapist told me—that I can't live my sister's life through the lives of other women called Nina.

TWENTY-FOUR

Stay!

The soft, sibilant whisper lulls me from my sleep. Instead of feeling afraid, the lingering echo of the word fills me with lightness.

"Nina," I murmur.

The sense of her, strong, silent, acts like a balm to my troubled mind.

"I'm not going to leave you," I promise her silently. "I'm going to get to the truth. If it wasn't Oliver who killed you, I'll find out who did."

I expect her to leave. But she stays, and I drift easily back to sleep.

I wake late, luxuriating in the aura of peace cocooning my body. I search the reason for this unexpected feeling of wellbeing and remember how I sensed Nina's presence in the night. I have no trouble believing her spirit was there, that—like my sister was—she's trapped between this life and the next, waiting for justice to be done. I throw back the covers, driven by new purpose. I'm not going anywhere, I have a promise to fulfill.

My cell phone beeps, a message from Leo.

You didn't tell me if I should come home tonight. My heart sinks. I take a moment, then text him back I'm sorry, I need more time. I wait anxiously for his reply, feeling guilty that I don't want him here. It comes—**It's fine, I understand. I'm here if you need me xx.** Tears fill my eyes. We were good together, me and Leo.

I find myself thinking about Thomas. I've already worked out that he must be around forty-four years old and I'm still wondering about his relationship with Helen. I've noticed a tenderness in his eyes whenever he mentions her name and I can't imagine what it must be like—whether she's a friend or something more—to know that time is running out for her. Leo thinks it's only because my sister was called Nina that I've taken Nina Maxwell's murder to heart, but he's wrong. If my husband or brother was wrongly accused of murder, I'd want the truth to come out. And from the relatively little time I've spent in The Circle, I'm convinced there's a truth to be found.

I call Thomas.

"I heard something," I say.

"Oh?"

He listens while I repeat what Leo told me about Nina helping out people in The Circle, including the husbands of her close friends.

"Thank you for being so open with me," he says when I get to the end.

"The only reason I'm telling you is because something strange happened. When I was leaving Lorna's house the other day, after I'd asked her about Nina, I could have sworn she whispered 'Don't trust anyone' in my ear."

"She's probably right. The more I look into Nina's murder, the more secrets I think there are."

"Yes, but that's not the point. She told me her husband wasn't there, so I thought it was strange that she felt the need to whisper. Then, not long afterward, when I got home, I saw him coming out of the garage. So I think she might have lied. Although he could have been in the garden, because he had his gardening shoes on."

"How did Lorna seem when you spoke to her?"

"Not frightened exactly, but definitely uneasy. Maybe she was worried that Edward—if he was there—might not be happy that she was talking to me. Unless there was someone else there, someone who didn't like Lorna speaking to me." I pause. "I'm sorry, I need to go."

"Is everything all right?"

But I've already hung up, my heart plummeting at what I've just realized. Tamsin had turned up on my doorstep two minutes after I'd left Lorna's that day and had warned me against asking her questions. I thought she'd seen me come out of the house and had guessed my motive for going there. But what if she'd been there all the time? She might have gone to see Lorna to warn her against speaking to me and I had chosen that very moment to call round. Had she been listening to our conversation from somewhere close by, is that why Lorna had been so nervous? It would explain how Tamsin knew what I'd been talking to Lorna about.

I sigh, uncomfortable with the position I've put myself in. Having a foot in each camp—wanting to help Helen get to the truth behind her sister-in-law's murder, and wanting to make friends here—is becoming increasingly difficult.

Eve rings at the door.

"Come in," I say, happy to see her. Then, over her shoulder, I see Tamsin walking quickly across the square, toward her house, and my bubble of happiness bursts. Maybe Eve's visit isn't as innocent as I thought.

"How are you?" she asks, following me to the kitchen.

"I'm fine. What about you?"

She pulls out a chair and sits down. "All good. I was going to come and see you on Tuesday, toward the end of the morning, but I saw you leaving the house."

"Yes, I went out to lunch."

She nods. "With a friend?"

I laugh. "Of course with a friend. Who else would I go to lunch with?"

She shifts in her chair. "I don't know—the reporter maybe?"

I pull out the chair opposite her, playing for time. Did she see Thomas when he came by yesterday?

"The reporter?" I ask.

"Yes, the woman who told you about Nina's murder."

"Oh." There's a hair on the table and I surreptitiously sweep it onto the floor, my brain screaming *ignore! ignore!* because the more I stress about it, the more hair I'll lose, a wretched vicious circle. "No, I went to lunch with my friend Ginny."

"Has she been back in contact with you? The reporter?" She catches my frown. "Sorry," she says, embarrassed. "Asking for a friend."

"If Tamsin isn't careful, I might think she has something to hide," I say mildly.

"It's normal that she's worried, Alice. We've only just begun to put the murder behind us and we don't want it being dragged up again." When I don't say anything, she sighs. "Look, after Nina was murdered and before Oliver was arrested," she says, choosing her words carefully, "when we'd only just found out that Nina had been having an affair, I think all her friends had a moment when they wondered if their husband could have been that person. It might only have been a moment, but it was there. And then, after we'd looked at our own husbands, we began looking at our friends' husbands and wondering if it could have been one of them. It was horrible, Alice. We were all at it, secretly trying to work out if someone from the Circle had been having an affair with Nina."

"Why would you think that?" I say, disingenuously.

She gives a little shrug. "Nina was very popular. She loved helping people and was very generous with her time. God knows how many hours she spent with Will, helping him rehearse his lines. She'd done some acting in the past, amateur dramatics, that kind of thing, and she was so happy when she discovered that Will was an actor. I'm not a jealous person and I never minded him going to see her, I was just glad that she could help him because, to be honest, I found listening to him repeating his lines a bit tedious. But, I admit, when I heard she'd been having an affair, there was that tiny moment of 'Oh God.' And although we've never discussed it, I think Maria and Tamsin probably had the same thought about their husbands."

"Why?"

"Because when Tim decided that he wanted to specialize further, Nina helped him look at various options, and it's down to her that he chose psychotherapy. And Connor was always bringing his whiskies for Nina to try because she was about the only person in The Circle who really knew about whiskey. Her parents owned a distillery before they retired and she used to joke that she was practically brought up on the stuff. She and Connor bonded over their Scottish roots, I guess." She leans forward and looks at me earnestly. "But what you have to understand is that nobody minded, not Oliver, nor any of us wives. We all loved Nina and we were glad that she had the time, with Oliver being away a lot, to help our men with their various projects. And it wasn't just men; she ran a yoga class for expectant mothers one evening a week at her house, which she started when Tamsin was pregnant with Pearl. She also ran a book club once a month. People were always in and out of her house. Sometimes Will would be there and Connor would show up with one of his whiskies so she'd call me over and the four of us would sit and chat for a couple of hours."

"You never suspected that she might have been having an affair?" I say, glad she has openly told me what Leo already had.

"Never. That's why it was such a shock."

"I can't imagine what it must have been like, everyone suspecting everyone else."

"It was terrible, especially as our first thought was that the man, whoever he was, was also her murderer. It sounds awful, but it was a relief when Oliver was charged. A terrible shock—but also a relief. We knew who had killed her, we could get on with our lives. We had nothing more to fear. If Nina had been having an affair, it didn't matter who the man was as he was no longer a suspect in her murder. It wasn't important to know his name, especially as Nina was dead. What was important was knowing that the person responsible for her murder wasn't going to come back and kill anyone else."

"You still believe that Oliver was responsible, then?"

"Yes."

"Because it's convenient to believe it." I make it a statement but I say it gently. "What if Nina's murderer is still out there somewhere?"

Eve looks uncomfortable. "I don't think he is." She takes out her phone and checks the screen. "Sorry, Alice, I've got to run," she says, standing up. "Hair appointment. See you tomorrow for coffee at Tamsin's."

Her relief at being able to get away is tangible. "Yes, see you there."

I shut the door behind her, mulling over what she told me, more convinced than ever that Nina's murder isn't as straightforward as Eve would like me to believe. Somebody is hiding something.

But who?

TWENTY-FIVE

I'm expecting Eve and I to walk to Tamsin's house together the next morning. But when I glance out of the window I see her hurrying down her drive, as if she needs to be somewhere fast. I check my watch; it's just ten o'clock and we've been invited for ten-thirty so she must be going for a run first. Except that she isn't wearing her running gear.

I hurry upstairs to Leo's study and watch Eve as she crosses the square. When she's nearly at the end, instead of carrying on toward the main gate, she veers to the left, heading straight for Tamsin's house. Realizing that I've got the time wrong—Tamsin must have said ten, not ten-thirty—I run downstairs, find my trainers and leave the house quickly, surprised that Eve hadn't come to get me. But maybe she thought I was already there.

By running, I arrive just a couple of minutes after her. Like some of the other residents, Tamsin and Connor have enclosed their porch and as I open the outer door, I can hear her and Eve talking in the hall, on the other side of the inner door. I'm just about to knock when I hear my name.

". . . Alice actually say that the reporter hadn't contacted her again?" Tamsin is saying.

"No, not exactly."

"Did you ask her where she went on Tuesday?"

"She said she went to lunch with a friend."

"Do you believe her?"

"Yes, why wouldn't I?"

"But she didn't say that the reporter *hadn't* been back in contact with her?"

"No. She kind of evaded the question."

"I'm worried, Eve. What if she's trying to find something out?"

"Like what?"

"Like who really killed Nina."

I freeze.

"Oh Tam, you're not going to start all that again, are you?" Eve sounds as if she's stifling a sigh.

"Oliver didn't kill Nina, Eve."

My heart thuds.

"You make it sound as if you have proof." Now there's an edge to Eve's voice. "Do you, Tam, do you have proof that Oliver didn't kill her? Because if you don't, maybe you should just accept that he did."

"He used to go and sit in the square."

"Who?"

"Oliver." Tamsin sounds near to tears. "Nina mentioned it to me once, she said that sometimes, after a long day at work, he would park the car in the drive and go and sit in the square for a while, to clear his head. Sometimes, if she saw him go in, she would join him."

"But—did you tell the police?" Eve sounds scared and I take a step back, uneasy about what I might hear. I want to leave, I should leave, and come back later, once they've finished their private conversation. But I'm worried they'll hear me walking back down the drive and I can't really hear anything now that I've moved back, not clearly anyway. And then—I draw in my breath so sharply I think they must have heard me. My heart thuds again. Did Tamsin really say something about Connor having an affair with Nina? She can't have—but she must have, because now Eve is telling her that she needs to speak to him. And then she's saying something about Will, and I catch the words "see Nina" and "gap in the fence" and my mind reels even more.

"I think everyone is capable of murder, if they feel threatened," Tamsin says, her voice so shrill that I catch her words in their entirety.

I don't hear Eve's reply but then I hear my name. Thinking I'm about to be discovered eavesdropping, my heart almost stops. But instead of the inner door being flung open, their footsteps disappear down the hall and I'm weak with relief until I realize that I still need to face them. I don't know how I'm going to do it, how I'm going to sit down and have coffee with them, not just because of what I overheard but because of the shame I feel at having listened in the first place. But I have to go through with it.

I wait a moment, then wipe my sweaty palms on my jeans, take a deep breath and knock.

Tamsin opens the door.

"Sorry, I'm late," I say, panting slightly to make it sound as if I've been running.

She gives me a look, as if she knows I've been standing in the porch for the last five minutes.

"You're not late. I said ten-thirty."

"Oh, sorry." My cheeks flush. "It's just that I saw Eve leaving her house, and I thought I must have got the time wrong. Shall I come back later?"

She opens the door wider. "Don't be silly. Come in."

"Thanks."

I ease off my trainers slowly, playing for time, even more flustered now. I follow her down the hall to the kitchen. It's beautifully minimalist, all neat lines and no clutter anywhere. Compared to my kitchen, with its stacks of cookbooks lying on the worktop and a fridge-door full of photographs, it's pristine. And calming. I feel suddenly confident. I can do this.

"Hi, Alice." Eve gives me a wave. "Welcome to Tamsin's super-tidy house."

"It's lovely," I say, looking around. "And admirable, considering you have two young children."

"I need the house to be tidy. It's the only thing I feel I can really control, the only thing where I'm in charge." Tamsin gives a little laugh. "The only part of my life that is mine."

There it is again, that streak of vulnerability. She comes over with a pot of coffee and I give her a smile.

"I think we all feel like that sometimes, that we've lost control. I know I did when I found out about the murder."

She stiffens, and I wish I could take the words back. I shouldn't be bringing up the murder now, not after what I just heard.

"In what way?" Eve asks, coming to the rescue.

"Everything that I thought was true, wasn't. The house wasn't what I thought it was, Leo wasn't who I thought he was. I could see the future that I'd built up in my head crumbling before my eyes. Things were happening that I had no control over. I know that sounds dramatic but it was horribly destabilizing."

"And now?" Tamsin asks. "Do you feel back in control?"

"I'm getting there. I've managed to stay in the house on my own, although I can't bring myself to sleep upstairs yet. And yesterday, I told Leo I needed space, so he's staying in Birmingham this weekend."

Tamsin raises an eyebrow. "And he accepted it?"

"Yes. For now."

She pushes a plate of homemade flapjacks toward me. "And wouldn't you rather do that—leave?"

"It's not an option anymore," I say, taking one.

"Why's that?"

"Tam," Eve warns gently.

Tamsin shrugs. "Sorry. It's not that I don't want you to stay. I'm curious, that's all. If you're sleeping downstairs, you're still not at ease in the house."

"You're right, I'm not totally comfortable yet. But I'm working on it."

Eve exchanges a quick look with Tamsin. "If that reporter

contacts you again, she'll be surprised to know that you're still living there," she says.

It's clumsy, but Eve is only trying to find out what Tamsin wants to know. I decide to boot the elephant right out of the room.

"Don't worry, if I ever hear from her again, the only thing I'll tell her is to leave me alone," I say.

"So you haven't heard from her since the day she told you about the murder?" Tamsin asks.

"No."

Tension seeps out of her, relaxing her body, reminding me of a balloon deflating. She reaches for a flapjack, breaks a piece off, pops it into her mouth, then breaks another piece off, and puts that in her mouth, as if she's famished. Tamsin starves her emotions, whereas I feed mine, something I hadn't realized until now. When I think about it, there have been quite a few times when I've stood in front of the open fridge, feeding my anxiety, trying to appease it, make it go away.

There's a beautiful family photograph perched on top of a sleek gray dresser, of Tamsin, Connor and their two little daughters.

"Amber is the image of you," I say, studying it.

"And Pearl is the image of Connor," Eve says.

"Yes, I can see that, she has his eyes." I turn to Tamsin. "Your hair was much longer back then."

She reaches for another flapjack. "It used to be as long as yours but I cut it after Nina died."

"Gosh," I say.

"I'm not really sure why I did it, all I know is that it was stronger than me. Nina had had her hair cut off so maybe I instinctively thought that whoever killed her had a fetish about long hair and I was protecting myself, in case he came back and killed me. Or maybe it was just a subconscious desire to honor Nina in some way. Amber cried and cried when she saw it and I had to promise I'd grow it long again." She gives a resigned smile. "I've still got quite a way to go."

"I used to have really long hair," Eve says. "Ages ago, when I was about seventeen. I cut it because I wanted to look older. I'm too small to have long hair, it made me look like a doll. It was darker in those days too."

"Did you have it dyed white at the same time?"

"Yes. I didn't intend to but the hairdresser suggested it. Will went mad. He hated my short hair at first. Now he loves it, right down to the pink tips."

"I'm thinking of cutting mine," I say.

Tamsin frowns. "Why? It's so lovely and long."

"It's falling out. After my parents and sister died, I lost it in clumps. It was horrible, I found it really distressing. And now it's happening again."

"Is that why you've been wearing your hair up?"

"Yes."

"Is it when you wash your hair that you lose it?" Eve asks. "Because I can recommend a really good shampoo."

"No, not really. I mean, I don't notice it coming away in the shower, or even when I comb it through after—at least no more than usual. But I keep finding it all over the house, especially in the kitchen, which is just about the worst place, because it can get in the food. It won't be so noticeable if my hair is shorter. Anyway, short hair must be so much easier to maintain."

"Don't you believe it. This—" Eve points to her hair, "takes a ton of gel and a lot of patience to achieve."

I turn to Tamsin. "Eve said you used to be a model. Is that when you met Connor?"

"Yes. We met at a party during London Fashion Week. I wasn't at all interested in him, he was too brash for me, so when he asked what I was looking for in a man, I told him I wanted someone who would take me to the theater, listen to classical music with me and spend hours reading books by my side. I felt safe saying that; it was a polite brush-off because I didn't think he'd be interested in any of those things. But he told me I was in luck and a couple of days later, he sent me a ticket for *The Tempest*. I really wanted to see *The Tempest*, so I went along. Then came the concerts and the weekends away, where we would spend rainy afternoons curled up with a book. He suited me so perfectly that there was nothing to stop me falling in love with him." She takes a sip of coffee. "I should have told him that I wasn't looking for a man, then he'd have left me alone."

"But it's lovely that you both enjoy the same things," I say, surprised at the vehemence of her last remark.

She shakes her head. "We don't. As soon as we were married, the trips to the theater, the classical concerts, the books—all that came to an end. If there's something I want to see, he tells me to go with a friend." She gives a little laugh. "It's hard to realize that the man you married never really existed at all."

"I know what you mean," I say quietly, thinking of Leo. "Not that Leo and I are married."

"Didn't you want to get married?" Eve asks.

"It never really came up. Leo doesn't believe in marriage anyway. He says he's never known a happy one."

"Me and Will are happy," she protests.

"Oh, shut up," Tamsin and I say simultaneously, and the three of us burst out laughing.

Eve and I walk back across the square together, then go our separate ways. In the study, I sit at my desk. I'm meant to start working but I can't stop thinking about what Tamsin said, that Nina once told her that Oliver would sometimes go and sit in the square when he came home from work. I wish I knew if she had told the police, I wish I'd been able to hear her answer to Eve's question. But she must have told them, it would have been criminal not to. And then I remember what she said about Connor having an affair with Nina. Did Tamsin keep back information that might have helped Oliver's case, to protect Connor? Except I can't be sure she did say that he'd had an affair with Nina.

Then there was Eve's comment about the gap in the fence between our houses. Was she insinuating that Will would have been able to come and go between theirs and Nina's without being detected? And why had Tamsin said that everyone is capable of murder if they feel threatened? Did someone know that Connor, or Will, was having an affair with Nina and threatened to tell? Did Tamsin, or Eve feel threatened because they thought their husband might leave them for Nina? Connor, Will, Tamsin, Eve—they could all have had a motive for killing Nina.

Suddenly ashamed at how easily I'm able to consider that one of our neighbors, all of whom have been perfectly lovely to me, is capable of murder, I lay my head on my desk with a groan. I don't even know Connor or Tim very well, my fault for not going to Maria's last Friday. I think for a moment, then lift my head from the desk and reach for my cell phone.

"I don't suppose you and Will are free for supper tomorrow evening?" I ask Eve.

"We are," she says, sounding pleased. "Is Leo coming back, then?"

"No, it'll just be me. That is all right, isn't it?"

"Of course!"

"I'm going to invite Tamsin and Connor, and Tim and Maria too. And maybe Paul and Cara," I add, remembering that it was Paul who told Leo about Nina helping her neighbors. "What do you think?"

"I think it's a great idea. Are you sure it won't be too much?"

"No, it'll be fine. I'll make something easy, like a curry."

"And Will and I will bring tiramisu, another of his grandmother's recipes!"

"Great, thank you."

Maria and Tim are free, Cara and Paul aren't, and Tamsin needs to see with Connor. She calls me back to confirm that Connor hadn't planned anything for the two of them.

"I preferred to check, in case he'd bought tickets for the theater as a surprise for me," she jokes.

"Perfect," I say, laughing. "I'll see you at seven, then."

TWENTY-SIX

In the middle of the night, I sense someone there. *It's only Nina*, I remind myself, before fear can take hold.

"I think your murderer's is still out there," I tell her. *"And I'm going to find him."* But in my mind, it isn't Nina Maxwell's face I see, it's my sister's.

I remember this when I wake up and a terrible uncertainty consumes me. Who am I doing this for? Is it because my sister never got what I considered justice for her death that I'm determined it won't be the same for Nina Maxwell? I'm not even sure what it is that I'm doing. How can I justify secretly helping to look into a miscarriage of justice when there might not even have been a miscarriage of justice?

Then a letter arrives, pushed through the door by the postman. It's so unusual to get a handwritten letter that I spend some time studying the envelope, trying to guess who it's from. I don't recognize the writing; it's slightly shaky, so maybe it's from someone elderly. Lorna comes to mind but when I open it, and unfold the single sheet of paper inside, I understand straightway.

Dear Alice,
I wanted to write and thank you personally for accepting to listen to what he had to say regarding Oliver and Nina. I

know you may not be able to help, or even wish to help. But I want you to know how grateful I am for your willingness to consider that Oliver might not be guilty, when those who knew him well were so quick to condemn him.

Please forgive me for not writing more, and for my appalling handwriting, I know that Thomas has explained my situation and that you will understand.

I sincerely hope we will get to meet each other one day.

With warmest wishes,
Helen

For a moment I wonder how Helen got my address, then remember that her brother had lived here. I feel horribly emotional as I slide the letter back in its envelope, the doubts I had about helping Thomas fading as quickly as they came. It's not as if I'm going to tell him my theories about Connor or Will, or anyone else. I'll only tell him what people have said, and leave him to draw his own conclusions. If Oliver didn't kill Nina, and someone else is murdered, I'd never forgive myself for being too afraid of upsetting people to do the right thing.

I already have most of what I need for supper this evening, because I went shopping in Stoke Newington last night. But I forgot the coriander, so I shrug on a jacket and head to the local shops.

I cross the square quickly, waving to Tim and his boys as I pass the play area. A chill wind I hadn't reckoned with drags tendrils of hair from my clip, and I button my jacket to the neck, wishing I'd worn something warmer. I'm soon at the greengrocer's, where I add a huge bunch of deep purple grapes, and some pears, apples and oranges to the coriander I need. And as I have grapes, I buy a couple of creamy cheeses at the delicatessen next door. There's a flower stall a little further along and on impulse, I buy a bunch of pale pink roses for Lorna. I'll take them round later; maybe I'll be able to catch her on her own.

Feeling the need for a coffee, I cross over to a café I've been to before. As I get nearer, I see Tamsin sitting in the window, a steaming mug in front of her. I start to move away but, suddenly aware of my eyes on her, she lifts her head. I smile awkwardly and raise my hand in a wave, as if I'm just passing by. But, jumping up, she pushes through tables and comes to the door.

"Do you have time for a coffee?" she calls over the noise of the traffic.

"Why not?" I say, glad that she's asked.

I love this café, with its vibrant hum of conversation interspersed by the hiss of the coffee machine, the clatter of crockery, the *ting!* of cutlery on plates. It's warm and crowded, but not so crowded that we can hear what the people at the next table are saying. The air is heavy with the scent of coffee and freshly baked cakes.

"You've been busy," Tamsin remarks as she takes my bags from me and pushes them under the scrubbed wooden table. "Is it for tonight?"

"Some of it is."

She nods approvingly at the roses. "I like a girl who buys herself flowers. If I didn't buy myself some, I'd never get any."

"They're not for me, they're for Lorna. She looked a bit down the last time I saw her."

"That's nice of you."

She lifts her bag onto her lap, pushes her cell phone, red leather gloves and white bobble hat into it, making room on the table, then takes out her purse.

"What can I get you?"

"Oh—thank you. Your hot chocolate looks delicious so I'll have the same, please."

She's back a few minutes later with a mug in one hand, and two plates precariously gripped in the other, each bearing a slice of cake. One is definitely chocolate but the other I'm not sure about. Coffee, maybe?

"And walnut," Tamsin says when I ask. "You choose."

"Gosh, thank you, I wasn't expecting cake. They both look amazing—why don't we do half-and-half?"

"Perfect!" There's something almost childish about her delight as she cuts each cake down the middle.

"Are we celebrating?" I ask. "It's not your birthday, is it?"

"No, but it feels like it."

"Has something happened?"

She takes her time answering. "Connor and I had a long talk last night about something that's been bothering me for a while, and well, it wasn't what I thought it was. So now I'm feeling kind of good about everything."

"That's great," I say casually. But I'm on high alert after what I overheard yesterday. "It's always good to get things out in the open, otherwise misunderstandings can build up."

She nods slowly. "I'm glad I've seen you because I feel guilty about bad-mouthing him yesterday, when you came over for coffee, especially as you'll be seeing him tonight. He's not all bad—he's a brilliant father—but we're very different people, something I didn't realize at first."

"I guess we all try to fit the ideal of the person we want to impress," I say, thinking back to what she said about Connor pretending, when they first met, to enjoy the same things as her.

"That's exactly what he said. He said he fell madly in love with me and tried to be the perfect man for me. He couldn't keep it up, that's all." She picks up her fork and breaks off a piece of the chocolate cake. "It's not just that, though," she says, pausing with her fork halfway to her mouth. "I've always suspected that he had an affair with Nina but I never dared ask him because I was afraid of what he would say, of what I might find out. Now, I wish I'd asked him ages ago and saved myself a lot of anguish." She lifts her fork the rest of the way. "This is delicious. Try it."

"So he didn't have an affair with Nina?" I ask, attacking my cake.

"No. But he wanted to."

"Oh." I put my fork down. "How do you feel about that?"

"Surprisingly fine, because it's cleared up something that's been eating away at me for a long time." She turns her plate and makes a start on the coffee cake. "A few months before she died, Nina began distancing herself from me," she says, telling me what I already know from Eve. "I thought I'd annoyed her by asking her to refer me to her therapist. She had been helping me sift through my emotions—as a friend, not a therapist—and I felt that I needed the professional help she couldn't give me. I was worried she'd taken offense, especially when she never came back with a name."

"I had therapy after my sister and parents died and I don't know if I'd have made it through without it. But—Nina saw a therapist?"

"Yes, a lot of therapists do. Some because they feel they need it, some because they believe the experience of being in therapy makes them a better therapist. I think for Nina it was a mixture of both." She stabs at her cake. "Anyway, the reason she no longer wanted to see me was nothing to do with her being annoyed with me, but because of Connor. He used to take his whiskies over for her to taste and I was fine about it, I hate whiskey so I was glad he had someone who shared his passion. But one night, he tried to kiss her. She pushed him away but the trouble with Connor is that he can't take no for an answer. When he insisted, she threatened to tell me. He begged her not to and, in the end, she agreed not to say anything. But she did a complete character assassination on him, said she despised him for even thinking he could cheat on me."

"And he took it? The character assassination?"

She looks at me appraisingly. "I know what you're thinking. You're wondering if maybe he was angry with her for what she said, and killed her."

"No, I wasn't thinking that at all," I say, my cheeks hot, and not just because I'm worried about someone overhearing our conversation, despite the distance between the tables. It's the way she said it so matter-of-factly that shocked me. Also, I can't ignore the possibility—because Lorna's words are never far from my mind—that this is another conversation that has been staged. "I was thinking that you're amazing for not minding that he kissed Nina."

She pushes her empty plate to one side and sits back in her chair. "I do mind, of course I do. But the relief of knowing that Nina only dropped me because she felt awkward around me somehow means more than knowing that Connor kissed her." She fixes me with her green eyes. "Can you understand that, Alice?"

I nod slowly. I can, because Leo lying to me, and about me, has affected me just as much, if not more, than the thought of Nina being murdered in our bedroom.

"And Connor told you all this?" I try not to sound skeptical.

"Yes."

"Well, it's great that you've worked it out between you," I say.

She nods happily. "We've agreed to start over, put it all behind us." She looks at my slice of coffee cake. "Aren't you going to eat that?"

I laugh and push my plate toward her. "Go ahead," I tell her. "I need to get going, anyway."

TWENTY-SEVEN

Leo calls me when I'm on my way home but by the time I've shifted my bags into one hand, tucked the flowers under my arm, and taken my cell phone from my pocket, his call has gone through to voicemail. I listen to his message and feel relieved when he says that Ginny and Mark have invited him for the weekend, because I've been feeling guilty about him being alone. My phone rings again and I smile when I see that it's Ginny.

I put my bags between my feet while I talk to her. "Yes, I know, Leo is spending the weekend with you," I say, because I know she'll feel that she has to tell me.

"That is all right, isn't it?" she asks anxiously. "Mark said we should invite him."

"Yes, of course, it's lovely of you."

"I don't want you to think we're taking sides."

"I don't. You said I could stay with you, remember?"

"What about you, are you doing anything nice?"

"I'm having Eve, Tamsin, Maria and their partners over for dinner. I'm doing a curry, nothing major."

"Sounds lovely."

"I have to go, I'm on the way back from the shops and it's freezing. Let's catch up after the weekend."

"Definitely! I'll call you on Monday."

I start walking again, my mind going over my conversation with Tamsin. I can understand her relief now that she knows Connor didn't have an affair with Nina, because it must have been terrible to have that hanging over her. But if she didn't tell the police about Oliver's habit of going to sit in the square to protect Connor, shouldn't she be wracked with guilt? She didn't seem to be, so maybe she did tell the police and they dismissed it. Or it's as I thought, and both conversations—the one I overheard yesterday and the one I had just now with Tamsin—have been fabricated for my benefit.

As I cut across the square to the house, I happen to look up, and see the blur of a face at the study window. My heart plummets. Leo must have come to get something before going to Ginny and Mark's. I wish he'd mentioned in his voicemail that he was coming to the house. If he had, I'd have gone for another coffee so that I wouldn't have to see him. I don't want him putting pressure on me to let him come home.

I put my shopping down in the hall, expecting him to appear at the top of the stairs.

"Leo!" I call. There's no answer so I go upstairs and push open the door to his study. It's empty. I check the guest room, because it's at the front of the house and maybe I got the wrong window, calling for him as I go. I stop in the doorway of our bedroom. It seems empty but there's something in the air—the scent of his aftershave maybe—that tells me he was here. The bathroom door is ajar. I head toward it nervously.

"Leo, are you there? You'd better not be hiding behind the door to scare me!" I try to make my voice jokey but inside I'm shaking at the thought he might jump out at me.

I give the door a shove and it smashes back against the wall with a bang. The noise ricochets through the house, a gun being fired over and over again. Stupidly, I've managed to scare myself even more.

I hurry back through to the bedroom, coming to a momentary stop when I see that the framed photograph I keep on the chest of drawers, of me and Leo in Harlestone, has been laid face down. *Pathetic!* I think, as I go downstairs, the drumming of my feet igniting my anger at the stupid game he's playing. He must have gone down to the kitchen as soon as he saw me walking across the square.

Gone completely, it seems, because there's no sign of him any-where. I can't believe he actually left by the French windows and sneaked around the side of the house as I was going through the front door to avoid seeing me. *But didn't you want to avoid him?* a voice asks. *If you had known he was coming, you would have waited in a café until he'd left.*

The voice calms my anger. It's sobering to think that Leo doesn't want to see me any more than I want to see him.

By 7:20 everyone has arrived. Tamsin and Connor are the last; they had trouble getting the girls to bed before the babysitter arrived, Tamsin explains, giving me a kiss.

"Until I tanned their wee hides," Connor growls.

I look nervously at him, wary of the scowl on his face.

Tamsin smiles. "Don't worry, he's joking."

Connor leaves to go and talk to Will and Tim and I find myself thinking about Lorna. When I took the flowers around earlier, it was Edward who came to the door. I hoped he would invite me in, but he kept me on the doorstep, telling me that she was having a nap. Which means I'm still no nearer to knowing what she whispered, or if she whispered.

I mentioned in my text message to Tamsin and Maria that Leo wouldn't be here tonight, so there are no awkward questions. Eve and Maria are in deep conversation and I leave Tamsin to join them while I get her and Connor drinks. I don't usually make snap judg-ments but there's something about Connor that makes me wary. I'm surprised that he and Tamsin are a couple. She's beautiful, fragile, while there's something almost brutish about him. He's a big man, muscle, not fat. It's easy to imagine him overpowering someone.

"You seem miles away." Connor's eyes find mine and I realize he saw me watching him. I search for something to say.

"I was just wondering why you didn't ask for a whiskey, given that your job revolves around it."

"That's why I don't drink it socially. I love whiskey, but I drink too much of it for work purposes. Does Leo like whiskey?"

"Not really. He's more a G&T man."

I give him the beer he asked for and take a glass of wine to Tamsin.

"Lovely," she says, taking it gratefully.

"I'll just go and say hello to Connor, otherwise he'll think I'm ignoring him," Maria says.

Tamsin waits until she leaves. "I was telling Eve earlier about bumping into you this morning, and our subsequent chat," she says.

Her choice of words jars slightly. It's as if she wants me to know that she's told Eve I know about Connor and Nina.

"I hope you also told her about the two slices of cake we demolished."

She grins. "That too."

I look around for my glass, which I'd put down to go and answer the door. It's on the table and I go to fetch it because the more time I spend with Eve and Tamsin, the more confused I feel. There always seems to be an undercurrent of something I can't quite explain.

Still, it's a fun evening. Connor and Will are the perfect foil for each other. Will tells jokes and stories with a nervous energy and Connor's interventions are witty and ironic. He's also surprisingly laid-back. Tim is quieter, and perfectly lovely, jumping up to help me fetch and clear plates, totally at home in my kitchen, which must be the same as theirs, because he doesn't have to ask where anything is. *It's not possible that any of them murdered Nina*, I think, and again feel ashamed that I could have thought that one of them might have. Connor catches my eye and looks steadily back at me, as if he's read my mind and knows that my motive for inviting them tonight wasn't just to be neighborly. For some reason—maybe for that reason—I feel slightly afraid of him.

"Tamsin said that you found out about Nina from a journalist," he says, and the conversations that had been going on around us comes to a sudden halt.

"That's right. I'd rather have heard it from Leo, then it wouldn't have been such a shock when the reporter asked me what it was like living in a house where a murder had taken place," I say.

"Why didn't Leo tell you?" Connor's eyes are the same tawny color, I notice, as his hair. If he were an animal, he would be a lion.

"Because he knew that if he did, I wouldn't want to live here and he really wanted this house. So, in a way, he did the right thing, because once I knew, it was too late to leave."

"Why?" He's curious, not aggressive.

"Because I already felt invested in my life here. And I don't like to give up easily."

"That's good to know," he says, raising his glass toward me.

"Well, we're glad you're still here, aren't we, Will?" Eve says.

"Definitely. I can't think of anyone better to replace Nina and Oliver than you and Leo."

There it is again, the slightly awkward phrasing, this time from Will. Or is it just me being overly sensitive?

"By the way, did you ever discover who the man was, the one who gate-crashed your party, pretending to be me?" Tim asks.

"He wasn't really pretending to be you, I don't think. He just used the fact that I thought he was you to get into the house. But no, I haven't managed to find out who he was. I'd completely forgotten about him, to be honest."

"It's strange nobody saw him," Tamsin muses.

"I don't think he stayed around long enough."

"Then what was the point of him coming along?"

I take a sip of wine to steady my nerves. "Your guess is as good as mine," I tell her.

She exchanges a smile with Eve that I don't much like. Thankfully, Connor launches into a joke and everyone relaxes into the evening again.

I don't know if it's the effect of there being so many people in the house, but later, when I close the door behind them, the silence seems heavier than usual. I stack the dishwasher, unnerved by the memory of Leo's clandestine visit. Why did he come? Was it to fetch something from the locked filing cabinet, something that he didn't want me to see? Is that why he left in such a hurry?

I delay going to bed, annoyed that Leo's secret visit has managed to destroy the relative peace of mind I'd managed to cultivate over the past few days. My dreams are a mix of him and Nina, and when I half-wake in the middle of the night, it's Leo I sense standing at the foot of my bed, not her. I go back to sleep but suddenly find myself sitting bolt upright in the bed, trying frantically to catch on to something that had occurred to me as I slept, something to do with what Ginny had said about Leo having had an affair with Nina. And then I realize—the woman who had come to Harlestone, supposedly wanting to know what it was like to live in the village, had had long blond hair.

TWENTY-EIGHT

I don't want to disturb Leo's weekend with Ginny and Mark but I'm desperate to speak to him about Nina Maxwell. My mind tells me that he couldn't have known her but my heart wonders if that was why he wanted this house so much. The thought that he didn't just know her, but had had an affair with her, won't go away and a chill goes down my spine when I remember what Thomas said, about a murderer returning to the scene of the crime. I chase the thought quickly; Leo might have concealed the murder from me but he's not a murderer.

I don't want to disturb him at work either so I wait until the end of the afternoon to send him a text.

I need to speak to you, when is a good time?

Now, he replies, and my phone starts ringing.

His eagerness is unsettling. I'm not ready, I wanted to get my thoughts in order first.

"How are you?" he asks.

"Fine. Did you have a good weekend?"

"Yes, it was good to be with Ginny and Mark. What about you, how are you getting on staying in the house by yourself?"

"I feel fine here now."

"Right."

There isn't anything particular in his voice but I don't like that a tiny part of him might be thinking that I got over my squeamishness a bit too quickly.

"Sometimes, something bad happens and then something worse comes along—like someone you trust lying to you—and the first thing doesn't seem so bad after all," I say.

He sighs. "What did you want to speak to me about?"

"Nina."

"Your sister?"

Is he doing it on purpose? "No, Nina Maxwell. Did you know her?"

"No." He sounds puzzled.

"OK, so did you ever meet her?"

"Isn't that the same thing?"

"The woman you were talking to in Harlestone one day, the blond woman who supposedly asked you what it was like to live in the village. Was it Nina?"

"What? No. Why would you think it was Nina Maxwell?"

"Did you have an affair with her?"

"Who?"

"Nina."

"Are you serious?" Now he's angry. "For God's sake, Alice, where has this come from? You really think that I had an affair with Nina Maxwell? I didn't even know her!"

"Then who was the woman who came to Harlestone? And don't tell me she was someone who wanted to know what it was like to live in the village."

"All right." There's a pause. "She was one of the clients I told you about, who were harassing me."

"Why was she harassing you?"

His voice becomes cold. "I'm not going to explain my business dealings over the phone. Anyway, I'm glad you called. I need to get something from my study—is it all right if I come over?"

"What, tonight?"

"Yes, now."

"Aren't you in Birmingham?"

"No, I had to be in London today."

"All right."

"I'll see you in half an hour."

He cuts the call and I stand with my cell phone in my hand, thinking over the conversation we just had. There was something off about his request to come over. He tried to make it sound as if it had been in his plans all along, but it came across as a spur-of-the-moment decision, brought on by my mention of Nina. Besides, if he needed to come over, he would have called me to ask, not waited until I called him. Worry gnaws away at me. What if he *had* known Nina?

It's only a week since I last saw Leo, but he looks like someone I used to know, not because he hasn't shaved for a couple of days but because of the awkwardness between us. He's taken off his jacket and left it in the hall, as if he's expecting to stay for a while. It makes me feel that I should offer him a drink but I don't really want to.

"Hi," he says.

"Hi."

He waits and when I don't say anything more, he shrugs. "I'll go and get what I need, then."

"OK."

He returns to the hall, and I hear him rustling in his jacket. Moving quietly to the door, I see him go upstairs, two steps at a time, his wallet in his hand. A moment later, there's the familiar screech of one of the drawers in the filing cabinet being pulled open. So, he keeps the key to the cabinet in his wallet.

In his wallet. Why not in the drawer of his desk, or on top of the filing cabinet, where it would be easily accessible? Are his client files really so important that he doesn't want anyone, including me, to be able to get to them? Or is he hiding something there, something that the little key, taped to the underside of his drawer, would open?

A few minutes later, he runs down the stairs, fumbles with his jacket, then comes into the kitchen, a couple of files under his arm.

"Did you forget to take them when you came over on Saturday?" I ask.

He puts them down on the table. "What do you mean?"

"The files. Why didn't you take them with you when you were here on Saturday?"

"I was with Ginny and Mark on Saturday."

"Yes, but you came here first, I saw you in the study. And then, as soon as you saw me crossing the square you left."

He shakes his head. "Not me."

"I saw you, Leo!"

"Alice, it wasn't me, I swear."

"Where were you when you called me?"

"At Ginny and Mark's, in my bedroom." He frowns. "Are you saying you saw someone in the house?"

I think back to the blur of a face I'd seen at the window. I don't want to believe that I scared myself into thinking there was someone in the house when it was only the late-September sunshine casting its glow on the upstairs window.

"I thought I saw someone in your study, but maybe I was mistaken."

"Did you check the house?"

"Yes, and everything was fine." I decide not to mention the faint smell of aftershave in the bedroom. He's only been gone a week, it's not surprising that there are still traces of him. And maybe I knocked the photo of us over when I was vacuuming, and hadn't noticed. "But if you could check the windows, I'd be grateful."

"Sure."

He starts to head off and I feel mean not offering him a drink.

"Would you like a glass of wine?"

He retraces his footsteps. "Thanks."

I take a couple of glasses from the cupboard, find a bottle of red wine, open it, pour it.

"Thanks." He takes a sip. "I hope you were joking when you asked me if I had an affair with Nina. I didn't know her, I promise."

"It's all right, I believe you."

He pulls out a chair and sits down. "The woman who came to Harlestone—she was a journalist. She wanted to interview me about my job for an article she was writing. I'd already refused twice by phone so she thought she'd accost me in person."

"Wouldn't it have been easier to accost you at your London flat rather than travel all the way to Harlestone? How did she know you'd be there, anyway? How did she get my address?"

He takes another sip of wine. "I have no idea."

"I'm not being funny, but your job has never struck me as particularly exciting, at least not exciting enough to devote column inches to."

"Certain aspects of it are. Risk management is a hot topic at the moment."

I nod, because maybe it is.

I ask him about his weekend with Ginny and Mark and he asks about mine with the neighbors. Stupidly, I tell him that because of the face I thought I saw at the window, I found it hard to sleep.

"You shouldn't be here on your own, Alice."

"I'm fine."

He toys with his glass. "I'd like to come back."

"I need more time."

"How much more?" He leans forward, finds my eyes. "I love you, Alice. I want to be with you, not stuck in a dingy flat in Birmingham."

"You don't have to be in a dingy flat."

"That's not the point."

"It is. It's as if you're trying to make yourself as miserable as possible."

"I am miserable!" When I don't say anything, he sighs. "Do you want me to check the upstairs windows as well?"

"Yes, please."

He drains the rest of his wine. "I'll do them first."

I follow him into the hall, my arm brushing against his jacket as I stand at the bottom of the stairs. I pause, then make a split decision.

"I'll wait here in case you need anything," I say. "A screwdriver or something."

"OK."

I wait until he's disappeared up the stairs and into the guest bedroom, then wait a few minutes more.

"Is everything all right?" I call, my hand already in his jacket.

"So far. I just need to check our bedroom."

There are three windows in the bedroom, plus the one in the en-suite, which should give me enough time. I take out his wallet, open it, leaf through it quickly. At first, I think the key isn't there but then I find it, tucked in one of the two smaller slots at the front, normally reserved for stamps. I slip it into my pocket.

"All OK?" I call, pushing his wallet back into place.

"All good." My heart misses a beat—his voice is close, too close. I look up and see him standing at the top of the stairs. Can he see my hand inside his jacket? He starts coming down and I take a quick step back.

"By the way," I say, looking for something to distract him from the guilt I'm sure is showing on my face. "Did you know there's a gap in the fence between ours and Will's? Oliver used to lend Will his lawnmower and they used the gap to get back and forth between the gardens. There's one on the other side too, apparently, because Oliver used to cut Edward's grass for him."

"No, I didn't know. But it's a good idea to have them there." He pauses. "Do you think I should be offering to cut Edward's grass?"

"Eve said that Geoff does it now."

While I worry that he might need to open the filing cabinet again before he leaves—because if he can't find the key, he'll guess that I've taken it—he checks the downstairs windows.

"What time is your train back to Birmingham?" I ask, needing him to leave.

"I have to be in London again tomorrow, so I'm staying with Ginny and Mark tonight."

"They must be waiting for you to have dinner."

He gives a quick smile.

"It's all right, I'm leaving."

"I'm sorry," I say, guiltily. "I wish I didn't still feel angry with you. But I do."

I wait until he's left, then take out my cell phone and call Ginny.

"You know when you called me on Saturday to say that Leo was staying the weekend with you? Where was he when you called me?"

"Um—upstairs in his bedroom, I think. He told me that he'd left you a message to tell you he was staying with us and I realized I hadn't told you that Mark had invited him, and I didn't want you to think we were taking sides. Is everything all right? It's not because he's still here, is it? But he had to be in London today, and again tomorrow."

"No, it's absolutely fine, it's lovely of you to have him," I say.

"Are you sure you're all right with it?"

"Yes. It's just that on Saturday, I was out and when I got back, I was sure he'd been here. But he said that he hadn't, that he was at yours."

"Yes, that's right. He arrived on Friday evening and didn't go out all weekend. Mark offered to take him golfing on Saturday with him and Ben but he had work to do and spent the day in his bedroom."

"Great. Thanks, Ginny. Let's have lunch again soon."

"Call me when you know what day."

"I will."

I cut the call, feeling bad for not believing Leo when he said he hadn't come to the house. I take the key from my pocket, the one I sneaked from his wallet, and drop it into a little earthen pot that stands on my desk. I'm not going to use it, I can't. I'm not that sort of person.

TWENTY-NINE

I'm running up the stairs. I need to open the filing cabinet but I can hear someone moving silently through the rooms downstairs. I reach the study, take the key from my pocket, my fingers fumbling as I insert it into the lock. It won't turn, there's something wrong. I take the key out, try again. I need to be quick, he's checking the rooms, looking for me. The key still won't work. I jiggle it and it turns. I pull open the drawers carefully, my breath coming in short gasps, aware of soft footsteps on the stairs. The first three are full of client files. I tug the bottom one open; it seems empty but I crouch down and reach into the shadows at the back of the drawer. It's there, the metal cash box is there.

The footsteps are coming along the landing now. I close my hand around the box, lift it out, place it on the floor. The door of the guest room creaks as he pushes it open and checks inside. I don't dare breathe as I insert the tiny key in the lock. I need to hurry, he's almost here. I unlock the box; the door behind me pushes open slowly and I crouch lower, hiding myself. I lift the lid and a scream of pure terror unfurls from deep inside me. But before I can give voice to it, a hand clamps down on my mouth, silencing my scream before it's even begun.

I start awake, my breath coming in ragged gasps, residual damage from the dream I just had. I reach out a trembling hand and switch on the lamp, remembering that as I tossed and turned in the throes of my nightmare, I was aware, on another level of my subconscious, of Nina watching me. I had wanted to call out, ask her to save me from what was to come. But I hadn't been able to.

I throw back the covers and get shakily out of bed. I'm no longer sure I can do this, stay in the house by myself. The temptation to call Leo, and ask him to come home is so strong that I take my cell phone through to the kitchen with me. I'm in desperate need of a drink, something soothing, so I pour milk into a mug and find the chocolate powder. The comforting hum of the microwave soothes me and I try and recall what the metal cash box of my nightmare had held. But it's as elusive as the face of the man who stifled my scream.

I manage not to call Leo, but it's five o'clock before I feel ready to go back to bed. Although I sleep late, I'm uneasy for the rest of the day, rattled by my nightmare. The discovery of more of my hair in the kitchen, and in the bathroom, depresses me further. I'm still losing it steadily.

There's a ring on the doorbell. I go to answer it and find Eve, on her way for her morning run.

"I wanted to thank you for Saturday evening," she says. "Will and I really enjoyed it."

"I enjoyed it too," I say, smiling as she hops from one foot to another on the doorstep, already in warm-up mode. "It was lovely to meet Connor and Tim properly. Do you want to come in?"

"No, thanks, I need my run." There's a pause. "I'm not being nosy or anything, but it's hard not to see things here. Is Leo back?"

"No, he came to pick up some files."

"How is he?"

I pull a face. "Managing to guilt-trip me by feeling hard done by."

"That's not fair. He should have been upfront with you about the house in the first place."

"I know. But if he had, I wouldn't be here. I wouldn't have met you, I wouldn't have met any of you. Don't you think it's amazing, the way fate works?"

She stops moving and looks at me curiously. "Do you think it's your destiny to be here?"

"Yes. I'm a great believer that fate takes you where you're meant to be."

"For a purpose, you mean?"

"Yes, although I'm not sure what that purpose is."

"You're not trying to find the truth behind Nina's murder, then?" Behind the question, her eyes are innocent.

"But if everyone believes that Oliver killed her, surely there's no truth to be found?" I say, puzzled.

"Except you don't really believe that Oliver is guilty." *Neither does Tamsin*, I want to say, but as I wasn't meant to have overheard their conversation, I can't. "That's what I don't understand, Alice. Why do you think he didn't do it? It's not as if you knew him."

"You're right, I only know what everyone here has told me about him and that's what I find hard to reconcile; the picture you've painted of him and the violence of the crime. But I'm not trying to solve any mysteries. First of all, it's not my place, and secondly, if everyone is happy that Oliver killed Nina, there isn't anything to solve anyway."

We're interrupted by Will coming out of the house.

"Still here?" he calls over, looking at Eve in amusement. "I thought you were desperate for a run."

"I am." She starts to move off. "Bye, Alice!"

She jogs to meet Will at the bottom of the drive. They exchange a few words and she plants a kiss on his mouth before disappearing into the square. Will gives me a wave and follows at a more leisurely pace. I watch them go, acknowledging once again that the more time I spend with the people who knew Oliver and Nina, the more I feel that something is off. Eve said she knew that Leo was at the house yesterday because it's hard not to see things in The Circle. Yet Nina had apparently had an affair for several months before she died and no one, not one person, had seen someone going into her house more frequently than they should have. Which means that Nina either met up with him outside The Circle, or they were able to sneak into her house undetected—which points the finger right at Will. He'd have been able to come and go as he pleased, using the gap in the fence without fear of detection. Although Eve works from home, she goes for a run for at least an hour every morning, and spends every Thursday with her mum. If Will had wanted to, he had plenty of opportunities to go and see Nina while Eve was out.

It doesn't take me long to accept that I am the sort of person who will snoop through her partner's affairs. The key to the filing cabinet is an itch I can't get rid of. I've tried to distract myself by keeping my head down and working, but by the time I break for lunch on Wednesday, I can't ignore it any longer.

I take the key from the earthen pot and go up to Leo's study. There's no point unsticking the smaller key from the underside of the drawer in his desk if there's nothing in the filing cabinet except client files. I unlock it; the first three drawers hold exactly that—a neat row of client files lying snugly in their hammocks. I bend to open the bottom drawer and when I see that it contains client files too—not as many as the first three, because they're pushed to the back, leaving room at the front for new files—I begin to feel a bit foolish.

And ashamed. I sit down on the floor, embarrassed that a part of me had actually wanted to find something. But I need something more, because if I'm to leave Leo, I'm worried that his lie of omission, plus his lie about me—both of which have changed the way I feel about him—won't be accepted as a good enough reason, not just by Leo but by others I care about, like Ginny, Mark and Debbie. In their eyes, maybe those lies aren't so great. I still care for Leo but the trust has gone. I told him, the day we spoke about my friend, that if I couldn't trust him, I couldn't be with him. He knew, yet he still took the risk.

The bottom drawer is still open and, disheartened, I give it a shove to close it. Something shoots out from under the files; I just have time to see it before the drawer slams shut, pulling it back underneath. My heart in my mouth, I crouch down, open the drawer and reach in under the hammocks. My fingers touch something solid. I pull it toward me, expecting a book, a desk diary maybe. What I get is a black metal cash box.

I stare at it. Apart from the color—I had imagined it red, like the one I had as a teenager—it's exactly the sort of box I'd imagined the key fitting. And then I remember the nightmare I had, how the box had been black, just like this one, and how what I saw inside had caused me to scream—a scream that had been silenced by a hand over my mouth. I scramble to my feet and look nervously toward the door. Voices reach me from the road outside, a parent speaking, a child laughing in response. They calm me; it's the middle of the day, there are people around, nothing bad is going to happen if I open the box now, in broad daylight.

I unstick the tiny key from the underside of the drawer in Leo's desk, telling myself that it might not fit the lock anyway. When I lift the box from the filing cabinet, I'm surprised at how light it is. I move it a little and something slumps against the side, a small book, a diary or journal maybe. My heart thumps, Nina heavily on my mind.

I place the box on the desk and insert the key. It fits. I turn it and lift open the lid.

At first, I think it *is* a diary. But it isn't, it's a passport, one of the old blue ones that are no longer valid. I feel a rush of adrenaline. Was this Nina's? I pick it up gingerly, my fingers already shaking, because why would Leo have Nina's passport? I turn to the page where the photograph is, and forget to breathe. Taken twenty years earlier, yet instantly recognizable, it's not a photo of Nina, but of Leo. And then I see the name, and once again, the world I thought I knew crumbles around me. The passport is in the name of Leo Carter, not Leo Curtis.

I grope behind me for the chair and sit down, vaguely aware of someone ringing on the doorbell. Why would Leo tell me his surname is Curtis when in fact it's Carter? I remember then, the way he looked as if he was about to pass out, the day I confronted him about the murder, when I asked him who he was. I had meant—who was he that he could lie to me? But he must have thought I'd discovered his true identity.

The doorbell rings again, sending panic surging through me, because Leo must have noticed that the key has gone from his wallet and has worked out that I've got it. I jump to my feet; what am I going to say to him about why I took it? And then I realize—if he has a passport in a different name, he must have something to hide, something far worse than sneaking a key from a wallet.

THIRTY

I go downstairs, taking the passport with me, a sick feeling in the pit of my stomach, dreading the confrontation I'm about to have with him. I open the door and take a sudden step back. It's not Leo, but Thomas.

"Oh." I should have realized that Leo wouldn't ring on the bell, he has keys. But why is Thomas here? Did we have an appointment?

"Alice, I'm sorry to disturb you but could I come in?"

He seems almost as flustered as I feel.

"Um. Yes, I suppose so." I open the door wider, realizing how ungracious I sound. But my mind is still spinning with the discovery of Leo's passport.

He comes into the hall and I close the door behind him.

"Can I ask—did you get a letter from Helen, Oliver's sister?"

It's hard to focus. "Yes. Yes, I did."

"I'm so sorry. I saw her last week and she said she wanted to write to you. I intended to check that you were open to receiving a letter from her. But when I saw her this morning, she told me that she'd already written and had asked her carer to post it." He looks at me anxiously. "I hope she didn't put pressure on you in any way."

"Not at all," I tell him. "It was a very sweet letter. It must have cost her a lot physically to write it."

He nods. "She's so weak she can barely hold a pen. She can't hold a book either and she loves reading. Thank God for audio books." He frowns slightly. "Is everything all right? You look shaken."

"That's a good question. I don't really know." Even to my ears my voice sounds strangled. "I've just discovered something very strange."

"Is there anything I can do to help?"

"No, thank you, it's fine." I reach around him, intending to open the door so that he can leave, and find myself pausing. He's a private investigator, maybe he can help me. "Actually, do you have a minute?"

"Yes, of course."

"I really need a coffee. Would you like one?"

"I'd love one."

He follows me to the kitchen.

"Have a seat. How do you take your coffee?"

"Black, please, no sugar."

He sits down. I'm still holding Leo's passport so I put it on the table and go to make the coffee. My movements feel heavy, and I have to concentrate on getting the capsule into the machine. I take the cup over to the table, then go back for mine.

He waits until I'm sitting down opposite him, then nods at the passport. "I haven't seen one of those for a long time."

I pick it up. "It's Leo's—my partner's. He told me he didn't have a passport and I just found this in a drawer."

"Perhaps he meant he didn't have an up-to-date passport. These haven't been in use for years."

"It's not that. It's in a different name."

He frowns. "Then—are you sure it's his?"

"It's his photo. It's the name that doesn't match." I pick up the passport and turn to the relevant page. "His surname is Curtis, here it says Carter."

"Could I see?" I hand it to him. He studies it for a moment then looks over at me. "You could always check it against his birth certificate."

"I wouldn't know where to find it."

"Hm. What about his bank cards? Are they in the name of Curtis?"

"Yes, I suppose so. I mean, I've never noticed."

"What about his mail?"

"Um, I don't know. I've never actually seen any mail for him." I look at him, worry creasing my brow. "Is that strange? We weren't living together before we moved here, he had a flat in London so his mail went there. And since we moved here—it was only a month ago but he should have received some mail here, shouldn't he?"

"I would have thought so."

I raise my cup to my lips, trying to push away the black cloud of terror looming behind my eyes. My hand is shaking so much that coffee spills everywhere.

"Sorry," I say, horribly aware of the tears pricking my eyes.

He reaches out and takes the cup from my hand, then goes over to the sink and comes back with a cloth.

"Can I make you another coffee?" he asks, mopping up the mess. "Or would you prefer some water?"

"Water, please."

He goes back to the sink and I hear the sound of running water, then cupboard doors being opened and closed as he looks for a glass. His movements are measured, giving me time to compose myself.

He brings the water over to me. "Thank you," I say, taking the glass gratefully. Our hands brush and I pull away, confused by the electricity shooting through me at the feel of his skin.

He sits down. "If I can do anything to help."

I take a shaky breath. "I think Leo might have known Nina."

He doesn't seem shocked, just looks at me intently, and it crosses my mind that maybe he's known all along that Leo knew Nina. Maybe that's why he came to our drinks evening, maybe he wanted to see up close the man he believes is responsible for her murder. Is that the reason he's been visiting me, hoping I'll let something slip? The sense of impending doom makes my heart race so fast I feel dizzy.

"Why do you think that?" he asks. His voice is calm and some of my terror subsides.

I tell him about the blond woman who turned up in Harlestone.

"And you think it was Nina?"

"I don't know. I mean, I didn't see her face or anything, I just noticed she was blond."

"Did you ask Leo about her?"

"Yes. At first he told me she was a client who was harassing him—"

"Is he a lawyer?"

"No, he's a consultant. In risk assessment."

He raises a dark eyebrow. "And he gets harassed by clients?"

"That's what he said. But later he told me she was a journalist who wanted to interview him."

"Do you remember when this was?"

"Not long after we met, so late January, early February last year." I pause, remembering that Nina had been killed at the end of February.

He nods. "Where does Leo work?" He's in full investigator mode now.

"In the Midlands. But he used to work in London."

"Do you know if he saw a therapist?"

"I don't think so. But I only saw him at weekends, he stayed at his flat during the week, so maybe he did."

He looks up then and the concern I see in his eyes makes me afraid. I can't help it; afraid for Leo, afraid for me, I feel close to tears again.

"Maybe she was just a journalist who happened to be blond," he says.

"I know. And I'm sure she was. It's just that Leo knew about Nina being murdered here before he bought the house but he didn't tell me."

This time, he can't hide his surprise. "That must have been—"

"Devastating," I finish for him.

"Did he say why he didn't tell you?"

"He said he knew I wouldn't agree to live here if I knew about the murder and he really wanted this house."

"Why this particular house?"

"For obvious reasons, it was cheaper than other properties we'd looked at so he made out that it was because I wouldn't have to sell my home in East Sussex to help buy it. But he also admitted that he wanted this house because it's in a gated residence. That's when he told me he was getting harassed by clients, something he'd never mentioned to me before." I raise my eyes to his. "I did ask him if he knew Nina. He said he didn't and I believed him. But that was before I found his passport."

"Would you like me to look up Leo Carter, see what I can find?" Maybe he sees the panic in my eyes; although I want to get to the truth, engaging a private investigator to look into the man I'd been hoping to spend the rest of my life with is a huge step. "I don't mean as a private investigator," he says quickly. "I mean as a friend. Here, now. I can google him, see if anything comes up."

"Yes," I say. "Could you?"

He takes out his phone. "There probably won't be anything," he says reassuringly.

"And if there's not?"

"Then you'll need to speak to Leo." He smiles to lessen the tension. "Maybe he just didn't like the surname Carter."

I watch, barely daring to breathe as he types into his phone. I keep my eyes fixed on his face, not on his screen, looking for a sign that he's found something. It remains immobile, professional. I'm aware of his fingers scrolling down, then stopping. He reaches for the passport, opens it to the photo page with one hand. His eyes flicker from screen to photo and back again, staying there for a while as he reads.

I'm afraid to ask. "Have you found something?"

He raises his eyes to mine.

"I think you might want to read this," he says quietly, passing his phone to me.

I look down at the screen, my heart thudding, and see a photo similar to the one in Leo's passport, along with a news story about Leo Carter being sent to prison in 2005 for two years. For fraud.

My heart slows to a dull beat, keeping rhythm with the thought throbbing in my head. *Leo went to jail?* It's so far away from what I thought that I have trouble focusing on the words in the article, something about him having been a compliance officer for an asset management company. Panic whirls in my stomach.

"I don't understand," I mutter.

He clears his throat. "Unfortunately, in my line of business, changing identity to conceal a criminal background is fairly commonplace." He pauses. "Leo didn't mention it to you?"

"No."

"You need to speak to him."

I nod. "I know."

"Then perhaps I should leave." He gets to his feet. "Please, don't get up, I can see myself out." He walks to the door, then stops. "If you need anything, anything at all, you have my number."

THIRTY-ONE

Silence shrouds me like a blanket. I sit without moving, trying to work through the emotions that assault me mercilessly, one after the other—disbelief, bewilderment, fear and anger. It's the cold that finally moves me to my study for a sweater. I can't find one so I put on my robe, tying it tightly around me.

I haven't called Leo, I couldn't bring myself to. Again, it's not a conversation I want to have with him over the phone and he's in Birmingham until tomorrow evening. I want to talk to someone. Normally, I would have called Ginny because she's nearer and could have come over. But she's too close to Leo, so I call Debbie.

"I'm so sorry, Ali," she says, stunned at what I've told her. "Coming on top of him not telling you about the murder, you must be devastated."

"I am," I say, brushing away the tears that I haven't been able to hold back. "I feel so lost. I told him everything about me, everything. I didn't hide anything, I was one hundred percent honest. That's what makes it so hard."

"I know," Debbie says. "Why don't you come and spend a few days here, clear your head a bit?"

"I'd love to, but I need to speak to Leo first. He's not back in London until tomorrow evening. I was going to ask him to go to

Ginny and Mark's like last week but I'll get him to come here. He's going to think I've forgiven him for not telling me about Nina."

"Would you like me to come to you?"

"It's lovely of you to offer but I need to speak to him alone."

"Let me know how it goes and if you need anything, just shout."

"Thanks, Debbie."

It takes me a while to call Leo.

"Alice?" Once again there's that hope in his voice, that I'm calling to ask him to come back.

"Are you working in London on Friday?"

"Yes."

"Then you can come home tomorrow evening."

"Really? Brilliant. Would you like to go out for dinner?"

"No, it's fine. See you tomorrow."

"Yes—thanks, Alice."

In the morning, I find it impossible to concentrate on the translation I'm meant to be doing. My stomach jitters at the thought of seeing Leo this evening. He texts me when he arrives at Euston and suddenly, I'm scared. I have no idea how he'll react when I tell him that I know who he really is. I don't think he would harm me but who knows what he's capable of when he's already been capable of so much?

I press my face to the window and call Ginny. I haven't been out at all today. In the square, a fierce wind whips the fallen leaves into a frenzy. Under the nearest tree, a small child, his little arms outstretched, tries to catch them, and they fall around him like extra-large confetti. His parent is filming the scene on his phone. It's Tim, I realize, with his youngest son.

"Hi, Alice," Ginny says cheerfully. "How are you?"

"Leo's arriving any minute now," I say, my eyes still on the little boy.

"Yes, I know, he told me you said he could go back."

"Only to talk."

"Oh."

"I hate to ask but would you mind coming over? It's just that I might need some back-up."

"Is everything all right?"

I turn from the window. "No, not really, but I'll explain when you get here. Could you leave now? It'll give me time to speak to Leo on his own first."

"I hope it's not what I think it is," she adds sadly. "I love you both."

I want to tell her that it's worse than she could possibly imagine.

Even though I'm expecting him, the sound of his key in the lock makes me jump. There are the usual sounds from the hall; the rustle of his Barbour being shrugged off, then his jacket, the chink of coins as he throws it over the newel post.

"Alice?"

"In here."

He comes into the kitchen. He's wearing a sweater I've never seen before. He's had his hair cut and the stubble he had five days ago is thicker, almost a beard. It makes him look younger. It makes him a stranger.

"How are you?" he asks.

"Not great."

I'm sitting at the kitchen table, like I was last time, when I confronted him about the murder. His passport is balanced on my knees, out of sight.

There's a scrape as he pulls out the chair opposite me.

"Has something happened?"

Questions crowd my mind. There's so much I want to ask him, too much.

"Is there anything you want to tell me?" I ask, needing him to come clean, because then, there might be hope for us.

"Apart from being sorry I didn't tell you about the murder?"

"Yes, apart from that."

"No, I can't think of anything." He rubs his hand over his chin. "I mean, I'd like to know how much longer you're going to hold it against me, because we can't go on like this." He leans forward, his eyes pleading. "I love you, Alice. Can't we put this behind us? I made a mistake. I'm sorry. Can't that be an end to it?"

"I'm going to ask you something, and this time I'd like the truth. Do you have a passport?"

He sits back, fake puzzlement on his face. "You know I don't. I told you that."

I can't look at him, I can't believe he's thrown our relationship away.

"What about a birth certificate? Have you got one of those?"

"Yes, of course."

"Can I see it?"

"I don't have it here."

"Where is it?"

"It's in a safe, in the bank."

The pause was slight, but I noticed it. "In a safe? I didn't know you had a safe." He doesn't say anything, just stares at me mutely. "Why don't you start by telling me who you are?" I say.

"What do you mean?"

It goes on a bit too long, the pretense that he doesn't know what I'm talking about. Tired of his lies, I take his passport from my knees and lay it on the table.

"I found this in your filing cabinet."

The change that comes over him is dramatic. His eyes dart around the room, looking for somewhere to hide and, realizing that there's nowhere to go, because I'm sitting right in front of him, they come to rest on me. The panic I see in them sends waves of adrenaline coursing through my body. For one horrible, frightening moment, I think he's going to lunge at me across the table.

The silence as we stare at each other becomes unbearable. My heart is racing so fast I think I might never be able to breathe again. Behind me, there's a tiny *drip-drip* from the tap in the sink. I focus on it, counting each drop. When I get to ten, I swallow painfully and force words out.

"Is your real name Leo Carter?"

It's there in his eyes, the knowledge that he's cornered. He puts his elbows on the table and buries his face in his hands.

"Leo." His despair makes him oblivious. "Leo," I say, raising my voice.

He lifts his head. His tear-streaked face is ashen. "You must hate me."

I can't cope with his pain. I push my chair back and move to the sink, turning the tap so that it no longer drips. "I could never hate you," I say to his reflection in the window.

He rubs at his face. "I shouldn't have lied to you, I know. But I couldn't tell you the truth, I was too scared that if I did, you wouldn't want to be with me anymore."

I turn back to him. "What is the truth?"

He sighs heavily. "When I was young and stupid, I worked for an asset management firm. I allowed myself to be influenced by a couple of guys I worked with and spent a few months in prison for fraud."

"How many months?"

"Four or five." I keep my eyes fixed on his face. "Maybe a bit more," he admits.

"I looked you up, Leo. I looked up Leo Carter. You spent two years in prison."

He shakes his head. "No. I was released early for good behavior." I don't say anything. "But you're right, it was more than a year, I'm not sure—"

I walk over to the table, hating that he still hasn't got it. "It doesn't matter how long you spent in prison, whether it was two months or two years," I say. "What matters is that you're still lying to me."

The desperation on his face is hard to witness. "I'll tell you everything, I promise. That woman, the one who came to Harlestone, I wasn't lying, she was a journalist. She wanted to write about the irony of someone who was once convicted for fraud advising clients on risk management issues. She kept on asking me and each time, I refused, because I didn't want you to find out what I'd done." New tears fall from his eyes. "Don't you see, Alice? I've turned the bad stuff I did into a positive. I'm making amends."

"Which is great, Leo," I say. "But it doesn't change the fact that at heart, you're dishonest." I stop, struggling for the words to tell him why it feels like the ultimate betrayal. "What I can't get my head around is why you didn't tell me the truth when I told you everything about me. Everything."

"But I went to prison!"

"Exactly. You paid the price for what you did." I turn at the sound of a car pulling up outside.

"Where are you going?" he asks.

"To open the door. Ginny's here."

"Ginny?"

"Yes, I asked her to come."

"But we haven't discussed anything yet."

"There isn't anything to discuss."

"Alice, please!"

"I'm sorry, Leo. It's over."

I go and open the door. Behind me, I hear Leo sobbing and I hate myself for not being able to comfort him.

"Is Leo still here?" Ginny asks anxiously, coming into the hall.

"Yes."

"What's happened?"

"I'll let Leo tell you," I say, reaching for my coat. "It's his story, not mine." I give Ginny a hug. "I'll call you later."

In the square I sink onto a bench and let the vicious wind whip tears from my eyes.

THIRTY-TWO

Ginny calls me.

"Where are you?" she asks.

"Sitting in the square."

"Coming now."

"I can't believe it," she says when she arrives a couple of minutes later, looking as shocked as I still feel. "I can't believe Leo spent time in prison."

I shove my hands deeper into my pockets, only realizing now how cold I am. "It's why he could never admit to having a passport. He must have changed his name officially, because he bought the house in the name of Leo Curtis."

"I'm so sorry, Alice, this is awful for you."

"How is he?"

"Upset, broken."

"Why do I feel guilty?"

"Because you still care for him."

"Maybe. But I can't forgive him."

"Because of his crime? I mean, fraud is terrible but it's not as if he murdered anyone."

"You're right, he didn't. But it's not that."

"Is it because he spent time in prison?"

I nod slowly. I wish I could explain to her why it matters so much, but I can't.

"What are you going to do?" she asks.

"Go back to Harlestone, I suppose. I'll ask Debbie if I can stay with her until I can get the tenants out of my cottage." Tears fill my eyes. "Six weeks, Ginny. Leo and I barely lasted six weeks."

She puts her arm around me. "Why don't you come and stay with us for a while?"

"That's lovely of you but I'm going to ask Leo if he'll let me have the house for another couple of weeks."

"But—won't he want the house? Especially as he's going to be working in London from Monday."

"Why? Has the Birmingham job finished?"

"Yes."

"Oh," I say, deflated. "Could he stay with you for a bit, do you think?"

"Of course. But why do you need the house for another couple of weeks? It won't take you long to pack up your stuff, will it?"

"No, but I need time to work out what I'm going to do."

"Can't you do that from ours? You can stay as long as you like, you know that."

I shake my head. "I want to be here."

She looks curiously at me. "This wouldn't be about the murder, would it?"

"What do you mean?"

"Leo says you've become a bit obsessive about it."

"No, it's not about the murder." I hate that I'm lying to Ginny. "I want to be able to say goodbye to everyone properly. Anyway, I don't think it's unreasonable to ask for a couple of weeks, given what he's done."

"You're right." She links her arm through mine. "Come on, let's get you back. You're freezing."

We leave the square and cross over to the house.

"Do you think Leo will stay in The Circle?" I ask Ginny.

"I think he intends to."

It doesn't seem fair, somehow.

She leaves me in front of the house with a hug. "If you need anything, you know where I am."

Leo is waiting for me in the kitchen, leaning against the worktop. I go and lean against the sink so that I'm facing him.

"I wish there was a bigger word than sorry," he says. "But there isn't."

"I'm sorry too," I say.

"What for?"

"That it hasn't worked out."

He nods. "It's all right. I always knew this would happen once you found out."

I push myself upright. "But not if you'd been upfront with me from the beginning!" I say, upset that he doesn't seem to understand. "If you'd told me about your prison sentence when we first met, everything could have been different."

"It wasn't a risk I was prepared to take." He gives a wry smile. "I've never been able to own up to my mistakes, I've always preferred to lie my way out of trouble. At least, that's what my therapist told me."

"You saw a therapist?"

"Yes. But not anymore. My parents found her for me when I was released from prison."

Something jars. "Are you really estranged from your parents?"

He sighs. "How could I introduce you to them when I was using another name? You would have found out pretty quickly that they were Mr. and Mrs. Carter, not Mr. and Mrs. Curtis."

I don't know why I feel shocked. "Don't tell me. They're loving parents, you had a pretty decent upbringing."

He ducks his head. "Something like that."

"And they don't know about me."

"I'm sorry."

I throw him a look of disgust. "It's bad enough that you lie about yourself. But that you lie about other people—you should be back in therapy, Leo, you still need help." I pause. "Are you going to stay here, in The Circle?"

He takes a glass from the cupboard and I move from the sink so that he can get to the tap. "Yes. I told you, I love this house, despite its history," he says, his back to me.

"I was wondering—I know it's your house, but would you let me stay here a couple more weeks? I'd like a bit of time to get used to the idea of going back to Harlestone."

He takes a drink of water, then turns to face me. "I thought you'd be overjoyed to be going back."

"No, not really. It feels like a failure, to be honest."

"I'm going to be working in London from Monday. But don't worry, I won't get in your way."

"I'd like two weeks on my own. Ginny says you can stay with her and Mark."

I feel his eyes on me. "Why do you need two weeks on your own?"

"I told you, I need to get used to the idea that I'm going back to Harlestone."

There's a rattle as he places his glass in the sink. "So it's not because you're still trying to solve a murder that's already been solved?"

"I'm not trying to solve it. But as I've already told you, I don't believe that Oliver killed Nina."

"Why are you so sure that he didn't?" he asks, perplexed.

I look for something to tell him. "I read an article. Apparently, Oliver's sister has always maintained his innocence."

"Well, of course she's going to say her brother is innocent! Are you telling me that because of an article you read in a newspaper, you've decided to go on a one-woman crusade to clear Oliver's name? You should leave things alone, Alice."

"So you think it's all right that the real killer got away with it?"

He throws his hands up in exasperation. "We're not going to get anywhere going backward and forward like this. You can have two weeks and then I want my house back."

"Thank you," I say. But he's already gone.

PAST

She's late. Again.

"How are you today?" she asks, once she's sitting down.

I smile. "Aren't I meant to ask you that?"

"Therapists are allowed to have off days too, aren't they?"

The fact that she's relaxed enough to joke with me is pleasing. Could it mean that she's finally going to tell me what I've been waiting to hear?

"No, I don't think they are," I say.

She laughs.

"Shall we begin?" I pull my pad toward me. "Over the last few sessions, we've been exploring the reasons for your unhappiness. You've told me about your childhood, your teenage years, your experiences in the world of work and we came to the conclusion that all those were mostly positive experiences. I think now we need to focus on when you first began to think about yourself as unhappy."

A small frown creases her brow.

"If you remember, during our last session, we touched on your marriage as a possible source of your unhappiness," I prompt.

"The thing is, I don't think I am."

"Sorry?"

"Unhappy."

I turn my head toward the window, giving her time to reflect on *what she's just said. Through the slats in the blinds, I can see brightly lit garlands strung across the street outside.*

"*I mean, how can I be?*" *she goes on.* "*I'm married to the most amazing man who would do anything for me, who gives me everything I want. That's what attracted me to him in the first place—that, and the fact that he was different from the men back home. He's a real gentleman.*" *She laughs nervously.* "*I know that sounds old-fashioned but it's true.*"

I turn my attention back to her and smile. "*There's nothing wrong with old-fashioned.*"

"*I think what I've been feeling is guilt. Guilt that I have so much. That's what has been making me unhappy, not Pierre. I love him.*" *She pauses.* "*You know that quote by Henry David Thoreau, about happiness being elusive?*"

"*Yes?*"

"*Do you think it's true?*"

"*I think it's worth careful analysis.*"

"*Then maybe I need to turn my attention to other things.*"

"*That's probably a very good idea.*"

"*The only thing is, I'm not sure where to begin.*" *She looks across at me.* "*I wish I didn't feel so anxious about everything.*"

I put my pen down, close my pad. "*Do you remember that during our first session, we spoke about relaxation therapy?*"

"*Yes. It sounds amazing.*"

I stand up. "*Why don't we make a start?*"

THIRTY-THREE

Debbie calls me the next morning.

"How are you?"

I don't have to pretend with Debbie. "Miserable. It's over between me and Leo."

"I'm so sorry, Ali."

"The worst thing is, nobody is going to understand why I left him. As Ginny pointed out, it's not as if he murdered someone. Everyone will think I've left him because he spent time in prison—which it is. But not in the way that they think."

"Does Leo understand?"

"I'm not sure that he does. After everything I told him, I don't think he really gets it. But you do, don't you, Debbie? You know why I can't be with him now."

"Yes," she says softly. "But, you know, if you want people to understand, you could tell them. You could explain why you feel as you do."

"I can't," I say, my voice tight. "I'd rather they think I'm unforgiving."

"Have you decided what you're going to do?"

"Short-term, Leo is letting me have the house for the next two weeks but long-term, I'm not sure. Could I come and stay with you for a bit? I'm not going to be able to get my cottage back until February so I'll have to find another solution until then."

"You can stay with me for as long as you like, you know that. We're hardly going to get in each other's way here. You can have the two bedrooms at the back of the house, make one into a temporary study, and in return, you can come for a ride with me each day, on Bonnie. How does that sound?"

Sudden tears fill my eyes. "Idyllic," I mumble.

"It's going to be all right," she says.

"I hope so."

"What are you doing today?"

"I don't know. I'm not sure where to begin. I feel a bit lost."

"Then why don't you take the day off, give yourself a break? I'm sure there's plenty to do in London. You're not going to be there much longer, you should do some sightseeing."

"You know, that's a great idea," I say, feeling brighter.

We chat for a while longer. Debbie suggests that I only take what I need from the house and arrange with Leo to leave behind my personal pieces of furniture—my desk, the dressing table which belonged to my mother, my sister's bookshelf and chest of drawers, my dad's chair—until I can move back to my cottage.

"Or, if he doesn't agree, you can store them in one of the barns," she says.

"I'm sure it will be fine. I don't want to leave Leo on bad terms, I'll still want to know how he is, how he's doing." I think for a moment. "I know I said I'd be down in two weeks, but if I decide to leave before, would that be OK?"

"You can arrive tomorrow as far as I'm concerned," Debbie says cheerfully. "Today, even."

"Thanks, Debbie, what would I do without you?"

We hang up and I decide to do as she suggested. I make a list of the places I really want to see before I go back to Harlestone and start with the Victoria and Albert Museum. Just sitting on the tube surrounded by people getting on with their everyday lives makes me realize, once again, how claustrophobic living in The Circle can be for people like me, who don't have to leave it every day to go to work. For those who do, coming home at the end of the day must feel like entering a haven of calm and privilege, an oasis in the midst of a teeming, bustling city.

I force myself not to think of Leo, not to think of anything except having a nice day out. On the way home, I bump into Eve.

"Hi, Alice!" she calls. She nods at the various bags I'm carrying. "What have you been up to?"

"I took the day off and went to the Victoria and Albert, it was amazing. And then I looked around the shops in South Kensington, treated myself to a couple of things, then went to a café and watched the world go by."

"It sounds perfect."

"I'm going to do some more sightseeing this weekend. The Tate Britain tomorrow, and if I've got time, I'll take the riverboat to the Tate Modern. I've reserved Sunday for Kensington Palace, with a walk around Hyde Park afterward."

"They've got a gorgeous tearoom there, in the Orangery. You should treat yourself."

"Good idea—why don't you join me?" I say, because I'm not going to be seeing her for much longer. "My treat for being such a lovely neighbor." I don't want to tell her that I'm leaving The Circle, because she would ask why and I haven't worked out what I'm going to say yet.

"I'd love that, especially as Will has rehearsals all weekend," she says.

"Great! Shall we meet there at 3 p.m.?"

"I think we might need to reserve. Would you like me to do it?"

"Yes, please."

The next evening, Thomas calls.

"I hope you don't mind me disturbing you at the weekend; I wanted to see how you are."

"I'm fine, thank you," I say, touched that he's called. "Well, not fine exactly because I'm still coming to terms with Leo not being the person he said he was. I'm trying to take my mind off it by exploring London."

"That sounds like a great idea. Where have you been?"

I tell him about my trips to the Victoria and Albert and the two Tate museums. "Tomorrow I'm going to Kensington Palace and for a walk in Hyde Park. What about you? Have you had a good weekend so far?"

"Yes, I have my son here. My ex-wife and I have Louis alternate weekends. I took him to Harry Potter World today, which exhausted me far more than it exhausted him."

I laugh. "Hopefully you'll have a quieter day tomorrow."

"I hope so. We'll probably end up going to kick a ball in the park."

"That still sounds energetic. Actually, I'm glad you called because there's something I've been meaning to ask. When you turned up on the doorstep the other day, was it only to ask if I'd received a letter from Helen? I mean, you could just have called."

"You're right, I could have. But when we spoke the week before, you hung up rather abruptly and I didn't know if I'd upset you in some way, or if what we'd been talking about had upset you. It played on my mind, so when Helen told me she'd written to you, I felt I had an excuse to call round and check that everything was all right."

"It wasn't you," I say. "I can't remember what we were talking about but it definitely wasn't anything you said that upset me."

"We were talking about your neighbor and wondering if there was someone who hadn't liked you asking her about Nina."

"Oh, yes." I pause, remembering it was the thought that Tamsin might have been listening at Lorna's that day. "I still don't know what to think. I can't believe she was worried about Edward hearing what she was saying, and the other suspect I had—well, I've dismissed her now. But I'm certain there are secrets here in The Circle."

"I'm sure there are."

Thinking of Tamsin has made me remember something that I've been meaning to ask Thomas. "Tamsin mentioned something the other day. Apparently, after Nina was killed, she cut her hair and she wondered if subconsciously, she was worried that if the killer had a fetish about long hair, he might come after her next. Do you think he did? Have a fetish, I mean?"

"It could be that. Or it could be symbolic. Throughout history, cutting off a woman's hair was often used as punishment for those thought to be immoral, as a shaming tactic. During World War Two, in France, it was the fate of many of the women who slept with Germans. They were seen as collaborators."

"So, if Nina's murderer thought she was immoral because she was having an affair, surely that points the finger at Oliver?"

"Or someone who wanted to have an affair with her and was jealous that she was having an affair with someone else. Or someone who was judging her for having an affair." There's a pause. "Sorry, Alice, Louis is waiting for me to read him a bedtime story. I'd better go."

"Of course."

I hang up, smiling at an image of him reading a story to his son. Louis. It's a nice name.

THIRTY-FOUR

It's raining the next day, so instead of going for a walk in Hyde Park, I head to the British Library, where I wander around in awe at the magnitude of the place. When I come across a bank of computers, I remember my conversation with Thomas the previous day and type in "hair fetishism." I read a few articles and then, on impulse, type in "hair fetishism in murders." Several links come up, to articles that appeared in a variety of French newspapers and as I scan them quickly, I realize that they all are about the same murder, which took place in Paris. My French is quite good and, as I read the first article, my blood begins to run cold. The victim, a thirty-one-year-old woman called Marion Cartaux, had had her hair cut off before she was strangled.

I study the photos of her. Like Nina, she had long blond hair. I look at the date of the murder—11th December 2017, approximately fifteen months before Nina was murdered.

It doesn't take me long to read everything I can find. I want to dig deeper but when I check the time, I'm already late for my appointment with Eve.

I hurry to the Orangery.

"Sorry I'm late," I apologize, tucking my wet umbrella under the table and giving her a hug. "I went to the British Library and got carried away looking at all the beautiful first editions."

"When I saw the rain, I thought you might change your plans."

"This is lovely," I say, looking around. "I'm glad you managed to get a table by the window."

"I nearly didn't get a table at all. Apparently, you have to book ages in advance. They'd just had a cancelation, so I was lucky."

We order tea and while we're waiting for it to arrive, Eve tells me that she couldn't sleep last night and almost called me for a chat, because she saw my lights on.

"I actually slept well last night," I say. "But there've been a few times when I thought there was someone in the house, and even though I know it's just my imagination," I add, because I'm not about to tell her that I believe in spirits, "I always leave the light on in the stairwell now." She frowns, so I carry on guiltily, "I know I shouldn't waste electricity but it makes me feel safer."

She shakes her head. "That's not why I'm frowning. It's just that there were a couple of times when Nina thought there was someone in the house. But as it was always when Oliver was away, like you, she put it down to her imagination. It used to freak her out, though."

My heart thumps. "When was this?"

"A few months before she died."

"Did you tell the police?"

"No, because it was only you saying the same thing that made me remember. As it happened when Oliver wasn't there, I thought the same as she did, that she was feeling vulnerable because she was alone in the house. I know if Will is away, I'm much more aware of noises in the house. Every creak could be a footstep on the stairs, that sort of thing."

I sit back to let the waiter place a stand of sandwiches, scones and cakes on the table, followed by two pots of tea. "What did Nina say, exactly?"

"Just that she would wake suddenly and think there was someone in the room. Then the feeling would disappear."

I reach for one of the teapots and fill her cup, not wanting her to see how much her words have affected me. If Nina experienced the same thing as me, maybe it's time to stop trying to convince myself that it's her spirit I've been sensing—and face up to the horrible reality that someone really has been coming into the house at night.

I don't say anything to Eve, but when I get home, I open my laptop and find a small boutique hotel not far from The Circle. I book myself in for four nights, then go upstairs to the bedroom where Leo and I used to sleep and begin filling a large canvas bag with a few basic necessities—pajamas, underwear, toiletries. I don't like giving up but I can't sleep in the house, not since my conversation with Eve. But if someone has been getting into the house, how have they been doing it? And why would they come back time and again and risk being seen? How do they manage to slip away undetected, without leaving the slightest trace of themselves? Whoever it is must have keys. As far as I know, only Leo and I have keys.

I open the wardrobe to get some jeans and T-shirts and give a sigh of exasperation. Once again, some of my shoes have been pushed to one side and I'm suddenly overwhelmed by memories of me and Nina playing hide and seek in the cottage in Harlestone. There were plenty of places to hide but Nina would always choose one of the wardrobes, knowing I'd be too scared to open the door in case she jumped out at me. Sometimes I'd get Dad to help and we'd creep quietly to the wardrobe where I thought Nina was hiding and, when I opened the door, he would roar and scrabble among the clothes like a tiger, giving her an even bigger fright than she would have given me. Sometimes we chose the wrong wardrobe and we'd all end up in fits of giggles.

I blink away the tears that happy memories of my family always bring. I miss Nina, I miss my parents, I miss all the things we were never able to do together. And then, as I stand there in front of the wardrobe, it hits me. Someone, at some point, has hidden inside it.

Stunned, I sink onto the bed. It has to be Leo. The day I thought I saw him at the study window, I had smelled his aftershave in this bedroom. I'd thought he was hiding behind the bathroom door but he must have been in the wardrobe. He told me he wasn't here, and Ginny had confirmed he was upstairs in the bedroom at hers when he called. Ginny wouldn't lie to me, so he must have sneaked out when she wasn't looking, while Mark was playing golf with Ben. Why didn't he want me to know he'd been here? I can't get my head around it. It's such a bizarre thing for a grown man to do, hide in a wardrobe. Would he even fit? It's extra deep, with a good space between the door and the rail, so maybe he would.

I go over and step inside, then turn myself around so that I'm facing the bedroom, and close the doors. There's plenty of room for me, plenty of room for Leo once he'd made enough room for his feet. And more importantly, if someone were to come into the bedroom now, I'd be able to see them through the slats in the doors. But they wouldn't be able to see me.

I push open the doors and step back into the room, freaked out at the thought of Leo hiding in the wardrobe. All I want is to get out of the bedroom, out of the house. I reach up to the shelf above the rail where my jumpers are folded in a neat pile. The one that I want— navy, to match my jeans—is at the bottom of the pile. I put my hand under it to ease it from the shelf without disturbing the rest of the jumpers and my fingers brush against something soft, like fur. I cry out and instinctively pull my hand back, shuddering at the thought of what I might have touched, thinking a dead mouse or a giant spider. I wait for my heartrate to slow; I want to be able to lift the pile of jumpers so that I can see what's lurking underneath, rather than pull the whole lot out, bringing whatever it is with them. The shelf is too high, so I fetch the chair from the corner of the room and place it in front of the wardrobe. I climb onto the chair and, steeling myself, carefully lift the jumpers.

A scream bursts from me and, losing my balance, I topple over the back of the chair, the jumpers flying from my hands as I crash to the floor. Horribly winded, I struggle to catch my breath, assessing myself for damage. My elbow and left leg are throbbing painfully and the back of my head doesn't feel good either. I take a moment, then force myself to my feet, using the fallen chair to lever myself upright, ignoring the needles of pain shooting through my arm. Tears of fright spring to my eyes. I want to believe that I imagined the swathe of long blond hair that was hidden under the jumpers but I know that I didn't. My mind spins with jumbled denials—*it can't be Nina's hair, it can't be, Leo didn't know her, he didn't kill her, he can't have, he wouldn't have*—which collide with the facts—*he wanted this house, this particular house*—and reach a terrifying conclusion—*he knew Nina, he killed her here in this house, he cut off her hair and kept some as a trophy. And now, he's returned to the scene of the crime.*

My fear that the hair is Nina's is greater than any pain I'm experiencing. I reach for my cell phone to call the police, aware that I'm going to sound crazy. Maybe I am crazy, maybe it was my imagination, maybe it was something else I saw. Shaking, I inch nearer to the wardrobe, craning my neck toward the shelf. It's still there, an amputated ponytail of long blond hair, tied top and bottom with red ribbon.

Except that Leo can't have killed Nina. And while I'm going through all the reasons why Leo can't be Nina's murderer, my eyes still fixed on the hair, my mind is registering that there's something not quite right about it. I move nearer for a closer look; the texture—unnaturally glossy—looks too perfect. I don't want to touch it—but I need to know, so I reach out and run a tentative finger along it. And breathe a sigh of relief. The hair isn't real, it's synthetic.

I slump onto the bed. Why has Leo hidden a ponytail of synthetic hair in the wardrobe, which anyone seeing it—anyone who knows what happened to Nina here in this house—might mistake for her hair? Did he put it there to frighten me? Did he see me take the key from his wallet that day and decide to play a little game with me in retaliation?

A cold anger takes hold. I'm tempted to call the police and tell them I've found a ponytail of Nina's in my wardrobe, tell them they should arrest my partner. But they'd come here first to check, and would see that it's synthetic. Maybe I should call Leo and pretend that I've called the police, frighten him a little. But he would laugh at my naïvety, tell me it was just his little joke. I'm dismayed at how little I know him, dismayed that he could stoop so low. Furious, I send him a message. FYI, the hair is pathetic! He replies almost at once. I didn't do it for you to like it.

I pick up my navy jumper from the floor but leave the others where they are, wanting to get out of the house as quickly as possible. My arm is still throbbing so I go to my study and peel off my T-shirt to check for damage. There's a huge lump below my elbow, where I whacked it against the chair as I fell, and I'm betting on a massive bruise appearing on my leg in the next few days. There's also a bump on the back of my head.

Needing some water, I head to the kitchen. There are more strands of my hair on the worktop and it seems like the last straw in an already lousy day. I go to brush them into the bin, and stop. Caught in the light coming from the fluorescent bulb fixed to the underside of a shelf, they are a pale blond, a shade paler than my hair. I pick one up carefully and roll it between my fingers. It isn't real.

Dropping it into the palm of my hand, I run back upstairs to the bedroom and take the ponytail from the shelf. It confirms what I expected; the hair I found on the worktop comes from the ponytail.

It's hard to get my head around this new twist in Leo's game; I never told him about losing my hair after my parents and sister died, so he wouldn't have known how much it would upset me to find strands of it all over the place. He must have had some other motive. Was I meant to think that it was Nina's hair? Has it been him creeping around the house at night, leaving hair for me to find? It can't have been, because that very first time, on the Sunday after our drinks evening, he was the one who heard someone in the house, not me. Unless he only pretended to have heard someone, so that in the future, I would blame the prowler for any nocturnal creeping I heard.

But why would he have done that? The answer comes to me almost immediately—so that, when I found out about Nina, if I didn't want to be with him because of his lie, I'd be too anxious to stay by myself. And he'd get to stay in the house while I moved out.

Except that it hadn't worked out like that. He had moved out and I had stayed. So he had upped his game and prowled the house at night, hoping to terrorize me into leaving. I remind myself that he's been in Birmingham most of the time, not in London. But I don't know that he actually stayed there. He could have been here, staying in a hotel at night and commuting to Birmingham each morning, just like he had before. I try and reconcile the Leo I know with a person who would creep around a house where his ex-partner is sleeping, to scare her into leaving, and can't. I'm being ridiculous. If Leo had wanted me to leave before now, he would have told me. After all, the house is his.

THIRTY-FIVE

The hotel is lovely, the room beautifully decorated in subtle shades of gray, with a gray marble bathroom and white fluffy towels. Relief washes through me. For the first time in weeks, I feel safe.

So that Ginny and Eve won't worry, I message them to say I'm going away for a few days and that I'll be back at the house on Thursday. I ask Ginny not to tell Leo and she promises she won't. If Leo knows I'm not there, he might move back in.

I toss and turn all night, and in the morning, I feel so empty that all I want to do is hibernate until I check out on Thursday morning. I'd intended to carry on working from the hotel but I don't want to think about anything, not my translation, not my parents or my sister, not Leo and his lies, not Nina's murder. All I want is to lie in the dark, with the curtains drawn, and switch off from everything.

For the next two days, I sleep, listen to podcasts, take long baths and order food from room service, telling the lovely girl who brings it that I'm feeling under the weather. At one point I find myself thinking about Thomas, and remembering that I haven't told him about the murder in France, I call him.

"Both women had their hair cut off," I say once I've told him about Marion Cartaux. "Do you think the two murders could be linked?"

"They could be," he says. "But it's more likely to be two murders committed by two different people with the same fetish. It's infuriating to think that nobody on my team—or me, for that matter—thought to look abroad. You'd make a very good investigator, Alice."

"Thank you," I say, pleased.

"I'll get my people to do a bit of digging and get back to you." I sense him hesitate. "Maybe I could come by tomorrow afternoon and let you know what I find? Or Friday, if you prefer."

"Tomorrow is better for me."

"Two o'clock?"

"Perfect."

I hang up. I could have chosen to see him Friday, because I'll be back at the house by then. But it seemed too long to wait.

The next day, I walk back to the house at the end of the morning, feeling bad that I'm looking forward to seeing Thomas when Leo and I have only just split up. But at this moment in time, he's one of the few people I can trust.

It's a crisp October day and apart from a handful of parents and children in the play area, the square is almost deserted. I glance over at Tamsin's house, wondering what her plans are for the morning, and see someone standing at one of the upstairs windows. I'm unable to make out if it's her or Connor but I lift my hand in a wave, knowing that whoever it is can see me.

"Alice!"

Turning, I see Will running to catch up with me, a brightly colored scarf around his neck.

"Hi, Will," I say cheerfully, hoping he didn't see me coming out of the hotel. If I didn't want anyone to know I was staying there, I should have chosen one further away from The Circle. "Have you been shopping?"

"No, just for a walk. I'm reading through a new script and I needed a break. Are you back already? Eve said you'd gone away."

Too late, I remember that I was meant to be away until tomorrow. "Yes, I just got back," I tell him.

He nods distractedly. "Eve really enjoyed the Orangery the other day."

"Me too. I don't know about Eve, but I ate far too much."

"I just wanted to say—Eve told me that there's been a couple of occasions when you've thought there was someone in the house at night?"

"It was probably my imagination," I say, wondering why he's mentioning it.

He gives me a quick look. "I don't want to worry you but I think Eve told you that Nina thought the same thing."

"Yes, she did."

"Then—are you sure you're happy staying there on your own? If Leo isn't coming back yet, you're welcome to stay with us."

"That's lovely of you but honestly, I'm fine."

He turns his blue eyes on me. "I'm sorry, Alice, I don't understand why you're willing to risk it, especially after what happened to Nina."

"But if Oliver killed Nina, how can I be at risk?"

"What if he didn't?"

I stop walking. "What are you saying, Will?"

He shoves his hands in his pockets. "Just that I've never been entirely happy with the theory that he killed her. I didn't know Oliver well, we'd only been neighbors for five months, but I knew him well enough to be as shocked as everyone else when he was accused of murdering Nina. But when they said his suicide proved his guilt—that I couldn't believe. I didn't say anything because as I said, everyone knew him better than me, so I thought there was something about him that I'd missed. Then you arrived and began questioning things, and now, I don't know. What if the real killer is still living among us, hiding in plain sight?"

He seems so genuine, so completely genuine. But at the back of my mind, there's a voice telling me that he's an actor, an incredibly good actor. If Eve told him of the conversation we had in the Orangery, did she also tell him what I said last week, that I no longer think there's a mystery to solve? Has Will just laid a trap for me?

"I'm really sorry if I've made you question what happened," I say, walking on, because I want this conversation to end as quickly as possible. "I didn't have all the facts at the beginning but now that I do, I honestly believe that Oliver killed Nina over the affair she was having. And if the police didn't think there was anything further to investigate, I'm not quite sure why I did." I give a self-conscious laugh, because I can act too. "Sometimes I wonder if it was just to make myself more interesting than I actually am—you know, to try and make my mark here in The Circle."

"Oh. Well, in that case, I guess I'll have to accept it too," he says, and I can't work out if he's disappointed or relieved.

We reach the gate opposite our houses.

"Good luck with the script," I say, heading toward my drive.

"Thanks, Alice. And remember, if you need anything, I'm just next door."

I give an involuntary shiver. It should have sounded comforting. But somehow it had felt like a threat.

THIRTY-SIX

Thomas turns up at two-thirty, wearing a dark blue suit and light blue shirt, and looking paler than usual.

"I've just come from Helen's," he says.

"How is she?"

"Not good. It's hard sometimes, remembering how she was."

"I'm sorry," I say, wondering again if he and Helen were more than friends.

We go to sit in the kitchen.

"We went out together once or twice when we were at university," he says, uncannily reading my mind. "But we realized we were better friends than girlfriend and boyfriend." He dips his hand into the inside pocket of his jacket and draws out his wallet. "This is us in better days," he says, taking out a photo. "I took it with me this morning, to show Helen."

I study it a moment. The younger version of him has longer hair, and his arm is around the shoulders of a girl with a pretty face and laughing blue eyes. They look so carefree that I wonder how hard it was for Helen to see the photo.

"She said she was glad she didn't know then that her life would be cut short at the age of forty-three," Thomas says. "Sometimes I wonder if Nina had the same thought, when she knew she was about to die."

I hand the photo back to him. "Don't."

"Sorry," he says, chastened. "I always feel down after I've visited Helen, but it's unprofessional to bring my low mood to work with me." I feel a momentary disappointment that he thinks of me as work. "Also, I didn't have time for lunch so I probably need sugar. I'm diabetic."

I jump to my feet. "You should have said, I thought you looked pale. Let me give you something to eat—what can I get you?"

"A biscuit or banana will be fine, if you have either of those."

"I do, but I haven't had lunch yet and I was going to make myself an omelette. Cheese and mushroom—will that do?"

"It sounds amazing, but I don't want to put you to any trouble."

"It's not a problem."

He takes out his phone and lays it on the table. "I'm afraid I don't have any news about the murder in France. I should hear back before the end of the week, though."

"I couldn't find anything about anyone being arrested for it," I say.

"I couldn't either. Which makes me think it's an ongoing case. That said, I still think it's a long shot that the two murders are connected, given that they occurred in different countries."

While I peel the mushrooms, I tell him about the conversation I overheard between Eve and Tamsin when I went to Tamsin's for coffee. I feel bad for telling him, but I want his take on it.

"Does Leo know about the gaps in the fence between your house and your neighbors?" he asks.

"Yes, I told him. He thought it was a good idea."

"I hope you don't mind me asking, but how are things between you?"

"He isn't living here at the moment."

"I'm sorry."

I turn away, not wanting to think about Leo. I tip the whisked eggs into two frying pans and begin cooking them slowly. The simple act of pulling the cooked edges into the center and letting raw egg run into the space left behind is strangely soothing.

"Have you met Tamsin's husband?" Thomas asks.

"Yes."

"What do you think of him?"

"I don't think he's a murderer, if that's what you mean."

"I know I'm not telling you anything that you don't already know, but appearances can be deceptive."

"You're right, I do already know that," I say feelingly, adding the mushrooms and a sprinkling of cheese to the eggs.

He gives a sympathetic smile. "But if Tamsin thinks he had an affair with Nina," he begins.

"He didn't," I say quickly, and launch into an account of my conversation with Tamsin in the café. "The thing is," I say when I finish, "I'm not sure how much of it was genuine."

"Oh?"

I fold the omelettes in half, pressing down on them lightly with the spatula to melt the cheese inside. "Just that a part of me wonders if I'm not being set up by Tamsin. When people asked how I found out about the murder, I told them that a reporter called me. And ever since, Tamsin has been worried that the reason the reporter contacted me is because the police are actively looking into the murder again. Even though I've denied it, I'm sure she thinks that I'm still in contact with the reporter. What if she's feeding me misinformation on purpose? Those two back-to-back conversations—the one I overheard, and the one I had the next day with her in the café—there's something off about them."

"It does sound as if Tamsin is doing everything to let you know that her husband didn't kill Nina. On the other hand, she also told you that he didn't take rejection easily."

"I know exactly how Eve and Tamsin must have felt when they heard that Nina had had an affair," I say, sliding the omelettes onto plates and carrying them over to the table. "Those few seconds last week, when there was the possibility of Leo having known Nina, were hard. Even Maria must have wondered about Tim, if only for a few seconds. And he's the least likely candidate."

Thomas looks appreciatively at the omelette. "This looks wonderful, thank you." He picks up his knife and fork. "I'm curious as to why you think Tim is the least likely candidate. He and Nina could very easily have bonded over their interest in psychology."

"Maybe, but he and Maria are a really solid couple. So are Eve and Will, which is why my money would have been on Connor."

I sit down opposite him and watch him surreptitiously from under my eyelashes while we eat. It feels right, him sitting here at the table with me.

"You know when you said that Nina having her hair cut off could have been some sort of judgment?" I say. "If someone *was* judging her, isn't it more likely to have been a woman?"

I regret my words immediately.

"Are you thinking what I'm thinking?" Thomas asks, reading my face.

"I don't know." But I am, it's just that I feel terrible for thinking it.

"Tamsin definitely had a motive," he says. "Not only had Nina turned her back on her, she also suspected that her husband was having an affair with her—"

"But she's always believed that Oliver didn't murder Nina," I interrupt. "She's thought all along that he's innocent. Why draw attention to the fact that someone else killed her, if she was the one who did it?"

"Because, as we've already worked out, she could be playing a very clever game. And didn't you overhear her say that everyone is capable of murder?"

Suddenly, it becomes too much. "No. No. I'm a hundred percent sure it wasn't Tamsin. I can't believe the thought even crossed my mind." I sit back in my chair, needing to physically distance myself from him, from everything that we're doing. But it's not far enough, so I stand and start gathering up our plates. "I'm sorry, but this isn't right. Can't we just accept that Oliver murdered Nina?"

"Like everyone here was happy to do," he says softly.

"Maybe it was him," I say.

He stands and takes the plates from me. "Maybe it was," he says. "But until I know for sure, I can't rest, for Helen's sake and for

Oliver's sake. Believe me, if I thought he was guilty, I wouldn't be investigating the murder. But there's too much that doesn't add up. Also, Oliver swore to Helen that it wasn't him. She says he wouldn't have lied to her and I believe her." He carries the plates over to the sink, then turns to face me. "I'm feeling more and more uncomfortable about having dragged you into this. I'm not sure—maybe it would be better if I leave?"

"No, please don't. But perhaps we could talk about something else."

"Yes," he says, relieved. "Good idea."

I don't know if it was the simple act of cooking for him that allows us to move to the point where we feel comfortable sharing information about ourselves. Thomas tells me he and his wife divorced three years ago and that he now lives in South London. I feel for him when he explains that he and his wife wanted to share childcare for their six-year-old son but because they didn't want to disrupt his daily routine, they agreed that his wife would be the main carer for the moment.

"All that will change when he moves school next September," Thomas explains. I've made coffee and we're back at the table. "His new school is nearer to where I live, so he'll be staying at mine every second week. I can't wait. I miss him so much."

He also tells me that he grew up reading Sherlock Holmes and, after studying Psychology and Criminology at university, he decided to become a private investigator instead of joining the police force, as he'd intended to do. In return, I tell him about me and Leo, how the move to London was meant to be our new start, how I feel guilty that I can't forgive him for lying to me and how bemused I feel for not realizing that he could.

"When you think about it, it's not surprising you found living together hard if you only used to see each other at weekends," Thomas remarks. "Two days a week over what—twenty months?—only amounts to around three to four months in real time."

"I never thought of that," I say, feeling slightly less guilty.

I also tell him about losing my parents and sister and admit that

I'm worried my sister is the reason I've become invested in Nina's murder.

"I think, if it wasn't for Nina—my sister Nina—I wouldn't be here, talking to you, trying to help you get to the truth. I'm confused about my motives, I'm worried they're not pure. I didn't know Nina, I shouldn't be this involved. But sometimes, when I think about my sister, or about Nina, they become intertwined. It's like they're the same person."

His eyes are full of compassion. "Do you think you and Leo are going to be able to work things out?"

"No, because there isn't any me and Leo, not anymore. Hiding his past from me is a lie too far. I can't be with him."

He nods slowly. "What are you going to do?"

"This is his house, not mine, so I'll be going back to Harlestone. He's agreed that I can stay here until next weekend. I think he felt it was the least he could do."

"Then—Helen was asking if she could meet you. I wasn't going to mention it yet because I didn't know if it was something you'd feel comfortable doing. But if you're only here for another week or so—" His voice tails off.

"I'd love to meet her," I say.

"Are you sure?"

"Yes."

For the first time since I've known him, he looks slightly awkward. "What about next Wednesday? Perhaps I could take you to lunch, and then we could go to Helen's together?"

I feel a rush of pleasure. "That would be lovely."

"And while we're having lunch, maybe you could explain to me how to get to Harlestone. Just so that I can let you know if there are any developments," he adds with a smile.

"I'm sure I could," I say, smiling back at him.

"Good." He looks curiously at me. "How did Leo take it when you told him it was over?"

"Resigned, I think. It's not just his lies, it's also the stupid thing with the hair."

"What stupid thing?"

"It's actually really embarrassing, which is why I didn't mention it before."

"What happened?"

Reluctantly, because it shows Leo in such a bad light, I tell him about the hair scattered around the house and how I found a blond ponytail in the wardrobe.

"The funny thing is, he was probably trying to scare me into thinking it was Nina's hair that I kept finding," I say. "Except that it didn't occur to me that it was. I presumed it was mine, because I lost a lot of it after my parents and sister died and I thought it was happening again, because of the stress of the murder."

"Is that why you always wear it up?"

I raise my hand and touch my hair self-consciously. "Yes, it's become a habit now. I also think Leo has been prowling around the house at night, another tactic to scare me. I can't be with a man who thinks it's all right to psychologically manipulate someone."

Thomas frowns. "What do you mean, prowling around the house? I thought you said he wasn't living here."

I give a dry laugh. "Exactly."

"I'm not sure I understand."

"Just that there have been a few nights when I've thought there was someone in the room, watching me. It was pretty terrifying the first couple of times, but as nothing ever happened, I managed to convince myself that there wasn't anyone there, that it was Nina's spirit I could sense." My cheeks grow hot. "I know that sounds stupid, but after my sister died, I used to sense her presence, especially at night, so it was easy to convince myself I was experiencing the same sort of thing. As I said, nothing ever happened and there was never any trace of anyone having been here, so I was fine with it. But then, the other day, Eve told me that before Nina died, there were a couple of occasions when she'd also thought there was someone in the house. Which kind of smashes my spirit theory."

"But why would Leo do that?"

"To scare me into leaving the house."

"But, as it's his house, he would have been entitled to ask you to leave."

"Yes—but maybe he wanted it to come from me, so that people in The Circle would think I was leaving because I was too scared to stay in the house, not because he was kicking me out. Everyone knows he didn't tell me about Nina. He needs to redeem himself if he's going to carry on living here."

"But if Nina experienced the same thing, it must be someone else doing the prowling." Thomas sounds perplexed. "Who else has keys to your house?"

"No one, as far as I know."

"Are you sure about that? It's quite usual to give keys to neighbors, in case of emergencies. My neighbor has a set."

"Leo never said that he'd given anyone keys but I can always ask him."

"Did you ask him about the prowling?"

"No, I forgot, probably because it didn't seem important compared to his other lie. But I asked him about the hair. I told him it was pathetic and he said he didn't do it so that I would like it. It makes me wonder if I ever really knew him." I give him a rueful smile. "Can we change the subject?"

By the time he leaves an hour later, I feel we're finally friends. I know he feels it too. As we stand at the door, saying goodbye, I don't think either of us wants the afternoon to end.

"Are you sure you still want to be involved in all this?" he asks, locking me with his eyes so that I can't look away.

"If Oliver didn't kill Nina, I want her killer brought to justice."

"No matter who it is?" he says softly.

I think of the people here in The Circle, some of who I consider friends. But then I think of Nina, of how she died and how she must have suffered. And of my sister, who didn't get justice for her death.

"No matter who it is," I reply firmly.

THIRTY-SEVEN

Before going back to the hotel, I call Leo. He's still at work but I'm no longer worried about disturbing him.

"Apart from you and me," I ask, plunging straight in, "does anyone have keys to our house?"

"Why—is there a problem? Have you locked yourself out? I can come over."

"No, it's not that." I take a steadying breath. "I'm going to ask you something and I'd like an honest answer. Have you been letting yourself into the house at night?"

"Sorry?"

"It's a simple question, Leo. Have you been letting yourself into the house at night and creeping around, trying to scare me?"

"It's also a bizarre one. Why would I do that?"

"To get me to leave the house."

"You really think that's something I'd do?" His voice is low and I remember that he's at work. "Anyway, I'm in Birmingham most of the time, remember?"

"But not all of the time."

"Can you hold on a moment?" I hear him say something to someone about needing to take a couple of minutes and then he's back. "Look, I might be dishonest but I'm not a psychopath."

"Really? What about the hair?"

"What hair?"

"The ponytail in the wardrobe."

"I have no idea what you're talking about."

"Come on, Leo, you admitted it!"

"Admitted what?"

I can't keep hold of my anger. I'm tired, so tired of his lies.

"Hiding hair in the wardrobe and spreading it around the house to make me think that it's Nina's!"

There's a long pause. "Alice. You're beginning to worry me. I honestly have no idea what you're talking about."

The calmness of his voice infuriates me further. "I messaged you! I told you the hair was pathetic and you said you didn't do it so that I would like it!"

"Yes, the shorter hair, my beard. It wasn't for you, I wasn't trying to impress you or anything. I just didn't shave for a few days and liked it, so thought I'd carry on letting it grow." There's a pause. "Can we rewind? To the part where you accused me of creeping around the house?"

My mind is still trying to catch up with what he said about the hair. "I'm not imagining it, Leo."

"I didn't say you were. I thought there was someone in the house after our drinks evening, remember?"

"After the first couple of times, I did think I was imagining it," I say. "Because nothing ever happened. But Eve told me that before Nina died, she used to think there was someone in the house."

"The first couple of times?" His voice rises in alarm. "How many times has this happened?"

"I don't know—four or five, maybe."

"And you've carried on staying there?"

"Yes, because nothing ever happened. As I said, I thought I was imagining it. But to get back to my original question, does anyone else have keys to the house?"

"Yes, Will and Eve. I gave Will a set after we moved in."

My heart plummets. "Right."

"You don't seriously think either of them have been letting themselves into the house to try and scare you?"

"No," I say, although my mind is screaming Will's name.

"What was all that about hair in the wardrobe?"

I cringe internally at the mix-up. "Sorry, I've got a call coming through. It's Debbie. Can I call you back later?"

"Sure."

I hang up. Debbie isn't calling but I need to think. I really need to think.

Ten minutes later, I'm on Eve's doorstep waiting for her to answer the door.

She flings it open. "Perfect timing!" I can hear voices coming from the kitchen. She opens the door wider. "Come in."

"No, it's fine, I don't want to disturb you, I just—"

She reaches for my arm. "Don't be silly, the others are here. It's a bit noisy with the children but I thought it was about time we had tea at mine."

"Great," I say, remembering that after their yoga session on Wednesdays, Eve goes with Tamsin and Maria to collect the children from school, and then they have tea together.

I follow her to the kitchen, which is full of people. Despite the cooler weather, the French doors to the garden are open and Maria's three boys and Tamsin's two little daughters run backward and forward, taking cake from the table and carrying it outside to eat. Tamsin and Maria are sitting at the table and Will and Tim are leaning against the worktop, mugs of tea in their hands.

"Hi, Alice," they chorus.

I give a little wave. "Hi, everyone." I look over at Will and Tim. "I didn't realize you were part of the Wednesday afternoon gatherings too."

"We're only honorary members this afternoon, because we both happened to be at home," Tim explains.

"And because I overheard Maria offering to bring one of her chocolate cakes," Will says. "You need to try some, Alice, it's the best."

"Sit down." Eve hoists herself onto the worktop next to the table. "Will, pass Tamsin a mug for Alice."

I pull out the chair next to Maria and she cuts me a slice of cake while Tamsin fills my mug with tea.

"Thanks," I say, trying not to think that at one time or another, I've suspected three of the people in the room of having murdered Nina.

"Did you have a nice time away?" Eve asks.

"Yes, thanks. Actually, that's why I came over—Debbie, the friend I was staying with, is coming to spend a few days with me and I'd like to give her keys so that she can come and go as she pleases. Leo said that you have a set?"

"Yes, hang on a second." Will goes over to the wall next to the fridge. "How is he, by the way?"

"Fine, thank you. Working hard as usual." I still don't feel ready to tell them that it's over between me and Leo.

"They're here somewhere," Will says, running his eye over a row of keys. He chooses a keyring and holds it up. "It's not this one, is it?"

"Those are mine," Tamsin says.

"I thought they were." Will frowns and turns to Eve. "Apart from your mum's spare set, Tamsin's seem to be the only ones here that aren't ours. Have you got Alice's?"

"No, I didn't even know we had a set."

"Leo gave them to me after they moved in. I put them here with the others." He turns back to the hooks. "Come and have a look, Alice, you'll recognize them better than me."

I leave my cake and walk over to where he's standing.

"Can you see them?" he asks.

"No."

"We did have them, because I remember seeing a label with number 6 on it. I don't remember Leo taking them back but maybe you could ask him."

"I just spoke to him, he was the one who told me you had a set."

Will scratches his head. "I don't know where they could be. Eve, did you move them, put them somewhere else?"

"How could I, when I didn't know we had any?" she says archly. She jumps down from the worktop. "Maybe they're in the study."

"Why would they be there?"

"I don't know but it's the only other place I can think of to look. Come with me, Alice."

I follow Eve to the study, and we search the desk and its drawers. But there's no sign of the keys.

"Weird," Eve says. "I'm sorry, Alice, I'll carry on looking once everyone has gone."

She doesn't sound too worried and another possibility adds itself to the ones already crowding my mind, none that I like very much. Could Will be lying? Maybe he's put the keys somewhere else, or they're in the pocket of the jeans he was wearing last time he went on a night prowl. But maybe it's not him, maybe someone saw our keys on the wall by the fridge and took them. I look over at Tamsin, then at Tim and Maria. They are all frequent visitors here.

"No problem," I say, except that it is a problem, because now I know that Leo isn't my prowler, I won't be able to sleep in the house when I leave the hotel tomorrow, not when a set of keys has gone missing.

I finish my cake, make my excuses and leave.

"When is your friend arriving?" Will asks, coming to the front door with me.

"Friday," I say.

"Well, let's hope we can find the keys before then."

Back at the hotel, my phone rings. It's Ginny.

"How are you?" she asks.

"I'm fine."

"Are you sure?"

"Yes, why?"

"I had a call from Leo. He's worried about you, Alice. He said you were accusing him of prowling around the house at night, and something he didn't understand about him spreading hair everywhere."

"It was a misunderstanding," I say. "And anyway, he's exaggerating."

"Hm." She doesn't seem convinced. "Are you still away?"

"Yes."

"I'm sorry, Alice, that's what I don't understand. You ask Leo if you can have the house for two weeks and then you go away."

"I'll be back tomorrow."

She sighs. "Are you going to tell me what's going on?"

"There's nothing going on. Sorry, but I really need to go. Can I call you in the morning?"

"All right, but—"

"Thanks, Ginny, I'll speak to you then."

PAST

I like my new client. I can already tell she's going to be more of a challenge but that's OK. She sits opposite me, her slim legs crossed, oozing confidence. She is a woman at peace with herself. But we all have darkness within us and the deeper it's buried, the more interesting it is.

I take my pad from the table and my pen from my pocket. I could use a laptop for my notes but clients still like to see a good old-fashioned notepad. The problem with using a screen, I guess, is that the client never really knows what we're doing behind it, whether we're taking notes or watching something on Netflix.

I begin asking her the standard questions and she raises an amused eyebrow.

"Really?" she says.

I frown and, chastened, she sits upright, uncrosses her legs, straightens her skirt, and turns her attention to giving me her answers.

"Why are you here?" I ask, when we get to the end. And then I give her the usual spiel about how anything she says won't go further than this room.

This room. I look around it, at the pale pink walls, at the window that looks onto the road outside. There are no blinds on the window shielding us from prying eyes, just curtains which I can't close, not at this time of the day. It's why I've made sure we're sitting toward the back of the room. Discretion, as always, is everything.

"I don't have any major problem," she says. "I just think that it would be good for me to be in therapy, to experience what it's like. And to talk. It's always good to talk, isn't it?"

"It certainly is," I agree.

So we talk, about her childhood—happy; her teenage years—no real problems; her career—she loves it. The one thing she doesn't talk about is her husband. I know she's married so that in itself is telling.

I put down my pad. "How long have you been married?" I ask.

She looks surprised, so I look pointedly at her left hand, at the thin gold band on her ring finger.

"I might be widowed," she says.

"Are you?" I ask.

"No." I wait. "Seven years," she says. "I've been married seven years."

"Seven happy years?" I ask.

"Seven ecstatic years. Not an itch in sight."

I suppress a sigh. She's disappointed me.

I lean toward her and fix her with my eyes. "Do you know what Henry David Thoreau said about happiness?"

Now she looks disappointed. She leans forward too, stares right back at me. "Yes," she says. "I know exactly what Thoreau said about happiness. And it's a load of bollocks."

THIRTY-EIGHT

The next morning, I check out of the hotel and cross the square to the house, my feet rustling crisp fallen leaves as I walk. I could have booked myself in for another couple of days but I don't like being bullied, and making me afraid to stay in the house is a form of bullying. So, I'm going to do what I did before, and stay awake during the night. If I hear anything, anything at all, I'll call the police.

It's cold, and there's no one sitting on the benches in the square, no one even walking across it on their way to work, which isn't surprising, given that it's half-past ten. It's amazing how conspicuous it makes me feel. For all I know, any number of people could be watching me from their upstairs windows. I raise my eyes and turn my head, scanning the houses as I walk, starting on the left-hand side with number 1 and carrying on to numbers 2, 3 and 4, then to Eve and Will's, past theirs to ours, onto Lorna and Edward's, then Geoff's, then Maria and Tim's. And stop. Because Tim is there, in one of the upstairs bedrooms, watching me watching him. I raise my hand in a wave, glad he can't see the shiver that runs down my spine, and he waves back. I pick up my pace, eager to be inside but as I go through the gate, Edward comes out of his house, his gardening shears in his hand.

"Good morning, Alice," he calls. "Been for a walk?"

"Yes, it's always lovely at this time of the year. How are you and Lorna?"

"We're fine, doing well."

"Actually, I wanted to tell you that I'm going to be leaving The Circle. But not Leo. He'll be staying."

"Oh dear, I am sorry," he says. "When will you be leaving?"

"I was going to leave next weekend but I might go earlier."

"Really? Right. Well, we'll be very sorry to see you go."

"Would you tell Lorna?" I ask.

"Yes, of course."

"I'll come and say goodbye," I promise.

"You do that. Lorna will be pleased to see you."

I flick my eyes toward Maria and Tim's house. Tim is still at the window. Edward follows my gaze and gives Tim a wave.

"Bye, Edward," I say distractedly. I start to move off but he shuffles closer.

"Don't tell anyone when you're leaving," he whispers. He pitches his voice back to his normal level. "Bye, Alice."

I let myself into the house, my heart thumping. First Lorna, now Edward. Two warnings, don't trust anyone and don't tell anyone. Who are they warning me against? Edward had seen Tim watching us. Is that why he said it?

I pace my study, thinking about Tim. There's nothing physically creepy about him and when they all came for dinner, he was perfectly lovely, helping me in the kitchen. But there's something slightly creepy about the way he always seems to be watching from the window. It could be perfectly innocent. He's studied psychology, and isn't psychology the study of people, how they act, react, interact? And if he's training to be a psychotherapist, it's normal that he finds people fascinating. Anyway, psychologists and psychotherapists help people, they don't kill them.

No sooner has that thought entered my head, something shoots forward from the recesses of my mind, a news story from a few years back about a woman and her therapist, who ran off together. It had made the headlines, because at first, the woman had been reported missing and when she hadn't been found after a few days, the media focus was that she had possibly been murdered. I can't remember why that changed, if she herself had come forward to say she had run off with her therapist or if someone had seen them together.

I find my laptop, open my search engine and type in "woman and therapist." There are several links to news articles, from June 2016. I click on one; it's more or less as I remembered—a thirty-year-old solicitor, Justine Bartley, left her office one lunchtime to go for an appointment with her therapist and never returned to work. She was reported missing the next day by her husband, after she failed to return home the previous evening. I trawl through other articles about the same story and discover why it had no longer become newsworthy. Justine's best friend told the police that Justine had fallen in love with her therapist and in the weeks leading up to her disappearance had become both excited and secretive. The friend also told the police that Justine had been experiencing problems in her marriage, hence the therapy sessions. Because no trace was found of her therapist—a Dr. Smith—her friend believed he and Justine had run off together, and the police seemed to agree that it was the likeliest possibility. I search for further news stories about the case, but like Justine Bartley, it never re-surfaced.

June 2016. Eighteen months before Marion Cartaux's murder in France. I don't get too excited. Apart from Justine Bartley having long blond hair, there is nothing to link her disappearance to the murders of Marion Cartaux and Nina, especially as nobody seems to think there was anything sinister in her having gone missing.

I carry on looking into Justine Bartley's disappearance anyway, watching videos of news bulletins and interviews. She was last seen turning into a street in Hampstead. Her phone had been turned off not long after.

I call Thomas.

"Did you know that Nina saw a therapist?" I ask.

"No, but I think it's quite usual for therapists to be in therapy."

"It's just that when Tamsin told me that Nina saw a therapist, I presumed the therapist was a woman. But what if it was a man?"

"Um—what if it was?" Thomas sounds puzzled.

"Do you remember the case about three years ago, the solicitor who went missing, Justine Bartley?"

"Yes, I think so. Didn't she disappear after going for an appointment during her lunch hour? Ah, I see where you're going with this—her appointment was with her therapist. I'm not sure that there's a connection with Nina, though, because didn't the police come to the conclusion that they had run off together?"

"Yes, but what if they didn't? I've just read up on the case and apparently, the police couldn't find any trace of a therapist called Dr. Smith. What if that wasn't his real name? Maybe they didn't run off together, maybe he murdered her."

There's a pause, as if he's wondering how to tell me that I'm being ridiculous.

"If you're thinking that Dr. Smith might have been Nina's therapist, I think—again—that it's a long shot," he says diplomatically. "But you could always check with Tamsin, see if Nina ever mentioned the name of her therapist, that sort of thing."

"I'll try, but Tamsin isn't always very forthcoming about Nina. I don't know if it's relevant or not but Tamsin asked Nina to refer her to her therapist, and Nina never came back with a name."

"Maybe she didn't get around to it or maybe she felt uneasy about Tamsin seeing the same person as her. But it's good to keep it in mind. I'll call Helen and ask her if she knows anything about Nina seeing a therapist. If we don't come up with a name, I'll speak to my police contact."

"Great."

"Thanks, Alice, let's speak soon."

I hang up, realizing I've already hit a problem. I can't call Tamsin and start asking her about Nina's therapist. I need to be subtler than that, see her face to face, chat about other things first. It would also be easier if Eve were there. Except that it's Thursday, and Eve spends Thursdays with her mum. The thought of not being able to speak to Tamsin until tomorrow is frustrating—and that's presuming that both she and Eve are free to meet up.

I think for a moment, then message Eve, asking if she's free for lunch the next day as I feel like getting out and there's a brasserie I want to try near Finsbury Park. I've eaten there before, with Leo, but she doesn't have to know that. I also suggest that we ask Tamsin and Maria to join us, if they're free.

Her reply comes in ten minutes later—it's a brilliant idea, she's already checked with Tamsin and Maria, they can both come if we meet at one o'clock, as that's the time Maria has her lunch break. Relieved that they can make it, I message her back with details of the brasserie and tell her I'll make a reservation.

In the middle of the afternoon, there's a ring on the doorbell and I run down to answer it, thinking it's Thomas, because it's about the time he usually calls. Maybe he's had news about the murder in France. I check my hair quickly in the mirror and open the door.

But it isn't Thomas, it's a young man with sandy hair and a confident smile.

"Ms. Dawson?" he asks.

I look at him warily. "Yes."

"We haven't met before." He holds out his hand. "Ben, Ben Forbes. From Redwoods, the estate agents."

THIRTY-NINE

It takes me a moment to swallow the disappointment of him not being Thomas.

"Oh, hello," I say, shaking his hand. He's younger than I expected, early thirties, I'm guessing, and very good-looking. "Well, it's lovely to meet you, Ben."

"I was at a property here in The Circle, discussing a possible sale, and I thought I'd come by and introduce myself seeing as we only met over the phone."

"I should have called you back to apologize," I say, embarrassed that I hadn't. "It never occurred to me that Leo already knew about the murder."

"Please don't worry. I'm just glad it didn't put you off living here."

"It hasn't been easy," I admit. "And I won't be here much longer. Another week and I'll be going back to Harlestone. Leo is staying," I add, in case he thinks that the house is going to be back on the market.

"Right." He doesn't seem surprised and I wonder if he already knows from Mark that Leo and I are splitting up. He peers behind me into the hall. "Ginny told me you knocked two of the upstairs bedrooms into one. It must be amazing."

It's on the tip of my tongue to invite him in to see it. But something holds me back.

"Why don't you drop in next time you're in the area? I'm sure Leo will be happy to show you around."

"I'll do that, thanks. I'm sorry it didn't work out."

"Me too." I give him a smile. "How's the golf going? You can't believe how grateful Ginny is that you're getting Mark out of the house at weekends."

He laughs. "He's becoming very good. Well, I'd better get on. Perhaps I'll see you again, if ever you're at Ginny's."

"I'm sure I will be. Thank you for coming by. It was nice to meet you."

"Likewise."

He leaves with a wave and I watch as he crosses over the road and disappears into the square.

I take out my cell phone and text Ginny—I just had a visit from Ben.

She texts back—Lucky you! How come?

He was in the area and wanted to introduce himself.

That was nice of him. He's lovely, isn't he?

I want to tell her that he is, but not as nice as Thomas, and I feel guilty that I can't, guilty that I've never told her about him, because I usually tell her most things.

I go back to my study but I can't concentrate on work because Ben's visit is on my mind. Is it weird that he turned up? Ginny didn't think it was, she said it was nice of him to call. I need to stop being suspicious of everyone.

Even of Will, it seems, because at eight o'clock, he comes to the door with a set of keys dangling from his finger.

"Found them," he says, smiling happily.

"Great!" I say. "Where were they?"

"On the side, among Eve's clutter. They must have fallen off the hook and got buried before anyone noticed."

"It happens," I say, because it does. "Thanks, Will."

When evening comes, even though I no longer have to worry about a set of keys being in the wild, I move to the sitting room. I plan to spend the night watching television. If I feel tired, I can doze on the sofa.

I don't have the volume on the TV turned up loud but at around three in the morning, I find myself muting it. There was a noise, from the kitchen, I'm sure of it. My heart in my mouth, I get up from the sofa and look around the room. If someone has got into the house, I need to stop them getting in here. They'll have heard the television, they'll know where I am.

Moving quietly, I take a low table and put it tight up against the door, then fetch a couple of lamps and put them on top of the table. If someone opens the door, the table and lamps will go flying, buying me enough time to dial 999.

I wait five minutes, my body tense with nerves, my phone ready in my hand, then wait five minutes more and when I don't hear anything else, I try and relax. But I can't bring myself to go and check if there was anyone there. I don't feel like going back to the film I was watching so I curl up on the sofa and wonder if it really is worth staying another week. The reason I asked for two weeks was because I hoped Thomas would have made some progress by then. And because, if I'm honest, I didn't want to never see him again. But now that he's said he'll come and see me in Harlestone, I no longer have to worry. It's probably better that I go. I told Thomas that I want Nina's killer brought to justice, no matter who it is. But what if it does turn out to be someone from here, how will I feel then?

At six o'clock, I open the curtains and look outside. It's still dark but there are lights on in some of the houses, people getting ready to go about their everyday lives. That's what I want, I realize, an everyday life, not one with secrets and lies, fear and mistrust. I'm going back to Harlestone today.

The feeling of a huge weight being lifted off my shoulders is incredible. I go back to the sofa and sleep until my alarm rings at ten. The table and lamps are still in front of the door so I put them back where they're meant to be and head to the kitchen for coffee. Now that I've decided to leave, I need to pack, call Debbie, Leo, Ginny, and Thomas. I can tell Eve that I'm leaving when I see her at lunch. For the first time in a long time, I feel happy. I don't belong here.

As soon as I walk into the kitchen, I know that something

has changed. I come to a stop, the weirdest of sensations coursing through my body. I was right, someone has been here, I can feel it on my skin, taste it on my tongue. I walk further in and take a careful look around. I can't see anything but something is definitely different.

My eyes fall on the French windows that give onto the terrace. I go over and try the handle—they're still locked. I stoop to examine the lock; it doesn't look as if it's been tampered with, but when I think about it, it's logical that whoever is getting in is getting in this way, because of the mortice lock on the inside of the front door. Even with keys, nobody can get in if I've locked it from the inside. There have been times when I've forgotten to lock it. But not recently. Since Leo left, I've been obsessive about it.

I go to my study and find the keys that Will gave me last night. There are only the two keys for the front door. The smaller one that would open the French windows isn't there. Did Will remove it before he gave the keys back to me? Or was it never there?

I call Leo.

"Is everything all right?" he asks, as if he knows that it isn't. It puts me on my guard. Everything puts me on my guard. I'm suspicious of everyone and everything.

"Why shouldn't it be?"

"It's just that you seem a bit all over the place at the moment."

I bite back an angry retort. He's right, I am.

"The keys you gave Will—were they only for the front door or was there one for the French windows?" I ask.

"Um—only for the front door. There are only two keys for the French windows, the one we keep in the drawer in the kitchen and the spare in my study."

"Where in your study?" I ask, already checking the kitchen drawer to see if the key is there. It is.

"In my desk, top drawer on the right. Is there a problem?"

"If someone *is* getting into the house," I say, running up the stairs, "the only way they could get in would be through the French windows, as long as I've locked the front door from the inside." I get to his study and open the right-hand drawer. The spare key is there.

"Or through a window," he says.

"They'd make too much noise. Are you sure there aren't any more keys for the French windows?"

"Quite sure. Ben gave me all the keys he had."

"Ben?"

"From Redwoods."

"But you changed all the locks, so the keys he gave you wouldn't work anyway."

"I changed the locks on the front door, but not on the French windows. It didn't seem worth it."

Alarm bells clang in my head. "So," I say slowly. "How do you know that Ben didn't keep back a key for the French windows?"

"Why would he do that?"

"If the only logical way someone could get into the house is through the French windows, someone else must have a key, because the two that we know about are both here, I just checked."

"Don't tell me—you think Ben kept one back and has been breaking into the house." I can hear the resignation in his voice.

"Don't sound so skeptical. I'm only thinking that because he came here yesterday."

"What—Ben did?"

"Yes."

"Why?"

"He said he was in the area and wanted to introduce himself."

"Maybe he was just being nice."

"Or maybe he had an ulterior motive. He sort of hinted that he wanted to come in and see the work we had done upstairs."

"You didn't let him in, did you?"

"No, I told him to come back when you were here. It seemed a bit strange and then, last night, I was in the sitting room and I heard a noise in the kitchen. There's no sign of a break-in or anything and nothing is missing. But now I'm wondering—what if it was Ben?"

"That's a huge jump to make. I mean—what would his motive be, if nothing is missing?"

"Maybe he knew Nina—"

"No." Leo's voice is firm and for a moment I think he's telling me that he knows Ben didn't know Nina.

"But what if he sold Nina and Oliver the house?"

"Alice. This has got to stop."

"What?"

"Your obsession with this murder. It's bad enough that you've suspected me and almost every one of our neighbors of having been involved. But when you start accusing our estate agent, when you don't even know if he knew Nina—it can't go on."

"I'm not going to stop until I know who's been creeping around the house at night," I say fiercely. "Because somebody has."

"Then find proof. If you have proof, we can call the police. But we need proof. We can't just tell them that we *think* somebody has broken in, they'll laugh at us. So, until you find something missing, or something that isn't as it should be, we can't do anything." He pauses. "I'm going to come back, Alice. You shouldn't be there on your own."

"It's all right, I'm leaving. I'm going back to Harlestone."

"When?" His relief is evident.

"Today, at the end of the afternoon. I've got lunch with Eve, so I'll leave after. You can move back in tomorrow."

"I'm really sorry it's come to this," he says quietly.

My eyes fill with tears. "So am I."

FORTY

I find two suitcases in the garage and start filling them with the clothes I have in the study, then head upstairs, because I need some jeans and jumpers to get me through the next few weeks. My jumpers are still scattered on the floor from when I fell off the chair. It's bad enough that I accused Leo of leaving a ponytail of blond hair in the wardrobe, thank goodness I didn't accuse him of hiding inside it. But somebody did and they were here the day I saw the face at the window, I smelled their aftershave. I thought it was Leo's, because he has several different ones and I don't always recognize them.

The thought of someone being in the wardrobe, watching me, when I was looking for Leo behind the bathroom door, makes me feel sick with retrospective fright. And what about the day after our party, when Leo had thought there was someone in the bedroom? The next morning, I had found my shoes pushed to one side so had there been someone hiding in the wardrobe that night too?

"For God's sake, Alice, get a grip!" I say the words aloud, trying to make myself see sense. Nobody in their right mind would hide in a wardrobe if people are sleeping close by. The only thing I'm sure of is that someone has been coming to the house. What does he do when he's here, other than drape strands of hair for me to find? Are there other signs I've missed?

I sit down on the bed, remembering the things that have never quite added up, like the time I couldn't find my white sundress before it suddenly turned up, a couple of days later, smelling fresh and clean. But no one would sneak into a house, take a dress, wash it, and put it back in the wardrobe. Not unless they wanted to see how much they could get away with before anyone really noticed.

My mind continues its processing. I take out my phone, call Leo again. He'll be at work now but this is urgent.

"I know this is a really stupid question but after the party, did you wash my white sundress for me?"

"Er—no."

"And the cards we got from everyone, that I put on the mantelpiece in the sitting room. Did you put them lying flat, for a joke?"

"No."

"OK. So did you leave a white rose for me on the window sill by the front door?"

"When?"

"It doesn't matter when, I only want to know if it's something you've ever done."

"No."

"You've never left me a rose?"

"No."

"Great, thanks."

I hang up, think for a moment, then call him a third time.

"Sorry," I say, "I won't call you again, I promise."

"It's OK." He pauses. "Was I meant to have left you a rose?"

"No. I just wanted to thank you for the champagne you left for me in the fridge. I forget at the time."

"What champagne?"

"The Dom Pérignon."

"Dom Pérignon?"

"So it wasn't you?"

"No. Are you saying someone put a bottle of Dom Pérignon in our fridge?"

"It was probably there from when we had drinks," I say

hurriedly. "Somebody must have brought it along and stuck it in the fridge."

"A bottle like that would have jumped out at me," he says. "Alice, what's going on?"

"Just trying to work things out."

I hang up before he can ask any more questions.

I leave my clothes and run downstairs, wondering how many other calling cards I missed. I'm sure he left one for me last night in the kitchen. I stand in the middle of the floor and turn slowly on the spot, scanning the room, looking for something that shouldn't be there.

"Where are you?" I cry in frustration. I go back to where I was standing this morning, when I first sensed that something was different, just inside the door. This time, I keep perfectly still. Only my eyes are moving as I make a detailed, inch-by-inch search, letting them travel slowly over each of the worktops, then up and down the cupboards, back and forth along the shelves, along the rack where the saucepans hang, over the cooker, the ovens, the fridge. But I can't see anything out of place.

I send a text to Debbie to tell her I'll be arriving this evening. For a moment, I wonder whether to cancel lunch with Eve and the others and leave straightaway, but while half of my brain is telling me that I'm in danger, the other half is telling me that everything I'm imagining can't be true. Anyway, I don't want to leave without seeing Eve. I might not have known her for very long but I feel close to her in a way that I can't explain.

Debbie replies that she'll have a bottle of wine ready. I message Ginny and tell her that I've decided to go back to Harlestone today, and that we'll speak over the weekend. And then I call Thomas.

"Am I disturbing you?" I ask.

"It's fine, I can take a few minutes. Have you managed to find the name of Nina's therapist from Tamsin?"

"No, and I'm not sure it's even relevant. Sometimes I wonder if I haven't gone a bit mad. I mean, isn't it a little crazy to link a disappearance three years ago with Nina's murder, just because the word therapist came into it? Even the murder in France—it's ridiculous to think it's connected to Nina's, just because both women had their hair cut off. Leo told me I need to let go of my obsession with Nina's murder and I couldn't be angry with him because he's right, I am obsessed. I'm so obsessed that I've suspected everyone that I know of being involved, even though everyone tells me that Oliver killed her."

"I'm sorry," he says quietly. "You don't know how much I regret dragging you into my investigation—which, to be honest, I probably would have closed by now, despite Helen." He sighs. "You're not the only one questioning your motives."

"What do you mean?"

"Just that sometimes, I wonder if I've only been keeping it open so that I can carry on seeing you."

I feel a surge of happiness. "You can carry on seeing me anyway."

"But only because you're no longer with Leo. Until you made that decision, I only had the investigation as a reason to see you."

"Are you saying that you think Oliver murdered Nina?"

"No, I don't think he did. I think her killer is out there. But I don't think I'm ever going to find him. Too many people are lying, and untangling that web of lies is proving impossible. And if they're not lying, they're covering something up."

"Like a conspiracy, you mean?"

"Yes. And if several people in The Circle are all covering up for each other, the only way we'll ever be able to get to the truth is if someone breaks rank."

"It's just as well I didn't tell you my other theory," I say.

"Which is?"

"Do you really want to hear it?"

"I haven't given up totally yet."

"OK. It's that Ben is somehow involved."

"Ben? I haven't heard of a Ben. What number does he live at?"

"No, Ben from Redwoods. The estate agent who sold us the house."

"Wow," he says. "OK." There's a pause. "I'm not saying you're wrong," he adds hastily, "I'm just wondering how you got there."

"You know I think that someone has been getting into the house at night? Well, I think they've been getting in through the French windows at the back. Leo told me Will had keys to the house so I got them back from him and there were only two keys on the ring, both for the front door. I checked with Leo and he said Will never had a key to the French windows, that there were only two, and both were in the house. And both are in the house, I checked. It means that if someone is getting in through the French windows, there must be another key."

"And you think Ben has it?"

"Only because he would have had keys to the house so that he could show people round and the only lock we haven't changed is the one on the French windows. And because yesterday, he turned up here."

"What—he came to the house?"

"Yes."

"Did he say why?"

"He said he'd been at a property here in The Circle, discussing a possible sale, and wanted to introduce himself. But he also hinted that he was interested in seeing the work we had done upstairs."

"Did you let him in?" He can't quite hide the worry in his voice.

"No."

"Thank God. Do you know his surname?"

"No, he mentioned it but I can't remember."

"It doesn't matter, I can look it up on the website. Redwoods, you said? Hold on a sec—here he is, Ben Forbes. Do you know when Nina and Oliver moved into the house?"

"No, why?"

"Because maybe it was Ben Forbes who sold it to them."

My heart starts beating faster; he's had the same thought as me. "Do you think there could be a connection?"

"That's what I'm going to find out. I'm willing to look into anything just to be able to tell Helen I've left no stone unturned. I want this over and done with, Alice."

"Me too," I say. "Which is why I'm going back to Harlestone

today. I'm too worried to stay in the house now, anyway. But don't worry, I'll come back next Wednesday to meet Helen."

"And to have lunch with me," he says.

"That too," I say, smiling. "I need to go, Thomas, I'm having lunch with Eve, Tamsin, and Maria, although I'm not sure there's any point trying to find out who Nina's therapist was."

"See how you feel. What time do you think you'll be back?"

"By four, I should think."

"Then maybe I could come and say goodbye. Next Wednesday seems a long way off."

"I'd like that," I tell him.

"Good." His voice is warm. "I'll see you about four, then."

FORTY-ONE

On the way to the brasserie, my cell phone rings. It's Ginny.

"What did you say to Leo?"

"About what?"

"The murder."

"Um—" I don't know what to say in case Leo told her what I said about Ben. And she and Mark both really like Ben.

"I'm only asking because he's spent the whole morning reading articles about it online."

"Didn't he go to work?"

"No. He said you were still convinced there'd been a miscarriage of justice and that it wasn't like you to take on a cause for no reason at all. He was trying to find the article you read that made you decide the husband wasn't guilty. And now he's trying to speak to Ben, I'm not quite sure why. Something about wanting to know if he sold the Maxwells the house."

I feel a twinge of alarm. I'm touched that Leo wants to help but I feel bad that he's wasting his time looking for an article that doesn't exist. And what if Ben is involved in Nina's murder, and Leo's questioning spooks him?

"I think he just wants to know when the Maxwells moved to The Circle," I tell Ginny.

"That's all right, then."

"I'm sorry, I have to go. Lunch date with Eve, Tamsin, and Maria."

"Good luck," she says.

"I need to tell them I'm leaving. I'm sure Tamsin will be relieved." She laughs and hangs up.

They're waiting for me when I arrive at the brasserie, seated at a round table. They've left me the place opposite Tamsin, so I give each of them a quick hug and sit down between Eve and Maria.

"Sorry I'm late," I say, while Maria pours me a glass of wine. "I was busy packing."

"I thought your friend was coming to stay?"

"No, I've decided to go to hers instead. But not just for the weekend. I've decided to go back to Harlestone for good."

Eve pauses, her glass halfway to her lips. "Really?"

"Yes."

She puts her glass back on the table. "Oh."

"What about Leo?" Maria asks.

"He's staying here."

She puts her hand on mine. "I'm so sorry, Alice."

"Me too." Eve looks as if she's about to cry.

"Don't worry," I say, leaning into her. "I'll come back and see you."

"But you won't be next door," she says mournfully.

"I'm going to miss you all. You've been so welcoming." I pick up my glass. "Come on, let's drink to our continuing friendship."

Maria passes me a menu and we choose our meals. Eve asks me if I'm going to be able to get my house back in Harlestone and I tell her that I'll be staying with Debbie until I can sort something out.

"Is there any chance of you and Leo getting back together?" Tamsin asks.

"No," I say, reaching for my glass. "I don't think so."

"Because he didn't tell you about the murder?"

"It's not always black and white," I tell her. "Just like the murder."

She groans. "You're not going to start going on about that again, are you?"

"I just want to know one thing," I say quickly, "and then I won't ask you anything else."

"What?" she asks warily.

"You said Nina saw a therapist. Male or female?"

"Male."

"Did she ever mention his name?"

She arches an eyebrow. "That's two questions. No, I did ask her for it, but as I told you, she didn't give it to me."

"Do you know where his practice was? Was it local?"

"It doesn't matter where it was because he came to her," Eve intervenes before Tamsin can tell me I've run out of questions. "That's why she stopped coming to yoga with us. It clashed with her therapy sessions."

"Yes, but she only arranged to have her sessions on a Wednesday afternoon so that she would have an excuse not to see me," Tamsin points out.

I frown, remembering that Nina had started avoiding her about four months before she died.

"So the therapy sessions were a new thing?"

"Yes."

"And he came to see her at the house? Is that usual?"

"I know it's not the same, because I'm a speech therapist," Maria says. "But I wouldn't normally go to a client's house unless they can't get to me for some medical reason."

"I don't suppose Tim would know the name of Nina's therapist," I say, turning to her. "I know he decided to specialize in psychotherapy largely because of Nina. Maybe she mentioned a name to him?"

"I can certainly ask him. But why do you want to know? If you're leaving, wouldn't you rather see a therapist nearer to where you'll be living?"

"It's not for me," I say. And then I stop, because I don't know what reason I can give for wanting to know the name of Nina's therapist.

But it's too late. "Don't tell me—you think her therapist murdered her," Tamsin drawls, an amused look on her face.

"No, but I don't believe Oliver did. And neither do you," I add, infuriated that she's laughing at me.

"I've never said that."

"Yes, you did! The day you invited me for coffee, I overheard you talking to Eve and you said that you had never believed that Oliver killed Nina."

Her green eyes flash with annoyance. "I guessed you were there, listening in the porch, but it's good to have it confirmed that as well as everything else, you're also an eavesdropper." She glares at me across the table. "I'm glad you're going. We'll be able to get on with our lives now."

"Tam." Maria puts a hand on her arm.

"So you don't mind that Nina's killer hasn't been caught?" I say angrily. "You know it wasn't Oliver but you prefer to sit there and do nothing, say nothing?"

Tamsin flushes. "Well, you've certainly done plenty. We were all happy before you came along and decided to stick your nose into something that had absolutely nothing to do with you. You didn't even know Nina, or Oliver, so why the hell did you get involved?" She looks appraisingly at me. "Shall I tell you what we all think?"

"No, Tam," Eve pleads. But Tamsin is too far gone to listen.

"You're a fantasist, Alice. You invent a whole load of crap and then you start to believe it. We knew it the moment you pretended that a man had turned up at your drinks evening, a man that nobody saw except you, a man that nobody spoke to except you. That's why we didn't care whether or not you found out who he was. We knew he was just something you made up to make you appear more interesting than you actually are." She gives a snort of disgust. "You even admitted to Will that that's what you do."

"I didn't make him up!" I say furiously.

She looks at me pityingly. "We know, Alice. We know that at one time or another you've suspected us or our husbands of killing Nina, we can see right through your invitations to lunch and dinner, right through the questions you ask, right through the lies you tell. You're dangerous. You need to get a life, before you destroy everyone else's."

I wait for Eve or Maria to come to my rescue. But Eve, who would normally do her best to smooth things over, doesn't say anything.

The silence becomes unbearable. Tamsin pushes her chair back. "I've just remembered I need to be somewhere," she says, her voice tight.

I push my chair back too. "No, you can stay, I'm going." I grab my bag from under the table. "If you must know, the reason I got involved was for Oliver's sister. I was doing it for her. But as nobody else seems to care—not even you, Nina's best friends—well, why should I?" I start to move away and then stop. "And by the way, I didn't make the man up, the one who came to the party. Lorna admitted to letting him in, remember?"

I manage to hold on to my tears until I get to the street outside. Then I dissolve. I walk quickly to Finsbury Park, my head down, my scarf pulled up around my ears, and crumple onto the first bench I find. Is that what I am, a fantasist? When I look at all the things I've allowed myself to believe over the last few weeks, I'm ashamed. Tamsin's right, at one time or another I've suspected all of them of being involved in Nina's murder.

My cheeks burn when I think of them laughing at me behind my back. What Tamsin said about me getting a life—it hurt more than anything because she was right about that too. I haven't really had a life since my parents and sister died. It's why I launched myself so fervently into helping Thomas and Helen. I needed something in my life, something to make me feel alive, make me feel that I was doing some good because most of the time, I just exist. But I've taken it too far. When I think of Leo and Thomas, both of whom are trying, at this very moment, to find out if Ben had something to do with Nina's murder, I'm scared. I need to tell them to stop.

I get a grip by thinking about Nina—my sister, not Nina Maxwell. I can almost hear her telling me to stop feeling sorry for myself, to accept that I had a kind of brain-storm, and move on. She's right, I need to move on. By the time I get home, it will be almost three o'clock. I'll just have time to throw the rest of my stuff into a case before Thomas arrives. In a couple of hours, I'll be on my way to Harlestone, and Nina Maxwell and my time in The Circle will just be a memory.

FORTY-TWO

I start walking back to the house, part of me wanting to blame Leo for what happened at the brasserie. If he had been upfront with me about the murder, I would never have come here. The only good thing to have come out of my time in The Circle is Thomas—if our friendship manages to survive when there isn't the investigation to bind us together. It worries me that it might not.

My phone rings. I take it from my bag, hoping it will be Thomas. It is. I stop walking and move to the side.

"Alice. Am I disturbing your lunch?"

"No, I'm on my way back to the house." I press a finger to my other ear, shutting out the noise so that I can hear him better.

"Good. Would you believe that one of your neighbors was in Paris at the time of Marion Cartaux's murder?"

My heart plummets. "I'm not sure I want to know who."

"Don't worry too much, because her murderer is behind bars, awaiting trial. He gave himself up a few months ago."

"Oh. Well, that's good, isn't it?"

"Normally, I'd say yes. But not everyone thinks that he did it. He's an SDF—a homeless person—who had been out of prison for a year at the time of the murder. Unfortunately, there are more cases than the judiciary would like of homeless people pleading guilty to just about anything so that they can get back inside. Being on the streets is far more frightening to them than being in prison."

"But he might have done it."

"We'll only be sure after his trial, once his account of events has been verified."

"So, which of my neighbors was in Paris at the time of the murder?" I ask.

"William Jackman."

I close my eyes. "I wish I hadn't discovered that gap in the fence between our gardens."

"It doesn't mean anything yet. I thought I'd let you know, that's all. Did you manage to get the name of Nina's therapist?"

"No, but it was a man. And she didn't go to him, he came to see her. That's not very usual, is it?"

"No, it isn't. But without a name, there's not much we can do." There's a pause. "Are you all right? You sound a bit down."

"Let's just say lunch didn't go according to plan. I'm glad I'm leaving today. It's the right decision."

"Would you rather I didn't come over? You must have a lot to do before you leave."

"I just need to throw some clothes into a case. I'll come and get the rest of my stuff another time. So please do come over. It will be nice to see you."

"If you're sure."

"I am."

"I'll see you in around an hour, then."

I've barely hung up when my phone starts ringing again. It's Tamsin. I give an angry laugh and let it ring out. It's taken Eve and Maria thirty minutes to persuade her to call and apologize, because I'm sure that's why she called. The phone starts ringing again, another call from Tamsin. I let it ring out again and a minute or so later, I get a message telling me I have a voicemail. I'm in no mood to listen to it, nor to the next voicemail she leaves me.

Five minutes later, it's Eve who calls. I'm still sore that she didn't say a word to defend me so I don't answer her either. I know I'm being unfair; she and Tamsin have been friends for years, it's normal she would take Tamsin's side. But I don't want to speak to her, especially now that I know Will was in Paris at the time of Marion Cartaux's murder. Thomas said it probably doesn't mean anything. But still.

I reach The Circle and trudge across the square to the house. School has finished for the day, so there are quite a few people heading toward the play area. Although there's a chill in the air, the sun is out and despite everything, I smile to see children clambering over the wooden climbing frames. The rest of the square is deserted. As I go through the gate opposite the house, I see Edward going into his garage and give him a wave. My eyes are drawn involuntarily to Maria and Tim's house; once again, Tim is standing at the upstairs window. He gives me a wave and I wave back. It's funny that he doesn't try and hide the fact that he's watching the square. Most people, even though they're doing nothing wrong, would jump back guiltily, or at least turn away once they've waved. But he just carries on watching.

I gather my things together and put my case and handbag by the front door, ready to leave once I've seen Thomas. There's a ring on the doorbell. I look up sharply; it's too early for it to be him. What if it's Eve? If it is, I won't let her in. I can't, not with Thomas due to arrive.

I latch the chain before opening the door.

"Oh, hi," I say, unsettled to see Tim standing there. He's dressed in his usual jeans and rugby shirt and I find myself wondering if he's ever played rugby.

"Hi, Alice, I thought I'd come over and see you myself," he says, giving me a smile. "Maria called to ask if I knew the name of Nina's therapist, she said you were asking about him?"

"Yes, but it doesn't really matter."

He looks relieved. "Oh good, because Nina never mentioned it to me." He pauses. "Maria said you're leaving?"

"That's right, I am. Which is why I don't have time to invite you in," I add, in case he's wondering why I'm speaking to him through the chain on the door. "I need to finish packing."

He takes a step away from the door. "No worries, I need to get on myself. I'm sorry it didn't work out, Alice. Hopefully we'll see each other again."

"Thanks, Tim," I say. "I'm sure we will."

I close the door behind him and go to the kitchen. I lean against the worktop, thinking about Nina helping Tim with his psychotherapy studies. I had presumed she helped him study for exams, looked over his essays, that sort of thing. But what if it was more hands-on? What if the help she gave him was based on role-play, where she took the role of a client and Tim took the role of the therapist?

I push away from the worktop, feeling as if I'm on the brink of something. Could it be Tim who Nina saw on Wednesday afternoons, when Maria went to yoga with Eve and Tamsin, then on to pick up the children up from school? It would explain why she wouldn't give Tamsin the name of her therapist, if it was Tim she was seeing.

I stop, disgusted with myself. Tamsin is right, I am a fantasist. But not a total one. I know, one hundred percent, that someone has been getting into the house.

I go to the fridge to get some juice. As I close the door, my eyes, already looking toward my glass, swivel back to the fridge, caught by something that shouldn't be there. They come to rest on a small, passport-sized photo stuck in the middle of all the other photos, and my heart doesn't just miss a beat, it stops. For a moment, I can't breathe. I know who it is in the photo, I just don't want to believe it.

I run into the hall and take my cell phone from my bag.

"Thomas, are you on your way?" I try to keep my voice calm but I can't.

"Yes, I'm not far. Why, what's happened?"

"I just found a photo of Nina on the fridge."

"Nina?"

"Yes, Nina Maxwell. I knew this morning that someone had been in the kitchen but I couldn't see anything different, I could sense it but I couldn't see it, I was too far away," I say, my voice high with panic. "But just now, I was right up close to the fridge and there it was, stuck among the other photos. I don't know what to do," I add breathlessly.

"Have you touched it?"

"No."

"Then don't. I was just speaking to my contact in the police about Ben Forbes. You're not going to believe what we discovered. We were right, there is a conspiracy."

"What do you mean?"

"It seems that not only did Ben Forbes sell the Maxwells their house, he's also a friend of Tim Conway."

I freeze. "He just came here," I say.

"What? Tim Conway did? Why?"

"Because I asked Maria to ask Tim if he knew the name of Nina's therapist and he came to tell me that he didn't. But I've been thinking—what if he was the therapist that she was seeing? Her sessions were on Wednesday afternoons, Maria is at yoga on Wednesday afternoons. And Nina used to go to yoga, but she stopped four months before she died." I can hardly catch my breath.

Thomas's voice is calm but urgent. "Alice, I'm going to hang up now. The police might arrive before me but I'll be there as soon as I can. Until then, if anyone comes to the door, don't let them in."

FORTY-THREE

My mind spinning, I lock the front door from the inside, check that the chain is in place and hurry upstairs to Leo's study to wait for Thomas. I'm trembling, shaken by the knowledge that Tim has been the one coming to the house at night. Everything points to it, including the way he was so at home in my kitchen the day he came to supper. He must have got a key to the French windows from Ben, then used the gap in the fence between ours and Edward's to get into our garden—maybe there's even a gap in the fence between his garden and Geoff's to make things even easier.

The questions keep coming. Was Ben also involved? If Tim murdered Nina, was Ben his accomplice? And how much does Maria know? Is she completely innocent, or is she part of a conspiracy that includes Eve and Tamsin, even Will and Connor? Unless Ben murdered Nina. Maybe he became obsessed with her when he sold her and Oliver the house, and they had an affair. Did he kill Nina and then tell Tim what he had done? Is that when the cover-up started? Or has everyone been in it together from the start, wanting Nina killed for reasons of their own and setting up Oliver to take the blame?

The thought that I might have been manipulated left, right, and center by the people I thought were my friends is overwhelming. Lorna tried to warn me, she had told me not to trust anyone. But I had plowed ahead, unwilling to believe that people would lie to me. I should have listened to Edward too; instead of telling nobody I was leaving, I ended up telling everyone.

The sense of impending danger is incredible. I keep my eyes on the gate at the other end of the square, knowing I'll only be able to relax when I can actually see Thomas. I feel a momentary anxiety. Maria will have gone back to work but what if Eve and Tamsin see Thomas as they walk back across the square from the restaurant? I imagine the two of them nudging each other when they see the tall, good-looking stranger striding along. Will they watch to see where he goes? What if they see him come to the house?

It doesn't matter if they do, I realize. I don't have to explain anything to them, I'm not even going to be here. I won't have to admit that he's the man who turned up at the party, I won't have to tell them that I kept him a secret because I've been helping him investigate Nina's murder—a murder which has now been solved. I think of Helen, how thrilled she's going to be that at last, she'll have justice for her brother.

And then I see them, Eve and Tamsin, coming into the square. I wait for them to turn toward Tamsin's house but they stop in the middle of the path. *Move!* I urge them. *Go!* They're huddled together, deep in conversation but that won't stop them seeing Thomas. He's not the sort of man to go unnoticed.

Except—he has. Not just at the party but also all the other times he's visited me. There must have been people around as he walked across the square on his way over, or on his way back, but no one ever mentioned seeing a tall, dark-haired stranger, despite everyone knowing that I was trying to trace a man who fitted that description. Because nobody really believed he existed.

Tamsin rummages in her bag for something. She begins to move toward her house, Eve following behind. I breathe a sigh of relief but at that moment, Tamsin turns and looks toward the house, her cell phone clamped to her ear. I move from the window, hoping she hasn't seen me. My cell phone, which I've got in my hand, starts ringing, making me jump. It's her.

A ring on the doorbell sets my heart racing. Thomas told me not to open the door to anyone. It might be the police; he said he was going to call them. Maybe they've come in an unmarked car. I push my cell phone into my pocket and run downstairs.

"Alice, it's me." Thomas's voice comes through the door.

I open it quickly, blinking back the tears that have sprung to my eyes.

"It's all right," he says, catching sight of my face. He lays a steadying hand on my arm. "I'm here now."

"I watched for you coming across the square but I didn't see you."

"I walked around the outside, I always do. I don't like to draw attention to myself. Is that your phone ringing?"

"Yes, but it's only Tamsin."

"Are you sure? It might be the police. I gave them your number."

"Yes, look." I show him my phone.

"Don't you want to answer it?"

"No, it's fine." We move to the kitchen. "We had a row over lunch. I told you, she hates me asking questions about Nina." I point to the fridge. "There's the photo."

He peers at it. "I wonder why he put it here?"

"It's a calling card," I explain. "I realized this morning that there were other things I missed, things that I put down to Leo, like a rose on the window sill, a bottle of champagne in the fridge, a photo turned upside down. Each time, he does something—there must be other things I missed. It's like a game. He's been playing with me." I look up at him. "What did the police say when you told them about the photo and Tim's connection to Nina?"

"I left everything with my contact there and he went to speak to his superiors. I'm surprised they're not already here."

"Let's have coffee while we're waiting." My phone starts ringing again and I groan. "Tamsin again. Maybe I should just answer it, get it over and done with?"

"You may as well. But don't take any stick from her. I'll make the coffee."

"Thanks." I take the call, loving that he feels comfortable enough to take over.

"Alice, don't hang up!" Tamsin's voice comes urgently down the line. I don't say anything, just wait for her to continue. "You said you were doing this for Oliver's sister."

"That's right," I say, hoping she feels guilty.

"Oliver didn't have a sister."

I laugh. "Nice try." Thomas turns from the sink and gives me a smile, pleased to hear me stand up for myself.

"Look, I knew Nina and Oliver really well and he told me he was an only child," Tamsin says. "Nina also mentioned it, his lack of a family, because his mother died when he was young and his father lived abroad."

"Don't call me again, Tamsin."

"Wait, there's something else! The man that you said turned up at your party?" My heart sinks. She and Eve must have seen Thomas walking around the outside of the square. "If it's true that Lorna let him in," Tamsin goes on, "if he did exist, why did you never think that he might be Nina's killer? Shouldn't he have been the first person you thought of, instead of suspecting us? Because why would he have turned up at your housewarming, otherwise?"

For one terrible moment, the world stops moving.

"Alice?" Tamsin's voice comes down the line. "Are you there?"

Thomas looks over at me, gives me a smile. It jolts me back to reality.

"As I said, don't call me again," I say, cutting the call.

I put my phone in my pocket, wishing I could have told her that Thomas is a private investigator looking into Nina's murder and that he's found her killer.

"I take it her apology wasn't good enough?" Thomas says.

I shake my head. "No, it wasn't."

"I don't suppose you managed to find out anything about her therapist?"

"Only what I told you. But he's hardly relevant now, as Tim is the culprit." I smile at him and he smiles back but Tamsin's words won't stop crashing through my brain. *Oliver didn't have a sister.*

I take out my phone. "I need to tell Leo what time I'm leaving so that he can move back in, he's been hassling me to let him know. I was going to leave in about an hour but maybe I should wait, in case the police come."

"Why don't you tell him you can't give him a time, so he'll have to wait until tomorrow?"

"Good idea," I say, already texting Leo.

Can you find out if Oliver had a sister? It's urgent, really urgent.

He texts back almost immediately. **You told me he did. And how am I meant to find out?**

"I knew he'd moan," I say with a rueful smile. "He's not happy about having to wait until tomorrow."

"Tell him he doesn't have a choice."

"All right."

I don't know! I text back. **Just find out. Please!**

I'll do my best. Btw, I spoke to Ben. He didn't know the Maxwells. He's only been with Redwoods two years. Ours was the first house he sold in The Circle.

My heart begins a slow, dull thud in my chest. I look over at Thomas, Tamsin's voice echoing through my brain.

Why did you never think that he might be Nina's killer?

"What did Leo say?" Thomas asks.

"That I win," I say, putting my phone face down on the table so that he won't be able to see what Leo says when he texts me back about Oliver having a sister. "He'll wait until tomorrow."

"Good."

He finishes making the coffee and brings it over to where I'm sitting.

"Did you tell Helen that I'm looking forward to meeting her on Wednesday?" I ask.

"I did, and she said to tell you that she's looking forward to it too." He pulls out the chair opposite me. "I've been thinking—I know it might seem a bit—well, early—but I'd love you to meet my parents at some point. And Louis."

"I'd like that," I say, lifting my cup to my lips. I try and sort through the thoughts careering through my mind, colliding with each other, canceling each other out. Thomas had shown me a photo of him and Helen at university together. No, he had shown me a photo of him with a young woman.

"It will be great if you can tell Helen you've found the person responsible for Nina's murder. If it does turn out to be Tim," I say.

"I'm a hundred percent sure that it's him."

"What would his motive have been?" I raise my eyes to his face, a face I've come to know well, the green specks in his eyes, the way his hair falls onto his forehead. He looks too kind, he has a son, he has parents, he wants me to meet them. He can't have murdered Nina, it's not possible, how would he have even known her? Unless she hired him to investigate Oliver. Or Oliver hired him to investigate Nina, because he suspected her of having an affair. The one thing I do know is that Thomas Grainger is a private investigator, because I checked out the address he gave me. Unless he lied, like Leo did. Maybe his name isn't Thomas Grainger. Maybe he's not a private investigator. Maybe he doesn't have a son, or parents.

"Who knows?" he says. "Maybe he fell in love with Nina when she and Oliver moved in here. Maybe they had an affair, and when she tried to end it, he killed her."

Is that what happened, I wonder? Is that his story? Did Thomas, if that is his name, have an affair with Nina? If he did, when and how? How come nobody saw a stranger, coming regularly to the house? But then, Thomas has been visiting me once a week for the last five weeks and nobody saw him coming to the house on any of those occasions, not even Eve, and she lives next door. And I realize—she wouldn't have seen him because, apart from today, Thomas always comes to see me on Wednesday afternoons, when Eve goes to yoga with Tamsin and Maria. Nina used to go with them but she stopped, because on Wednesdays, she saw her therapist.

And that's when I know.

He is the therapist.

PAST

I know as soon as I arrive that something has changed. The smile she gives me isn't as wide as it usually is, and doesn't quite reach her eyes.

"Is everything all right?" I ask, once we're both sitting down.

"Not really."

"Oh?"

"Much as I've enjoyed our sessions, I'm afraid I'm not going to be able to continue with them," she says.

I can't believe it's happening again. Just when I think I've got them, they slip away. I don't understand; I've always taken such care in choosing my victims, watching them for months, waiting for the right moment to insinuate myself into their lives. Because of the circumstances I found myself in, this one was always going to be more problematic. But I can't believe I've got her wrong too.

"May I ask why?"

"Because you're not a therapist," she says. "You may have studied psychology, but you're not a psychotherapist."

I sit back in my chair. "What makes you say that?"

"You ask too many questions."

"If I've asked questions, it's because I'm trying to get to the bottom of your dissatisfaction with life."

"That's the other thing that gave you away—your insistence that I'm unhappy. At first, I thought it was part of our therapist-client training, but I've come to realize that you're working to your own agenda. Which is dangerous." She leans forward, fixing me with her eyes. "It's also intriguing. In fact, I think what we should be exploring is why you want me to think I'm unhappily married."

"I've observed you, Nina. For months."

"I think, if you look back on our sessions, I've never given the slightest indication that I have anything but a happy life."

"Before that," I say. "Before our sessions even started, I observed you."

She frowns. "What do you mean, observed me? When?"

"If you're so happy with your life and your husband," I say, ignoring her question. "How do you explain the string of men that come to your house when he's away?"

She bursts out laughing. "I hope you also observed the string of women who come to the house. Really, is that the best you can do?" She gives me an amused smile. "Shall I let you into a secret? I've known from our third session that you're not what you say you are and the only reason I continued to see you is because you make a great case-study. If I'm stopping these sessions now, it's because I've come to the conclusion that you have a personality disorder that I don't have the expertise, or the wish, to explore any further. At best, you're manipulative, at worst—well, I'd say you have psychopathic tendencies. It's why I never gave Tamsin your number, because you could have done her untold damage and she has enough problems as it is." She stands up. "I'd like you to leave. But you should know I'll be reporting you to the relevant bodies so that you'll be banned from working as a therapist, if you ever decide to set up a practice somewhere."

Another one who thinks she can reject me, who wastes my time, who leads me on, fiddling with her hair during our sessions, teasing me.

I get to my feet and leave without a fuss.

"Don't come back," she says.

"I won't."

But, of course, I do go back. I go back that evening and ask her for the book that I lent her, which I know she keeps in the bedroom, because I've seen it there during my night-time visits.

She goes to get it and I follow her silently up the stairs.

The book is **Walden,** the author Henry David Thoreau.

One way or another, Thoreau always works.

FORTY-FOUR

Thomas smiles at me. I put my cup down, smile back at him.

"I'm just going to get a sweater," I say, pushing my chair back. "It's turned a bit chilly."

"Can I get it for you?"

"No, it's fine, there's one in my case. It's in the hall."

I go out to the hall and open my case, tugging the zips hard so he'll be able to hear. Then I crouch down, find my house keys in my bag and slip them into my pocket.

"Do you need help?"

I look up and see him filling the doorway.

"No, thank you." I put my hand into the case and tug out a pale blue sweater. "This will do."

My heart is thumping as I stand up. I shouldn't have bothered taking my keys, I should have got out of the house while I could. But I had wanted to lock the door behind me, lock him in so that he couldn't come after me. With him standing there, it's too late. If I make for the front door, he'll know that I've guessed and will be on me before I've even opened it. I have no choice but to go back to the kitchen.

He sits down but I stay standing. I want to take my phone from where I left it on the table but it's too far away for me to reach. I pull the jumper over my head but it snags on the clip holding my hair up. I undo the clip and tug the jumper down. My hair gets stuck so I reach up and pull it free. Something flickers in his eyes.

"You have beautiful hair," he murmurs.

I force the words out. "Thank you."

"By the way, you got a message from Leo."

I freeze. How does he know it's from Leo?

"It's all right," I say. "I'll look at it later."

"Aren't you going to sit down?"

"Yes, of course." I pull my chair further out.

"I can tell you what it says, if you like." The hairs on the back of my neck, and then on my arms, prickle with fear. I stay as I am, halfway between sitting and standing.

"It says," he goes on, looking me straight in the eyes. *"Oliver didn't have a sister."*

It happens so fast. He lunges toward me but I get there first, picking up my chair and hurling it across the table at him. Caught by surprise, he cries out. But I'm already gone. I get to the front door and as I open it, I hear him come into the hall. Slamming the door shut behind me, I take the keys from my pocket, almost dropping them in my panic, and lock him in. I expect him to start hammering on the door, and when he doesn't I realize he's gone to look for another way out. The key to the French windows is in the kitchen drawer, it'll take him a while to find it.

I start running down the drive then stop, my eyes darting. I don't know where to go. I was going to go into the square, get help from someone there but there's no one around. I don't have long. I need to find somewhere with a phone so that I can call the police. I look toward Eve's house then remember she's at Tamsin's. I run up the drive to Edward and Lorna's.

I press on the bell, over and over again.

"Lorna, Edward!" I call, hammering on the door. "It's Alice! Can you let me in? It's urgent!"

I hear them shuffling as they come into the hall. "Please hurry!" I urge. I don't want to alarm them but I need to get inside.

There's the sound of bolts being drawn back. The door swings open and I burst into the house, smashing it back against Edward. I barely give him a second glance, my eyes caught by Lorna standing further down the hallway, her face white with fright.

"Sorry, Lorna," I say. "It's urgent." I turn to Edward hurriedly. "Can I use—" The words die on my lips. Standing behind Edward, his hand gripping the back of Edward's neck, is Thomas.

The blood drains from my face as he pushes the door shut with his free hand. "How did you—?"

"Get here?" He sounds amused. "Out through your French windows and in through ours."

I stare at him in confusion. "Yours?"

"Yes." Now he laughs. "I did say I wanted you to meet my parents."

His *parents*. I look in shock at Edward, and my shock quickly turns to fright. His face is dangerously red and his eyes are slipping out of focus. Adrenaline surges; I need to get help. I take a step back, look toward the door. But I'm too late. Still holding Edward, Thomas reaches out with his other hand and grabs me by the throat.

He waits until fear registers in my eyes, then tightens his grip.

"You're hurting me," I gasp.

The last thing I hear is his laugh.

When I come back to consciousness, I find myself tied to a chair. My instinct is to struggle free but I sense someone behind me and everything comes rushing back. Survival mode kicks in. *Don't let him know you're awake.* My mouth is dry; I swallow carefully, quietly, and have to stop myself crying out from the pain in my throat.

I try and regroup my thoughts but it's difficult when battling fear is my primary concern. Fear for Lorna and Edward—where are they? Fear that I might not get out of this alive.

Did he say Lorna and Edward were his parents? In a way, it makes sense. He must be the son they said died four years ago, in Iraq. What had he done to make them deny the existence of their only child? Justine Bartley had disappeared three years ago after going to meet her therapist. If Thomas was Nina's therapist, was he also Justine Bartley's therapist?

I inadvertently swallow and, unprepared for the pain, a groan escapes my lips. A hand winds itself in my hair and my head is pulled back, stretching my neck, making the fire in my throat worse. I close my eyes. I don't want to see his face.

"Awake, are we? Good!"

"Stop, John, please!" I recognize Lorna's voice and open my eyes, moving them in her direction. I can just about see her, crouching down beside Edward, slumped against the wall. "Your father needs an ambulance. It's his heart."

"Be quiet!" Thomas snaps. I'd thought at first that Lorna was speaking to someone else. But of course, Thomas isn't his real name.

He tugs my head back further, causing my swollen throat more injury. The pain is excruciating but I refuse to let him see how much it hurts.

He bends over me, bringing his face close, so that I'm looking right into his eyes, upside down.

"Guess what's going to happen now?" he says.

You're going to kill me.

I hear a noise, a noise I recognize as a pair of scissors being sliced open and closed. Lifting his arm, he brings them into view and I remember what happened to Nina.

"You're going to cut my hair." It comes out in a hoarse whisper.

"That's right." He moves his hands to either side of my head and pushes it forward, so that I'm looking straight ahead. At first, I think there's another woman in the room with us, until I realize it's my own reflection staring back at me from a gold-framed mirror, speckled with age, set up on a table in front of me.

I quickly work out that the room I'm in corresponds to my study in our house next door. The two windows have been boarded up; the only light comes from two ornate lamps, placed on either side of the mirror. As I watch, he takes hold of my hair, lifts it high above my head and slowly, gradually, lets it fall around my shoulders. I watch him in the mirror and shudder at what I see. He looks so different to the man I knew—or thought I knew—that it's like looking at someone else. Somehow, it makes it easier.

He separates a length of my hair, about an inch thick, from the rest and, like before, holds it high above my head. Opening the blades of the scissors around it, he moves them downward, stopping now and then as if deciding where to cut it.

"Here, or here?" he muses. Our eyes meet in the mirror. He waits for a reaction so I stare back, not giving him one. With a sudden movement, he moves the scissors down to within an inch of my skull and saws through the length of hair. I don't move, I don't flinch, not even when he drops it onto my lap. I'm too worried about Edward to think about what Thomas is doing. I can't see him at all now, I can only see the top of Lorna's head as she crouches beside him. It comes back to me then, how Lorna and Edward had wanted to move away after Nina's murder but Edward had had a heart attack. Was it from the shock of knowing that his son was a murderer? Had Thomas been staying here at the time? Or maybe all the time. Maybe he has been living here, in this house, in secret. It would explain why I hadn't seen him walking across the square earlier, why nobody has ever seen him walking across the square, not even on his visits to Nina. Because all that time, he had been living right next door.

"Why did you kill Nina?" I ask.

"Why don't you tell me what you think?" he says. "I'd love to hear another of your theories."

"You killed her because you were having an affair with her and she wanted to break it off." He doesn't say anything. "What about Justine and Marion? Did you have an affair with them too?"

He grins. "I saw what you did there. But you're wrong. I didn't have an affair with them. Or with Nina."

"But you killed them."

"Correct."

"Why?"

"Because they didn't know their own minds. Not like you, Alice."

"What do you mean?"

He smiles, lifts another length of hair. "Where shall I cut this one?"

"Wherever you like." Again, he snips it near my skull and drops it onto my lap. I can't pretend I'm not distraught at the sight of uneven clumps of hair sprouting from my scalp, but I keep it to myself. "Are you really a therapist?"

"How can I be a therapist if I'm a private investigator? Oh, wait—maybe I'm not a private investigator." He waves the scissors around. "The trick is to be who people want me to be. A therapist worked well for the others. For you, I had to think of something else. You needed a savior, a redeemer. Someone you could help, so that you could atone for your sins." He looks triumphantly at my reflection in the mirror. "I'm right, aren't I, Alice? You were the one driving the car the night your parents and sister died."

I stare at him, not letting my gaze waver, not letting him know that he's right. He lifts another length of hair and I focus on the sound of the scissors sawing through it to stop the sounds that have haunted me for almost twenty years, that will haunt me for the rest of my life, the screech of brakes, the tearing of metal, the screams of pain and fear.

"It's a shame you decided to leave The Circle so abruptly," he continues. "It was fun listening to all your different theories about who killed Nina. I could barely keep up with your suspicions. A headless chicken came to mind. You suspected your friends, their husbands, the man you were meant to love, even the estate agent." The scissors slice through my hair again. "You're not a very nice person, Alice. You do realize that, don't you?"

"Compared to you, I'm an angel," I say scathingly, to hide the shame I feel at his words. "You used your knowledge to manipulate me into thinking everyone had something to hide. I suppose it was you who told Lorna to tell me not to trust anyone."

"No, foolishly, she did that of her own accord. But I overheard her and made sure she paid for it."

I give him a look of pure disgust. "Were you born evil or did you become evil?"

"Why don't you tell me what you think?"

I swivel my eyes to where Lorna is crouching. She looks terrified.

"I'm guessing a normal family background so it must be rejection by a woman, or women, that made you hate us so much." I pause. "It was the woman in the photograph you showed me, wasn't it, the one you told me was Helen? She had long hair—and I think she was blond." I curl my lips in a pitying smile. "Is that what happened—she rejected you and you couldn't cope? Are you really that pathetic?"

He laughs, a harsh, detached laugh. Why had I never heard him laugh like that?

I've needled him. Ramming the scissors into my hair, he begins making furious cuts close to my scalp, nicking my skin so that I can't help but flinch.

"Where did you get the key to our French windows?" I ask.

"It was on the set of keys that Nina and Oliver gave to my parents. I kept them, hoping they would come in useful." He sighs in pretend despair. "Leo really should have changed all the locks, not just those on the front door." Then he grins. "I love that you thought I was Nina when I visited you at night."

I hate that he heard me talking to her, hate that he has seen me in all my weaknesses.

"How pathetic of you to hide in the wardrobe," I sneer.

"John, I think he's dead." Lorna's trembling voice breaks through Thomas's amusement. The scissors stop moving. "I think your father's dead."

I watch in the mirror as he walks over to where Lorna is standing. He bends down, then straightens up, a look of confusion on his face, which he quickly hides.

"I think you might be right," he says, feigning nonchalance.

Lorna bursts into tears. "We need an ambulance," she sobs. "Please, John."

"Why, if he's dead?" His voice is harsh.

He comes back to where I'm sitting, powerless in the face of his suppressed anger at his father's death. I want to comfort Lorna, get her away from Thomas. But tied to a chair, I can't do either of those things. I can't do anything. For the first time, it hits me. I am going to die.

"They moved here to get away from me." He starts to chop at my hair again but his heart has gone out of it. He might have been prepared for my death, but not his father's. "They didn't tell me they were leaving Bournemouth. When I came back from Paris, after I killed Marion, I had to hire a private investigator to track them down—which is where I got my idea for you." He pauses, drops another length of hair onto my lap. "You came along at just the right time. My sights were set on Tamsin, I had her lined up, ready to go. I knew from Nina that she was looking for a therapist but she didn't want to share me with anyone." He laughs again. "I was her little secret, just like I was yours. I knew Tamsin would need a therapist even more once Nina had died, so it was perfect. But then she cut her hair."

"You came here, to The Circle, after killing Marion?" I say, backtracking, needing to keep the conversation going, because as long as we're talking, I'm alive.

"Yes. It was ironic, really. My parents chose London, thinking it would reduce them to needles in a haystack, plus a gated community, thinking they'd be able to keep me out. But it proved the perfect hiding place for me."

"He wouldn't let us go anywhere, he kept us prisoner," Lorna says, her voice stronger now. She moves nearer, coming into my vision. "He locked us in here during the day, in our bedroom at night. There wasn't anything we could do, he was too strong for us. We were only allowed to put the bins out, or do a bit of gardening at the front of the house, so that people would see us from time to time and not worry about us. But never together, he always kept one of us hostage. When Edward went to hospital with his heart attack, John told him he would kill me if he said anything to the doctors. He wouldn't let me visit Edward, I had to pretend to the hospital that I was too frail to make the journey."

"But you're not frail, are you, Lorna?" I say, trying to catch her eye in the mirror, needing her to understand that if we're going to get out of this, she has to be strong. But she's too deep in her own story.

"He made me lie to the police. I had to pretend I'd heard Oliver and Nina arguing, pretend that she'd admitted to me that she was having an affair. I had to say that I'd seen Oliver go straight into the house the night she was murdered." She clutches her pearls, a lifebuoy in the tumult of her emotions. "He must have seen Oliver go into the square and took his chance to go and kill Nina. I didn't know, I didn't know what he'd done, not until he came back and told me exactly what I had to say to the police if they came knocking. He threatened to kill Edward if I didn't, he was always threatening to kill us." The tears come back. "Oliver and Nina never argued. They loved each other."

Thomas shakes his head angrily. "No. Nina did not love him, she loved me. She couldn't see it, that's all. Just like those other two bitches. But you were different, Alice. If only you'd given me a little more time. We were so close."

"What do you mean?"

He stoops, bringing his face up against mine. "Admit it, Alice," he says softly. "You were beginning to fall in love with me."

I look at our reflections in the mirror, captured within its ornate frame. We could be a photograph.

"Lorna," I say, my voice firm.

Her eyes lock with mine and I look toward the scissors, still in Thomas's hand but within her grasp, hoping she'll get the message. But Thomas sees and with an almost childish laugh, raises them high above his head.

"She's not going to help you, Alice. I'm her son."

He's right, I know that. Lorna is no match for his strength anyway. She wouldn't be able to wrestle the scissors out of his hand, let alone use them against him.

"Did she turn me in to the police after I killed Justine, after I killed Marion?" Thomas goes on. "No, she didn't. Did she cover up for me after I killed Nina? Yes, she did. Blood is thicker than water, Alice. Justine, Marion, and Nina were just that—water."

"But Edward wasn't," I say. "Edward was blood. And you killed him."

I've struck a chord. "I didn't kill him!" he shouts.

"Well, technically, you did."

Lorna screams then, not a scream of fear, or of suffering, but a scream of white-hot anger that goes on and on and on. It comes from deep inside her, canceling out a mother's innate desire to protect her child, no matter what they do. And Thomas, sensing that something has changed, freezes for a few precious seconds, just enough time for me, still tied to the chair, to spring up and back, smashing into him. He crashes to the floor and I land heavily on top of him. Caught unawares, the scissors fly from his hand.

"Lorna!" I cry. She stops in mid-scream and stares, seemingly paralyzed, at Thomas and me on the floor. He grapples with the chair, trying to throw the weight of it off him. But I force my body downward, pinning him underneath me.

"Lorna!" I call again. "Get help!"

With a roar of anger, Thomas gets his arms around the chair and throws it off him, slamming me to the floor. The air is expelled from my lungs and as I lie helpless, he throws himself across my chest, compressing it. His hands move to my neck, his face contorted with fury. As the pressure builds in my throat, I realize that even if Lorna does get help, it will be too late for me.

I hear him grunt and the weight of him on my chest increases. But his hands lose some of their grip and I twist my head to the side, gasping desperately for air. His hands slacken more, then fall from my neck and, at the same time as his head crashes onto mine, I become aware of a dull rhythmic thud, repeating itself over and over again.

SIX MONTHS LATER

There's a knock at the door, so timid that it barely registers.

I place my book on the scrubbed pine table, and wipe suddenly clammy hands on my jeans. Even though I've been expecting Eve, I'm still horribly nervous about seeing her. What if she knows?

It's all right, I remind myself, as I walk to the door. *She doesn't know. Thanks to Lorna, nobody will never know.*

I thought I would die that day, crushed by the weight of Thomas's body across my chest. Although I'd managed to twist my head to the side, I couldn't get air into my lungs. Lorna had gone into shock, paralyzed by what she had done. My strangled gasp pulled her back. She tried to lift Thomas off me but he was too heavy for her.

"Pull me out!"

Understanding, she got her hands under my arms and freed me just enough to release the pressure on my chest. The rest is a blur; the police arriving, the gentle questions, the walk to the ambulance, the shocked faces of the people huddled outside, brought by the sight of an ambulance and a police car screeching into The Circle. And Eve and Tamsin, staring at me in stunned disbelief as I followed Lorna to the ambulance, realizing there was more to what they were witnessing than Edward having died.

It dawned on me then, how everyone—not only the police but also Leo, Ginny, Debbie, and all who lived in The Circle—would know how I'd been taken in by the stranger who had come to our house six weeks before.

"They'll all know," I wept in anguish to Lorna as we sat in the ambulance, waiting for it to leave. "They will know how stupid I've been. I can't bear it."

And Lorna had reached for my hand under the blankets that had been wrapped tight around us. "All anyone needs to know is that you came to see me and Edward to say goodbye, and were taken captive by a man, who you recognized as the man who turned up at your drinks evening," she whispered. "When the police ask, that's what you tell them. They don't need to know anything else, nobody does." I stared at her, not daring to believe it could be so simple. "It will be all right," she promised, giving my hand a squeeze.

I took it, this lifeline she had thrown me, and clung on to it. I made the end of my story the beginning, and never mentioned the name Thomas Grainger. He had existed only for me; nobody needed to know how stupidly gullible I'd been. As far as the police and everyone else was concerned, it was as Lorna had said; I had gone round to say goodbye to her and Edward, and had found a man there, who I recognized as the man who had gate-crashed our drinks evening. He had Edward by the throat and before I could react, he attacked me. When I regained consciousness, I found myself tied to a chair and while he hacked at my hair, he told me that he was Edward and Lorna's son, that he had killed Nina Maxwell and that I would suffer the same fate. And I'd thought I would die, until Lorna saved me.

This small part of the truth is all anyone knows.

Eve looks different. The pink tips have gone from her hair and her face is fuller.

"Thank you for agreeing to see me," she says awkwardly.

We stare at each other for a moment. Then my emotions take over and I pull her into a hug.

"It's so good to see you," I say, and she sinks against me.

"Really?" There's a catch in her voice.

"Yes," I say. "I've missed you."

"I've missed you too." She moves back, searches my face. "How are you?"

"I'm good," I say. "Getting there."

She nods, then grasps my hand. "I need so much to apologize," she says, her voice anguished.

I frown. "Apologize?"

"Yes. I feel awful about everything. We all do." She gives an awkward smile. "I don't suppose I could sit down, could I? I'm pregnant and it's been a long drive."

"Oh, Eve, that's wonderful, congratulations!" Spurred into action by her lovely news, I lead her to the kitchen and pull out a chair. "Here, have a rest while I make some tea."

She looks around, captivated.

"This is lovely, Alice. I love that plate rack, and your amazing Aga—and is that a bread oven?"

I can't help laughing at her enthusiasm. "Yes," I say, turning to fill the kettle.

"Your cottage is gorgeous, I'm not surprised you found leaving it hard. When did you move back in?"

"Two months ago. I stayed with Debbie at first."

"You must be happy to be back."

"I am. I feel safe here."

She tips her head to one side, observing me. "Your hair. It suits you."

"Thanks." I raise my hand to my head. "I always wanted to know what it would be like to have short hair and now I know." I don't tell her that I hate it, that every time I look in the mirror, I see Thomas Grainger standing behind me, his face contorted with malice. But I'm getting good at blinking the image away; I refuse to let him carry on impacting on my life.

I glance at her neat little bump.

"When is your baby due?"

"At the beginning of August."

"Wow. In four months. I'm so pleased for you, Eve. Will must be delighted."

She laughs. "He is. You'd think he was the first man to become a father."

I take mugs from the cupboard and milk from the fridge. "So, how is everyone?"

"Struggling," she says and I nod, because I know this from Leo. "Maria and Tim have already left; they put their house on the market almost at once, for less than it was worth, and managed to sell it relatively quickly. Tamsin and Connor will be the next to leave. Then Will and me. We're trying to stagger it so that the price of the houses isn't affected too much. But we'll still be selling at a loss."

"I'm sorry," I say.

She gives me a little smile. "It's not your fault." But she's wrong, it is my fault. If I hadn't been so gullible, it wouldn't have come to this. Shame heats my cheeks, and I busy myself making the tea so that she won't see.

"We feel so bad, Alice, and not just because we didn't really believe that a strange man had turned up at your party. We feel terrible about Oliver. We accepted too easily that he was guilty. We needed so much to believe that her killer had been caught so that we could carry on with our lives. We took the easy way out and that's hard to live with."

I carry the mugs over to the table and sit down opposite her. I want to say something to comfort her, but I can't find anything.

"Leo said that you saw Lorna," Eve says, breaking the silence that has grown between us.

"Yes, a few months ago."

"How is she?"

I give a slight smile. "Struggling. She's living with her sister in Dorset while she's awaiting trial."

"They'll be lenient with her, won't they?"

"I hope so."

While Eve sips her tea, my mind goes back to the day when Lorna and I were in the ambulance together. She had been so strong. A sort of euphoria had set in; she had managed to free herself, she had managed to save me. It hadn't yet hit her that Edward was gone forever, and that she had killed her son. That although one nightmare was over, another was about to begin.

When I'd next seen her, two months later in Dorset, it was very different. She was huddled in a chair, her sister hovering behind her. She seemed to have shrunk to half her size, and aged by ten years. It was hard to see her so diminished.

"Oliver killed himself because I betrayed him," she whispered, her eyes blurred by tears. "He said I was the mother he never had and I betrayed him. I betrayed you too. John made me write that letter."

It took me a while to remember the letter I received, supposedly from Helen, the letter that had given me new resolve just when I was beginning to have doubts about helping solve Nina's murder.

I took her hand. "It doesn't matter."

She told me then, how it had all started, how even as a child John would quickly become obsessed by a particular person; first, the little girl who lived next door, then classmates at school, to the point where the mothers and teachers had worried words with Lorna before putting a distance between her child and the others. As a teenager, he developed a dangerous obsession with one of his teachers, and it had come out during his police interview—when, at fifteen years old, he'd been cautioned for stalking her—that he had interpreted innocent actions on her part as a sign that his love for her was reciprocated. One example he gave was that she would sometimes release her hair from its ponytail and let it swing around her shoulders for a moment before attaching it again, in what he believed was a secret and intimate message to him. Lorna and Edward sought help from doctors and therapists and John was diagnosed with Obsessive Love Disorder. He cleverly played along, leading everyone to believe that his obsessive personality was under control.

During his university years, Lorna and Edward rarely saw their son and after graduating in 2003, he disappeared from their lives completely. It was the start of the Gulf War, and without news, Lorna and Edward convinced themselves that he had joined the army. One night, thirteen years later, he turned up at their Bournemouth home. He told them that he had come to stay for a couple of weeks and when they asked him if he was in the army, he told them that yes, he'd been fighting in Iraq. He was charming to the neighbors, telling them that he was home on leave, and was going to build his parents the terrace they had always wanted. For three weeks, he worked long into the evenings until he left as suddenly as he came, taking their car with him and leaving his behind.

"Did you have any idea why Thom—" I caught myself, "John, was building the terrace?" I asked Lorna, because after her interviews with the police, the terrace at their former home had been dug up. Human remains had been found, later identified as Justine Bartley.

She shook her head violently. "We knew there was something not right but not that, never that. All the time he was with us, we hadn't felt safe. He was aggressive, threatening, and we were frightened of him. We told ourselves it was because of his experiences in Iraq but deep down, we knew that he had never been in the army and that the darkness in him came from something else. It was a relief when he left and we were scared that he would come back, so we decided to move somewhere he wouldn't find us." She touched her hand to her pearls and I was glad to see this old gesture of hers, glad that there was still something left of her previous self. "We told our neighbors we were moving to Devon and moved instead to London. And when we arrived, we told everyone our son had been killed in Iraq. I know it sounds terrible, disowning our son like that but—" Her voice trailed off. "And then, one day, we woke up and found him waiting in the back garden."

"Is that when he began keeping you prisoner?"

She nodded and repeated what she had already told me while I'd sat tied to the chair. "He kept to the bedrooms at the back of the house and at night, we could hear him moving around. He never seemed to sleep. But often, at six in the morning, he would wake us and lock us in the downstairs room and only let us out at lunchtime, so we thought that was when he probably slept." She paused to gather her thoughts. "I wasn't allowed out of the house, only Edward was, to put the bins out and do some gardening at the front, to keep up appearances. He would put his hands around my neck and squeeze until I could barely breathe and tell Edward he would strangle me properly if he tried to alert anyone to what was going on. We were allowed to answer the door but he would stand behind us, listening to everything we said." Her hands moved to the pink patchwork blanket covering her knees and began plucking at it. "The day that you came over, asking about Nina, he was listening to everything. I tried to warn you, I tried to tell you not to trust him, I couldn't give you a name because I knew he wouldn't be using John. I knew he'd gone to your drinks evening, he'd seen the invitation on the WhatsApp group and after what he did to poor Nina, I was scared for you." Tears rolled down her cheeks as she quickly dug a tissue from her sleeve.

"I thought you said that I wasn't to trust anyone," I told her.

She dabbed at her eyes. "No, I said 'Don't trust him.' But he knew I had whispered something to you and he was so angry. I swore that I hadn't but then he found out that I had and he hit me."

"It was me," I said, appalled that I had been the cause of such violence. "I told him you'd told me not to trust anyone. But Lorna, there's something I don't understand." I moved closer. "When I told you and Edward that a man had turned up at our drinks evening, why did you say that you had let him in to The Circle? Wouldn't it have been better to deny all knowledge of him?"

"I was going to, but then you said that Leo wanted to go to the police and I panicked. John was there, listening, and I was scared that if he thought the police might turn up, asking questions, he would kill us in case we gave him away."

There was something else that had been puzzling me but I wasn't sure she could give me an answer. "I don't understand why he pretended to be a private investigator looking into a murder that he himself had committed. It seems such a risky thing to do."

"I suppose it was the only way he could think of to hook you in, tell you that he was looking into a miscarriage of justice and ask you to help him. He would never have expected you to get to the truth. It was why he was willing to take the risk."

"But if I had told everyone about him?"

"He must have known that you wouldn't," she said and I blushed, realizing how well he had read me. "And even if you had, it wouldn't have mattered. The private detective would have disappeared into the night. But he would have found some other way to get to you," she added, and I wondered how he had got to Nina, if it had been a card through the door advertising his services as a therapist to therapists. "It was a game to him, everything was about manipulating people into thinking he was something he wasn't, like pretending to our neighbors in Bournemouth that he was the perfect son, and that the reason he hadn't been home for years was because he used his leave to help war orphans. He was so charming that everybody believed him. Even Edward and I believed him at first." She paused. "Perhaps that was because we wanted to believe there was good in our son, even though he scared us. But we never imagined he was capable of evil, not until he told us he'd killed Nina. I hate myself for lying for him, for telling the police that I had heard Nina and Oliver arguing, that Nina had told me she'd been having an affair. But he threatened to kill Edward if I didn't and somewhere underneath it all, he was still my son." Her hands began to shake. "I can't believe what I did, I can't believe I killed him."

I held her hands between mine, stilled the shaking. "You saved my life," I told her. "That's what you did. You saved my life." I leaned to kiss her. "Thank you."

It didn't seem enough. But what do you say to a mother who killed her son, who severed, so violently and with such finality, the umbilical cord that bound them together, to save the life of an almost-stranger?

She rallied then, became suddenly stronger. "Then if I saved your life, will you do something for me?" she asked. "And for Edward, because he would have wanted it too."

"Of course," I said. "Anything."

"Live it." I looked at her uncomprehendingly. "Live the life you have. You've spent the last twenty years living in the past. Now you have a whole life ahead of you. Don't let guilt consume you. We all make mistakes."

Some more than others. I can make any number of excuses for myself. Despite therapy, I have never recovered from killing my parents and sister. The judge's refusal to send me to jail, even though I begged him to, robbed me of my need to be punished and I've been punishing myself ever since. Leaving Harlestone, where everyone knew my story and came together to stop me from sinking into despair, meant that I was left without my support group. But I had Leo, the only other person I had confided in, because there were meant to be no secrets between us. He knew everything, including my anguish at not being properly punished. It's why, when I discovered that he had served a prison sentence, it wasn't his criminal record that made me unable to forgive him, but jealousy. I was jealous that he had been able to atone for what he did and move on with his life, while I was stuck in the past. Already floundering because he hadn't told me about Nina, I became even more disorientated and turned to the one person I felt I could trust, the one person who represented stability when distrust and suspicion, created unwittingly by Lorna's whispered warning, began to color my friendships with those around me. But the only thing I can really blame Thomas Grainger for is instilling fear into me with his night-time prowling. For the rest, I played right into his hands.

Eve and I talk a while longer. It's almost the same as before, but not quite. And that's OK, because I know it can never be the same, not when I haven't told her the whole truth. It's the same with Leo; I still see him, we are still friends and he's made it clear that he'd like us to be together again. But how can I if I'm keeping secrets from him, when I couldn't forgive him for keeping secrets from me?

Sometimes, I think he knows there's more to what happened than the version I gave him. The last time he was here, he caught hold of my hands and pulled me to him.

"I would never judge you," he said softly. "How could I, after the things I kept from you?"

Eve leaves me with a hug, promising to let me know when the baby arrives.

"Tamsin would love to see you," she says and I wish I could tell her that I owe Tamsin a huge debt, because if she hadn't told me about Oliver not having a sister, I doubt I'd be here. I'm sure Thomas intended to kill me that day to stop me from leaving The Circle, that he would have led me upstairs on some pretense, and I would have suffered the same fate as Nina, Marion and Justine.

"I'd like that," I say truthfully, although I'm not sure it will ever happen. "Give her my love."

I walk slowly back to the kitchen. It's not always easy doing as Lorna asked, but I'm glad I agreed to see Eve. I sit down at the table, happy to get back to the book I was reading, then pause. Leo will be calling later to see how it went. I've already taken one huge step today; maybe it's time to take another and finally tell him the truth about the man who turned up at our drinks evening.

The truth, and nothing but the truth.

ACKNOWLEDGMENTS

First and foremost, thank you to my amazing agent, Camilla Bolton. After five books together, you are so much more than my agent. I'm proud and honored to call you my friend.

Thank you to Kate Mills at HQ and Catherine Richards at St. Martin's Press for your precious input and unwavering support. And to all my other editors abroad, more than forty of you now! Your continued faith in my books is humbling.

Huge thanks also to the following:

The teams who work with my editors to proofread, design, promote, and market my books. I wish I could mention each of you by name. But you know who you are, and I also hope you know how grateful I am for your hard work and enthusiasm.

My fellow authors, who kindly take time out from their busy lives to read my books. In particular, I would like to thank Louise Candlish, Jane Corry, and Tim Logan for their generous quotes in relation to *The Therapist*.

The bloggers and readers, who give up their precious time to read and review my books.

My friends, both in France and in the UK, for always being interested in what I am writing, and for buying my books when they are eventually published.

And, of course, my thanks to the wonderful members of the Curran and MacDougall families, most of all my husband, Calum, and my daughters, Sophie, Chloë, Céline, Eloïse, and Margaux. You hold me up.

Turn the page for a sneak peek at
B. A. Paris's new novel

Available Fall 2022

ONE

PRESENT

I sense the shift of air beneath my nose a millisecond before something—thick, sticky tape—is clamped over my mouth, silencing the scream that would have ripped from me. My eyes snap open. A dark silhouette is bending over my bed.

Adrenaline surges. *Move! Grab the knife!* I twist my arm toward my pillow, but a hand slams onto my wrist, holding it still. Pulled from the bed, I kick out. But my feet flail uselessly, find only air. I try to focus but my mind is spinning. Why did I fall asleep? I should have been expecting this.

My arms are pulled behind my back, my wrists bound together. I try to twist away but something is pulled over my head, material, rough and tight, a hood of some kind. Panic spreads through me like wildfire. *Don't. Keep calm, Amelie. You know what this is.*

He pushes me from the room, my feet tangle, I stumble, he jerks me upright. Under the hood, my head is filled with the frantic pulse of my heartbeat. I fight back the fear. *I can outwit him; I've done it before.*

The soft carpet beneath my feet gives way to the cold polished floor of the landing. My toes bump the edge of the carpeted runner; in my mind I see its intricate green and red pattern of leaves and animals. I inhale the chemical smell of glue from the tape and a mix of a cough and a choke burns my throat. I draw a breath, and the material from the hood sucks into my nostrils. *Where is he taking me?*

The grip on my shoulders tightens a little; there's a slight pulling back. Instinct tells me we are at the top of the stairs and I hesitate, afraid to fall. Pushed forward, I find the first step, then move downward until the soles of my feet touch the cold checkered tiles of the hall. We move down the hallway to the left, my ragged breathing amplified in the eerie silence. I know where we're going. He's taking me to the basement, where the garage is.

I turn, wrenching my body away from him, and for a precious moment, his grasp on me weakens. But it's not enough; I'm hauled back into place, and pain flashes up my arms. Angled to the right, more steps down, the space narrows, the air shifts, becomes cooler.

And then, an influx of sounds, stifled by the hood but recognizable still—scuffling feet, a muffled whine, a sense of others there waiting. I push back, then stop. The scuffling, the whine—they didn't come from me. My mind reels. *It can't be, it's not possible.*

But I know the voice behind the smothered protests—Ned.

This is not what I thought it was.

TWO

PRESENT

Under my hood, my eyes dart, looking for a way out of this night-mare. *Think, Amelie, think!* But my mind is paralyzed. *What is this? Who are they?*

I hear the clunk of a car trunk opening. There's more scuffling; Ned's muted protests become louder. A grunt and a thud; have they put him in the trunk? My body tenses; I can't be put in there with him. Then, without warning, I'm pushed into the interior of the car, facedown in the space between the seats, my knees forced up against the thin material of my pajamas. Heavy shoes push against my back, holding me down when I try to get up.

At first, I attempt to keep track of where we're going. But I quickly become disoriented. I concentrate instead on drawing small sucks of air into my lungs. My stomach heaves; I'm breathing too fast. I close my eyes, imagine I'm outside in the cool night air, looking up at the sky, the stars, the infinite space. Gradually, my breathing calms.

Later, hours it seems, the car slows, the road becomes rougher. My mind has wandered. I force myself to focus; I know that for sur-vival, every second counts. The car rocks; I picture a dirt track under the wheels, a forest around us. I should be more afraid. But I'm not scared of dying, not anymore. Not after everything.

There are sudden thuds from the trunk and cries of pain from

Ned. He must be terrified—but shouldn't he have been expecting this? Hunter, his security guard, brutally murdered three days ago, replaced by Carl, an unknown quantity. Where was Carl while we were being abducted? For this to have happened, there has to have been a massive breach of security. *All eyes on Carl.*

The car comes to a halt. Doors click open, the boots are removed from my back. I'm pulled from the footwell, made to stand. The cool August night air wraps itself around my legs; goose bumps rise on my arms. There's the smell of dirt, foliage, tree sap.

I hear Ned being dragged from the trunk. We're pushed forward, Ned in front; I can hear him mumbling. The ground is sharp under my bare feet, stones digging into soft flesh, like shingle on a beach. I wait for the softer undergrowth of bracken, the crisp snapping of twigs. But the stones become smooth slabs, a path of some kind. *Not an execution then. At least, not in a forest.*

We stop. I hear the creak of a door pulled open, the scrape of wood along the ground, not a door to a house, an outbuilding perhaps. Propelled forward into a blast of cold air, I tremble. It's not a shed; it's a dungeon or basement, its thick walls untouched by the warmth of the sun.

I'm shivering now despite the crush of bodies around me. A door opens somewhere in front, another scuffle, Ned frantic, my foot trampled as they move to contain him. I hold my breath, wait it out. A door slams, followed by thuds as Ned throws his body against it, raging from behind his gag. *Be quiet. It's not going to help.*

We move on, climb stone steps; I count them, twelve in all. Then, at the top, the worn stone under my feet becomes warm wood, softer against my skin. A door is opened; I'm moved forward.

There's a movement behind me and I steel myself for a blow. Instead, the hood is pulled up and off my head. My hair crackling with static, I draw a deep breath in through my nose, then blink and blink again, waiting for my eyes to adjust to the darkness. But there's nothing. No flicker of light, no paler shade of black.

Without warning, there's a tug on my hand, strong fingers on my wrists. A cry of alarm builds, pushing against my throat. *Not this.*

I kick back and my feet connect with flesh and muscle, but whoever is behind me holds me tighter. Then, a sawing sound and the rough scratch of a knife echo around the room until suddenly, there's an audible snap. The pressure on my wrists releases and the momentum trips me forward. Before I can turn, there's the slam of a door, the click of a lock.

That's when I realize: From the moment the man came into my bedroom, our abductors haven't said a word.

Philippe Matsas

B. A. PARIS is the international bestselling author of *Behind Closed Doors, The Breakdown, Bring Me Back,* and *The Dilemma.* Having lived in France for many years, she and her husband now live in the United Kingdom. She has worked both in finance and as a teacher, and she has five daughters. *The Therapist* is her fifth novel.